Whore of Babylon

AZARIA FROST

Contents

Chapter 1

She tore the darkness with a scream.

Her sister was there in an instant, calming her with a soft embrace. The night terrors were less frequent than they used to be, but Eliana still could not shake them off. Two years had passed since the conquest, but memories of the horrors she had witnessed still lingered.

Kisha rocked her back and forth, stroking her hair and singing softly.

Her racing heart gradually returned to normal and she sank back into sleep, the arms and voice of her sister becoming their mother's. In her dream, she strained for a glimpse of her mother's features. As always, all she saw was a pair of kind eyes in a shadowy face.

By the time the golden light of dawn washed across Eliana's bed, Kisha was gone. Barely awake, tears welled in the younger girl's eyes as she remembered that next time the nightmares came, her sister would not. Today was Kisha's wedding day, and she would wed the conqueror of Nippur.

Forcing back the tears, Eliana rose from the bed and went to the copper washbasin in the corner of the room. Splashing water on her face, she tried to banish the traces of the dream from her mind: she had last seen her sister's bridegroom nearly two years ago as he cut down a pair of shepherd boys who had tried to hide their flock from the invaders. Just twelve and fourteen years old, they had been Eliana's playmates. Laughing and chasing through the dusty streets one day; dead the next. Her final sight of them had been their corpses piled anonymously atop the mounds of others who had perished, entrails dangling grotesquely from their slit bellies, glistening greenish in the heat of the day.

He had slain the boys personally, taking a knife to the throat of the younger while his second-in-command, the one they called 'the Brute', plunged his spear into the stomach of the other. The elder had pleaded for mercy, the words bubbling up in blood and dying on his lips.

Those two boys haunted her dreams; now her gentle sister was to marry the monster who killed them.

She would not cry, she had promised herself and sworn it to Enlil, the great god of Nippur. There was not a man in the city who could claim to have ever seen her shed a public tear, even during the darkest hour of the conquest. She would weep when the ceremonies were complete and the house emptied of guests, but not before.

Eliana dried her face and slipped on the dress she had laid out the night before – an ochre-coloured silk that shimmered and ran through her fingers like water. It clung to her body, a second skin, highlighting her newly blossomed woman's curves. She clipped a belt of painted leather around her slender waist, smudged some vermillion onto her lips and combed jasmine oil through her black curls until they gleamed like obsidian.

The reed mats rustled underfoot as she made her way down to the walled garden where the wedding would take place. Kisha would be preparing herself, so it fell to Eliana to see that everything was ready.

The little garden was a riot of colour – the date trees planted all around its edges were almost ripe, fruit hanging heavy in so many shades of vibrant red and orange that it would rival even Utu, the sun god himself, when he lifted his head in the morning.

On the ground, the mustard was in flower, dazzling yellow heads nodding in the breeze, interspersed with spidery green garlic and onion plants and the feathery leaves of chickpeas.

Little fish leapt in the decorative pool at the garden's centre, creating a lilting music.

She took a deep breath, savouring the peace.

The servants had been busy. Banners and streamers of bright cloth festooned the trees, and benches and tables had been set out ready beneath them. The altar had been brought out and placed before the pool, dressed for celebration.

Though what there was to celebrate, Eliana wasn't quite sure. Her sister hadn't chosen this marriage, and their father had been powerless to resist it. She could tell that, beneath her usual calm exterior, Kisha was terrified. Once she disappeared behind the glazed walls of the Red Palace, she would be beyond the help of any but the gods. Enlil had failed to protect his city from the invaders, why should he protect one of his daughters from its conqueror?

The mighty god had been punished for his failure to act – the Babylonians had stripped him of his powers over Nippur, neglected his dwelling place in the House of the Mountain, and set their own god up in his place. The wedding would be conducted according to the rites of Marduk; Enlil would have no part in the ceremony.

'Was it the old dream again?' asked a soft voice behind her.

She jumped. Her father had drifted up silent as a feather on the breeze. She turned with the smile she always saved for him, 'Yes, Father. Sorry I woke you. It comes less often now.'

'Good,' he nodded, resting a light hand on her shoulder. He looked at her intently, 'You look quite beautiful, Eliana. Like your mother's shade made flesh again.'

His face was etched with grief, the lines even deeper than usual. Adab had been like a shade himself since his wife had died in childbirth more than ten years ago. When they married she had imbued him with her lively spirit. When she passed on, it passed with her. He had never even named his little stillborn son.

Eliana covered her father's hand with her own.

'I always thought I would wish she could be here when you girls got married. For the first time since the conquest, I am glad she is not here to see this.'

'It would break her heart to see it,' Eliana agreed, feeling the old familiar pinch of loss. 'A wedding should be a happy occasion, especially one where a member of our family is joined to a prince.'

Her father heaved a sigh, 'Fetch me when he arrives. I must make ready.'

His hand slipped from her shoulder and he drifted away towards his office.

She watched him go, wishing she could remember what he had been like before her mother died. It had happened when Eliana was just four years old, and her sister had stepped into the maternal role at the age of nine. She was fifteen now, and Kisha twenty, but it felt like she was losing her mother all over again.

Her sister had always been the one who soothed her when she was frightened, scolded her when she was naughty, and loved her unconditionally. Their father had been distant for as long as Eliana could remember, but Kisha told stories of when he was a lively, bold man, full of energy and fond of music. Both their parents had died that night, in all the ways that mattered.

Adab had never once reprimanded his younger daughter – she had been a grubby child, preferring to run barefoot through the streets playing at soldiers with the shepherd boys than dolls and dress-up with the other girls of her age. Whenever she had come home dusty and bruised, her tunic torn and lip split from fighting, her father would just ruffle her cloud of tangled black curls and send her off for a wash. It had been Kisha who would clean her up, mend the tunic, soothe the bruises and chide her for unladylike behaviour.

Even now, she loved to run and climb, though she had learned the wisdom of words over fists, and choosing her battles carefully.

There was little left to do downstairs, the servants had everything in hand. Eliana set off in search of her sister. She found her in a sun-drenched room at the front of the house.

She stopped at the door, her breath taken away.

Draped in a crimson silk gown fringed with gold beading, Kisha was at her most beautiful. Her hair was elaborately braided, topped with a traditional feathered headdress. A thick collar of gold set with garnet encircled her throat, and matching earrings skimmed her shoulders – wedding gifts from her husband-to-be, given when he selected her as his bride.

On any other day, she would have looked radiant, but hollow eyes betrayed her.

'Oh, Kisha! You look so beautiful.'

'So do you,' she smiled sadly. 'You should take care that you don't attract yourself a husband today too.'

'I wouldn't mind that,' said Eliana honestly, 'as long as he's not a Babylonian. I could never be as brave as you – I couldn't wed one of those beasts.'

Tears welled in Kisha's eyes, 'I'm not brave, Elly. I don't have a choice. I'm too cowardly to kill myself. Even if I tried, he would kill you and father in retribution. He won't be denied. You've always been the brave one.'

'No,' Eliana shook her head, fighting back her own tears, 'I'd have killed myself before going through his selection process. A brave woman lives; cowards die.'

In a few short hours, Kisha would become the wife of Samsu, the only surviving son of the mighty Hammurabi, King of Babylon. That all-conquering monarch had already annihilated most of the ancient city-states of Sumeria. He was building himself an empire, and even Nippur, the holy seat of the great Enlil, father of the gods, was not safe once his gaze had lighted upon her.

A prince feared by all who knew his name, notorious for his cruelty, Samsu had breached the city walls and sent his men swarming through like wasps. Any man, woman or child who stood against him was put to the sword, if they were lucky. Many were not so fortunate. Fathers were forced to rape their sons and daughters, or else watch the soldiers do it with daggers. Mothers were taken as whores, children as slaves. The two shepherd boys that had been Eliana's playmates had suffered little in comparison to some. Any who resisted were mutilated and hung from the city walls to fester, lingering until Ereshkigal claimed them as servants in the underworld that was named for her.

The city was utterly subdued – its people now lived in terror of their ruler. The survivors had immediately been set to constructing a great palace for Samsu – a luxurious complex of bath houses, apartments, gardens and council chambers faced with glazed red brick. The building work had been completed just six moons ago, and Samsu had begun to look for a concubine.

He was already married, but his wife was rarely seen in public and it was whispered that she was an old woman, at least of an age with Eliana's father, with a son the same age as her husband. Samsu needed a young wife – one who could provide him with heirs.

He had sent out a decree – all unmarried maids between the ages of sixteen and twenty-one were to be brought to his palace for examination. Eliana, just fourteen years old then, had been spared the trial. Kisha, a rare beauty of nineteen and betrothed to a scribe at the civic offices, had been dragged forcibly away by the soldiers. She did not return for four days.

When she was brought back, it was with a gold-and-garnet collar, and a swollen, tear-stained face.

She could not be made to talk about her time in the Red Palace – all she would say was that it had been a humiliating and degrading experience, and that she had been singled out from than a hundred girls to become Samsu's concubine. She had passed tests in obedience, modesty, docility, beauty and cleanliness to win the honour she never sought.

The other girls had not fared much better – Samsu gave the officers of his army their pick of his leavings.

Isin, her former betrothed, was not mentioned again. Eliana still came across him at the market sometimes. He would always ask after Kisha with a tragic lovesickness stark in his eyes, and swear eternal servitude if he could ever do anything to help.

That tragic look haunted Kisha's eyes now. Eliana went to put her arms around her; they held each other in silence for a long moment.

Hearing the arrival of guests below, Eliana broke away reluctantly, feeling the pressure of time. 'Here, let me help you with your paints. You can't go to him looking pale and frightened.'

She pushed her sister gently down onto the stool and took up the powder, carefully covering the dark circles under her eyes. Dusting saffron onto Kisha's cheeks to give them some colour and adding a dab of vermilion to the lips, she stood back to take in the effect.

'Better!' she smiled weakly. 'Now don't you dare to cry again, or I'll have to start over!'

'I won't,' said Kisha. 'I'll save my tears for tonight. He likes it when people show they're afraid of him – he calls it humility.'

*

The tension in the house was palpable.

There were less than half as many Babylonians as Sumerians. They might have been dressed for a trip to the market, garbed in plain military tunics with daggers hanging from their belts. The Sumerians eyed the weapons uneasily – it was unheard of for guests to attend a wedding armed for battle. The blatant disrespect spoke volumes: this marriage was as much a travesty to them as it was to the city.

In contrast, the flower of Sumerian society had turned out for this wedding – priests, scholars, city officials and their families. Every available space was filled with gaily dressed people. Despite being dressed for a festival, they wore the faces of funeral-goers. The atmosphere was solemn, with none of the high spirits usually seen at such a ceremony. Kisha, with her kindness, charity and graciousness, was a great favourite in the community, and not one of the Nippurites present would willingly have seen her married to a barbarian.

These people had come to show their regard for the family, not for celebration and levity.

As *Ensi* of Nippur, Eliana and Kisha's father Adab was held in the highest respect by the Sumerians. He had charge of the day-to-day government and maintenance of the city, administration of taxes, and dispensation of justice. The people esteemed him as a fair and capable man.

When the invaders had flooded through the city gates, he had immediately gone to surrender to Samsu – it had cost him his pride, but he had been able to assure the safety of his daughters and retain his position. By securing his place, he could continue to work for the good of the people and the smooth running of the city, rather than abandoning them to a stranger with foreign ways. Nobody blamed Adab for submitting where others had resisted – rather, they admired his quick thinking.

From across the room, the Babylonians looked contemptuously at the Sumerians as less than dung beneath their sandals. Not one of the soldiers had brought a wife or child for the festivities. They stood apart in their own group, speaking the common tongue, Akkadian, with guttural accents. A servant boy stood nearby, clutching a jug of sweet date-wine and trying to make himself invisible. He did not dare look directly at the men, but stood with his head bent, watching up through his lashes for any sign that they needed their drinking bowls refilled.

Between them, the Babylonians had already consumed more wine in their short time at the house than all the Sumerian guests could be expected to drink from their first arrival until the end of the wedding feast. With every swallow they were becoming more raucous and more vocal in their dismissal of the natives.

'This cesspit!' one of them slapped his thigh. 'I'd jump in the canal before I brought my sons here – I'll not have them go soft and weak like these savages!'

His companions roared with laughter, wine spilling from their bowls and staining their tunics as they pushed each other.

Eliana bit her tongue hard, praying to the mother-goddess for the wisdom and the strength to swallow back the words that threatened to leap from her mouth. It could only go badly for her if she spoke angrily to the Babylonians. She walked by quickly, sandals slapping against the bare tiles, feeling their eyes on her as she passed – a whisper of jasmine with sinuous hips.

Crossing the garden, she took a seat next to Kisha on the bench by the pool. She took her hand and squeezed it hard.

Kisha barely seemed to notice, gazing into the pond with distant eyes.

Eliana did not need to ask what she was thinking to know that Kisha envied the fish – free to spend the day frolicking and leaping, no need to be concerned about invaders, duty or family. No memory of the past, no fear of the future.

Occasionally, a Sumerian guest would approach the sisters to offer Kisha their half-hearted congratulations on her prestigious marriage, anxious to be seen to be doing so. She wore her public face, smiling and thanking her friends graciously. Eliana watched, wondering how many of the guests would even think of her sister again after today.

When they were alone, she could hardly bear Kisha's pensive silence, but there was nothing more to be said between them. Contenting herself with holding her sister's hand, she turned her face towards the house, darting anxious glances at the office door through the throngs of people. Samsu was closeted alone with her father, discussing final details of the dowry.

People milled around the garden, wandering in and out of the house. The Sumerians were brightly coloured butterflies, flitting furtively from one flower to the next; the Babylonians were watchful hawks, waiting for any misstep, any excuse to swoop and swallow them whole. Servants moved through the crowds, flowing smoothly around the guests like river waters around a stone, offering fruit platters and date-wine.

The platters were nearly empty by the time the door finally opened. Adab emerged alone, gesturing to the servants to have the guests take their seats. He walked over to his daughters, stopping in front of Kisha, offering her his hand. Placing hers in his, she stood to face him.

They looked into each other's eyes, as though each was trying to memorise the other's face. *As if*, thought Eliana, *they never expect to see each other in this life again.*

There was a threatening prickle behind her eyes and a tightness in her throat. She swallowed hard.

'I would not have chosen to put you through this ordeal for anything on this earth,' their father whispered, his face drawn taut with grief.

'Peace, Father,' said Kisha softly. 'It is not for us to determine our own fates – we go where the gods send us. We must accept and bear it as best we can.'

Adab nodded, his eyes shining with unshed tears. Kisha's were dry. Eliana's heart swelled with pride in her sister. *No amount of weeping will change this*, she told herself firmly.

'Good luck,' said Adab.

Kisha stretched up to place a gentle kiss on her father's cheek.

The guests were in place – Babylonians on one side, Sumerians on the other. The priest waited beside the altar.

Eliana and Adab took up their places on the front bench, and Kisha moved to stand before the altar. She folded her hands before her and bent her head, eyes on the ground.

A steward banged his staff on the floor for silence, 'His Royal Highness, Samsu, Crown Prince of Babylon.'

A hush fell as the door swung open and Samsu strode out.

He had not altered much in the time since Eliana had last seen him. He still stood half a head above any of his officers, built of solid muscle encased in copper skin burnished by the sun. A tangle of dark hair hung down past his ears, framing a square jaw and slightly crooked nose that had been broken once too often. He wore the same military tunic as his men, showing off the battle scars on his powerful arms and legs, luminously pale against his dusky skin.

His most striking features though, were his eyes. On another man, they might have been beautiful. On Samsu, they were cold, hard and black as jet, glittering cruelly in the midmorning sun.

There was a hint of swagger in his stride – the movement of a man who knows he has the entire world at his feet. He stalked down the aisle between the Babylonian and Sumerian sides, looking neither left nor right, fixing his gaze directly on the altar.

Eliana recoiled as he passed, the mere sight of him was still enough to give her fearful chills.

As he approached, Kisha sank to her knees, sat back on her heels and touched her forehead to the floor in a full Babylonian bow. The faintest ripple of surprise passed over the Sumerian guests.

Eliana was expecting it. Kisha had been schooled in the Babylonian marriage rites before being brought home from the Red Palace, and had practiced her movements with her sister again and again. She was expected to make a full submission before her husband, and remain there until he raised her up by his side.

He stood before her and held out his hand. She took it, rising gracefully to her feet, keeping her eyes on the floor.

'Raise your head,' he commanded in a voice as rough and harsh as pumice stone.

She lifted her gaze no higher than his shoulders, allowing him a full look at her face without ever meeting his eyes.

Samsu grunted and nodded his approval. 'Well, get on with it!' he barked at the priest.

The priest began to chant a strange prayer unknown to the Sumerians, invoking the blessings of Marduk. The Babylonians sang the response as the Sumerians shifted uncomfortably on their benches.

Eliana gripped her hands together in her lap as she stared at the ground. Enlil had no part in this ceremony, no place in the new Babylonian Nippur, but still she hoped against hope that he would step in at the last moment, make his displeasure known, smite Samsu with a thunderbolt – anything. She prayed silently.

Grain was sprinkled over Kisha, accompanied by a prayer for her fertility and the bringing forth of sons. The priest took a length of rope, binding Kisha's hand to Samsu:

'We here present pray you now, almighty Marduk, to help this woman to be a good and honest wife. We bind her to this man, from now until the end of time. May she be fecund, loyal, and above all, faithful. May your wrath strike her down if her heart ever strays from her husband. Keep her obedient, humble, pious and reverent in all ways, that she may be pleasing to this man you set above her.'

Pouring oil from a little clay jar into a golden cup, the holy man added a sprinkling of powder and ignited the mixture with a taper. A brilliant blue flame flared from the little vessel.

Eliana gave an involuntary gasp of awe along with the rest of the Sumerians, while the Babylonians sniggered rudely.

The priest dipped his fingers into the oil and anointed first Samsu's forehead, then Kisha's, and then the length of rope that tethered them. Untying the rope, he repeated the strange prayer which had opened the rites.

The moment the last response had been sung, Samsu turned on his heel and walked away. Closing in around Kisha, the soldiers of his personal guard walked through the house and out to the street, forcing her to move with them.

Eliana watched for a moment, frozen as if in a nightmare. The deed was done, and they were taking Kisha away. They had not even let her say goodbye!

Running after them, Eliana opened her mouth to shout to her sister, determined to say a proper farewell whether Samsu willed it or not, when somebody snagged her wrist and dragged her backwards. It was Isin, Kisha's beloved. He put his fingers to his lips and shook his head, his eyebrows drawn together in pain. He was right, of course, it would do no good to scream and shout and make a scene. She shrugged him off and chased after her sister in silence.

Outside, Samsu had already mounted his horse and set off up the road to his Red Palace. A soldier gripped Kisha around the waist, lifting her as easily as a doll, and set her up on a saffron-red mare.

She just had time to turn and catch a last glimpse of her family, eyes wide with fear, before her horse was led away.

The Sumerians looked at each other, outraged as the Babylonian party moved away – to take the bride so suddenly, without even giving her a chance to say goodbye to her family! To make such a swift exit, with none of the traditional toasts to the couple's good health or taking part in the wedding feasts! The Babylonians were barbarians indeed.

The feast went ahead without the guests of honour. Eliana struggled to maintain her composure, sitting to the left of her sister's empty place, her father to the right of Samsu's. It was a grave and sober affair, but Adab had decided that it would be unseemly to waste the lavish, exquisite dishes when so many in the city were starving. The farming community had still not recovered from the deaths of so many of its menfolk during the invasion.

She choked down the delicacies, but they made her stomach turn. Finely spiced gazelle, goose stuffed with garlic, fresh fish baked with leeks and mustard… it all seemed to turn to ash in her mouth.

When the last guests finally departed with whispered thanks and condolences, Eliana began to help the servants clean up – she needed to keep herself occupied, to keep the tears at bay. She felt numb, dazed. Her hands shook so badly that she dropped a beautifully painted alabaster jug. It smashed in the dirt, the last remnants of its wine seeping away into the ground. The servants, not unkindly, sent her away.

Her father had shut himself away in his office, so she took herself off to her room. Shedding the day's finery, she changed into a simple tunic, fumbling with trembling hands.

She threw herself face down on the bed. The tears came slowly at first – a trickle, sliding silently down her face and into the blanket. Then a stream. Then a torrent. She took great, shuddering breaths, coughing as she sobbed, feeling as though she would never have enough air in her lungs again. Her sister's face swam up in her mind, that last pleading look in her eyes as she was led away – the last hug and words of farewell that they had been denied ran through Eliana's head again and again in all the different ways they might have happened. She yearned to feel her sister's protective arms around her just once more, bitter with the knowledge that she would never have that comfort again.

The blanket was soaked with her tears and her sweat as she cried until, at last, she had exhausted herself enough to fall into a blessedly dreamless sleep.

*

The house felt desolate and empty without Kisha there to brighten it with her laughter. Eliana had no company but the servants, and they remained frustratingly distant and deferential. She drifted miserably from one room to the next. The house became a yawning chasm that swallowed any happiness she might have felt, leaving only bitter loneliness.

Desperate to make herself useful somehow, she began going with her father to the civic offices during the day to see if she could help with any small duties. He tasked her with listening to the complaints of the cityfolk and giving him a summary of their concerns.

She soon discovered a talent for listening. But more than that, she really cared – and the people recognised and appreciated it. Her father had devoted his life to making their city a better place, and she was determined to do the same.

Though the city no longer belonged to her people, Eliana found solace in it. Not content with waiting for the Nippurites to come to her with their problems, she started going out into the city herself. Every day she visited traders and farmers, walked the roads and canals, visited the slums. Seeing the city first-hand, she found, she could be of much more use to her father – reporting where taxes would be best spent, and assessing where the people were most in need.

Nippur was crowded. A constant haze of dust hung over the city centre, kicked up by hundreds of sandalled feet. A thousand scents seasoned the air – rich spices from the east mingled with new leather, and the stink of the beasts of burden who carried the goods, mixed with the distinctive smell of the unwashed. On the busiest days, one could barely stop at a market stall without being jostled along by impatient elbows and overwarm bodies.

On these days, Eliana preferred to stick to the canal paths, judging where repairs were needed. Though the city was busy, it had less of the enthusiastic energy that had characterised Nippur's market in years gone by. The wounds had healed, but the scars remained.

Even when they were quiet, the streets were a labyrinthine tangle, impossible to navigate if the traveller did not know the way. More than once, Eliana had found herself lost in the back streets whilst looking for one place or another that her father had asked her to visit.

It was a searingly hot day when Adab asked his daughter to go to a bakery in one of the poorest areas of the city. Reports were being made of the baker adding chalk to his flour to pad out the bread. Eliana was to buy a loaf and bring it back to the offices for examination, but she had missed a turn somewhere, and, try as she might, she could not bring herself back to a landmark she knew. She was hopelessly lost.

She leaned against the crumbling wall of an abandoned house in a narrow alley, grateful for the shade. Her feet ached and her throat was dry with the dust of the street. Wiping the sweat from her hairline with the backs of her fingers, she tried to think of a strategy to find her way out.

There was an uncomfortable prickle at the back of her neck – it could have been the heat of the day, but she had the uneasy feeling that she was being watched.

She glanced around, and caught the faintest flicker of movement in the shadows. She prayed it wasn't a soldier, or one of Samsu's spies.

'Come out,' she called, her voice cracking a little in her parched throat. 'I'm a friend.'

Slowly, inch by inch, a ragged creature came into view. A tangled mass of dark hair all but covered her face, and her gown was threadbare, torn in places, and hanging off a spare frame. Eliana could see from the girl's spindly arms that she was a beggar; when she pushed back her hair, her eyes seemed huge in an emaciated face – Eliana's heart wrenched with pity.

'What do you want?' the girl asked, her hands nervously plucking at the fabric of her gown.

Eliana confessed, 'I'm lost – can you help me find the way to Epu's bakery?'

'It's not far,' said the girl, warily. 'What do you want there? The bread is awful.'

'That's what I need to investigate, I'm Eliana – the *Ensi*'s daughter.'

The girl backed off a step. 'What will you give me, if I help?'

'What do you want?'

She shrugged, 'Food, mostly. My family all died in the conquest – I've got nothing.'

'Take me to the bakery and then back to the civic offices – I'll make sure you get a proper meal,' Eliana smiled reassuringly.

'Swear by Enlil?'

'I swear it by Enlil and all the gods.'

The girl nodded and beckoned for Eliana to follow. Together, they made their way to the bakery in just a few minutes: squeezing through a tight passage between two houses and rounding a couple of corners. Eliana concluded her business quickly, and was back at the civic offices in no time at all. As the girl tore at her meal, she glanced up from time to time, as if expecting someone to come and snatch the food from her at any moment.

When she had finished, she stood up and made to leave without a word.

'Wait!' cried Eliana.

The girl turned back, looking at her quizzically.

'You were so much help today – I would still be lost if it hadn't been for you.'

She shrugged.

'Would you help me again? I could give you food every day.'

'Every day?' the girl's eyes widened.

Eliana nodded earnestly, 'You know so much more about the streets and communities than I do – I'd be so grateful.'

'I don't need your gratitude, my lady. I can't eat that.'

'Well meet me at the market an hour after sunrise tomorrow and I promise you'll have more than gratitude.'

Unexpectedly, the girl gave a shy smile – it transformed her face, lighting her eyes with joy. 'Thank you, my lady. My name's Mari – I'll see you tomorrow, as you say.'

She turned and ran, as if afraid that Eliana would change her mind, or say that it had all been a joke. As good as her word, Mari was waiting at the market the next day, and every day thereafter.

The two girls worked hard, traipsing the city all day – Mari to earn her dinner, Eliana in the hopes of exhausting herself enough to sleep at night.

Their friendship had only a couple of moons to prosper.

They had been working together for weeks, and not once had Mari been late or failed to come. She was as reliable a person as Eliana had ever met, and they were becoming fast friends.

Standing at their usual meeting spot an hour after sunrise, Eliana couldn't help but be struck by the quietness of the city. The streets were less busy than usual, and there was no sign of Mari. The sun rose higher in the sky, and still there was no sign of her. By mid-morning, Eliana had to accept that she wasn't coming.

Worried, she hurried to the civic offices to see her father. He always knew what was happening in the city. She ran up the steps into the cool complex of clay brick, accosting the first scribe she saw.

'Where is my father, please?'

He knew her by sight, as did all the scribes and officials. 'He's in a meeting with some foreign merchant, my lady. The man wants a licence to trade here – it could take some time.'

Eliana made a little noise of frustration and hastened to her father's office, taking a seat on a bench in the courtyard outside of it, tapping her foot impatiently. It seemed like hours before the door swung open and a stout, pale man with an outlandish beard shook Adab's hand over the threshold and left.

As soon as the man was out of sight, she marched into the office and closed the door behind her.

'Eliana – what's wrong?'

'I came to ask you the same question!' she burst out. 'What's happened in the city today? The streets are so quiet, and Mari didn't come. Something must have happened.'

'Hush! Calm yourself. Something has happened – Samsu wanted to reduce the number of beggars in the city...'

'Beggars that he created!'

'... and so he arranged a sweep of the streets. Overnight, he has cleared away all the able-bodied orphans and needy. They have been claimed as slaves, taken to work in the palace.'

Eliana could have burst with indignation, 'So he's taking native Nippurites and forcing them into slavery in their own city?'

'Yes.'

'And we're doing nothing about it?'

Adab shrugged, 'There is nothing we can do. He is the Prince, and this was his decree.'

This only inflamed her impotent hatred of Samsu. Every friend she had, he took from her. In the eight moons since he had stolen her sister away, Eliana had only been permitted to visit her once.

They had sat together in the garden – Eliana was not allowed inside the palace – and exchanged banalities and pleasantries. She could not discover anything of her sister's life inside the palace, and didn't dare to ask. They had sat in the shadows of two huge guards, set to stand watch over the pair and report back on every word. Eliana had talked of her work in the city, trying to improve people's lives; Kisha had been pale, quiet and withdrawn, remarking only on the weather and Eliana's dress, and asking after their father.

Eliana didn't mind that her sister was reserved, but it worried her. It was impossible to tell whether Kisha was simply quiet because of the guards, or something more was going on. She would not speak more than three words in a row. Could she have changed so much in just five months of marriage? Eliana did not push her; just to hold her hand and be in her company again was enough.

But that visit had been three moons ago, and she had not been permitted to see Kisha since. Now Mari had disappeared behind the high red walls too. Eliana had not heard anything of or from her since she was taken; it was hard not to fear the worst.

She pushed herself even harder during the days, travelling the streets alone, wearing out her sandals more quickly than ever before, but still sleep did not come easily. She would usually lay awake long into the hours of Suen's watch – the moon god pouring his light through her window to pool on her bed. Lying under the blanket, she would watch the shadows slowly travel the room, falling asleep shortly before Utu took his turn in the sky and brought the dawn.

It was on a night such as this that, drowsing, she was startled by a quiet cough under her window. She sat upright, wondering if she had half-dreamed it, listening intently.

The cough came again, followed by an unmistakeable whisper: 'Eliana!'

She sprang from the bed and ran to the window, peering out. The shadowy figure below pulled down the hood of his cloak for a moment, showing his luminously pale features in the moonlight – Isin!

'Meet me in the garden,' she hissed.

She threw on a cloak and hurried soft-footed down to meet him, leaping lightly over creaky floorboards. She found him sat on the very bench where she had last sat with Kisha.

'What are you doing here at this time of night?' she whispered.

'I can't be seen near you – I scribe for Samsu now.'

'So?'

'He can't know I've been here, and I don't want to raise his suspicions. He doesn't trust me – I think his spies have learned about my engagement to Kisha.' His voice broke a little as he said her name. He sat with his back to Suen, his face in shadow, the god's light only illuminating his reed-like form and long-fingered hands. 'I have a message from her.'

'You've seen her?' Eliana asked desperately, clutching at his hand. 'How is she?'

'I haven't seen her, as such. Her maid got a message to me to pass along. No man is allowed near her except for the most trusted of Samsu's inner circle – he is very protective of his property.'

'Then what's the message?' she had to hold herself back from grabbing Isin and shaking it out of him.

'She just begs you to come and see her. She… she says she's in fear of her life.'

Eliana stifled a gasp. 'Samsu?'

'No, actually. As I said, he's very protective of his property. I think it's his wife and her pet bodyguard. They whisper that she is cruel to Kisha; that she'll stop at nothing to get rid of her.'

'I thought she was a harmless old woman? I've never even seen her.'

He shook his head, 'Not so old – no more so than your father. Harmless unless you cross her. She sees Kisha as a threat. Samsu only married your sister to get heirs, and Susa wants her own son to inherit, though he has no more Babylonian blood than she does.'

Eliana stared at the moonlight playing across the ripples of the pool, deep in thought. 'I'll go to her tomorrow. I'll find some excuse.'

Isin stood, 'Don't mention me, or Mari.'

'Mari?'

'Kisha's maid.'

Eliana breathed a sigh of relief – she could have kissed Isin for that piece of news. Mari was safe, and Kisha had a friend at her side.

Isin said, 'Samsu wants Kisha to forget that she ever had a family – he wants her loyal to him alone, completely dependent on his good will. Don't mention a message at all. It will bring none of us any good.'

Eliana embraced him, 'Thank you for coming. I know the risk you're taking.'

He nodded, 'Anything for Kisha.'

Stealthy as a shadow, he disappeared through the side door of the garden.

Eliana returned to bed. If she had been wakeful before, she was fully alert now. Her heart broke as she thought of her sister. In her mind, possibilities chased each other, each more chilling than the last. Her imagination ran wild through the gloom of the unknown.

She lay awake until Suen was fully abed and Utu's pink-gold light filled the room before drifting into a brief, uneasy sleep of sheer fatigue.

Chapter 2

It was mid-morning before she stirred again. Knowing how little rest she had had recently, her father ordered the servants not to wake her, and left for work alone.

As she opened her eyes, the memory of Isin's message came flooding back. She sat up abruptly and looked out of the window – the sun was high; it was approaching noon.

Washing quickly and pulling on a plain gown, she picked up a pair of sandals and moved silently along the hallway. Her heart beat so loudly that she feared it would give her away as she went down the spiral staircase, across the entrance hall and through the front door. She breathed a sigh of relief as she stepped out into the street – she hadn't encountered a single servant. No-one would tell tales on her to her father.

Sliding her feet into the sandals, she set off for the Red Palace, her feet finding their way without the help of her mind. She was so busy mentally rehearsing what she might say to get into the palace that she barely noticed the friendly faces smiling and greeting her along the way. She grinned and waved back as though her body were a puppet being controlled by someone else.

It would be better not to give a definitive reason for needing to see Kisha, she decided. She couldn't think of anything both plausible and pressing enough to gain her entrance. If she claimed to have a message from their father, they could say that she didn't need to deliver it in person. Or worse, they might drag her before Samsu to let him decide whether Kisha needed to hear it. If she said their father was gravely ill, it could be discovered as a lie immediately. Adab was no trader whose illness and absence could go unnoticed – he was visible in the community every day. All of the other excuses she could think of, she knew they would just scoff in her face and turn her away.

But she could not think of that now. If she failed, she did not know what she would do – defeat was not an option. She just couldn't countenance it. Kisha needed her, and she would travel through the underworld itself to reach her sister if she had to.

Her eyes snapped back into focus as she rounded the corner and the dazzling mountain of the palace came into full view, the glazed tiles reflecting the midday sun and making the whole building seem aflame. The complex was enclosed by walls as high as trees, with just two gates on the perimeter.

The main gate was set into the north wall, wide enough for six horses to pass abreast. It was for officials, nobles and royalty – certainly not the sister of the second wife. Eliana veered off to the left, making for the eastern gate – a smaller opening that allowed suppliers and servants to come and go without looking unsightly.

Two guards flanked the gate, standing to attention despite the crushing heat of high noon. She didn't recognise either of them from Kisha's wedding. Spears in one hand, leather shields in the other, they stared into the distance.

Eliana's heart sank as hope of success began to ebb away. Summoning all her courage, she approached the smaller of the two, trying to carry herself with an air of importance. He looked down his wide nose at her, a sneer playing about the corners of his lips.

'We don't give to beggars here – get lost, or you'll find yourself at work in the kitchens.'

She drew herself up to her full height so that her eyes were level with his, and Wide-Nose had to tilt his head back to keep looking down at her. 'I am no beggar. I am Eliana, younger daughter of Adab, *Ensi* of Nippur, and sister to your *Lugal*'s wife.'

The second guard gave an unpleasant snort of laughter, like an impatient horse. 'You mean the concubine.'

Refusing to rise to his bait, she ignored the slight. 'I must see my sister – it's urgent.'

Wide-Nose gave her a hard prod in the shoulder with his index finger, moving her back a step. 'Push off. The concubine is not receiving visitors.'

'Why not?' she demanded.

'We don't have to explain our master's orders to little girls,' said Horse-Snort.

'But, please… it's a matter of life and death!' tried Eliana, desperately.

'It will be, if you don't disappear.' Wide-Nose took a menacing step towards her.

She turned and fled, hoots of laughter following at her heels.

There was no way forward with those two – she would have to try something else. She fumed as she made her way home: 'little girl', 'the concubine', 'beggar'… the insults echoed in her ears. She was not fooled – Kisha would not send a secret message one day, then refuse visitors the next. Something was deeply wrong.

She would not give up so easily. She would have fought the guards if she'd thought there was any chance of success.

Kisha's apartments were on the western side of the complex, she knew. When they had sat together in the palace garden and talked of the weather, she had mentioned how much sunlight they got in the evenings. Eliana resolved to go back after dark, hidden under Suen's cloak of night, and scale the west wall. She could find Kisha's rooms from there.

The afternoon passed at an agonising crawl as she tried to find ways to keep herself occupied and her mind off what the night might bring. When she thought about it too hard, her breath quickened, her palms slickened and it felt like a wild animal was trying to gnaw its way out of her stomach.

It was not the thought of what she must do, but the consequences of failure that made her so fearful.

It was servants' work, but she went down to the garden to tend the plants. It soothed her, gave her something to concentrate on. She had never been above getting her hands dirty – she couldn't bear simpering girls who were afraid to get mud on their sandals or earth under their nails.

When she could no longer clearly see her hand in front of her face, she returned to the house. Her father was still out – he often worked late into the night.

'Would you like dinner, my lady?' asked the nervous boy who had served the Babylonians at the wedding. He was carefully not looking at her dirt-smeared tunic and scuffed sandals.

'No, thank you. I'm so tired… I shall just go to bed.' Her stomach was too unsettled with nerves to contemplate food.

She went up to her room and pulled out a man's tunic of black linen, the shorter skirt allowing more freedom of movement than one of her own fringed gowns. Eliana was well-known in the city for often wearing men's styles – more practical for her sort of work than women's. To help her blend into the shadows, she withdrew a hooded cloak of black wool along with a pair of soft-soled slippers of kidskin to muffle her footsteps. Anyone catching a glimpse of her in the dark would think they saw a *gidim*, a restless shade of the underworld.

Setting the clothes aside, she went to kneel at her shrine to Enlil, praying him to implore his son Suen to guide her in the dark, and the mother-goddess to reunite her with her sister, and the healer god Enki to see that her sister was safe and unharmed.

By the time she had finished her prayers, Suen was high in the sky, the city blanketed in night. She pulled on her shadow clothes and slipped out of the house. The moonlight gave the road a waxen look. She set off at a jog; her heart was pounding before had taken a single step.

The Red Palace rose from the flat plains like the castle of the underworld, a mass of black against the sky. Keeping well back from the front of the palace and its north gate, she circled to the west and headed for a grove of trees growing near the walls.

She picked her way through and pressed into the shadow of the wall that loomed above her.

Lithe as a cat, she scaled the nearest tree. The bark was cool and smooth beneath her feet as she edged out on a sturdy branch that was almost of a height with the wall. Her heart pounded in her throat as she took a deep breath, adjusting her balance. She judged the distance and, putting all her faith in Enlil, flung herself towards the wall.

Her midriff made contact with the top of the wall, knocking the breath out of her with a hammer blow to the ribs. She clung on, hanging for a few long seconds, steadying her breathing before pulling herself up, ready to drop down the other side.

She lowered herself until she was hanging by her fingertips, before hesitating a moment. In the darkness, there was no telling what she might land on. She must trust the gods to guide her fall. There was no turning back now – she did not have the strength to pull herself back up from this position.

Letting go with a rush of fear, she hung in nothingness for an agonising moment before her feet connected with soft earth and her knees folded beneath her. Fragrance filled the air around her.

With a long exhalation of relief, she said a silent prayer of thanks as she crouched in the flowerbed, getting her bearings, listening for any sign that she might have been heard.

There was no sign of life anywhere. The gods were on her side. She crept along the wall for a little way, alert for anything out of the ordinary. When she was calm, confident that she would not be detected, she made her way out of the shadows and into the open. Moving quickly and stealthily, she was guided by the light of the moon, avoiding the path that would crunch underfoot.

She froze in place – thinking for one heart-stopping moment that she had heard footsteps. The wait was agony. She held her position. Had she heard something, or was her imagination playing with her? Was that shadow moving?

With every nerve tingling, she took off at a run, leaping and weaving around obstacles, towards the dark mass of the palace. *I'll be alright*, she told herself over and again as she ran, *Enlil is with me – I'll be alright*.

But the gods are cruel, and mortals merely their playthings. Suen dipped behind a cloud, hiding his face, plunging the garden into complete blackness.

Eliana missed her footing and fell with a shriek and a resounding splash into an ornamental pond.

The sudden plunge took her breath away, the icy water gripping at her chest and throat. Her cloak was instantly saturated, soaking up the water like parched soil – the weight dragged her beneath the surface. She floundered in panic, flailing her arms, struggling for purchase on the soft edges. Her pulse hammered in her ears as she battled the instinct to breathe in.

Somebody seized the cloak and dragged her from the water. Not stopping to see who it was, she broke free of the fabric with a twist and a jolt, sitting down hard on the ground. She scrambled to her feet with no idea where she could run to in the dark enclosure. The only thought in her mind was to escape, get away, run. Anywhere.

Before she could even right herself, two strong hands grasped her under the arms and hauled her into the air. The two palace guards marched with her suspended between them, one clutching her sodden cloak in his other hand.

As if to mock her, the moon came back out from behind the clouds.

A blind panic overtook her as she realised where they were going. Her wet hair covered her face, a smothering cushion. Her heart raced like a pursued gazelle as she screamed over and over again, not knowing where help might come from in this place.

Twisting, kicking, fighting – it availed her nothing. The two held her as easily as a basket of barley. They carried her into the palace; she had no time to notice the opulence of her surroundings. She could think of nothing but shedding the vice-like grips around her arms.

They burst into a great chamber, lavishly decorated with glazed tile mosaics, gilding, fashionable cedar furniture from Lebanon… all unnoticed by the girl who was no longer screaming, but putting every ounce of her energy into fighting.

Through her sodden, matted hair, she saw an indistinct figure sat at a desk, working by the light of half a dozen blazing torches. It was too late. The sight of him chilled her to the core – the resistance went out of her as she stiffened in the grip of terror.

The soldiers threw her into a heap on the floor before the desk; she trembled with cold and dread.

Samsu didn't glance at her, but looked up at his guards from the tablet he was reading with a mild expression.

'An intruder, sir. She broke in. We fished her from one of the ponds near the west wall.'

'I see. And just who would be stupid enough to break into my palace and expect to leave it alive?'

Eliana lay still on the floor, curled up, wet and shivering. Her stomach had turned to water – she was afraid she might be sick.

'Come on, girl. Who are you?'

She pulled herself to shaking knees and pushed back the mass of dripping hair to show her face.

He raised an eyebrow.

'Well, you surprise me,' he gestured to his guards to leave. 'I thought you might try something to respond to your sister's message, but it never occurred to me that you'd be this stupid. You are supposed to be the clever one.'

Her heart sank; he knew about the message. Scowling, she lifted her gaze to meet his.

She barely had time to draw breath before a vicious strike across the face sent her reeling; her head hit the tiles hard, momentarily blacking out her vision.

When her eyes focused again, Samsu was upon her. He coiled a hand into her hair and pulled her up until her face was level with his. She cried out in pain and fear.

His breath reeked of garlic and sour wine as he hissed, 'Insolent girl! Who do you think you are, to look me in the eyes like an equal?'

That harsh black gaze travelled her body, from the bruise blossoming on her cheek where his rings had bitten her, down to where the wet linen clung to every curve of her body.

Visibly aroused, he dropped her to the floor, snarling, 'You think you are my equal? Bow!'

She rolled to her knees and touched her forehead to the floor as she remembered Kisha doing at the wedding.

'Good, now you will stay like that until you are told to get up.'

He moved behind her and grabbed the hem of her tunic, ripping it with his hands to expose her backside and female parts, the tearing fabric making a sound like the growling of an angry dog.

She balled her fists, fighting to control herself, her breathing. She thought she might faint. She almost wished she *would* faint so that Samsu would not have the satisfaction of seeing her so afraid. So that, whatever happened next, she might not remember it.

She tried to pull her knees in closer to her chest to better cover herself. Samsu delivered a swift, stinging crack across her buttocks, leaving the throbbing imprint of his hand.

'Do – not – move,' he barked, his general's voice echoing from every tile. 'Your father has spoilt you – let you run wild. But at *my* hands, you will learn a woman's place.'

She held back a sob as her blood raced, pounding like a war drum inside her head.

He knelt behind her, so close that she could feel the warmth of his breath against her damp skin as he inspected her. She gripped her hair in her hands, fighting back the sickness and shame in the pit of her stomach. The stories of his actions during the conquest raced through her mind. Her scalp burned as she pulled her hair harder, trying to distract herself from thoughts of what might come next. She shuddered in revulsion, every muscle clenched against the expected invasion of her body.

She whimpered.

He laughed, pulling the ruined tunic across her bare backside. 'My guards will take you back to your father.'

Her hopes soared.

'You will remain there under guard during the day tomorrow, and be brought to me in the evening for your first lesson in obedience.'

A sob forced its way up her throat, all her relief snatched away. She had dared to hope that she might escape with her honour, if not her dignity.

He began to walk away. 'Be sure to bathe tomorrow,' he called back over his shoulder. 'I shall not tolerate you smelling of pond water. And do not think of trying to escape. These are experienced soldiers, men of war – they will not hesitate to deal with a wilful girl.'

The door closed behind him, the dull sound reverberating around the hall like a nail being hammered into a coffin. She collapsed onto her side as panic took her again – struggling to fill her lungs, hating herself for showing weakness.

A pair of hands pulled her roughly from the floor. Blackness claimed her; she knew no more until she was dumped over the threshold of her father's house.

Chapter 3

At first light, she made her bid for freedom.

She could not meekly submit to her fate as her sister had. If she failed it would be because the gods willed it, but she had to try something, anything to save herself.

The purplish predawn light was barely enough to see by, but she would not go by night and risk losing the moonlight again. Samsu's guards barred the main door, so she made her way to a little-visited room at the back of the house. Overlooking nothing but a barren orchard and the dusty track to Nippur's west gate, she could be sure that nobody would spot her by accident. She picked her way through broken furniture and long-forgotten storage chests, towards the window.

Throwing the shutters open, she tied a thick-woven hair rope to a torch bracket set into the wall and tossed the other end outside where it hit the ground with a dull thud.

She watched for long moments, waiting for the soldiers to come running.

Nothing.

Over her back, she slung an old leather bag containing a couple of wineskins, some bread and a handful of fruits. She eased backwards out of the window, wrapped her feet in the rope and lowered herself hand over hand until her sandals touched the earth. She looked towards the west gate with a surge of triumph – she was free!

A blow to the face sent her staggering backwards before she had even had time to disentangle her feet. The heavy rope caught at her ankles and brought her crashing to the ground.

Dust filled her nostrils; unshed tears of pain, surprise and disappointment shimmered in her eyes. Tasting blood, she brought a hand to her face, checking that she still had all her teeth. It took a moment to realise that she had bitten her tongue as she fell.

A strong hand seized her arm and hauled her up. A dagger appeared at her wrist. She clenched her fist instinctively.

'Next time you try to run, we'll see how well you escape with just one hand,' hissed Samsu's thug. 'The prince only needs one of your hands to pleasure him.' He ran it lightly over the fragile skin of her wrist – a thin red line blossomed where the blade had been; the blood welled up and trickled down over her fingers. It stung a little, but she stared him in the eyes and did not flinch.

If he was disappointed, he did not show it.

He strode around to the front of the house, dragging her behind him, and threw her back inside.

'Stay!' he commanded, as if to a dog.

The door slammed behind him. Eliana pulled her knees to her chest and let the despair engulf her.

Dawn broke, the household woke, and still she sat there, steeped in misery.

A gentle hand found her shoulder. She jumped and looked up.

Her father looked down at her, concern written in every line of his face. He helped her to her feet and steered her towards his office.

She took a seat on the bench opposite his desk, dropping her head into her hands. Her hair formed a comforting curtain around her, shutting out the world.

Adab took a seat behind his desk. 'What happened?' he asked in a soft voice.

The story came tumbling out in a waterfall of words.

Her father's face crumpled, 'So now he is to steal away both my daughters.'

Eliana sniffed, 'Can't you... is there any way... can you do anything at all?'

He sighed and rubbed at his forehead, 'You know I cannot. No more than I could do anything to protect Kisha.'

The words barely registered in her mind – as he said, she had known it anyway.

A tear rolled down her face. She could see only one way out – it was as if she had exhausted herself in a maze of streets, only to find herself in a narrow alley ending with a high brick wall. Her voice broke as she said, 'Then, will you kill me?'

Her hands trembled as she asked – she had no real desire to die. Being alive was exhilarating, sensual, full of people to meet, things to learn, lives to touch. Death was so final. Once she entered the spirit world, there could be no return.

Though his face betrayed nothing, he wrung his hands in his lap. 'I would gladly give you an honourable death to spare you the ordeal that lies ahead. Better to let Enlil claim you for the underworld where you can be with your mother than send you to be Samsu's plaything,' his voice cracked as he spoke, filling Eliana with guilt for asking it of him. 'I would even... even kill myself, so that we can all be together. But could you do that to Kisha – leave her all alone in the world with Samsu?'

'No,' she whispered.

'I still have work to do in Nippur – the people need me. You know that if I ended your life, deprived the prince of his whim, he would take vengeance on me... or on Kisha.' Adab's mouth twisted in pain as he was forced to choose between the safety of one daughter or the other.

Her father and her sister were all she had in the world, she would not see them suffer for anything. She hung her head, defeated.

Standing, he embraced her. 'I must be off to work, Eliana. I shall pray for you. And I shall pray that we meet again.' He kissed her atop her black curls, still dusty and tangled from the night's adventures, and left the room.

The door clicked softly shut behind him. From the other side, she heard a strangled try. It was the anguish of a man who lived to help people, but could not protect his own daughters – the sound of it tore her apart.

She sat a long while after he was gone, contemplating her options. If her father killed her, Samsu would wreak his revenge on her family. If she killed herself... nobody else would be culpable.

First, she would need a blade. Adab had carried a dagger, once. It hadn't been seen for many moons – Sumerians were no longer permitted to carry weapons under the new regime – but if he still had it, Eliana knew it would be in this room.

She began with his desk, carefully moving stacks of clay tablets and reed styluses, looking beneath everything that moved. When she found nothing there, she searched the gleaming cedar chest that stood near the door. There was still no sign of the blade.

It was as she was trying to think where else in the house it might be stored that she spotted an old iron chest, half-buried under a pile of old linen. Rummaging through, she found what she was looking for; buried at the bottom, rusted by lack of care.

Cradling it like a newborn, she carried it back to her room.

She sat on the bed, breathing deeply as she stared at it, trying to imagine how it might feel to have the cold metal plunge into her flesh.

'It is the only way,' she told herself. 'To deny him satisfaction, to save my honour. To spare myself. It is the only way. If I do the deed myself, he cannot punish my family.'

Speaking the words aloud did nothing to convince her of their truth.

She took up the blade. It was an old one, the carved stone handle worn smooth by countless generations of her forefathers' hands. The iron was spotted with rust, but it was usable and sharp enough for her purpose. She touched her thumb to the edge to be sure.

She would show him, she decided. He might rule Nippur, but he would never rule her. He could conquer her city, but never her spirit.

Placing the point below her ribs, aiming squarely up at her heart, she clasped the hilt in both hands and took a deep breath. Her last breath.

Her senses sharpened. The noise of the city carried through her window on spice-scented air. She turned to look out, the sun high in the lapis blue sky. A pleasant breeze stirred her hair. Every part of her felt alive.

A voice echoed in her mind – her own voice, from the day of her sister's wedding: *A brave woman lives, cowards die.*

Was she a coward? Was that how Kisha would remember her? How would she feel when… when she heard the news? She would understand, wouldn't she?

Eliana shook her head, trying to banish any doubts; she turned back and gripped the hilt harder. Of course Kisha would understand – anybody could see that she'd be better off dead.

She pressed the point into the soft flesh under her breasts and felt a prickle. A small bead of blood welled up to stain the front of her tunic.

Looking at the blood – the blood of her father, of her sister – her hands trembled again. Could she be sure that Samsu would leave Kisha and her father in peace? He was a monster – he might punish them in spite of their innocence. How could her shade ever find rest if they suffered for her selfishness? She would be doomed to roam the land forever as a *gidim* – it would be a fate worse than living.

She dropped the blade to the floor, knowing that she couldn't do it. Kisha *needed* her; she had sent that message for a reason. Suddenly overcome with exhaustion, she lay back on the bed, tears sliding into the dirty mass of her hair. She had been awake, alert and nervous for more than a day and a night – her body finally defeated her mind, and she slept.

*

The sun was low and the evening cool when Eliana awoke. The despair was gone, replaced by a calm resignation. What would be, would be. If the gods had decreed it, no action of hers could change it.

She rose and bathed as ordered. A new plan formed in her mind – not so much a plan of action, as a plan of acceptance. She would go to him pretty and beguiling, sweet and obedient, and hope for more gentle treatment. If he saw no defiance in her, perhaps the game would lose its sport and he would send her home.

It was a vain hope, but one she must cling to.

Drying her hair with a sheet, she combed jasmine oil through it until the thick curls sprang back to her waist and held their shape. When she turned, her hair danced sinuously around her like a living being.

She applied the usual cosmetics – powder to her face, colour to her lips and cheeks to make her eyes sparkle. By the time she slipped into her best saffron silk gown and put on a pair of beaded sandals, the light had begun to fade.

As a final touch, she clipped on a gold bracelet, inset with lapis lazuli and ivory – the last relic she had of her mother. Under normal circumstances, she would not have defiled it by wearing it for such an occasion, but she knew that she might never return home again, and she wanted to keep it with her.

She paused in the doorway and looked back at her room – the neat little bed with its colourful woven blanket, the iron chest containing her gowns, the cosmetics table with its clay pots and jars, the copper washtub and her holy shrine to Enlil. It was not much, but it was all she had. She fervently hoped to see it again.

Making her way downstairs, the front door already stood ajar and Samsu's bullies waited inside.

One gave a snort of laughter when he saw her. She flushed deep crimson, but kept silent, her head up and her eyes focused.

She took a last glance around before walking out into the street. There was no sign that her father had returned home in time to see her go. She supposed he could not bear it.

The walk to the palace felt never-ending, like a torment of the underworld: a road that one was destined to travel for eternity, stretching on and on to some terrible destination, the dreadful anticipation mounting with each step.

More than once, her courage almost deserted her and she glanced off the road, plotting which route she might take, calculating her chances if she were to flee.

If the thought of what Samsu might do to her father and sister wasn't enough to put her off, the memory of her recent escape attempt was. Touching her fingers to her lip, she winced; it was still swollen from the morning's blow.

The high red walls came into view – she could see them as nothing other than the red brick walls of her tomb. She felt numb inside as she wondered whether she would ever be on this side of them again.

On reaching the palace, the guards at the eastern gate nodded them through – they were clearly expected. As they passed through, Eliana saw a glint of recognition in Horse-Snort's eyes and a barely repressed smirk of amusement on his lips.

Her hand twitched, longing to slap the smugness right off his face, but her guards marched her on too quickly.

Instead of leading her towards the audience hall of last night, they took her south. Kisha had said that Samsu's private apartments occupied most of the southern side of the palace.

Her heart skipped a beat – she had been hoping she would see Kisha first.

She was taken to a lavishly appointed bedchamber. The men pushed her inside, then turned to stand sentry outside the door, leaving her to take in her surroundings.

The centrepiece of the room was the bed: enormous, with four great posts of cedar at each corner, intricately carved to depict men and women in the throes of passion. They turned her stomach with their lewdness – she could not imagine how any such act could bring pleasure. Between the bedposts were strung delicate hangings of gossamer silk, blood red. Matching curtains hung at the windows, breathing with the breeze.

A magnificent Persian rug was laid near the terrace over the glazed red floor tiles; it was a luxury Eliana had never seen before, a clear sign of the conqueror's wealth. Embroidered cushions were deposited at intervals around its edges, and a collection of clay writing tablets cluttered the middle. Torches burned in iron brackets around the room... illuminating the two guards stationed inside.

Their eyes never moved; they didn't acknowledge her presence in any way. They might have been carved of stone, except that she recognised the face of one: Samsu's closest companion, his second-in-command, his Brute.

She shrank back a little and felt her cheeks grow pale under their artificial colour.

Tearing her gaze away from his impassive face, Eliana looked around once more, wondering where to arrange herself for him to find, to appear to her best advantage. There was the bed, where she would look most beguiling... but she did not want to him to think her wanton, or to give him ideas if it was not in his head to have her. Perhaps the cushions... she turned to take in the whole room, feeling lost.

Behind her, Samsu emerged from the terrace, silent as a prowling wolf. He cleared his throat softly.

She jumped and whirled to face him. Her hand, now shaking, flew to her heart as if to physically slow its wild beating.

He gave her a brief, appraising glance, his expression inscrutable. His left hand was relaxed by his side – in his right, he carried a bullwhip. He approached slowly, boot heels thudding menacingly on the tiles.

Just in time, she remembered to lower her gaze to the floor.

'Kneel,' he said. He did not need to raise his voice.

She knelt, back upright, hands folded in her lap. A sharp kick connected with her ribs, driving the air out of her.

'Properly!' he barked.

She touched her forehead to the ground. His boot had left a smear of dust on her silk, and she could feel a bruise flowering on the delicate skin of her ribs.

He sneered, 'Look at you, with your painted face and whore's garb. Did you think to seduce me? Imagined that I would have you and send you on your way?' He did not require an answer. With a harsh laugh, he continued, 'I told you that you would learn a woman's place, that I would teach you obedience. You won't escape by playing the whore. Believe me, girl, I have lain with more whores than you've had gowns. I know all their tricks. And so shall you, before I'm finished.'

Eliana's stomach clenched, all hope of winning gentler treatment with acquiescence gone.

'You will learn to obey whatever command I give, without question or hesitation.' He thrust his dusty boot under her face. 'Lick it clean,' he ordered.

Looking at the boot with revulsion, she wondered how many proud spirits Samsu had trampled beneath it. She hesitated a moment too long – he brought it up to collide with her chin, sending her sprawling backwards. He placed the boot heavily on her chest, pressing his weight down to expel the air from her lungs as he shouted, 'Are you deaf, girl? Lick it!'

His voice rang from every surface, every syllable loud and menacing, sending a knife of fear through her artificial calm and into her gut.

Trembling and struggling to draw breath under the crushing weight of his boot, she stuck out her tongue and gave a tentative lick, repressing the urge to gag.

He lifted his foot off her and placed it on the floor, allowing her to pull herself back into her bow and continue. Her jaw ached from his kick to her chin, and the dust of the street dried up her saliva, making each stroke more difficult than the last. She closed her eyes and tried to forget where she was – she thought of Kisha, wished for her sister's arms around her.

By the time she finished, her mouth was arid as the desert and her tongue felt coated in wool.

Finally satisfied, he withdrew his foot. 'Good,' he nodded. 'Now, remove your dress.'

Her cheeks burned with shame and she felt a knot of tears gather at the base of her throat – she would not shed them. She would not show him that he frightened her. He would not win so easily.

As if it were not bad enough to undress before Samsu, she felt the interested gazes of the two guards boring into her. She swallowed hard and slid off the shoulder straps, allowing the silk to fall to the floor, standing tall and proud in nothing but her unblemished skin and her mother's bracelet, her eyes as dry as her mouth.

Samsu's eyes drank her in. 'Now, prostrate yourself on the floor... no, not the rug, you arrogant child – it's too good for the likes of you. On the tiles.'

Shivering as her bare skin came into contact with the cold clay tiles, she lay face down, arms outstretched. She saw his shadow flickering in the torchlight as he bent over her, shuddered as he ran calloused hands down the length of her body – fingertips grazing the edges of her nipples, tracing the dip of her waist, trailing the crack of her buttocks and into the crease between her thighs, all the way down to her feet.

He exhaled deeply. She held her breath.

'Up.'

She pulled herself back to her knees, forehead still touching the floor, feeling sick with vulnerability and dizzy with the effort of hiding it.

He chuckled, 'You're getting the hang of this. Now,' he grabbed her bruised chin hard, directing her gaze towards the Brute, 'suck his cock.'

Her head snapped up of its own accord; she stared at him in horror.

'I can't!' The dismayed words were out of her mouth before she could stop them. She threw herself back to the ground, trembling in anticipation of Samsu's wrath. 'I'm sorry!' she cried.

The words were barely spoken before the whip cracked across her buttocks sharp as a lightning bolt. She almost choked on the cry of pain.

The sting of the first stroke had barely dulled before a second and a third landed on the same spot, splitting the skin so that blood trickled down her thighs.

He seized her by the hair and pulled her up, 'You can, and you will! Who are you to tell me "I can't"? To disobey me? You will wrap those pretty lips around his cock, or I will cut them off!'

With a mighty shove, he sent her stumbling towards the Brute, every step sending a fresh knife of pain through her injured behind. She fell to her knees in front of him.

He hoisted his tunic up to the waist to expose himself.

Eliana stared in horror – she had never seen male parts before, except on sheep and dogs. He was already erect; purplish with swollen veins. He gave a grunt of impatience, dug his fingers into her hair and pulled her mouth forcefully down onto it, thrusting in and out so deep that she thought she would choke or suffocate.

Her first instinct was to bite, but there was no doubt in her mind that she would pay for that transgression with all her teeth. For a split second, it almost felt as though it would be worth it to humble this monster and bite his manhood clean off for this humiliation… then her mind filled with images of the atrocities he had committed unprovoked during the conquest. She could expect no quick and easy death if she acted impulsively.

She pulled back against his hand, trying to reduce the thrust. Some of her hair came away in his grip.

He broke his rhythm, pulled her head back for a brief, blessed second, before slapping her hard across the face and continuing harder than before, filling her mouth and throat.

The gagging sound she made only spurred him on. He moved faster and faster, until, with a grunt and a shudder, his seed came spilling down her throat. She fought and tried to pull away, but he held her firmly in place; she had no choice but to swallow or drown.

As soon as he let her go, she fell to her hands and knees and the liquid came flooding back up. She gasped and retched until her stomach had expelled every drop, then collapsed shivering to the floor.

She heard Samsu's voice as if from a distance, amusement plain in his tone as though he'd been watching a troupe of travelling performers. 'How did she do?'

'Well enough,' said the Brute, straightening his tunic, 'for a novice. She can be taught.'

'Very well, go to her father tomorrow and pay him whatever you think she is worth. She will live here at the palace – a maid to my concubine by day, and a whore to me by night. That is what you wanted, isn't it, Eliana? To be with your beloved sister again?'

She could not have summoned the strength to answer even if he had demanded it.

'Perhaps,' Samsu added, 'if you ever learn humility and obedience, you could be something more than just the whore to the Prince of Babylon. Once we have broken that unfortunate pride and spirit.'

She curled tighter in the foetal position, praying for an end to it, aching all over from the assault and longing for nothing so much as a soft bed behind a sturdy door.

He continued, 'To speed up the process, my officers may borrow you for... training, whenever they please; but your virginity will be kept for me alone.' His voice hardened, 'I will take it when you have nothing else to give.'

Turning away, he made a dismissive gesture with his hand. 'Lesson one is at an end. I trust you learned something. Ashan, take her to the concubine's apartments.'

The other officer stationed in the room, who had not moved an inch throughout the whole show, nodded sharply and strode to where Eliana lay.

'Get up!' he hissed softly.

She tried to pull herself to her feet, but her body was in shock and her legs would not support her weight. After three attempts, she gave up and folded back to the ground.

Ashan bent and scooped her up, not ungently, and carried her from the room towards the western quarter of the palace. She opened her eyes and looked up at him through a haze of pain and misery, but she could not focus, so closed them again.

'Give him what he wants,' the soldier whispered. 'Don't resist him, it will all go easier for you.'

The pity in his tone was more than she could bear; silent tears began flowing down her face.

He deposited her on her feet before a wooden door, half holding her up, half propping her against the wall as he knocked.

After long seconds, the door swung inwards to reveal Mari, her face pale and hair dishevelled, just roused from sleep.

'Ashan?' she whispered.

He pressed a finger to his lips and gestured towards Eliana. Mari barely stifled a gasp of horror, taking the other girl's weight and staggering into the room with her.

Ashan quietly closed the door on the women and made his way back to his place at Samsu's side.

Chapter 4

'Eliana!' Kisha gave an anguished cry when she saw her sister. 'Mari – what happened?'

'I don't know, my lady. Ashan just brought her to the door and left her here.'

Eliana did not open her eyes as she leaned heavily on Mari. 'S – Samsu.' She croaked out, her voice still hoarse from vomiting. She swayed – Kisha rushed in to catch her under the other arm.

'We'll put her in my bed. Gods, she's freezing. Why is she unclothed?!' Kisha had never seen her strong baby sister in such a state.

Mari gave her a meaningful look. 'Perhaps it is best not to ask questions when the answers would only distress you.

Between them, they got Eliana onto Kisha's bed as she drifted in and out of consciousness.

'Bring warm water,' Kisha said, 'and arnica and thyme.'

Mari moved quickly, and they were soon tending Eliana's wounds with expert care. Mari washed her, while Kisha applied arnica to the bruising on her sister's face and ribs, and oil of thyme to the wound behind where the whip had split the skin. They dressed her in a warm woollen bedgown of Kisha's and manoeuvred her under the blanket as she slept, limp and still as the dead.

Their work done, Mari gathered up the medicine and returned to her little room that adjoined her mistress's. Kisha climbed into the bed, wrapped her arms around Eliana and held her as she slept.

The following morning, Eliana struggled to remember where she was. Waking with her sister's familiar arms encircling her, she could almost believe that the last eight moons had been an awful nightmare. She made to snuggle closer into Kisha's warmth – and found that every muscle ached.

She slowly became aware of a dull throb in her face, a pain when she breathed in too deeply, and a sharper pain in her backside. Her throat was raw and inflamed when she swallowed.

The memories of last night came surging back. She tensed, taking a deep breath and exhaling slowly, concentrating on calming the flutter of panic in her stomach.

'Elly?' came Kisha's sleepy voice from behind her.

'I'm awake,' she whispered, rolling onto her back, wincing at the pain.

Kisha sat up and looked at her sister, 'What are you doing here?'

'I came to see you. Or, I tried to. I got your message through Isin. But they turned me away at the gate, so I broke in...'

'Oh – you silly thing! Just like you – brave and daft!' Kisha clutched Eliana's hand.

'... I fell in a pond and they caught me. Now Samsu wants to make me his whore.' She almost spat the final word, the indignity of it catching in her throat.

'And if he wants it, it will happen,' said Kisha sadly, crossing her arms over her stomach.

'It will not,' Eliana set her jaw in the way she always did when she was determined. 'He'll never have loyalty or obedience from me. I'll find a way out of this place for both of us.'

'Hush!' Kisha covered her sister's mouth, eyes wide with fright. 'You mustn't say such things! Even the walls have ears, here.'

'I don't care,' Eliana sulked. 'I'll fight him with every breath. I'll even kill him if I have to.'

'Stop it! Now listen, Eliana: as *Ensi*'s daughter, you were always allowed to be free in your words and your ways, but if we're going to survive in this place, you need to learn to still your tongue. You'll get all three of us killed.'

'He wouldn't kill Mari too, surely?'

'No,' Kisha let the blanket drop away from her chest.

Eliana gaped – her sister's belly was huge and round. 'You're having a baby?'

'Samsu's baby. He leaves me alone now that I'm carrying his child. If I give him a son, maybe we'll be safe.'

'How long to go?'

'Just two moons – I fell pregnant quickly. Samsu was... generous, with his attentions.'

'So, when I visited you in the garden...?'

'I was three moons gone, yes.'

'And you didn't say anything!'

'What could I say? Every move, every word was being watched. I hadn't even told Samsu at that point.'

'Oh, Kisha!' Eliana put her hand on her sister's stomach, hoping to feel movement.

'He's sleeping at the moment, my little prince,' Kisha smiled. 'I'll grab you when he kicks.'

There was a tentative knock at the door.

'Come in!' called Kisha.

Mari entered, clutching a tray. 'Sorry my lady, I heard voices and thought you might be up.'

'We are,' Kisha beckoned. 'Come and eat with us.'

Placing the tray on the bed, Mari perched on the edge. 'You look much better than last night, my lady,' she said to the younger girl.

'I'm no lady,' said Eliana bitterly. 'I'm to be a whore. A toy for Samsu and his officers, and no less a slave than you are. You can call me by my name.'

There was an uncomfortable silence.

Kisha reached for the tray and poured a bowl of warmed honey drink. She took a sip, then offered it to her sister. 'Try, it's lovely.'

Eliana waved it away. 'I don't want anything.'

'You must have something, my… Eliana,' Mari said. 'You'll need your strength to recover from those injuries, and to bear anything more that's to come.'

She could have wept, then, at the futility of it all. These wounds would heal, but how long until Samsu sent for her again? Days… hours?

Kisha placed light fingers on her arm, pressing the bowl into her hands. 'Drink,' she said.

Eliana took a long swallow, the warm, thick drink soothing her aching throat. She looked into her sister's loving face, and felt at home.

'Whatever's to come,' she said, 'I can bear it. As long as I have you, Kisha, I can withstand anything they throw at me.'

Kisha smiled, kissing Eliana's rumpled curls. 'Come on, let's finish breakfast and get down to the bathhouse. Then I'll show you around – it's not all bad, living in a palace.'

*

The ladies' bathhouse was a beautiful building constructed of white stone over a natural hot spring. The sisters stripped off and eased into the blissful, soothing waters as two silent slave girls appeared and began to wash and massage them. They didn't blink at Eliana's injuries – Samsu's ways were well-known amongst the women of the palace.

Eliana finally began to relax as the girl's strong fingers worked at her tender muscles. It was never far from her mind that there would be terrible times to come, and unimaginable experiences to endure – but she would spend more time in Kisha's company than Samsu's. She would only ever have to make it through a few hours at a time before she could return to her sister.

It was a price she was willing to pay.

They sat quietly throughout the bath, enjoying the peace and the simplicity of being in each other's company again. Mari had been a great help to Kisha, but was no replacement for the sister she had raised.

When they finally climbed out, the slave girls dried and dressed them. It was an unusual experience for Eliana, who had always done everything for herself. It wasn't entirely unpleasant.

They made their way back towards the apartments, chattering merrily.

Kisha suddenly fell silent. She froze in her tracks.

'What is it?' hissed Eliana.

'Shh! Bow, Elly!' Kisha lowered her head and bent from the waist, stepping back off the path.

Eliana scoffed – she wouldn't bow before she knew who was supposed to be worthy of her respect! She looked up the path and saw a little party approaching, headed by a richly dressed woman old enough to be their mother. Scurrying behind her was a portly woman of a similar age, and beside her walked two guards. Even from a distance, Eliana recognised the taller of the two as the Brute. She felt physically sick to look at him, wanting to vomit all over again. The mere sight of him brought back all the fear and shame of last night.

As the woman approached, Eliana saw that she was small and spare. Her purple silks were neatly tailored to her tiny frame, fringed and beaded with gold. A golden diadem embedded with amethyst sat atop her brow.

But more striking than her clothes was her face. It was a face lined by bitterness and set with permanent displeasure. She might have been a beauty, once, but those days were long past.

She stopped in front of the sisters and looked Eliana up and down. 'Well, at least the concubine knows her place.' She turned to the Brute, 'And who is this impudent piece of work?'

'The new whore, ma'am.' He replied, all deference and courtesy.

'Ah,' she turned back to Eliana. 'I have heard of you. You are the concubine's sister.'

It wasn't a question. Eliana held her silence and gazed steadily back.

'Well, whore; my husband is a man of unusual appetites. He will break you and mould you into a copy of your spineless sister before tiring of you and packing you off to a city brothel. A common thing like you, it shouldn't take long.'

'He won't break me,' said Eliana calmly.

The woman raised her eyebrows. 'Girl, I have been married to the prince since he was six years old. I practically raised him. He was the sort of child who would break a cat's hind legs for the sheer amusement of seeing it haul itself about on its front paws. I guarantee he will break you, and I look forward to the day.'

She swept past imperiously, forcing Eliana to take a step backwards or be collided with.

Balling her fists, Eliana forced herself to keep calm as the Brute strode past. He looked at her with a lecherous hunger in his face. Her stomach cramped in disgust, and she was glad she had only eaten a small breakfast.

Kisha held her bow – the Brute deliberately barged into her as he passed, sending her staggering in the dirt.

Eliana rushed to catch her sister, now more easily knocked off-balance with her heavy, cumbersome belly. With an angry hiss, she let out the breath she had been holding in and looked after him.

'Leave it,' ordered Kisha. 'You won't do us any good by arguing with him. Besides, it's all at her instigation.'

They carried on slowly up the path. 'That was Susa, then?' asked Eliana.

'Yes – she hates me. If my child is a prince, he will displace her son from the line of succession. She has been trying her best to make me miscarry, but the child is strong. When… when I sent you that message… I was afraid for my life, and baby's. She had a boy knock me down a flight of steps – I bled so heavily that I thought, well, you know…'

Eliana gripped her sister's hand, not trusting herself to speak.

'But it was all alright,' smiled Kisha. 'The baby is clinging on tightly. I wish I hadn't sent that message, then you would be safe. But I'm still glad to have you with me.'

'Why is she so awful?' Eliana burst out.

'It's as she said – she was married off to Samsu when he was six years old, and she more than twenty. She's an Elamite princess. King Hammurabi conquered her father's kingdom two decades ago and took her hostage – he married her off to his son to ensure their good behaviour; no matter that she had her own son, a boy of an age with her new husband!'

Eliana was silent. She supposed that being love-starved for so many years would leave anybody bitter and resentful. She would not allow it to happen to herself, whatever Samsu had in mind for her.

'Never mind,' said Kisha. 'You had to meet her eventually. Now that's all done with. Come on – I'll show you our gardens.'

She quickened her pace, dragging Eliana back to their rooms before they could encounter any more trouble.

*

Eliana slipped her arm through Mari's as they walked barefoot through the garden. Kisha tired easily in this late stage of pregnancy so was resting indoors, out of the heat.

The air was heavy with perfume you could almost taste, the flowers in full bloom.

They set the garden aflame in hues of red, orange and yellow, carefully arranged to exquisite effect, bordered by leafy greens and sprays of purple. Planted in banks, they were perfectly spaced to create pathways designed to lead the wanderer from one delight to the next. Eliana felt like a butterfly as she flitted from blossom to blossom, exclaiming over the beauty of this petal or the sweetness of that scent.

She picked a few posies. The girls paused on the bridge over the stream that wound its way through the little patch of paradise, its waters channelled from the canal that nestled beside the palace. Two levels created a gentle waterfall; beneath the tumbling waters sat a statue of Enki, the god of fresh water, of mischief, and of male potency. Dressed in the skin of a carp, wrapped around with his double helix snakes and wearing the horned crown of divinity, the stone effigy looked terrifying and laughable all at once.

Eliana leaned over the bridge, pulling petals off her flowers to drop in the water, watching them swirl away. She sighed. 'Such beauty here, but at such an ugly price. You know, I think I could cope with just Samsu by himself. It's him teamed with the Brute I can't endure.'

'I know.' A shadow crossed Mari's face.

Eliana looked at her, squinting against the sun. 'He hasn't... violated you too?'

'No, nothing like that. Worse.' Her voice cracked a little; she cleared her throat.

'What could *possibly* be worse?'

'He... he murdered my family.'

'I'm so sorry.' Eliana reached out and placed a hand on the other girl's arm.

'I'm fine,' Mari smiled through tear-filled eyes. 'Really. I'm glad they're not alive to see me brought into slavery.'

'What did your family do? You know, before.'

'We were shepherds. My two brothers would take the flock out to graze, and I would help mother at home.'

Suspicion crept over Eliana. 'Your brothers – how old were they?'

'Twelve and fourteen. Why?'

The colour drained from Eliana's face. 'I… just wondered.'

Mari did not notice, brushing a tear from her cheek. 'What's done is done. It's been nearly three years – I've grieved for my family, and now I'm glad they're not here to see what our city has been reduced to.'

The girls linked arms again and made their way slowly back to the terrace that led into their apartments. Eliana still could feel a slight tremble in Mari's arm.

Kisha was up when they returned, working at her loom. She was more than halfway through an elaborate rendering of Inanna, the goddess of the morning and evening, standing on the backs of two lionesses against an eight-pointed star.

She looked up and smiled when the girls came in. 'So, what do you think of our little garden?'

'It's gorgeous,' Eliana sighed. 'I can see myself spending many hours out there.'

Picking up Kisha's lyre from its stand, she plucked at a few strings.

'Oh, play us something, Eliana!' said Mari. 'I can't play a note, myself. It was never very important for a shepherd's daughter to be musical.'

Mari settled herself onto a floor cushion with a basket of mending, while Eliana perched on the bench next to Kisha, who continued her weaving.

It had been some months since she had played properly, but her fingers soon loosened up and began to dance across the strings – picking out the soothing song that Kisha would sing to calm her nightmares.

When the song ended, she stilled the strings and looked out across the terrace. Utu was beginning to lower his great golden head to the horizon, and the sun's rays gilded every petal in the garden. Eliana took a deep breath of the flower-scented air. Harmony reigned.

I could find some happiness here, she thought. *For the first time since the conquest, I could really be happy – with my sister, my friend, and my little niece or nephew.*

Her thoughts were interrupted as the door to the apartment flew open with a crash. Eliana's heart plunged as the Brute strode in.

Kisha cried out in fear at the first sight of him, crossing her arms protectively over her belly. Mari and Eliana stood up defensively, ready to shield her.

He went straight for Eliana – the vile lechery she had read on his face that morning was stark in his eyes again.

She realised his intention too late and turned to run – he grabbed her by the wrist so hard that she felt her bones bend under his grip. He began to drag her towards the bedroom.

'No!' she screamed, pulling away. 'No! NO!'

He stopped, twisting her arm up behind her, making her shout with pain. He brought his mouth close to her ear, but didn't trouble to lower his voice. 'You can be sure that your words this morning about Samsu not breaking you will get back to him. I promise you, he'll take them as a personal challenge. You should be thankful that it's only me come to give you a lesson… for now. He said that I could take you for training whenever I like, whore, and I'm taking him at his word. Now,' he chuckled, 'let's put that loud mouth of yours to better use.'

She cast a pleading look at Kisha as he pushed her past. Kisha stared in mute horror, hands gripping the sides of her loom so tightly that her knuckles looked in danger of splitting the skin.

Mari stood in silence, knowing there was nothing she could do.

Keeping her arm in its painful twist, the Brute forced Eliana ahead of him. He threw her into the bedroom, slamming the door behind them.

Chapter 5

With a self-satisfied smirk on his lips, the Brute pulled down his tunic and left the apartment.

As soon as his back was turned, Kisha and Mari ran to the bedroom.

Eliana lay on the bed. Her gown was torn across the chest, and there was a new bruise on her cheekbone and fingerprint bruises on her exposed breast. Her eyes were blank and staring – if it hadn't been for her ragged breathing, they would have feared the worst.

'Are you ok?' asked Kisha, uselessly.

She shook her head. 'Bowl, please,' she whispered.

Mari was back in an instant with a ceramic bowl, vibrantly painted with fruits and vines.

Eliana did not notice the bowl's beauty, but turned her back on the others, pushed two fingers down her throat and vomited neatly into it, eyes streaming with tears as her throat burned and convulsed. Mari vanished again, this time reappearing with a drinking bowl brimming with cool water.

Accepting it, Eliana drained the bowl.

'Mari, will you take me down to the bathhouse?'

'Again? It's almost full dark.'

'It's ok, Mari.' Kisha nodded.

'As you say, my lady,' she said, before turning back to Eliana. 'Can you walk?'

She nodded. Kisha slipped a loose wool gown over her sister's shoulders to cover her modesty.

She walked unassisted to the bathhouse, Mari holding a torch before them to light their way. When they arrived, it was blissfully deserted. Not even the slave girls were in attendance at this hour.

Mari slipped the torch into a bracket and helped Eliana to ease out of her gown.

The injured girl climbed stiffly into the water and picked up a piece of pumice. 'Help me wash? Please.'

Taking it, Mari began to rub the stone over her back.

'Harder.'

She increased the pressure slightly.

'*Harder!*' Eliana insisted.

Hesitating, Mari said, 'I'll take your skin off if I rub any harder.'

'Good!' spat Eliana. 'Scrub off any part of me that he touched.'

Mari laid the pumice aside and began to rub the tension from Eliana's shoulders with her hands instead. 'You're very brave, you know.'

'I'm not. If I was brave, I wouldn't let it happen. I'd fight him off.'

'We both know there's no choice in this. Neither of us would be here if there was. But I think you're right – Samsu won't break you.'

Eliana turned to look at her, 'Do you think? I wish I was so certain.'

She nodded firmly. 'It will take more than violation of your body to break you – your strength and courage is in your mind. If I could have just a fraction of what you've got, I'd be a better person.'

'You are a good person,' said Eliana, surprised. 'Kisha couldn't have done without you these last few months.'

'I know, and despite that, I'd still flee if I thought I wouldn't get caught,' Mari said, her voice catching on her misery. 'What kind of person does that make me?'

'It makes you human.' It was Eliana's turn to comfort Mari. 'It's only natural to want to save yourself. I would rather they hurt me than Kisha, but she's always been the best thing in my life. I'd do anything to protect her.'

'I wish I could be as loyal as you.'

'You would, if it was your family. You didn't ask for any of this.' She shrugged Mari's hands off and dipped her head under the water, coming up with her curls flattened and plastered to her scalp. Taking up the soap, she washed her hair and body quickly, trying to wash away the Brute's smell while Mari went off to look for sheets.

By the time she was clean and dry, Eliana felt more like herself – just exhausted.

Her sister was already in bed when they returned. She crawled in behind, draping an arm over Kisha's firm, rounded belly, hand resting lightly on the bump.

She gave a deep sigh.

'Alright?' Kisha asked, sleepily.

'I suppose.' Eliana stared into the darkness. 'Do you think this will happen every day?'

There was a long pause. 'You'll learn to bear it.'

'What if I don't?'

Kisha covered her sister's hand with her own, pressing it hard against her belly. 'You will – I know you. Besides, this little prince needs his loving aunt by his side in such a big, dangerous world.'

As if in response, a little foot struck out at Eliana's hand. She shrieked and sat up. 'He kicked me!'

In the dark, Kisha grinned. 'See, he knows you already. If that's not something to fight for, I don't know what is.'

*

The days fell into a steady routine. Samsu's officers would visit several times a day to take their pleasure in various ways – it didn't take long for the girls to think of a way to spite them.

Mari began to wait near the door, listening for the distinctive ring of boot heels on tiles. She would give a signal when she heard the approach, and Eliana would dart out via the terrace, quick as a startled rabbit, clambering up a tree to the safety of a high branch, hidden by the wide flat leaves.

They giggled amongst themselves at how this enraged the officers – particularly the Brute. His were the assaults that Eliana was keenest to avoid. The others were brusque and took what they came for – it was only he who seemed to take pleasure in added viciousness.

He would storm in, demanding, 'Where is she?'

'Last I knew, she was heading off to the bath house,' Mari would reply, sometimes varying it to 'in the garden' or 'walking in the courtyard'.

Kisha kept quiet, still too timid to draw his notice if she could avoid it.

The Brute would bluster and rage uselessly, making his dire threats; but in the end, he always left without his prize, and Eliana could come down feeling smug and triumphant.

She didn't always come down – it was pleasant up in the tree. She could stretch out along the branch, hidden from prying eyes by the foliage, and gaze up at the wide blue sky. For that short time, she could pretend that she was free as a cloud, could drift wherever she pleased… intangible, uncatchable. It was her favourite daydream.

Kisha laughed and called her a little monkey to prefer the tree-dwelling life over the comfort of a palace bed, but beneath the jest, she understood.

This little trick worked for five days as though the god of mischief himself had gifted it to them.

On the sixth day, the Brute would be cheated no more. When Mari gave her excuse, he narrowed his eyes as if to better see through her deception.

'If the whore is *unavailable*,' he growled, 'I shall have to take my pleasure elsewhere.'

From up on her perch, Eliana heard Mari scream as he dragged her away. She scrambled down and sprinted back to the apartment, but it was too late. By the time he returned her, she was white-faced and trembling, her dress stained with blood where he had split her lip with a heavy blow.

He did not try to claim Eliana when he saw her stood in the middle of the room, staring at him with her chin raised in defiance, daring him to take her. He merely gave her a triumphant look, threw Mari in a shaken heap on the floor, and left without a backwards glance.

'Mari!' Eliana ran to her, dropping to the ground by her side. 'What were you thinking? We agreed that if you were in danger, you should just give my hiding place away!'

'I know,' she said in a quivering voice. 'But I thought you shouldn't have to go through this alone...' she tailed off.

'You brave thing! I thought you said that you wished for more courage? That is the most courageous thing anyone has ever done for me.'

'I'd be dead if it wasn't for you. I was starving on the streets before you asked for my help in your work for your father. If not for you, I'd have come to this anyway.'

'I won't let it happen again,' Eliana swore. 'I can't have you hurt on my account. They have taken my dignity and my freedom, but they won't take my pride. I couldn't sleep at night if I knew you were being tormented in my place.'

'No... if this is what it takes to spare you just a couple of attacks, I'll do it.' Mari's frightened eyes and pale face belied her plucky words.

'You won't.' Eliana was resolute. She was serene on the surface, but underneath, she was seething – furious that he should stoop to harming her maid just to get to her. Though she was not sure why this should be surprising.

'There's more,' Mari whispered. 'Susa is paying the guards. That's why they're coming so often.'

Eliana's jaw dropped. That really was surprising. She knew that Samsu's consort had taken an instant dislike to her, but this went beyond anything she could have imagined. If she had hoped for some feminine solidarity from another woman who had suffered at the hands of men and circumstance, her illusions were instantly shattered.

'That's low,' she muttered. 'What a revolting thing to do.'

'I – I suppose she wants to get rid of you. If you fall pregnant, Samsu might marry you too, and her son will be moved another step from the throne.'

There was a knock at the door. For a heart-stopping moment, Eliana thought that the Brute had returned to claim her after all.

She calmed as she remembered that the Brute never did anything as courteous as knocking.

Kisha took a few tentative steps towards the door, but Eliana held up a hand and went herself.

She opened it a crack. There in the entrance stood a man in the military tunic of an officer of Samsu's army; she immediately recoiled a step, but there was something different about him. His eyes had none of the hardness and cynicism of the others', and there was compassion in his gaze.

His black hair fell in tousled waves to just below his ears and what she could see of his body was finely honed. A strong jaw, straight nose and chiselled cheekbones made for a face that any girl would look twice at. Eliana was annoyed to feel an attraction in the twist of her stomach as their eyes met.

He bowed slightly, 'Apologies for disturbing you, my lady.'

She looked at him warily – this was not the treatment she was accustomed to. Expecting him to make a lunge for her any moment, she edged backwards a little further.

Holding his hands up, he said, 'I mean you no harm. I came to let you know that the prince wishes to see you tonight. I'm to fetch you at sundown, and I thought you might appreciate some forewarning.'

Still suspicious and expecting a catch for this kindness, Eliana gave a brief nod. 'Thank you, sir.'

He inclined his head, turned on his heel and strode off. She closed the door behind him.

'Ashan is a good man,' said Mari. 'You can trust him. He carried you here the night you arrived. He did not take advantage when you were at your most vulnerable, and you can be sure that he's the sort of man who will never willingly hurt an innocent.'

'A rare man indeed, at this court,' observed Eliana, remembering the shadowy figure who had lifted her from the ground when she could not rise.

She fell silent as she turned her thoughts towards sundown.

*

Dressed in a moss-green linen gown fringed with white, Eliana walked in silence beside Ashan as he escorted her to Samsu's chambers.

In the nicest way she could, Mari had insisted that Eliana wear this dress – the linen was easier to scrub than silk, and easier to repair if torn.

She was outwardly quiet and composed, mentally preparing herself for the fact that, for the immediate future, her body was not her own. At Kisha's bedroom shrine, she had prayed to Enlil for the strength to get through whatever was to come, and to Ninazu to heal her injuries quickly.

Ashan coughed quietly, 'How are you feeling?'

'Fine,' she replied. 'A little nervous, perhaps.' In truth, she was more than a little nervous, but until she knew more of this man, she would not say anything that he might repeat to Samsu to put her at more of a disadvantage than she already was. Samsu's guards were famously loyal.

'How do you like it at the palace?'

'Well enough,' she said carefully. 'It is good to be with my sister again.'

'So, you're happy here? You have everything you need?'

'Everything but my freedom!' she snapped. He was being kind, trying to take her mind from what was to come, but the questioning set her on edge.

Ashan fell silent.

'I'm sorry,' she said, a moment later. 'It's not your fault. Yes, I am happy enough here, thank you, between interruptions. The palace is certainly more luxurious than my father's home.'

'Luxury always has its price,' observed Ashan. 'There are things you can do to ease his temper.'

She gave him a sideways glance. 'Like what?'

'Well, when we go in, just bow. Don't wait to be told, just do it, and do it the Babylonian way. Stay there until he decides to honour you with his attention, and never speak unless spoken to.'

Eliana nodded. All this she had already learned from experience.

'Certainly never look him in the eyes. Only once a man reaches the rank of general is he allowed to do that. Hmm,' he paused for thought, wrinkling his forehead. 'Seem willing. Above all, never question him.'

They had reached the chamber door. She tried to commit all he had said to memory, though much of it grated against her nature.

He caught her hand and gave it a reassuring squeeze. A little overwhelmed by the kindness, and still sure not to make of it, she squeezed back.

Entering the chamber, Ashan moved silently to his post. Eliana took a few steps into the room and sank gracefully into her bow. She waited, nervous anticipation mounting in her stomach.

Samsu sat on one of his floor cushions, the Brute on another nearby. Together, they were discussing a tablet that Samsu held.

She waited, and waited.

It seemed an eternity. Her knees began to hurt from being folded in two on the unforgiving tiles. She began to wonder if he hadn't noticed her.

The two men tossed the tablet back onto the pile in the middle of the rug and walked over to Eliana, speaking about her as though she couldn't hear.

'And so, the whore is here again,' said Samsu.

'She looks like a peasant,' growled the Brute.

'She seems to be learning though. She bows and waits without making a sound. Does she come willingly yet?'

'No, sir. She runs, she hides, she screams, she fights. She is often conveniently absent when I visit for training. She has a lot to learn before she's worthy of a prince.'

'Oh, but this wildcat is worth the effort. As in a siege, the greater the challenge, the greater the satisfaction when you succeed.' He turned to speak to Eliana, 'I know what you said, about me not breaking you, girl. Not a single word you speak within the walls of this palace escapes me. In case you haven't noticed, I have not even tried to break you... yet. I've been allowing my soldiers to warm you up, teach you the rudimentary basics of pleasure and obedience while I serve out the term of a vow of chastity I made to Marduk. He speaks directly to me; he has promised me a son from your sister's belly if I abstain from the joys of the flesh until after the birth. Once my son is born, I will take on your training myself.'

Eliana tried not to shudder at the thought.

He continued, 'But my women must learn to be silent and quiescent. When you run from my men, you run from me, and that I will not tolerate. So,' he came to stand directly over her, 'to teach you a lesson, you will be flogged.' Her stomach tightened in fear. The Brute flexed his fingers in delight. Samsu turned to speak to him, 'How many times did you go to her rooms to find her missing?'

'Twice a day, for five days, sir.'

'Very well. Whore, you shall receive a lash for every instance of disobedience. Stand up.'

She stood on shaking knees. The Brute came up behind her and pulled her dress from her shoulders, tugging it to her waist, uncovering her breasts and back. He gathered her hair, twisted it into a knot and draped it over one shoulder, leaving her back exposed. He reached around and roughly grabbed one of her breasts in his calloused hand, giving it a painful squeeze.

Eliana flushed with shame and embarrassment – not to bare herself in front of Samsu and his henchman, who only saw her as a piece of meat, but to be displayed before Ashan, who treated her with compassion.

Over at his post, he stared straight ahead, giving no sign that he had noticed her nakedness.

Samsu led her to the bed, indicating that she should take hold of the bedpost as the Brute walked over to a chest, withdrew a bullwhip and handed it to his master.

She stared at it – a wooden handle with a lash of braided leather, ending in a cruel tip soaked in milk and hardened in the sun. A rising tide of terror engulfed her, and she gripped the post with all her strength, praying silently to every god in the pantheon who might help her, swearing to herself that she would not make a sound – she would not give them the satisfaction.

Seizing the whip, Samsu moved behind her and threw all his weight behind a vicious stroke across her shoulders – she screamed as the hardened tip embedded itself into her shoulder and tore out again. A warm stream of blood flowed down her back, soaking into the gown at her waist.

'One.'

There was a pause of several seconds as Samsu allowed the pain to subside and the terror of the next stroke to build, before letting the whip fly with a whistle and a crack, landing the second stroke just below the first.

Eliana screamed again, her back aflame.

At the third stroke, her resolve broke and she began to sob. She tried to carry herself out of her body, imagining herself up on her tree branch, gazing at the wide open sky.

By the eighth stroke, her knees had buckled. She collapsed to the ground, unable to move for pain.

'Get up,' commanded Samsu.

She shook her head. 'I can't,' she whispered.

'There are still two lashes left to give. You will stand for them.'

His tone brooked no argument, but she shook her head again in silence.

'Then it seems we have reached an impasse. I can stand here all night, waiting for you to rise again. For every minute that I wait, you shall receive another stroke.'

She could have screamed again, for sheer frustration. Whichever way she turned, he had her cornered. Drawing on reserves of strength she didn't know she had, she pulled herself back to her feet on shaking legs, bracing against the bedpost.

By the time he had finished, her back felt flayed open and her gown was soaked.

He dropped the bloodied whip to the ground and laughed. 'Now that you've been punished for your transgression, you must give this man what you denied him.' He gestured towards the Brute, who looked back at Eliana, an unbearable smugness imprinted on his features. He hitched up his tunic.

Eliana did not move.

'Go!' Samsu bellowed.

Still she stood there.

'Very well, perhaps you would like a few more lashes after all?'

She shrugged, slowly and deliberately, each tiny motion reigniting her agony.

Ashan's eyes flicked to her face, silently urging her not to rebel, but she would not allow Samsu to win. She could not bend to his whims, whatever dire retribution he promised. It would almost be a relief to experience the worst he could offer so that she would no longer have to live in fear.

Then Samsu did something truly shocking – he laughed. Long and loud and full, he laughed. 'You will be a challenge indeed; one that I shall greatly enjoy. He shall not force you, because you must learn to go of your own free will.'

Against all wisdom, her hopes leapt.

'If you do not care for your own safety, perhaps there is someone you care for more?'

Her heart sank.

'Asag!' he called.

A young man stepped into the room, so ugly that it was immediately apparent why he had been named for the monstrous demon whose mere presence made fish boil alive in the rivers. His hand was clamped around a girl's upper arm, his dagger against her prominent belly.

'Elly!' cried Kisha, pleadingly. Asag backhanded her across the face, and she fell silent.

The colour drained from Eliana's face, but her expression did not change. Samsu would not chance the heir he had bargained for with Marduk, just to spite her.

As if reading her thoughts, Samsu looked at her and laughed again. 'You think I won't hurt her, just because she's with child? Wives are easily found, and children just as easily made.'

Asag pressed his dagger harder against Kisha's belly, making a hole in her gown.

Looking at the frenzy in her sister's eyes, it was clear that Kisha believed Samsu would do it. If she believed it, so must Eliana.

She walked slowly to the Brute, every step a torment, her head held high. She knelt before him, hatred firing every part of her.

Taking him in her mouth, she thought only of why she was doing this. Of Kisha and her child.

When she gagged, the Brute was spent, and the ordeal finished, Samsu nodded, pleased. 'There. That was not so hard. You will learn to come willingly, or those you love will suffer for your pride. Get up.'

Eliana stood, considering covering her naked chest, but unable bear the touch of the fabric against her torn back.

Samsu snapped, 'Ashan! Return the women to their rooms. I am finished with them for tonight.'

Ashan strode past, beckoning to Eliana and prising Kisha from Asag's grip.

They made their way back by moonlight, without so much as a torch-bearer to light the path. Kisha clung to Ashan, Eliana following behind on shaking legs, sick and dizzy, her vision swirling.

He walked in silence, not looking at Eliana with her breasts still bared. There was an expression on his face that she could not place – perhaps it was shame.

Mari opened the door for them. Eliana went inside without a second glance at Ashan; if he would not speak to her, she certainly would not beg for his conversation.

As she lowered herself gingerly onto a bench, face down, she heard him mutter to Mari, 'Make sure you wash her wounds and anoint them with rosin rose so that they do not fester. We've lost many a good man on the battlefield from minor wounds, and she must live to fight another day. I'll get some white willow bark tincture from mother's physician and send it on, for the pain.'

Nodding and whispering goodnight, Mari came back into the room and lit a torch to find Eliana already semi-unconscious, weak with blood loss.

Ashan's face lingered in her mind's eye, the last thing she saw before she drifted into sleep.

Chapter 6

Mari and Kisha set to work as soon as Eliana was asleep. They gently cut the gown away from her and sponged the dried blood from her skin. While Mari tore an old sheet into strips, Kisha made a paste of St John's Wort and honey to prevent the wounds from festering.

Once the blood had been washed away, the girls were relieved to see that the injuries, though extensive, were fairly shallow. They carefully applied the paste and overlaid it with the cloth strips – they stuck to the honey, holding the bandages in place.

When Eliana awoke the next morning, she was furious to find herself all but bedridden. It was agony to move her arms and legs, and she could not get up without help. All her small pleasures were out of reach: running, climbing, walking in the gardens, playing the lyre. Her waking hours were spent lying face-down on a padded bench, chafing against the inactivity and raging against Samsu and his attack dog, his Brute.

True to his word, Ashan had sent a tincture of white willow bark for Eliana. She took it regularly to numb the pain and entice her body to sleep – anything to escape the crushing boredom.

Still, through her fog of misery Eliana was able to find one ray of sunshine: the guards left her in peace for a full week after her ordeal. The first one to come to the door had been given the rough edge of Mari's tongue and brought in to see the sleeping invalid. No more had come after that, not even the Brute.

Mari and Kisha tended her faithfully – washing her, keeping her fed and comfortable and trying to entertain her. It was like trying to entertain a tigress with a toothache; she snarled and snapped at any attempt to cheer her up.

She did not mean to be unpleasant. Being dependent on others went against every part of Eliana's nature and grated on her. She preferred to do things for herself rather than lounge around waiting for others to do them.

On the fifth day, she insisted on getting up. Her limbs were stiff and her back protested every slight movement, but she felt she would go mad if she stayed still any longer.

She took a slow walk into the garden, savouring the sunlight and the breeze against her skin. Turning her face up to Utu, she allowed him to bathe her in his warmth.

Just walking down as far as the stream exhausted her. She eased herself down onto the grass alongside the water and lay there in peace, rediscovering her serenity, listening to the thrum of insects' wings and the animated chatter of birds. She could almost imagine herself back in the garden of her father's house, when she was free.

The sound of a twig cracking underfoot snapped her attention back to the present. She pushed herself up on one hand, looking around, cursing as her wounds reminded her not to move so sharply.

'Who's there?' she called out, praying that it would not be the Brute who answered.

'Isin,' replied a thin voice.

'Isin!'

With difficulty, she pushed herself into a seated position. Isin emerged from behind a tree and dropped down beside her.

If he had been a nervous young man when he was courting Kisha, he was now positively rabbit-like – all eyes and ears, quivering and alert, poised and ready to flee at any moment. He had grown even paler in his period of service to Samsu, his body long and slender like the reeds he used for his scribing. Over-long hair flopped into his eyes; he pushed it away impatiently.

'I had to come – I know Kisha's time is near.'

'She has a little over one moon to go.'

'And how... how is she coping?'

'Very well, when Samsu isn't using her as a tool to force me to do what he wants.' That incident had shaken Kisha to the core. She hadn't seemed quite herself ever since.

Isin looked her over. Most of her bruises had healed with the help of Mari's arnica remedy, but she knew she was looking far from her best. 'How are you now?' he asked.

'Healing,' she replied, her tone not inviting further discussion.

'Good. Well,' he glanced around, checking for anyone who might overhear, 'I couldn't stay away. I wanted Kisha to have something that I was going to give her when we thought it would be my child she would bear.' He took out a little amulet of ivory bearing the carved head of Pazazu, the spirit known to protect in childbed against the she-demon Lasmashtu. 'It belonged to my mother. I meant to give it to Kisha when she was brought to bed with our child – I hope it will still work for her.'

Eliana took it and turned it over in her hand. 'This is so thoughtful, Isin, but will you not need it when the woman you do marry...'

He cut her off with a shake of the head. 'I don't intend to marry – Kisha has my heart and soul. As long as she lives, those parts of me are not my own to give away.'

She felt a pang of pity for this poor boy – so devoted and loyal, yet too weak to move on. He would never be happy while he clung to dreams of Kisha.

'Then thank you,' she said. 'I'm sure it will protect her when her hour comes. Do you have a message to go with it?'

'Only what I said about giving it to her for our child, and...

and tell her that I hope she has a boy, so that she'll be safe. And that I will always be here for her and the baby, though they are not mine. And… I still love her.' A tear rolled down his face.

Eliana cupped his cheek in her hand and wiped away the tear. 'I'll tell her,' she said, gently. 'Now you should go – you mustn't be caught here.'

He nodded, 'I know. Samsu swore he'd rip off my manhood if he ever caught me near Kisha. I was right to think he knew of our engagement.' Isin helped Eliana to her feet and kissed her forehead. 'I shall always think of you as my little sister,' he smiled, taking his leave.

When Eliana gave the amulet and the message to her sister, she had every reason to be proud. Kisha did not weep or wail, lamenting her lost love and the life that might have been; she simply pressed the ivory to her lips, held it a few seconds, and stowed it safely under her pillow.

*

Holding Kisha's hand, Eliana lowered herself into the water.

Seven days on from her ordeal, she had regained enough mobility that Mari declared it was time for the bandages to come off. The three girls had come to the bathhouse to soak the linen off.

Eliana breathed deeply, feeling the fabric beginning to grow heavy and peel off. Cautiously, Kisha took hold of one end and gave a gentle tug – the bandage came away easily.

When her back was free, she turned it to the others. 'How does it look?' she asked, a hint of nervousness in her voice.

'Not too terrible, actually,' said Mari. 'As long as you leave it alone to breathe and heal, you might escape relatively unmarked.'

Eliana exhaled in relief. 'I can cope with most things, but I'd rather not have permanent scars to remind me of them.'

There was more than a little vanity in her. She had always had such a flawless complexion – smooth, carnelian-coloured skin, always unblemished and well-cared for. Though she had never taken an interest in the boys who tried to court her, she knew she was attractive, with high cheekbones, rosebud lips, and a slender figure, all accentuated by the jet curls that tumbled to her waist.

Above all, she was well-aware that her eyes were her best feature, as well as how to use them. Black and sparkling with mischief, almond-shaped and tilted up at the corners, framed by long charcoal lashes – she had learned at an early age how to stop a man with a precisely-timed glance.

But now, beauty was her curse. Perhaps if she'd been born ugly, Samsu would have left her in peace.

Kisha washed the remaining honey from her back with tender hands, then took up the soap and helped her to wash her hair.

Producing a little jar, Mari beckoned Eliana from the water. She lay face down on a bench and gritted her teeth as Mari began to work oil into the still-damaged skin.

'What's this?' she asked.

'Calendula, lavender, rosemary and chamomile. My own blend – it should help to minimise the scarring.'

'You're a wonder, Mari,' smiled Kisha. 'I think you've missed your calling in life – you should have been a physician.'

'I think I am being one!' laughed Mari. 'My skills are certainly in high demand these last few weeks.'

She gave Kisha a quick massage too, working the tension out of her neck and shoulders. Then, clean, dried and dressed, the girls made their way back to their rooms, laughing arm-in-arm.

They stopped in their tracks as they entered via the terrace.

A plump woman with fine hair severely scraped back under a black-and-gold headdress was shaking out and re-folding Kisha's gowns. She worked as though it was usual for her to be here, as though she belonged in these rooms.

Whey-faced and pinch-mouthed with a scowl drawing all her features down, she looked older than her years, and she could not be a day younger than forty.

Kisha coughed politely, the woman looked up.

Getting a plain view of her face, Eliana recognised her as the woman who had followed Susa when they encountered each other that first day in the palace.

'Can I help you, Ani?' asked Kisha, voice strained with courtesy.

Ani inclined her head, 'I am here to help you, my lady.'

'You are?'

'My mistress sent me to be of any assistance I can in your final weeks of pregnancy. She was concerned that those about you are too inexperienced to be knowledgeable about such matters. Prince Samsu's heir must be brought into this world with all propriety and care.'

'I thank you and your mistress most kindly for your consideration, but Mari, Eliana and I are getting along just fine.'

'Nonetheless, the Princess Susa would have skilled hands about you when your labour begins. I am to remain here until after the birth of the child. The son of such a great man as the husband you share must be given the best possible start in life.'

'Then I must welcome you to our home,' Kisha smiled, as though nothing would please her better.

Mari took Eliana's arm and steered her into the bedroom before she could retort against the implied slight on their care of her sister.

'*Don't* say anything against her,' whispered Mari.

'Why not?'

'She is Susa's bastard sister – born of King Simash of Elam and some nameless slave, and taken hostage with Susa when Samsu's father crushed their kingdom. She is Susa's most trusted confidante. If she is here, it can only mean that Susa has sent her to spy and report back.'

Eliana clenched her fists at her sides, 'By what right does she place a spy in my sister's household?'

'By her right as Samsu's consort. Susa is a danger to this baby, and Ani is her puppet. If it is a boy, she will try to take him away to raise as her own, or simply find a way to remove him.'

Hands covering her mouth in horror, Eliana urged, 'Is there no way to just get rid of this woman? To refuse her a bed here?'

Mari shook her head. 'Susa has charge of all Kisha's domestic arrangements; it's her right as first wife and consort. If we try to interfere, she could just as easily have us two placed elsewhere – then Kisha would be all alone. All we can do is keep watchful – try not to leave Ani alone in the apartments, and certainly not alone with Kisha any more than necessary.'

Eliana blew out a long breath between her teeth, frustration clear in the set of her jaw. This Susa was a more formidable enemy than she had given her credit for – she didn't wage her wars as Eliana would, forthright and honest and blunt; instead, she used underhanded wiles to sneak and disrupt and spy.

Trying to wipe the disgust from her face and arrange her features pleasantly, Eliana went to join her sister at the loom.

*

The day after Ani's arrival, there came a knock at the apartment door.

'Only Ashan knocks like that!' exclaimed Kisha in delight.

Mari opened the door and Ashan strode in, wearing his customary military tunic and short dagger. He bowed to the three girls in the room; Ani had taken herself off to the kitchens to instruct the cooks on dishes for the expectant mother.

Kisha struggled to her feet and extended a hand to Ashan. 'Come, sit with me,' she smiled.

'You are very gracious, my lady.' He took a seat.

Eliana moved her stool nearer to the pair, anxious to be closer to Ashan. She felt a little safer in his presence.

He looked over at her and gave a curt nod, before turning back to her sister. It was like a slap in the face.

'You look very well, my lady. Do you have everything you need?'

'I do, thank you.'

'And your sister, has she recovered from her punishment? I'm told she was quite ill afterwards.'

'She has recovered well enough,' Kisha motioned towards Eliana, indicating that he could ask her himself. He ignored the gesture.

A little knot of anger gnawed at Eliana's belly – what had she done to annoy Ashan that he should suddenly turn so cold? They had not spent much time together, but she had thought he was different from the other soldiers. At least he had never come 'visiting' with them.

The anger turned to a little pang of bitterness as suspicion crept over her – could it be that he was just here to report back to Samsu on whether she was well enough to resume *training*? She gave a little shudder of fear. The movement drew his eye; he glanced her over, his expression unreadable, before turning back to Kisha.

Furious at the snub, Eliana went over to whisper with Mari, leaving Ashan and Kisha to talk alone.

'Have you seen the way he looks at me?' she began.

'How?'

'Not at all! He can't meet my eyes and he can hardly bear to glance at me! I thought he was decent.'

'He is! Perhaps you've misunderstood.'

Eliana gave her a look. 'Misunderstood? He doesn't look at me or speak to me, he acts as though I'm not here. How does one misunderstand that?'

Mari shrugged, 'Well, he's seen you naked – perhaps he's embarrassed? Maybe he prefers men!'

The two of them snorted with laughter; Kisha turned a mildly disapproving stare on the girls, quieting them.

'Maybe!' coughed Eliana, trying to cover her giggles. She sobered abruptly as a thought occurred to her, 'Or maybe it's because he's seen me at my weakest. He's seen me meekly do as I'm told by Samsu and the Brute, instead of standing up for myself. He's seen me vomit, he's seen me violated... I probably disgust him.'

The notion made her unexpectedly miserable. She shouldn't care, she told herself. He was just another extension of Samsu, and no concern of hers.

She looked over at him talking with Kisha. They were deep in conversation – Kisha smiled and rested her hand on her swollen belly as she spoke.

The door to the apartment swung open and Ani slipped back in so quietly that Eliana did not even notice her until she glided past.

Ani moved near Kisha – Eliana could pinpoint the exact moment that Ashan noticed her.

He did not need to look at her, but his body stiffened suddenly and his face closed up. Eliana saw the hurt in Kisha's eyes as he stood abruptly, while she was mid-sentence.

'I do apologise, my lady,' he said formally. 'I have suddenly remembered an urgent duty that I must attend to.'

He bowed and left so quickly that Kisha was quite concerned. 'I hope he's alright,' she murmured.

Only Eliana was positioned to see Ani's smug expression as he departed.

Ani took Ashan's seat, covered Kisha's hand with her own and began to give detailed instructions on what she must and must not eat in these crucial final weeks of pregnancy.

Eliana, trying to put her suspicions aside, picked up the lyre and began to pluck out a tune. Out of the corner of her eye, she thought she saw Ani shoot her a venomous glance before raising her voice above the music – it was so fast that she could scarcely be sure she'd seen it.

The next morning, two of the lyre strings were broken.

'Oh, such a shame,' commiserated Ani. 'You must have been too vigorous with them yesterday. If you like, I can get you some more when I next send a slave to the market.'

Eliana said nothing, studying the ruined strings. When the woman was out of earshot, she confided to Mari, 'They are not broken through overuse. See how neat the ends are? They have been cut, not frayed. It could only have been her.'

'It's just a couple of strings,' said Mari. 'Let it go – it's not worth the trouble of arguing over.'

The lyre strings were just the beginning of a series of unfortunate mishaps that befell Kisha's belongings.

When she sat down at her loom a couple of days after the lyre incident, she found that the threads were all knotted and tangled. Ani offered her sympathy, suggesting it must have been the wind, and insisted on helping Kisha to detangle everything.

The following day, a wine stain was discovered on her favourite ivory silk gown. It had been a costly item, and one Samsu was always pleased to see her wear.

Ani took the gown away, vowing to scrub the stain out if it took her all day.

These events began to take their toll on Kisha's nerves. 'It's ill-omens,' she whispered to Eliana, barely able to give voice to her fears. 'The gods are telling me that the baby's cord will be tangled, or there'll be a stain on his birth, or…'

'Hush!' exclaimed Eliana. 'It means nothing of the sort. It just means that someone is trying to frighten you, and you're letting them succeed.'

'I wish I could be as sceptical as you, Elly. But there's only the four of us here, and I trust you all completely.'

Her jaw dropped, 'Even Ani?'

'Even Ani,' Kisha was firm. 'I had my doubts about her at first, but she is so sweet and helpful that I cannot think ill of her. Why would she offer to remedy all the things that have gone wrong if she was the one to cause them? She'd just be creating more work for herself.'

Eliana was far from convinced, but she tried to avoid arguing with her sister at the moment. Kisha was normally so gentle, but the pregnancy was beginning to wear away at her nerves.

There was no doubt in Eliana's mind that Ani was acting on Susa's behalf, and reporting everything back to her. She also suspected that her own health was mentioned in the reports – after a week and a half of blessed peace, Samsu's officers renewed their visits to the apartments with more vigour than ever before.

It was no longer a shock to her when they arrived – it had become part of daily routine. Eliana no longer fought them; she was tired of injuries and bruises. When she submitted, she felt that a little part of her spirit had died. She was almost as disgusted with herself as with the soldiers.

One in particular didn't always remember to remove his belt and dagger beforehand. While he used her, Eliana would stare at the blade with a fervent longing, imagining how satisfying it would be to grab it, swift as a striking snake, and plunge it into the belly of her assailant. When he spilled his seed, she pretended that the warm liquid was his blood.

It seemed that she spent so much time in the bathhouse during these days that her hair was never truly dry before she felt unclean again and had to go back.

It was as Kisha had said – Eliana learned to bear the things she could not change, though it made the whole situation no less repellent for her. She could not grow used to it, but she could bear it.

She would always take a careful look at the face of her tormenter before he began, storing it away in her memory in case of any future chance of revenge. For now, she must submit, but she dared to hope for a time when she would have the power to punish them.

Many of the soldiers spoke to her almost politely before they used her, now that she no longer made life difficult for them. The only one who remained perpetually unpleasant was the Brute. Whether she fought or surrendered, he still humiliated her in every way that he could. Once, he had burst in whilst she was styling Kisha's hair, forced her to her knees by her sister's side and taken what he wanted there and then.

Kisha had held her hand throughout. There was uneasy comfort in that.

Eliana was sure that he would rape her if he were not so loyal to Samsu – she found herself almost grateful that he had reserved her maidenhood for himself. At least it delayed the inevitable.

After that event, Ani had insisted on taking over many of Eliana's duties. She would not risk it happening again, she said. Kisha must not be distressed by the sight of her whore sister servicing the men of the army.

Eliana had clenched her fists and gritted her teeth at this, but kept her silence only for the sake of her sister's pleading eyes.

She never saw Ani acting suspiciously, and she certainly had no cause to complain that the woman ill-treated her sister. It was sickeningly clever. Eliana longed to catch her in the act of vandalising something, just for the satisfaction of having solid proof with which to accuse her.

Mari always counselled caution. She was wary of Susa, and would give her no opportunity to remove Kisha's allies from her service.

However, even Mari's tact could be tested.

Ani had been with them for a fortnight when Mari went to change the sheets on Kisha's bed. She drew back the hangings, stripped the blankets and picked up a pillow to take it out for airing.

There, underneath, was the little amulet meant to protect Kisha in childbirth, the eyes of Pazazu staring up at Mari from two distinctly separate pieces.

Someone had broken the charm in two and replaced the halves carefully beneath the pillow.

When she saw what had happened, Kisha became as pale as the broken ivory, her eyes filling with tears; her voice remained steady. 'Such a pity – and all the sadder for what it meant to the giver of the gift. Do you know how it happened?'

'No, my lady,' Mari bowed her head. 'I just lifted the pillow and the pieces were there, broken.'

'What nonsense!' scoffed Ani. 'Even amulets do not magically break themselves in two. You must have been careless and knocked it to the floor while you were removing the blankets.'

'I did not!' Mari was indignant. 'I'm no liar! I tell you true, Kisha – I found it like this under the pillow.'

'It doesn't matter,' Kisha was tactful as she could be – not blaming her maid or correcting Ani. 'It is broken, and that cannot be undone. Please store the pieces away in my jewellery box, Mari.'

She turned back to the loom, shoulders hunched.

Watching from across the room, Eliana was sure she glimpsed anxiety in her sister's eyes. Kisha hated conflict, she knew, and was beginning to work herself into a panic over the omens for the birth.

*

Things returned to normal for almost a week, and no more of Kisha's possessions were damaged.

Then things took a more serious turn.

Mari came rushing into the bedroom, where Eliana was sat embellishing a baby gown with lapis beads as Kisha dozed on the bed. With a finger to her lips, Mari gestured for Eliana to come.

Setting aside the gown, she followed. There, on the dazzling white stone of the terrace, was a sight that made Eliana's stomach turn.

A grizzled black mongrel, a bitch, lay split almost in two. She was disembowelled, her entrails spilling from the monstrous gash in her belly. A fly crawled lazily across her dead, staring eye.

In itself, the dead dog was revolting. Worse was the statuette tied about her neck with a distinctive beaded necklace belonging to Kisha. Eliana had to squint against the glare of the sun to make it out – made of jet, it blended against the dog's black fur.

When her eyes focused, the unmistakeable likeness of Lasmashtu glared back at her.

She took an involuntary step backward. 'A curse?'

'Undeniably,' murmured Mari. 'We must clean it up before Kisha sees.'

They bent and took hold of a leg each; Eliana struggled not to retch at the smell. The day was a hot one, and the corpse had already begun to rot.

As she straightened to ask Mari where they would take it, Ani appeared in the doorway. Both girls looked at her, silently urging her to quiet. She stared back, malice in her clear gaze.

Taking a deep breath, she opened her mouth and screamed. Eliana could happily have hurled the dead dog straight into her smug face as Kisha came running.

Mari and Eliana instinctively moved to try to block Kisha's view, but it was no use.

'Ani, what on earth is…' she stopped in her tracks, gazing horror-struck at the bloodied mass behind the girls. 'What is that?' she whispered.

'Nothing, my lady!' Mari answered, her words running together in her rush to get them out. 'It must have been injured somewhere and crawled here to die.'

'Then… why is it wearing my necklace?'

Eliana kicked herself for not having removed the necklace and offensive statue before trying to move the creature.

'It's nothing,' she tried to reassure her sister. 'Just somebody playing a tasteless joke.'

'It's no joke.' Ani cut in. 'Is that not a statue of the childbed demon tied around the throat? It's as clear a curse as they come.'

Kisha staggered backwards, her mouth working in a soundless scream, her arms cradling her belly protectively. Her face crumpled in pain and she bent almost double.

A rush of fluid spattered the floor between her legs.

She dropped to her hands and knees, one hand still on her bump, and cried out in pain.

'Kisha!' Eliana ran to her sister. 'What's happening?'

'It's coming,' Ani answered, not moving.

Mari went to Kisha's other side and the two girls helped her up. 'We need to get her to bed,' said Mari. 'When the contractions grow stronger, we'll move her to the birthing chair.'

Once Kisha was settled in the bed and as comfortable as they could make her, Mari went running for water, linen sheets and all manner of medicines to try to ease the pain.

Eliana sat helplessly beside her sister, holding her hand and trying to distract her with chatter. Kisha was ashen and could not concentrate on the conversation. 'This baby is cursed,' she muttered. 'I'm going to die.'

'Don't be silly! Of course you're not going to die.' Eliana reassured her.

Mari returned with a tray of medicines, and some bread and honey. 'We won't let you die, my lady. Hundreds of women give birth every day – if every one of them died, none of us would ever have siblings! You have nothing to worry about.'

'Our mother died in childbirth,' Kisha spoke quietly to Eliana.

'I know,' she squeezed her hand. 'But you won't.'

Kisha did not argue, but turned her face to the ceiling.

Mari brought the bread and honey over. 'Eat,' she urged. 'You will need your strength when your body is ready to push.'

Ani sat on a nearby stool, watching intently, but made no move to interfere for good or for ill. The girls ignored her, and Kisha was too miserable to notice.

Then the waiting began.

The room was stifling in the heat of the day, and Eliana wanted nothing more than to go out into the garden and lounge beside the stream in the shade of a tree. But Kisha needed her. The baby would not be born for many hours yet, but her sister could not bear to be without her for even a moment.

As day dragged into night, Kisha's contractions grew stronger, more frequent and more prolonged. Around midnight, she sat up, leaning in towards her belly and crushing Eliana's hand as her body strained to be rid of its burden.

'It's time,' Mari nodded to Eliana. Between them, they moved Kisha from the bed and settled her into the birthing chair – made of elaborately carved cedar, it had strong arms to be gripped at the height of the pain, a reclining posture, and a hole set into the seat.

Still, Ani did nothing.

Eliana sent her a couple of accusing looks, but she stared back impassively.

Red-faced, Kisha gripped the arms of the chair and screamed.

'It's coming, my lady!' cried Mari. 'Push!'

'It's tearing me in half!' shrieked Kisha.

'No it isn't,' said Eliana firmly. 'Come on, sweeting – push! It'll all be done soon.'

The torches flickered in their brackets, making the shadows seem to come alive – dancing and writhing on the walls. Kisha's hair clung to her sweating body in lank strands as she heaved and struggled against the tiny body fighting its way out of her.

With a final scream, a shudder and a push, the baby slithered out of her and into Mari's hands.

Kisha collapsed back into the chair, panting.

'You did it, Kisha! It's done!' Eliana was jubilant for her sister, even as she gripped her hand, waiting for Mari to answer the unspoken question filling the air.

A moment later, the baby began to bawl.

'A healthy baby, my lady!' cried Mari as she swaddled the child and cut the cord. 'A perfect, healthy, beautiful girl.'

'A girl!' Kisha moaned. Tears ran down her exhausted face. 'No! No, no!'

Eliana's disappointment lasted only for a moment, until Mari placed the squalling infant in her arms to give to her sister. 'Look at her!' she smiled. 'She's gorgeous, Kisha. The very image of you!' She laid the baby at her mother's breast.

Only then did she think to glance over at Ani to see how she had reacted to the baby's gender.

The stool was empty. Ani had gone.

'Scuttled off to Susa the moment it was over,' Eliana whispered bitterly to Mari. 'We'll not see her in these rooms again, if the gods are good.'

Kisha cuddled her baby with a miserable expression that Eliana could not bear.

'This is a good thing, you know!' she said, with a bright grin that she hoped did not look as false as it felt. 'Think about it – Susa isn't interested in a girl, nor will Samsu be. She's all yours, Kisha! A little piece of you for us all to love. We won't have to worry about evil influences or people trying to take her away – she'll be just as inconsequential as we are.'

A half-smile tugged at the corners of Kisha's lips as she gazed down at her daughter. 'Yes, you're right. She's a little blessing.'

'What will you call her?' asked Mari.

'I suppose we'll have to wait for her father to name her,' said Kisha, sounding dejected again.

As if she had summoned him, Samsu marched into the bedchamber. He went straight to Kisha as if the other two were not even in the room. It did not take a genius, Eliana thought, to work out where Ani had run off to as soon as the baby's sex was announced.

'A girl?' he sneered.

Kisha nodded fearfully.

Samsu slapped her hard across the face. 'Next time, you will do better.' He turned to leave without so much as a glance at his daughter. 'Name her what you will,' he tossed the words back over his shoulder from the doorway. 'Raise her well and perhaps she'll be a useful pawn in an alliance someday.'

Eliana could not keep silent, watching him slap an exhausted woman on her birthing chair – one who held his own child, no less! 'She is strong and healthy, and so will her brother be, when the gods are good enough to send him to us.'

Samsu looked at her as though a rat had spoken. She stared back at him, both of them forgetting for a moment that she was not permitted to make eye contact with him.

Her bravery spent, her stomach twisted into knots of anxiety as he glared at her. She dropped her gaze to the floor.

'You seem well-recovered, whore,' he said softly. 'My pledge of abstinence to Marduk is at an end – I shall see you very soon.'

As he left the room. Eliana's hands were trembling – she had expected some violent reaction from him. His calm was more unnerving than his savagery.

'Thank you, Elly,' whispered Kisha.

She squeezed her sister's hand again in response, not trusting her own voice.

'So, does she have a name?' Mari asked again, eager to know.

'Sarri,' breathed Kisha. 'Our little princess.'

Chapter 7

The palace was quiet. It had been three days since the birth and there had been no visits and no summons for any of the girls.

It was a period of blessed respite as they learnt to care for Sarri, to adjust to her patterns of eating and sleeping. Eliana and Mari took it in turns to tend to Kisha and the baby – the new mother was still in some shock, and could not be persuaded to let go of her daughter for a full day after the birth. As her sister slept, Eliana had to gently remove Sarri from her arms in order to wash the child and change her underclothes.

Nor could Kisha be persuaded to leave the relative safety of their apartments. It was peaceful there, she said, and she could keep a constant watch over her baby.

Finally, on the third day, Mari resorted to bringing Kisha a polished obsidian mirror stone, to let her see her own reflection. The woman who stared back at her had waxen, sallow skin, hollow eyes and lank, greasy hair. She sighed, and agreed to a trip to the bathhouse, on the condition that one of them should remain behind with Sarri. Kisha would not have her taken from the apartment.

Eliana agreed to remain behind, eager for some time alone with her tiny niece.

As soon as they were gone, she picked Sarri up from the cradle. The baby gurgled and waved her hands a little before settling into her aunt's arms and going back to sleep.

Eliana stared at her in wonder, trying to imagine what sort of woman she would be. Breathing in the sweet, new baby smell, she gazed down at the fragile body with its miniature features and tuft of black hair. Sarri breathed evenly, taking deep, snuffling breaths.

She hiccupped. Eliana giggled quietly, trying not to disturb her.

Watching the child sleep, feeling her warmth, weight and utter dependence, she felt so full of love that she could overflow. She could not love this child more if it were her own – in the scrunched up, sleeping face, so like a scaled-down version of her sister, Eliana saw a reason to live. Whatever happened to her here, knowing that this child of her own blood needed a protector would be enough to see her through anything.

The love was tempered with a pang of sadness as she wondered if she would ever have her own child. While her imagination ran wild trying to work out what Samsu might have in store for her future, she could not be sure of anything. Her life was like a path winding into a dark forest and shrouded in mist – she could make nothing out for sure.

Would her child look like this one, she wondered. Or perhaps it would look like its father. Who would the father be? She prayed it would not be Samsu.

Most of all, she wondered if she would ever be free of the oppressive red glazed walls surrounding the palace. If she would ever have her freedom.

A knock at the door interrupted her thoughts. Mari had probably forgotten something and sent a servant back from the bathhouse for it. She replaced Sarri in the cradle and went to see.

Ashan stood framed in the doorway. He looked taken aback to see Eliana stood there – it was usually Mari who answered a knock. Some of the friendliness immediately drained out of his face. He shuffled a little from foot to foot.

'Hello, my lady,' he gave a stiff half-bow. 'Is Kisha here?'

'She's not, I'm afraid. She went down to the bathhouse with Mari. But she shouldn't be long – would you like to come in and meet the new princess?'

She had not forgotten his coldness, but she was determined to thaw him with her own warmth, whatever it took.

'Thank you,' he nodded. She stepped aside and he crossed the threshold and went straight to the cradle, picking Sarri up with such tenderness that one might think he handled babies more often than swords.

He cooed over her with a smile on his lips. *He would make such a wonderful father*, Eliana thought, with a little smile of her own. There was an unexpected rub of irritation as it occurred to her that he might already be a father. Perhaps he was married and had several children.

Once she had thought of it, she couldn't see how it wouldn't be true. He was certainly the best of the men she'd met here, and he was at least Samsu's age. Of course he was married, how had she not seen it before?

For no reason at all that she could explain to herself, she was annoyed with him; all her good humour drained away like rain into the ground. *I bet his wife is beautiful*, she thought bitterly. *And accomplished – probably a high-born Babylonian. She would have to be, to be worthy of such a man.* Though exactly *what* sort of a man he was, she couldn't put into words.

'So, you like children?' she made a half-hearted attempt at conversation.

'Yes.'

'She is beautiful.'

'She is.'

'Is she prettier than yours?'

'My what?'

'Your children, of course.'

'I don't have any.'

'Oh. Well, is your wife going to give you any soon?'

'I doubt it.'

'Oh.'

'I'm not married.'

'Oh.' Eliana was beginning to feel like an idiot, but the feeling was tempered with inexplicable relief.

There was a long pause. Still, Ashan did not look away from the baby. He held her and bounced gently up and down, back and forth.

Eliana broke the silence again. 'So, the palace seems very quiet these last few days.'

Ashan raised his eyebrows. 'Did you not know? Samsu has gone back to Babylon – an urgent summons from his father. He's taken most of his guard with him – there's only a skeleton staff here at the palace, and not many more left for the garrison. He's left me to hold the place in his stead.'

Eliana's heart leapt – she could have jumped around the room in sheer delight. Just one question lingered on her tongue, but she hardly dared to ask it...

'The Brute has gone too. I'm sure you wanted to know.'

'Thank the gods!' she exclaimed. 'How long will they be gone?'

'At least a moon. You have a few weeks of peace yet.'

She suddenly felt liberated and full of relief – so light and unburdened that she could lift off into the sky like a feather on the breeze!

Eliana laughed aloud, 'I can almost feel the weight of the shackles fall away! Oh, Ashan, you can't know how happy you've made me!'

He looked up at her then, his dark eyes so opaque that she could read nothing in them.

She barely noticed, babbling in her happiness, 'I always wonder why he keeps me here – he doesn't have anything to do with me himself. If he hates me, why keep me here?'

Surprised, Ashan said, 'Hates you? He doesn't hate you. He admires you.'

The smile fell off her face. 'Admires… me!' She nearly fell over in shock. 'What on earth would make you say that?'

'He's quite open about it. A couple of weeks ago he accused a soldier of cowardice – told him he could learn a thing or two about courage from you, and you just a woman. If you were a man, he'd have you in his army.'

She was staggered. 'But, why?'

'He's used to mindless obedience. That's what he likes, and what he frightens people into giving him. But he can't frighten you into submission so easily. You don't break, you don't give in or surrender unless you judge that it best. You balance your pride with protecting the people you love. He sees right through you, and so do I. He knows he hasn't won you yet, even when you go through the motions of obedience. He will keep you until he can win your unquestioning obedience and loyalty, as he wins his soldiers'. And I…'

Ashan tailed off. It was the longest speech Eliana had ever heard him make, she wondered if he had run out of words.

'You… what?'

'Nothing. It doesn't matter.'

Putting Sarri down, he turned to leave. Eliana felt an acute wave of irritation – she had been so close to breaking through that barrier he had erected around himself, and she was not going to let him leave it like this.

'What's changed?' she asked abruptly.

'What?' he balked at her direct challenge.

'Why have you gone from being kind and sweet and solicitous, to blanking me and even refusing to look at me? Do I disgust you – is that it?'

She stood with her feet apart, hands clenched on her hips in indignation, hair tumbling wildly around her face, her eyes glittering with ire – she was more beautiful in her anger than in perfume and silks, and she fired Ashan's blood.

In three strides, Ashan was stood before her, just a hand's breadth away. She looked up at him, still with her hands fisted on her hips; a heat rose up from her core to stain her cheeks as the very nearness of him warmed her.

He lifted his hand to her face.

She flinched.

A dozen emotions flitted through Ashan's eyes; anger chased embarrassment chased shame, and others she couldn't identify.

He moved his hand more slowly, bringing it up to stroke her cheek. Then, unexpectedly, he bent his head to kiss her.

She felt her insides dissolve as he brought his other arm around her lower back and drew her close. For all that she had experienced of men in the last couple of moons, she had never been kissed, nor treated with any kind of tenderness.

Ashan kissed her so gently that it took her breath away and made her legs tremble. Her lips parted for him. His tongue grazed hers. She exhaled, savouring the cinnamon taste of him as her heart raced and her stomach fluttered.

He broke away too soon. 'You do not disgust me, Eliana. I disgust myself. Samsu is not the only one who admires you. I owe all my fealty to him, I am a sworn general of his army. I have pledged an iron oath of devotion to him that binds me until death. And so, no matter how deeply I love you, I cannot protect you from him.'

'You – you love me?' She was so taken aback that she could do nothing but echo his words.

His expression changed in a heartbeat. He dropped her as though she burned him to touch. 'I should never have said that.'

Without another word, he turned and marched out.

'Why not? Ashan!' she called after him in desperation. He did not look back.

*

Their month of freedom passed in blissful peace. In the absence of Samsu's shadow, Kisha recovered from the birth and climbed out of her pit of depression. With her mother rosy and happy again, Sarri was thriving, and the four girls could finally make a harmonious home, free from fear.

Eliana adopted a little corner of the garden for her own, and spent several hours a day out there, cultivating the plants and herbs that Mari used most often, and growing mustard and garlic for seasoning at their own dining table.

During those hours spent alone with only her thoughts for company, Ashan's visit played on her mind.

While the days passed in idle contentment for Sarri, Kisha and Mari, Eliana was reliving Ashan's kiss, dreaming of his arms around her and the safety she had felt within them. Each time she remembered, all the sensations would come flooding back, tinged with the agony of knowing that it might never happen again. Uselessly, she found herself imagining ways in which they could be together: trysts, secrets and lies – all dishonourable actions that Ashan would never consent to.

The scenario that she dreamed of over and over again was the one in which Samsu contracted a fever or was assassinated before he ever made it back through Nippur's gates. She knew it was just a fantasy, but it was not beyond the realms of possibility, and so it gave her comfort all the same.

She still cringed a little, remembering the fury in Ashan's eyes as he realised what he had said, declaring his love for her and his loyalty to Samsu in the same breath. Her heart was torn – she delighted in his admission, revelling in the feeling of being wanted and cared for by one other than her own blood; and she was irritated with him, too, for giving her a hope that could never be realised, a longing that placed them both in danger.

Most of all, she wanted to confront him about his anger – was he annoyed with himself for saying something untrue in the heat of the moment? Perhaps he did not love her at all, only lusted after her.

If she was ever to sleep soundly again, she had to know.

But Ashan was cleverly avoiding being in her presence. He timed his visits to Kisha and the baby when Eliana was down at the bathhouse, or out tending her garden. If it had been once or twice, she might have believed it to be a coincidence, but once or twice a week for an entire moon was something more. She was convinced that he had set a spy to watch the apartments.

There were too many hours in a day to spend them all pining for Ashan. When she was not longing for him, she thought on his other revelation: that Samsu admired her.

She had been shocked beyond words to learn what he had said about her. Part of her wondered how much he truly admired her, and how much was just exaggeration for the sake of shaming the coward. She could well imagine him shouting into the poor man's face: 'You call yourself a soldier? My whore has more courage than you! If she were a man, I would have her in your place.'

Words meant to humiliate one, rather than to praise the other.

But still, she meant to take the insight and use it to her own advantage, if she could. There would be a fine line to tread between maintaining his admiration, and not earning herself further punishment. Above all, she feared he might do some permanent damage.

The way to keep her little family safe was undoubtedly with absolute compliance – but he would see through it in a heartbeat. If she could only keep Samsu's admiration there was a chance, however small, that she might soften him a little. His good opinion and goodwill meant nothing at all to her ego, but everything to the wellbeing of her loved ones. If he ever hoped to win her admiration and loyalty, he was as deluded as the Brute was vicious.

Eliana confided nothing of Ashan's visit to Kisha or Mari. Her sister would be horrified, she knew, and would likely try to keep her away from him altogether. Even the vaguest suggestion of affection would be enough to put everyone in the household at risk, and Kisha would do anything to protect her child. Once, she could have gone to her sister with anything, but Kisha had new priorities now.

She could not confess anything to Mari, either. Though the maid would happily gossip about Ashan, Mari would counsel caution, tell her to put her feelings aside – as if it were that easy! And quite aside from that, Eliana suspected that Mari had her own secret passion for Ashan.

No, she kept the memories sacred, locking them away in the recesses of her mind and bringing them out to pore over in her private moments – hugging the precious hope and comfort to herself.

After four weeks of torturing herself with desire and constantly seeking even as much as a glimpse of him, Eliana decided that he would avoid her no longer. She would not sit around and simper, waiting for him to come to her. She had been raised an *Ensi*'s daughter, and taught to be forthright and direct.

The image of the anger on his face haunted her – she must know if she had somehow destroyed the tender shoot of his affection instead of nurturing it. She must clear the air.

But first, she had to know where to find him.

'Mari!' Eliana beckoned her over. 'Do you know what is actually going on in the palace at the moment?'

'Business is much the same as usual,' Mari wiped her hands on her apron as she finished mixing up a tincture for Sarri's colic. 'Ashan holds audiences and makes decisions in Samsu's place.'

'But... what does he actually *do*?' Eliana persisted. 'I have lived here for almost three moons now, and I still don't know what happens inside the palace.'

'Oh – I'd have thought your father would have enlightened you on all that!'

'No, no,' lied Eliana. 'He kept most of the politics away from his daughters.' In actual fact, Adab had often discussed affairs of state with Eliana. Kisha had shown little interest, but his youngest daughter was bright and enquiring, and had a way of looking at the world with fresh eyes, solving problems in ways he never could have imagined.

'As I understand it, Ashan is an early riser. He gets up when Utu does, and sees to himself. Then two hours after dawn, the politics begin. There are council meetings, city inspections, consultations with the *Ensi*, petitioners, audiences... all the usual things that keep a huge place like this running, I suppose.'

Eliana nodded, looking eager and interested. Mari had told her all she needed to know.

The next morning, she rose in the pre-dawn haze, threw on her clothes and crept barefoot from the apartments, praying that Sarri would not wake in her absence.

Making her way down to the men's bathhouse, she found a discreet hiding place behind a statue in an alcove near the entrance. She secreted herself inside and waited, her heart pounding so loudly that she was sure it would give her away.

An eternity later, as Utu's first rays lightened the sky with a rosy tint, she heard the sound of bootheels on tiles. She froze, pressing herself back into the niche, waiting.

The man flashed past so quickly that she could not be sure it was him. Leaning out, she recognised his hair and build from behind and ran silently after him.

She caught his wrist, 'Ashan!'

With snake-like reflexes, he twisted on the spot, grabbing the hand from his arm and forcing it into a painful lock behind her. In the same moment, a blade appeared at her throat.

He recognised her almost immediately. Swearing an oath, he

let her go, snatched up her hand and dragged her back into the recess she had pounced from.

The space was small, and they were almost pressed up against each other. She rubbed at the thin line his blade had left on her neck.

He breathed hard as he looked down at her, trying to bring his heart rate under control. 'What did you think you were doing?' he hissed furiously. 'I could have killed you!'

'I had no idea you wore a dagger to the bathhouse,' countered Eliana.

'I wear a dagger *everywhere*. Why are you down here? You and I have nothing more to say to each other.'

Her anger rose to match his, 'Actually, we have a great deal to say to each other! You kiss me, tell me that you love me, then leave in a rage and take great pains to avoid me for a full month – do you really not have anything to say to me about that? Because I can think of a few words for you!'

'I should never have said it.'

'Why not? Was it untrue?'

'I should never have said it because it *is* true,' he spat back. 'Nothing but misery and danger can come of it, and I've shamed myself by coveting what is Samsu's.'

'I am not Samsu's – I will never be his. You know that as well as anyone.'

'He would beg to differ, and you may be sure he'd leave you with something to help you remember it, if he heard you say so.'

'He will take my body, but my heart is my own to give. I would choose to give it to you.'

'Well I would not choose to accept it. Eliana, too much is at stake, you must realise that.' His voice was harsh.

Her eyes filled with unexpected tears and spilled over. 'Of course I know that. But you did not give me a chance to tell you that I could love you too, if you would let me.'

Softening, he reached up and brushed the tears away with his fingertips. 'Brave girl – I can't let you love me. I couldn't be responsible for adding to your misery. I know you will never be Samsu's, but you must know that he will never let you be mine.'

Before she knew what she was doing, Eliana stretched up onto tiptoe and kissed him, wrapping her arms around his neck and burying her hands in his hair. He inhaled sharply, but did not pull away. With a deep groan, he leaned into her, pushing her gently back against the wall and pressing his body down the length of hers.

Reluctantly, he let her go, pressing his hands against the wall as if he needed to have them in plain sight. 'This can't be, and we both know it.'

'But… please don't stop being kind to me. Perhaps we can't be together, but we can be friends. I have precious few friends in this place, and I can't bear to have you against me.'

He tucked a stray lock of hair behind her ear. 'That much, I can promise. I shall always be kind to you while it's in my power.'

Raising her hand to his lips, he kissed it, backed out of the space and was gone.

As soon as he was out of sight, she raced back to the apartments on winged feet.

Creeping back in, she could hear movement in the bedroom. It was too late to get back into the bed unnoticed, then.

She resorted to her second plan and stole out into the gardens, away to her favourite corner. When Kisha and Mari found her missing, they would usually search for her here.

As she sat and waited to be discovered, her spirit soared. She had known that Ashan wouldn't compromise himself for a secret affair, but the outcome was the best that she could hope for. To know that he still cared for her, that he would not ignore her any more. That he was her friend in this glazed red prison.

It was enough that she would be in his company from time to time, knowing how he felt, and waiting to steal a glance. They could not be together, but she could depend on his continued kindness, and that was more than she could expect from anyone else.

Her joyfulness continued all that week and into the next. Even Kisha remarked on how much improved her mood was; Mari eyed her suspiciously, not daring to voice any of her fears in case they turned out to be true.

The bubble burst half a moon after her confrontation with Ashan.

Suen was high in the sky, and Eliana slept peacefully beside her sister, with Sarri in the cradle at the foot of the bed.

The door flew open with a bang, startling the sisters awake. Kisha sat up with a shriek, frightening Sarri, who began to wail. A huge figure brandishing a torch stood silhouetted in the frame, like a demon come up from the underworld.

Depositing the flame in a wall bracket, the unmistakeable shadow of the Brute strode around the bed to where Eliana lay. He seized her by the wrist and hauled her from the warmth of the bed, dropping her roughly to the floor.

Head still fugged with sleep, she didn't resist.

'Did you miss me, whore?' he hissed, the stink of wine on his breath. 'I missed you. We have just arrived back. Samsu will see you tomorrow night – if you please him, he'll keep you for his own. This might be our last night together.' The fire was reflected in his eyes, making them dance orange in his dark face. If it hadn't been for the all-too-real chill of the tiles beneath her, Eliana would have wondered whether this was a nightmare and he truly was a demon come to earth.

He used her in his usual way, with unnecessary force and still with the dust of the road clinging to his tunic. Taken by surprise and with a clouded mind, there was no fight in Eliana.

He seemed disappointed as he spent himself and threw her back to the ground.

Kisha had remained silent throughout, clutching the blanket to her chest to protect her own modesty; though the Brute would not so much as look at her without Samsu's permission.

Sarri still cried from the cradle.

Pulling down his tunic, the Brute turned to march from the room.

He kicked out hard at the cradle as he passed. It teetered for a moment, before crashing to the floor, spilling its precious contents. Kisha leapt up like she'd been branded, all modesty forgotten, scooping up the screaming infant and checking her all over for damage.

'Hush! Hush!' she soothed and tutted, once she was happy that Sarri had not suffered any real injury. The Brute had left the torch behind, and Eliana could see that Kisha was as pale and shaken as she was.

It was the first time that Kisha had forgotten to ask after her sister following one of the Brute's assaults.

Eliana barely noticed. As soon as she knew that her little niece was no more than rattled and upset, her mind returned to the Brute's words.

Samsu would see her tomorrow. If she pleased him, she would no longer have to suffer at the Brute's hands.

But she was no longer sure what would please him: courage or submission.

Chapter 8

Ashan arrived at dusk to take her to Samsu, but she was not to go alone.

He came in and bowed to Kisha, 'My lady, your husband insists that Eliana bring the princess this evening.'

Kisha's arms tightened around her daughter. 'No,' her voice was barely audible.

'I don't think it was optional,' said Ashan gently.

'No!' she was firmer this time. 'I don't care what you tell him, but she's not taking Sarri. You'll have to prise her from me.'

Eliana stood behind Ashan, poised and ready to leave. 'You know we won't do that. But Samsu won't just let it go.'

'I don't care. My baby stays with me.'

Ashan nodded, 'As you say. But I strongly advise against it. As your sister says, this will not be the last you hear of it, and it will go worse for you later if you refuse now.'

Sarri let out a little cry of protest as Kisha gripped her harder and shook her head.

'Very well.' Ashan swept out of the room with Eliana in tow.

As they made their way to Samsu's chambers, he asked her, 'What will you say to him?'

'I'll think of something,' she said. 'I can't just tell him she refused – I don't think he'd believe me, for a start. Motherhood has given her some conviction at last.'

'Well, good luck.'

'Thank you. Honestly, I almost hope that the Brute was right about Samsu claiming me for his own. At least I could be free of one of them.'

They arrived at the chamber door. Eliana took a deep breath, gathered her courage, and followed Ashan inside.

Samsu reclined on the bed, bare-chested, studying a map and picking at a bowl of dates beside him. Two guards were in the room, as usual: the Brute, and one other that she only knew by sight.

Moving into the centre of the room, she stopped, aware of his eyes on her. She counted slowly to five, before sinking into her bow.

She would show the humility that he demanded, but with just enough of a pause for it to be obvious that it was not spontaneous or genuine respect that made her bow.

'Well, whore. This is a poor start to the evening, is it not?'

Keeping her forehead to the floor, she held her tongue.

'You seem to have forgotten something. Where is the child?'

Eliana took the directness of the question for permission to speak. 'The princess has been a little unwell with colic this week. It is quite common in young children, but I judged it best to leave her with her mother so that she wouldn't disturb you with her crying.'

Samsu swung off the bed and walked towards her. '*You* judged it best? You think I keep you for your judgement?' He placed the heel of one foot carefully onto the fingers of her left hand as it rested on the ground beside her forehead. Gradually, he increased the pressure.

She bit her lip, determined not to make a sound even if he crushed her fingers to dust.

Impatient, he stamped, driving all his weight down on her slender digits. She gave an involuntary gasp, and was immediately furious with herself.

He gave a little chuckle. 'I always get what I want, whore. You must know that by now. If I want a cry of pain from you, that is what you will give me, whether you wish it or not.'

Turning to the Brute, he said, 'Go and fetch the child. Tolerate no argument from the mother – you can deal with her.'

While his attention was elsewhere, she clenched and flexed her hand. The fingers would be bruised, but didn't feel broken.

The Brute left, and she was once more his sole focus.

'Stand up.'

She obeyed immediately this time.

'Remove your dress.'

Unfastening the shoulder ties, she stared straight ahead, past Samsu. From the corner of her eye, she could see Ashan. It was easy to pretend that she was undressing for his benefit alone. Taking her time, she shrugged out of the gown and stepped to one side, leaving it pooled on the floor behind her.

Usually, when she was commanded to undress, she felt that she was leaving her dignity entangled in the discarded garments. Today, however, she felt the lure of her body – saw in Samsu's expression that she perhaps had some power over him after all, though she had yet to learn to use it.

He circled her like a vulture, examining her as critically as one might appraise a horse when making a purchase. Goosebumps prickled at her skin – whether from the chill of the evening or the mounting anticipation, she could not say.

Cupping one of her breasts in his hand, he squeezed hard, before rolling the nipple between his thumb and forefinger. She kept her face impassive, even as he repeated the action with the other.

When he tugged hard on both together, she winced.

He smiled, satisfied enough by her grimace. In one swift move, he pulled her against him; warm breasts and stiff nipples pressed against his bare chest. He reached around and grabbed her buttocks, kneading them like dough.

Every touch made her stomach churn. She longed to slap his hands away, like an insolent boy at the bazaar.

One day, she told herself, she would have the courage to do it.

His fingers snaked between her legs. The sudden touch made her jump and pull away – though she had been violated in other ways, that part of her body had thus far remained largely private.

Samsu took a step back. Gripping her hair with one hand, he gave a blow to the face that made her legs buckle beneath her. She cried out as he held her up by the hair.

'You *will* learn, girl.' He barked. 'You are a slave. No part of your body belongs to you, and I will do what I like with my own possessions. The person that you were is dead – you are my whore, and you have no identity beyond that. In fact,' he looked thoughtful for a moment, 'you shall have a new name to match your status. *Karkittu*, "whore" in the Babylonian dialect, lest you forget who you are.'

He dropped her to the ground and walked back to the bed.

Lying there in a crumpled heap, she raged inwardly, swearing to herself that he could do as he wanted with her outer shell, but her inner being was beyond his reach. She was desperate to reassure herself, afraid of how far he might go to strip down her sense of self and rebuild her to suit his whim.

As she lay in silent, miserable fury, shivering on the floor, the Brute returned, Sarri screaming in his arms.

'At last,' said Samsu. 'I know you care little for your own welfare, *Karkittu*, but I am sure you are anxious to make sure that none of your niece's innocent blood stains these tiles.'

Eliana sat up in a panic – she could well believe that Samsu would harm his own daughter just to make her obey. Her heart sank with dread as she saw the Brute standing at his post, cradling Sarri in one arm, poised with a dagger above her stomach.

'A-ha,' laughed Samsu, 'now I have your undivided attention, I see. So, with your sister's child here to ensure your good behaviour and no unfortunate injuries to my person, I am eager to see what you've learned. Come here.'

She stood.

'No,' he stopped her. 'Crawl.'

Dropping back to her hands and knees, she dragged herself the unending length of the room to where he stood beside the bed, feeling sick with the indignity and absurdity of the act. Tears of despair threatened, but she fought them down. She would not show him her tears.

'Good.'

She looked up at him. A broad grin split his face, like a child given a much-coveted toy.

He kicked her hard in the ribs, making her cough. 'Now, little *karkittu*, you know the rules about looking at your master. Sit up.'

She sat onto her heels.

Hitching his kilt up to his waist, he made it clear what he wanted from her tonight. What Eliana saw no longer shocked her – one was much the same as another. She fought the almost overwhelming urge to use her teeth as a weapon, instead tuning into Sarri's heartrending wails for her mother.

With the little princess's cries filling her ears, she took him into her mouth. Massaging the base with one hand as her tongue flicked deftly around the tip, she slid well-practised lips up and down the length of him, alert to the groans and shudders that told her when she was pleasing.

Thankfully, he lasted no longer than any of the others. Twisting his fingers into her hair, he held her head still as he spent with a gasp and an oath, forcing her to swallow his seed as had so many others before.

She would make herself vomit later, as she always did.

Samsu pulled away and staggered backwards to sit on his bed, panting a little. 'Give her the child,' he ordered the Brute. 'Ashan, you may return her to her rooms and send in the concubine. I have had my fun for tonight, now it is time for duty. She will have another child in her belly within half a year.'

He gestured to Eliana that she could get up. The Brute thrust Sarri into her arms, glad to be rid of the screaming child. She quickly crossed the room to retrieve her dress, then followed Ashan outside.

As soon as the door closed, she handed Sarri to him and put on her dress. As she took the baby back, he said to her, 'You did well.'

'Do you think he will be pleased?' she asked anxiously.

'I think so. I saw nothing to suggest otherwise.'

She blushed. It was mortifying to hear him acknowledge that he had been witness to the whole disgusting ordeal. She didn't speak again before they reached the apartments.

They walked in as Mari was finishing applying her arnica ointment to Kisha's face. The Brute had not been compassionate when she refused to hand over her daughter.

'Is she alright?' she cried, leaping up as soon as she saw the bundle in her sister's arms. She all-but snatched Sarri from Eliana.

'She's fine,' said Eliana indignantly. 'I wouldn't let anything happen to her, when her safety depends on my behaviour.'

'He wants you now, my lady. He is determined to get another child on you as soon as possible.'

Kisha's shoulders slumped. She handed her daughter back to Eliana, placed a kiss on the baby's forehead, and meekly followed Ashan from the room.

*

In her sister's absence, Eliana lowered herself onto a floor cushion, pulling her knees up and cradling Sarri in the warm crook of her arm. She would enjoy some time to cuddle her niece now – Kisha certainly wouldn't let go of her for quite some time after tonight's trauma.

The sweetly sleeping face was relaxed, unaware of the danger her father had put her in. Eliana envied her a little – babies lived only for the moment; their pasts were too short to trouble them, and their futures too distant. The future would not trouble this little one for years yet. She was utterly dependent on others to see that she had one.

Mari flopped down on the cushion beside her. 'You look as though you've got the weight of the world crushing you – was it so awful?'

'Hm? No, not so bad, not what he made me do. Nothing out of the ordinary. It's just her,' Eliana gestured at Sarri. 'This is no place for her. What sort of future will she have here?'

'Well, she'll be treated with a reasonable degree of respect, being Samsu's legitimate daughter. She'll be raised as a princess, and when she's ready, she'll be married into another royal family somewhere.'

'If there are any other royal families left when Samsu's father has built his empire,' Eliana scoffed.

'Hammurabi is very enthusiastic about expanding his borders.'

'Anyway, that's not what I meant. There will always be a shadow of fear hanging over her – that's not what any of us would wish on an innocent child.'

'True. She will always be a weapon for Samsu to use against you and your sister.'

'A life of luxury, but there will forever be a dagger hanging above her head. I wish I could smuggle her out of here, get her to safety. And she makes Kisha do stupid things too.'

Mari was quiet a moment; she looked thoughtful. 'Well… why don't you?'

'What?'

'Smuggle her out – get her to safety.'

Eliana glanced at her for a sign she was joking, but Mari's face was straight and deadly serious.

'Do you really think we could?'

'I think we could try. For her. She deserves better.'

'But who would we send her to? The only person in the city I would trust is my father.'

'Then send her to him.'

Eliana sat in silence for long minutes, turning the possibilities over in her mind as she gazed down at the little body in her arms. It was true that Sarri would never be safe here, and she would be better off raised as a merchant's daughter in the city than a royal princess in this palace. Her father could arrange for some pay off to be made to cover the girl's expenses – she need never know.

At length, she spoke. 'No… it's impossible really. For a start, Kisha would never agree. She'd die before letting us take her baby.'

'She's going to get herself killed anyway if she carries on being this stupid about her,' Mari was as blunt as ever. 'The way I see it, she doesn't even have to know until the deed is done. Wait until she's with Samsu, like now, and get her out.'

'I couldn't do that!' Eliana was shocked. 'Take my own sister's baby away without giving her a choice in the matter, or even so much as a farewell.'

'But it's in your niece's best interests,' Mari persisted. 'She would come to forgive you when she realised you saved her baby's life, and maybe her own.'

'My father may not agree either,' Eliana warned. 'He's as frightened of Samsu as any of us. His main priority is to keep his place so that the city and the people don't go to rack and ruin under some Babylonian thug.' Her heart ached a little as she thought of her father, alone now in his big house, with nobody but the servants for company. She hoped he wasn't working himself to death. She went on, 'And we'll also need someone with the freedom of both the palace and the city to take Sarri. Someone we trust.'

'Well, that part isn't a problem, surely?' Mari looked at her as if she had missed something obvious.

'Who? Ashan?'

Mari laughed, 'Ashan! No! Why would you think of him? He's a good man, but he'd never betray Samsu. No, Isin, of course.'

Eliana paused for thought, 'I suppose he did say he'd do anything for Kisha. In fact, he swore to care for the baby like his own. But those were just words spoken by a broken heart – he might feel very differently if we called on him to act on them.'

Mari shrugged, 'If you don't ask, how will you ever know?'

Completely torn between loyalty to her sister and a sense of care to her niece, Eliana's head was beginning to hurt as she tried to weigh up the rights and wrongs. Was it a greater wrong to leave an innocent in danger, or to destroy the sister who had loved her and raised her? For it surely would destroy Kisha if they took Sarri away – the child was her whole reason for being now. Mari had confided to Eliana that Kisha had stopped eating in the weeks before she conceived – too afraid for her family and of her own blood to take her life with a blade, she had hoped to starve herself gently to death.

The pregnancy had changed everything. Sarri was her entire reason for being.

With the stresses and events of the evening catching up on her, Eliana could not wrap her mind around the moral complexities. She rubbed her temple with her free hand; the arm cradling the baby was beginning to go numb from her weight.

'I'll think about it,' she said eventually. 'Taking a baby away from her mother isn't a decision we can make in a moment.'

Mari opened her mouth to reply, but at that moment Ashan came striding back into the room, escorting a subdued-looking Kisha.

Without a word, she went straight to her sister, plucked the baby from her arms and retreated to their bedroom. Eliana stood up, shaking her arm gratefully. She and Ashan exchanged a glance; Eliana longed to go to him, to feel his protective arms around her and his lips on hers again.

He bowed and left.

That night, Eliana barely slept; despite the exhaustion of her body, her mind was overactive, and she was filled with guilt that she should even consider what she and Mari had spoken of.

But, lying awake and straining to catch the sound of Sarri's breathy little snores, she was becoming ever-more convinced of the right course of action.

Chapter 9

'Let's do it.'

Eliana had wrestled with her conscience, but the baby's welfare had to come first. Sarri relied on her mother and aunt to give her the best quality of life they could, that was the nature of being a parent. Eliana had finally convinced herself that Sarri would have a better life away from the palace, away from Samsu.

She would have a chance to grow up free from fear, cherished by an adopted family and free to marry whom she chose when the time was right. Having thus far been denied that privilege herself, Eliana was all the keener that Sarri would not end up chained to a monster who would only take her for the dynastic advantages. She deserved a man like Isin, who loved her and was willing to go to the ends of the earth to help her.

Isin. He was the next obstacle to overcome.

'Are you sure?' whispered Mari. 'Once we commit, there's no turning back.'

'I'm sure. Get Isin to meet me at my garden at dusk – we'll be safe there.'

Eliana's garden was in a tranquil, secluded spot. Not so far from the stream that she couldn't still hear its soothing babble, but far enough to take her comfortably off the path and into a patch bordered by trees on three sides and a wall on the fourth. She felt safe there. When she sat with her back against the sun-warmed stone wall, nobody could sneak up on her. She had her plants to amuse her, the soft grass for a bed, and the sun for company as he drenched her little space with his rays.

Even shut away in the depths of the palace, she had found a place to call her own.

After the evening meal, she took the lyre and went to sit out amongst her herbs. The sky flamed as Utu began to lay his head to rest. She had intended to practise her playing, work on a tune she had been composing, but in the end it was irresistible. Stretching out on her back in a pool of sunlight, luxuriating like a cat in the warmth, she watched the sky as it dimmed from orange, to pink, to purple twilight.

A light cough came from the trees.

'It's safe, Isin,' she said in a low voice.

He stepped out from behind a date tree. If it was possible, he was even paler than when she'd last seen him. His eyes were large and bright in an almost emaciated face.

She gasped, 'Have you been ill?'

'Just heartsick,' he mumbled.

'You haven't been eating, have you? Here,' she stood and plucked a ripe fig from one of the trees.

He shook his head. 'I'm not hungry.'

Pressing into his hand, she insisted, 'Eat.'

Taking the fruit, he made no move to put it in his mouth. 'You didn't ask me here to ask after my health – what do you want?'

Eliana hesitated a moment, searching for the right words. 'It's Kisha,' she began.

'Well *obviously* it's Kisha – do you think I'd have come otherwise?' he snapped. Her shock must have been visible, for he immediately hung his head, flushing in shame. 'I'm so sorry *ahatatu*,' he used his pet name for her, little sister. 'I've been under a great deal of strain lately. I'm thinking of leaving the city altogether. It's clear I'll find no happiness here.'

'Will Samsu let you leave?'

'Willingly – he's granted me safe passage to Umma, and offered to give me an introduction to the *Ensi* there, on the understanding that I never return to Nippur.'

She pulled a face, 'And are you going?'

'I suppose so. There's nothing for me here. I'll never love anyone other than Kisha, and my career is limited here because of our previous relationship, though we've not laid eyes on each other in over a year. I might as well start afresh somewhere else.'

His thin shoulders shook with a barely repressed sob.

Not knowing what to say, Eliana put a hand on his back. She was shocked to feel the lumps of his spine standing up from his flesh through the pale linen of his scribe's tunic.

'What if... you could have a piece of Kisha to take with you?' she ventured.

Isin's head snapped up, his eyes suddenly alert and focused. 'What do you mean?'

'The baby isn't safe here, and Kisha constantly puts herself in danger on her daughter's behalf. We both know it's futile, Samsu will have what he wants whether she inconveniences herself first or not. It would be better for everyone if Sarri was taken to safety outside the palace walls.'

His jaw dropped, 'You can't be serious? What will happen when Samsu finds out?'

She shrugged. 'Who knows? It won't be pleasant, I'm sure. I'll take the blame, and if he kills me, then so much the better.'

'You can't seriously want to die, *ahatatu*?' he said softly. 'Life cannot be all that bad?'

'Life is as bad for me as it is for you. I'm a prisoner here – I'll never have the freedom of my own life or love, I'll never have a career, I do not even have my own body. My life is a long, flat road, stretching out before me in an endless monotony with no destination. I can take it or leave it.'

'We all leave it eventually.'

'Yes. Death is so very final… but Ereshkigal comes to us all, and with no prospects in life, what matter if she finds me sooner rather than later?'

'I wish I had your sense of purpose, Eliana,' he said seriously. 'No matter what happens to you, you always seem to know what to do next. I feel like a *gidim*, a shade trapped here with no future but existence.'

'But we are not all condemned to go on without a future – Sarri could have one, if you'll give it to her. You can take Kisha's child and raise her as your own – it will soften the blow for Kisha when she finds out what I have done. She'd be pleased to know you were raising her daughter in safety.'

'I suppose I have nothing to lose,' he said softly, his eyes lit with excitement.

'Then you'll do it?' Eliana could scarcely believe her ears. 'I can't thank you enough, Isin. You could be saving Sarri's life.'

He nodded, 'Well I have nothing to lose but my own life, and that is worth little enough.'

'Don't devalue yourself; your life is worth as much as any of ours. But I hope this will bring you happiness. We were going to ask you to take her to my father to find her a foster family, though we were afraid Father would just bring Sarri straight back here, out of fear of being caught. You have solved the problem for us.'

'It's nothing – send me word when your plans are in place.'

'It's not nothing. Giving a little girl a chance at life is far from nothing.' She stretched up and kissed him on the cheek. 'Thank you.'

She watched him depart, disappearing between the trees, and thought of how different life might have been if Samsu had chosen a different city to conquer. Kisha would have married Isin, and he would be Sarri's father in truth. Eliana would have liked him for a brother-in-law.

She had no idea who she would have married. Perhaps she would never have married at all, but it would be nice to have the option.

Minutes after Isin took his leave, Mari appeared between the trees, almost invisible in the darkness as night swallowed the garden.

'Did you see him?' she asked.

Eliana nodded.

'And?'

'He'll do it. He is moving to Umma, with Samsu's encouragement. He'll take her away and raise her there.'

A smile split Mari's face, 'That's better than we could have hoped for!'

Eliana allowed herself a smile in return. 'I know.'

'You must come now – one of Samsu's slaves has come looking for you.'

Her heart sank and the familiar hand of despair touched her, 'Am I summoned?'

'No, he has something for you.'

Intrigued, Eliana hurried back to the apartments with Mari.

The slave stood in the middle of the room, dressed in a soft black tunic as a marker of his status as a personal servant of Samsu. He held a cushion in his hands, draped over with red silk.

The room was now lit by half a dozen burning torches in brackets, smoke streaming upwards to stain the painted walls and high ceilings. The man bowed. She raised an eyebrow. No-one but Ashan ever bowed to her.

'My lady, the prince sends me with a gift and a message.'

'And your message is?'

'That you have satisfied your prince, and he is pleased to take you for his own, to the exclusion of all others on your part.'

Eliana heaved a great sigh of relief. She would only have one bully to deal with now.

'As a token of his ownership, he sends you this gift.' The man allowed the silk to slide to the floor.

Gold glittered on the cushion.

Wide and rich, set with semi-precious stones and exquisitely engraved, Eliana looked at it in horror.

A slave's collar.

He meant to shackle her in deed as well as in words.

The man set down the cushion and gingerly picked up the gift, 'May I?'

She nodded, struck dumb. Somewhere in the back of her mind was a dull urge to laugh – she could not recall the last time she had been speechless.

He moved behind her. The metal weighed her down as he placed it around her neck, cold and unyielding. The clink as the clasp snapped shut sounded to Eliana like a bolt being slammed home in its lock.

The slave fiddled for a moment longer, then stepped around to take a better look at the collar. In his hand, he held a small golden key.

Her pulse leapt and stomach contracted in panic as she realised what the key was for. She tugged desperately at the collar, which felt too tight around her slender neck, too heavy on her shoulders. It would not come off.

'It is locked, my lady. The prince will take the key. He will decide if and when to remove it.'

She covered her face with her hands, defeated. Abject misery swelled inside her, subsuming the panic. The collar already chafed at her spirit, soon it would chafe at her skin and she would be powerless to remove it.

The man bowed again and left without another word.

Eliana stood there helplessly, the flickering light of the torches bringing the gold about her neck alive.

With a sleeping Sarri in her arms, Kisha walked in from the

bedroom. She stopped in surprise, 'That's pretty, Eliana. Where did you get it?'

'Samsu. I'm glad you like it, because you'll be looking at it a lot from now on. It's my slave collar, done up to look like a rich necklace.'

'We all have our slave markings, little sister.' Kisha held up the hand bearing her wedding band. Mari lifted her gown to reveal the branding on her thigh. 'He likes to be able to identify his property.'

Eliana sagged onto a couch, crushed beneath the weight.

She could not sleep that night, feeling the discomfort of Samsu's touch whichever way she turned.

*

Within days, the collar had rubbed her neck raw. The skin beneath the edges cracked and bled and stung, no matter how much salve Mari applied.

'If you keep poking at it, it's never going to heal,' she said, frustrated.

Eliana didn't reply. She sighed and twisted her fingers to keep them busy while she waited for Mari. As soon as she was finished, Eliana sulked off to sit with her sister and niece.

The collar's weight was dragging her down mentally as well as physically. Her slim shoulders weren't made to bear the wide circlet of gold and gems. She was grateful that she wasn't a queen – to wear a gold and feathered headdress would be agony on the neck. Perhaps it was less painful when you were born to it, she considered, and she certainly hadn't been born to slavery.

'If I'd known it would be locked on, I would never have let him put it around my neck,' she complained to Kisha for the hundredth time. 'I thought I would only have to wear it in Samsu's presence.'

Her sister ignored her, concentrating on the babe in her arms.

'It's heavy, it hurts and I can barely sleep,' she fumed. 'I don't know what purpose he thinks it will serve to have me wear it all the time, except to make me miserable.'

'Oh, will you stop whingeing and whining and just *accept* it, Eliana!' Kisha snapped. 'Stop fighting and being such a pain all the time, and maybe he'll take it off some day. You can't talk it off, and I wish you'd stop trying!'

'Gods, what's wrong with you?' Eliana bit back.

'I've already got one baby to worry about; I don't want you being another! Sarri needs me, and I put all my energy into worrying about her – our futures, mine and yours, they're mapped out, they're here, but hers… I'm so afraid she'll be killed, afraid *all* the time, and you want me to be concerned about your necklace because it's a bit uncomfortable?'

'I – '

'Yes, I know you object to it, you don't like what it stands for, it hurts… but you should thank the gods for it. It's a barrier between you and the Brute – he'll never have you again while you wear that collar. And Samsu isn't interested in you at the moment either. He calls for me every night, and he will do so until I have another baby in my belly. You may not see it, but I'm still protecting you, Eliana. He's so preoccupied with me that he's got no time for you. Thank Enlil for your good fortune in not being called to his bed and stop complaining about something so *trivial!*'

Eliana was silent, a rare tear slipping down her face. She might cry in pain when Samsu and the Brute hurt her body, but it was uncommon for her to cry from this sort of hurt, and even less so for the hurt to come from Kisha. Her gentle sister had become another person since the birth.

She sloped off to her garden to cry out the confusion in private. It had been her comfort that here she could be with her sister

– the one thing she had longed for after Kisha was married. It was the thing that had sustained her through those early weeks. But now…

She was no longer sure that Kisha wanted her around. After Eliana sent Sarri away, Kisha would want her around even less.

The constant weight of the collar around her neck was nothing compared to the burden of guilt on her heart.

Lying beside the stream, her skin drank the coolness of the shade in the heat of the day. She no longer dared to spend too much time in Utu's direct gaze, lest the sun heat the metal around her neck and burn her.

She had no idea when she had fallen asleep, and no notion of the time when she woke up. The sky was fading fast and the first stars were out; the goddess Inanna, in her guise of the evening star, outshone them all.

Eliana hastened back to the rooms, chilled to the bone now, hoping that Kisha would be in a better mood.

To her great astonishment, Ashan sat beside Sarri's cradle. Kisha was nowhere to be seen.

He looked up as she entered, 'Ah, there you are! Kisha is with the prince, and Mari is busy. We couldn't find you, so she asked me to stay with Sarri.'

'She couldn't have looked for me very hard – I was where I always am.'

Ashan shrugged and gave a heart-melting smile, a dimple dancing in one cheek beneath his stubble. Eliana went to sit beside him.

'You can hold her, if you like.'

He didn't not need to be invited twice. Reaching into the cradle, he picked Sarri up as though she were a delicate fragment of porcelain and hugged her to his chest.

Eliana looked at him and wondered how she would ever keep her love for him a secret. Kindness ran to the very depths of his soul. She wondered whether he would approve of her plan to send Sarri away to safety.

On second thoughts, she doubted it. He was Samsu's man, and she must never let affection tint her perception of him. Decent and kind, he may be; loyal, he certainly was. If she acted against Samsu, she was sure Ashan would tell him.

Still cuddling the baby, he leant against the back of the couch. Tentatively, afraid of being pushed off, Eliana leaned into him, negotiating the collar that he had studiously ignored thus far, and nestled her cheek against his arm; it was soft and solid all at once, like a brick wrapped in silks.

He did not push her off, but leaned in a little.

She gave a sigh of deep contentment. If only life could be like this all the time. To be in contact with Ashan was to be in paradise, even if it was only temporary. They sat together in comfortable silence.

Mari entered, looking for thread to mend another hole in one of Eliana's gowns. She gave them an odd, pained look that Eliana couldn't make out, before retreating back to the bedroom.

Eliana paid her no mind; it was proof, she supposed, that the older girl had more than a passing affection for Ashan. She couldn't blame her.

After several minutes, Ashan stirred again. He leaned forward to replace Sarri in her cradle, then settled back into the couch and draped one arm around Eliana. She snuggled in.

'I suppose there are upsides to every situation,' smiled Eliana.

'What's that?' he murmured into her hair.

'If I hadn't been brought here for Samsu, I wouldn't have known you. I would relive all my moments with Samsu to have another such as this.'

'What would your life be if you hadn't come here?'

The question took her by surprise. 'I don't know. I suppose I would still be helping my father. I had no interest in a husband;

I've always just wanted to improve the city really, like Father. Leave a legacy in stonework, something for people to remember me by.'

He kissed her curls and said nothing.

'What about you? How did you come to be here?'

His arm tightened almost imperceptibly. 'It's a long story,' he said. 'The short version is that my father died when the prince's father conquered our city, and I ended up in Samsu's personal guard.'

Eliana laughed, 'That's not much to go on! Did you choose it, or is that just the way things worked out?'

'It doesn't matter. It is what it is.'

His tone told her that it was not a topic for easy discussion. Perhaps it was too painful.

He eased her off him and stood. 'It's time for me to bring your sister back. Try to be nice to each other – the palace doesn't need any more strife.'

She gave a rueful smile, 'I'll try, if she does.'

'That's all I ask.' He gave a little wink and bowed to her, as was his habit, and headed off to Samsu's apartments.

It was fully dark now. Mari came out to light the torches, making the wall paintings come to life in the alternating of dancing light and flickering shadow. Their magic was lost on Eliana. As she did several times a day, she stood over the cradle and gazed lovingly at Sarri, wondering if Kisha would ever forgive her for what she was planning.

*

Isin tendered his resignation, and Samsu was glad to accept. A date was set for him to leave the city in a fortnight's time, with an escort all the way to Umma and an emissary to introduce him to their *Ensi*.

Mari went between Eliana and Isin with messages as they laid their plan – she was the only one who had freedom of the palace, and could even venture out into the city market occasionally.

It was a freedom that Eliana had never realised she would miss. The heat that shimmered off every stall; the close press of bodies that jostled every step and exuded every human smell imaginable; the merchants shouting their wares over the constant thrum of chatter – a steady vibration, like putting an ear to a beehive.

When her father had sent her to the marketplace, she'd hated every moment. Now, she would give anything she owned to go again. On a still day, she could hear the noise of the city over the palace walls and see the dust dancing in the air, stirred up by hasty feet. It made her feel more of a prisoner than ever, and glad that Sarri wouldn't have to suffer confinement as she grew up.

Isin showed no signs of second thoughts – his messages were upbeat and positive, and he seemed to relish the idea of being a father to Kisha's child. They arranged that he should come to Eliana's garden at sunset the night before he was due to depart – Kisha was usually with Samsu at that hour, and Eliana would be able to hand Sarri over without causing any suspicion. By the time Kisha returned to the room, Isin would have left the palace.

Eliana considered hiding somewhere until the morning, perhaps up one of the trees – she had no idea how she would explain Sarri's absence. But her own disappearance along with her niece's would suggest that she too had escaped, and a city-wide hunt would be launched. If Isin was discovered, it would be the end of Sarri's chance at life.

Her only thought was that she could claim the physician had taken the baby for examination and would return her tomorrow – that would provide enough of a delay for Isin to get out of the city.

The more Eliana thought on the plan and the closer the day came, the more she tried to picture her sister's reaction and foresee the consequences of what she was planning.

It was not the thought of Samsu's punishment that scared her, though it would inevitably come out that it was she who had planned Sarri's escape, it was the thought that she might not be able to conceal the baby's whereabouts if he began to torture her. She would not put it past him – although he probably cared little about his daughter, it would be the principle of the thing. He would see it as defiance, and would punish her accordingly until he brought Sarri back.

And Kisha... her usually sweet and gentle sister had been unpleasant since the birth, but only because she was in constant fear for her child. If Sarri was taken away, would that fear be assuaged, or grow worse?

The more she looked ahead, the less she thought her sister would ever forgive her.

She knew that what they planned would be in Sarri's best interests, but she also had Kisha to worry about. And herself. Once Kisha understood what had happened, things could get very unpleasant in the apartments...

Eliana was torn. She had been resolved on her course of action, but it seemed that no matter what she did, there would be misery and pain.

It was as she watched her sister feed the baby on the night of the planned handover that she made her decision. Kisha gazed on her daughter, soft brown eyes brimming with love and wonder, as if she couldn't quite believe that this child had grown from her own body. As the baby suckled, Kisha gave a contented sigh.

'This is all I ever wanted from life,' she smiled.

Eliana was astonished. 'Confinement, restriction and an abusive husband?'

'No, a child. To be the sort of mother to her that our mother never had the chance to be to us.'

There was no reply that Eliana could make to that. She could not take the child away without asking Kisha.

Time was against her. Kisha would be summoned to Samsu's chamber at any moment and Isin would be making his way to the garden. It was too late to turn back, but if she could just talk to Kisha first, make her understand…

There was a knock at the door. Kisha put Sarri back in the cradle with a sigh as Mari answered it.

Ashan entered and gave his usual bow, 'Are you ready, my lady?'

'As I'll ever be.' Kisha adjusted her hair, took his arm and let him lead her out.

Too late.

Eliana approached the elaborately carved and brightly painted cradle. Sarri sucked on her fingers, peering up at her with inquisitive eyes. The little face was already becoming more expressive, and the tuft of fine black hair she had been born with nearly covered her ears.

Reaching into the cradle, Eliana couldn't bring herself to pick Sarri up, to take this sweet, trusting child away from her mother. She had been ripped from her own mother when she was an infant, and this one had no older sister to take care of her.

She pulled the baby's blanket up and tucked her in, hating herself for letting things go this far, setting off for her garden at a run. She had to let Isin know – he at least had to wait until she could talk to Kisha, it would not be more than a couple of hours.

Flitting light and barefoot over the grass, crossing the bridge and making her way through the twisting path between the trees, her heart was beating out of her chest as she thought of Isin's disappointment.

Ducking under a branch, she came out in her garden, 'Isin!'

She stopped dead. A high-pitched scream echoed around the garden. It took her a moment to realise that it was her own.

Eliana's knees gave out and she dropped to the ground.

Samsu sat with his back against the sun-warmed wall, in Eliana's own favourite spot. His face was a picture of tranquillity.

His hands and tunic were heavily bloodstained, and the knife in his hand dripped with gore.

The grass at his feet was red and sodden. Isin lay scattered in six pieces around the garden.

Her stomach heaved at the stench of the blood, so strong that she could taste its metallic tang.

'You're late,' Samsu said.

Eliana had no reply.

'I told you once that not a single word you speak within the walls of this palace escapes me. You were a fool to forget it.'

She could only stare back in mute horror.

'And now that I'm here, you have no words for me.' He pushed himself to his feet and came to stand over her, the blade still in his hand. 'I thought that you'd learned your lesson about obedience. How could you imagine that you'd be able to get my daughter out from under my nose without being noticed? You think that just because I don't see her, I don't have eyes on her? She is my blood, my first legitimate child. She will grow up like her mother – a beauty, meek and mild – and be an asset to me. You thought I'd let you and this petty scribe whisk her out from under me?'

Opening her mouth, no sound came out. She shook her head.

'And where is my daughter?'

'In her cradle,' whispered Eliana. 'I wasn't going to go through with it.'

'So, common sense won through.' Samsu's knife dripped. Droplets of Isin's blood spattered her hand and gown. The head had been severed from his slender body, and the blank eyes stared at her from a face that still wore an expression of surprise.

She retched, trying desperately to hold her stomach strong.

'*Karkittu*, if you ever wish to be more in this palace than a pretty pound of flesh, you must develop a brain. My daughter is my property. My wives are my property. *You* are my property.

I do what I will with what belongs to me – the sooner you learn it, the more pleasant your life will be.'

She shook her head again. 'You can have my body, but you'll never own my spirit.' The words were supposed to come out with strength and conviction, but they were scarcely louder than a sigh.

He laughed, grabbed her by the hair and pulled her to her feet. 'Still so stubborn!' Keeping hold of her hair and bringing his other hand to her back, he thrust his lips onto hers. His kiss was not tender, like Ashan's, but a crushing possession of her mouth. He bruised her lips and nipped sharply at her tongue, drawing the breath from her lungs.

Eliana was dizzy from lack of air before he released her, leaving a bloody handprint on the back of her gown. She staggered sideways a little, toward's Isin's dismembered leg. Giving a shriek, she reeled away again.

Samsu laughed at her. 'It can't hurt you, *karkittu*. That leg will never kick again.' He stepped over it and made for the path between the trees. 'Don't think that you've escaped punishment for your part in tonight. I'll have you obedient the next time we meet, or your body will be in more pieces than this one by the time I'm finished with you. You will go to the underworld in fragments if I have to be the one to send you there. But for now,' he ducked under the low branch, 'your sister awaits me.'

He disappeared into the foliage, leaving her alone with her fear.

Eliana dropped back to her hands and knees, eyes riveted on what remained of Isin. White balls of bone gleamed at the ends of each of his scattered limbs, protruding from the ragged flesh. An intestine snaked its way out of the hole in his torso where a leg had been. Her stomach lurched again, and this time she let it go, vomiting onto the grass.

There was the faintest breath of chill wind on the back of her neck – she stifled another cry, imagining that Isin's wretched shade stood behind her. Forcing herself up onto trembling legs, she made her way back to the apartments.

Ashan was waiting for her when she returned. She was a ghastly sight – pale as the moon and covered in Isin's blood where it had soaked the ground and dripped from the blade.

As soon as she saw him, the tears began to fall. He moved to her, masking his shock, wrapping her in his arms and making soothing noises.

'What's happened? Are you hurt?'

Between sobs, she gasped out the story.

Ashan tensed. 'Idiots, the pair of you. You are lucky that it was only he who died.'

She thrust him away, 'Lucky! I wish it had been me! I will live forever with that poor boy's shade at my shoulder, and his last grimace burned into my mind!'

'Eliana, Samsu has spies *everywhere*. People you don't see, people you'd never suspect. How you could ever think that this insanity would work is completely beyond me.'

'You're not helping!' she cried, turning away from him.

His voice softened as he placed a hand on her shoulder, 'What would help?'

'Get it out of my garden! Make it so that this never happened.'

'I cannot reverse time, sweet one, but I can put your garden right.'

She turned back into his arms, 'Would you? You'd really clean Isin up and lay him to rest? It's so gruesome – I can't ask you to do it.'

'Be pragmatic,' he said. 'How else do you expect the body to get out of the garden? Samsu certainly won't clean it up.'

'You don't mind?'

He shrugged, 'I'm sure it's no worse than the sights I've seen on the battlefield.'

Eliana shuddered.

Planting a kiss on her forehead, Ashan made for the terrace. 'I don't have time to do it before I have to fetch Kisha back, but I promise it will all be done by morning – I'll go now to see what needs to be done. Get yourself down to the bathhouse, wash off the blood and burn your gown. Kisha need never know.'

'Thank you,' she whispered, almost faint with relief.

She was grateful that Mari was nowhere to be found – perhaps she could put off explaining their failure again until tomorrow.

Chapter 10

Isin haunted her dreams.

More than a month after his murder, she still slept badly. The worst part of it was that she couldn't confide the reason for her restlessness in her sister, and Kisha was beginning to complain of Eliana's tossing and turning disrupting her own sleep. Eliana had to deflect her, saying that it was the collar still making her uncomfortable.

It was impossible to rest – Isin's shade stalked her relentlessly, blank glazed eyes fixed upon her, staring from a shadowy face.

And his wasn't the only shadow to haunt her – she was becoming afraid to leave the apartments, even to go to the bathhouse. Everywhere she walked, her footsteps seemed to have an echo; if she stopped to look round, she saw nothing. If she ever thought she saw a shape flicker around the corner behind her, it was so swift as to make her think she might have imagined it.

Dark circles had begun to form under her eyes, and she was nervy, jumping at every little motion or sound, much to the irritation of Mari and Kisha.

Of course, Mari knew why she was anxious, and tried to accommodate it. Eliana had had to explain to her why Sarri was still in the cradle. Both girls had been fond of Isin, and they wept together as they tried to puzzle out how Samsu might have discovered them.

Eliana tried desperately hard not to suspect Mari. If she had betrayed them then there was truly no-one in the world she could trust but her sister. From that day onwards, Eliana was careful what she shared with Mari.

The older girl was hurt by the sudden withdrawal – the puzzlement was plain to see in her amber eyes. Without hard evidence, Eliana did not like to accuse her of anything.

Ashan had been as good as his word. The morning following the butchery in the garden, there had been no trace of Isin but a few rusty-looking patches of grass where the blood had stained the greenery.

A good strong storm would wash it away, but Eliana stayed away from her little haven, letting the weeds claim her carefully cultivated herbs. She could not bear to sit there again, in her favourite spot against the wall, knowing that Samsu had profaned the place. The gods could send a flood to wash away the world, and still her former sanctuary would not be clean.

Eliana's seventeenth birthday came and went all but unnoticed. Her sister gave her a gold hairpiece adorned with sapphire-blue feathers that brought out the midnight hues of her hair, along with a belt of braided leather threaded with alabaster beads brightly coloured with cedar oil paints.

If she had hoped to receive a message from their father, she was disappointed. Neither girl dared to ask after him when Ashan came to visit. Ignorance was bliss, and both had learned not to ask questions when they feared the answer. They preferred to believe that no news was good news – it had been nearly four moons since the birth of Kisha's child, and they had still not received a message of congratulations.

Similarly, Eliana could not bring herself to ask anybody why Samsu had not yet sent for her. She fearing another flogging, knowing that her attempt to free Sarri could not go unpunished, but since he had collared her, she had not been summoned. At first, every passing day had tightened the knot of worry in the pit of her stomach; now she began to dare to hope.

At the end of every day of freedom from his attentions, Eliana knelt at the little shrine to Enlil in the bedroom, scattered dried rosemary over the altar, lit a taper and gave thanks.

The time did not pass slowly – Sarri was growing fast. She was beginning to sleep almost through the nights now, waking up only for a feed. During the daytimes, she was lively and interested; already she was holding her own head and starting to roll. This new agility took Eliana completely by surprise when she set her niece on the floor on her back to change her, twisted around for the clean napkin, and turned back to discover Sarri lying on her front, happily babbling away to herself.

If it had not been for the collar that still chafed at her spirit, though her skin had grown used to it, and Isin's restless *gidim* haunting her, she could have been as fully at ease in her rooms as when she lived with her father.

Even Kisha seemed cheerful again – she laughed more frequently, and went about singing to Sarri. The colour had returned to her cheeks and lips, the hollow look was gone from her eyes. They were lit with carefree good humour again, as her sister remembered them.

Eliana thought she knew why. She shared a secret smile with Kisha, as she shared her bed. Her own monthly courses had been and gone twice since Kisha's last moon blood. She had only bled once since the birth of her daughter.

Sending Mari away on an errand to the linen room, she went to sit with her sister at the loom. In the look that passed between them, there could be no doubt that each knew what the other was thinking.

Kisha's hands worked deftly over the warps, passing the wooden shuttle back and forth in a steady rhythm. 'You know, then,' she smiled.

'Are you sure?'

'Positive. I have the same tenderness, tiredness, nausea – I'm going to have another baby!'

It was all Eliana could do not to squeal in delight. 'This time, a prince for sure!'

'I'm certain of it.'

'I can't believe how fast it's happened – are you sure you're ready?'

Kisha grimaced, '*More* than ready. Perhaps once I tell Samsu, he'll stop honouring me with his attention and doing his duty every night, and I can go back to a peaceful existence.'

A familiar fear clenched at Eliana's stomach. If Samsu was not diverted by her sister, would he send for her instead?

'When will you tell him?' she asked.

'Tonight. Will you help me dress?'

'Of course.' Eliana hugged her sister – delighting in her fertility and the thought of another baby for the nursery.

That evening, she dressed Kisha in a gown of fringed carmine silk, dusted her lips and cheeks with vermillion and pinned her black ringlets up with silver pins and scarlet feathers. Leaving the neck bare, she dusted it with shimmering powdered pearl, and hung a heavy belt of silver medallions around her hips. Her waist was a little softer than it had been this time last year, but still slim and attractive.

She stepped back to admire her work. It was easy to see why Kisha had been chosen, of the three hundred girls brought to the Red Palace for Samsu's inspection. She was breathtaking – still only twenty-two years old, in the prime of her beauty, and looking healthier than she had done since Samsu's rule began.

'You look stunning.'

Kisha blushed.

There was a knock at the door – Kisha went to it herself, not wanting to keep Ashan waiting, and eager to have Samsu's response.

Eliana waited anxiously, alone in the fading light – Mari was down at the bathhouse, enjoying a few hours to herself at Kisha's insistence, to allow the sisters privacy to gossip as they prepared.

She did not have long to wait – Kisha was back within half an hour.

'He won't touch me now,' she grinned, 'he won't risk harming the baby.'

Something in her voice set Eliana on edge. 'Congratulations,' she said, almost through gritted teeth. 'Is there something more?'

Kisha's face fell a little as she admitted, 'He wants to see you tomorrow night.'

*

Ashan's knock came at the usual time; only this time, it was for Eliana.

She was dressed in a gown of leaf-green beaded and embroidered in gold, with the faintest dusting of vermillion on her lips and cheeks to hide her frightened pallor.

Kisha hugged her in silence – she had no more advice to give. She knew that whatever guidance she gave her volatile little sister, urging her to calm and placidity, it would be ignored the moment that Samsu said something to rile her.

Eliana left with Ashan. He was unusually quiet as he escorted her to Samsu's rooms, though she could find the way herself by now.

'Ashan?' she asked, tentatively. 'What's wrong? What should I expect?'

'He means to have you tonight,' he said, his voice clipped and tight. 'But I cannot tell you what to expect – he's had rather a lot to drink.'

'Well, this could be interesting then,' she tried to make light of it. 'I can't imagine him drunk.'

'You will not have to imagine it.'

They walked in silence until they reached the familiar door that always filled her with dread, the hands of the carved Babylonian gods seeming to reach for her, mocking her with grotesque faces from their lacquered cedar prison.

Even after she crossed the threshold, their eyes were still upon her, staring down in frozen contempt from bright murals, but she hardly noticed. She was astonished to see Samsu lounging half-dressed across his floor cushions, a jar of date wine still in one hand, staring at the ceiling with unfocused eyes.

She was so taken aback that she forgot to bow. The prince did not even seem to notice. Ashan went to his usual post, one of a pair of guards in the chamber, as ever. Slowly, as if his skull weighed more than the rest of his whole body, Samsu brought his head straight and concentrated his gaze on Eliana.

'You're poison, d'you know that?' he lurched to his feet, fingers reaching out for something to grasp onto and finding only air. He staggered a little.

'*Me*, poison?' Eliana didn't know whether to be shocked or laugh aloud at the absurdity.

'You're nothing but a wretched shade, come up from the underworld to torment me, are you not?'

Eliana was astonished, thinking that Samsu had run mad. 'No, I'm not. Whose shade would I be?'

'You are,' he insisted. 'How else could you have bewitched me? You take the form of the only person to ever love me and ensnare me with those eyes of dark fire that sear my flesh. I pray to Marduk daily to protect me from your spells.' He walked unsteadily to her and caught up a lock of her hair, twisting it around his fingers.

'I didn't ask for this! If you don't want me here then set me free!' she snapped back, without thinking.

'*Quiet!*' he barked. 'That was always your problem, Eshnunna.

If you had been obliging and acquiescent when you had the chance, you would still be alive!'

He sat abruptly on the bed and dropped his head into his hands. Eliana was stunned. When he didn't move and she could stand the curiosity no longer, she moved to stand beside him.

Placing a light hand on his shoulder, she asked gently, 'Who was Eshnunna?'

He shrugged her off. 'Don't touch me. Kneel. You do not stand higher than me.' His voice was still muffled by his hands and he did not look up.

She folded her legs beneath her and sat back on her heels, watching him with fascination, absorbing every moment of this glimpse of the man behind the monster.

'Eshnunna was my sister, and you are as like her as a resurrected spirit. She didn't know what was good for her either. Full of life and laughter, outspoken and rebellious. She raised me, much as your sister raised you – nobody else paid me much heed, the youngest of the three sons. Our parents were occupied with my two elder brothers as they fought over the title of crown prince; Eshnunna was the only one who ever cared about me. If she had just obeyed our father, she would still be alive today.'

'What happened?' whispered Eliana.

'She would not marry where she was bid; she was seventeen years old, in love with some trainee priest. She married him in secret. A royal princess, promised to my wife's father, Simash, King of Elam, and she threw herself away on a nobody. The disobedience could not stand – she left our alliance with the Elamites in tatters. It was the excuse they needed to declare war.'

He was lost in his own past, still speaking into his lap. Eliana sat in silence, not wanting to distract him from telling her more.

'Father had the priest thrown from the top of his own temple for despoiling a royal daughter. Eshnunna was inconsolable, secluding herself in her room at the top of the ladies' tower.

Father tried time and again to get her to come out – bribing, cajoling, threatening, begging… none of it worked. Finally, in a rage, he gave her a choice: come out within the hour, or be bricked up in there.'

'And she didn't come out?'

'No. Father was true to his word – he has never been one for idle threats. He sealed her inside. I went up there every day for a week to speak to her and try to keep her spirits up, not really accepting that she would never come out again. Then on the eighth day, I had no response but silence. I beat my fists bloody on that wall, to no effect. For all I know, she's entombed there still. Her name was never spoken by my family again.'

Without warning, his head snapped up, black eyes boring into hers, reading the pity there. Face twisting with fury, he struck swiftly as a hunting eagle, grabbing her by the throat, pulling her up and pinning her onto the bed, his hand uncomfortably tight on her windpipe.

She tried to keep her face impassive, to hide the fear that she knew he wanted to see.

'You look just like her,' he hissed. 'You sound like her, you act like her. It's like you do it on purpose, to torture me. But where she was warm and loving, you have only ice for blood.'

Eliana stared back, the pity washed away by hatred.

'You are not even supposed to be here, still,' he hissed. 'I intended to bring you here to teach you a woman's place – force you to the obedience that Eshnunna never learned, do for you what my father never could for her. Train you, break your pride, have you and send you home. If you had just *surrendered* you would be back with your father already; but even when you pretend to acquiesce, as you are now, you can't do it convincingly. If looks were blades, I'd be dead of a thousand wounds.'

He increased the pressure on her neck, making it difficult for her to draw breath.

'You are poison,' he repeated. 'I close my eyes, and all I see, all I feel, is you. Even when I don't want to touch you, it's like you're under my skin. Your voice pricks with a hundred thorns, and still I want to hurt you, just to hear you scream. Your pain thrills me, you arouse me with a look, even a look of hatred – but when I go to take you, all I see is Eshnunna.'

Curling his free hand into her hair, he gave a hard yank. Eliana cried out in pain.

Samsu laughed. A cruel sound, devoid of mirth. 'I can face and defeat any man in battle, but I needed drink to take you tonight,' he slurred. 'It's not my fault – it's yours, with your witchcraft. Well,' he fumbled at his tunic, 'you will be mine, or I will burn you as you burn me.'

Panic overtook her as he began to push at her dress – it took all her self-restraint to remain still.

His movements were sluggish, clumsy and laboured. After a moment, he lay still, breathing deeply, crushing her under his weight.

Eliana's heart leapt – could she really be so fortunate? She lay there for several minutes, waiting to see what would happen

There was nothing but his long, even breaths. He began to snore.

Almost holding her own breath, and moving painstakingly slowly, she eased herself out from under him. It seemed to take an eternity, but it was worth it to not wake him.

Inch by inch, she wriggled out until she was able to slither to the floor.

She stood beside the bed, looking down on at his prone body. Her gaze was irresistibly drawn to the blade at his belt.

Leaning over, she slipped it from its sheath. The iron reflected the torches as though lit by the sun – it seemed to glow in her hands. Thinking that she had never seen anything so beautiful, she fingered the blade, taking note of Samsu's exposed neck.

Eliana jumped as someone cleared his throat behind her, so quietly as to be almost inaudible. She wheeled around – Ashan stood there. With a jolt, she remembered the other guard at his post – Samsu never slept alone, he knew he was a hated tyrant in a conquered city, and was rightly paranoid.

'What are you doing with that?' he breathed.

'Thinking of using it on myself,' she lied.

Prising the blade from her fingers and placing it on a carved wooden table inset with ivory beside the bed, he took her arm and led her from the room, leaving Samsu snoring on the bed.

The door closed softly behind them – Eliana breathed a deep sigh of relief.

'The ordeal is postponed for another night!' she smiled.

'Thank your god for it,' Ashan replied gravely. 'Your luck will not hold out forever.'

She laughed, 'But won't he be furious when he wakes? What will you tell him?'

'He won't reference it. He holds drunks in contempt.'

'The wine certainly loosened his tongue. I didn't realise he hated me so much – I was afraid he'd gone insane for a minute.'

'For as long as I've known him, Samsu has always been touched by his sister's death. He grew up the neglected youngest child – ignored by disinterested parents and resented by a bitter wife almost 15 years his senior. His nature was never pleasant, but nothing in his life has helped to improve it.'

Eliana's mind worked, trying to piece the puzzle together. 'So, if he was the youngest of three sons, how has he come to be heir?'

'The two elder princes killed each other in their fight to be crown prince. They struggled bitterly against each other for Hammurabi's affection; with just two years separating them in age, he declared that the title would go to the worthiest son, rather than going to the eldest. Samsu was seven years younger, so never really in the running.'

'How did they destroy each other?'

'The eldest shot the middle son, the favourite, with an arrow while they were out hunting. He always swore he didn't do it, but Hammurabi didn't believe him. The King is a fierce advocate of equal punishment and justice for all, whomsoever they may be, so he banished his eldest son to Egypt. The boy met with a convenient accident along the way – slipping off his horse as they forded a river. A week later, he washed up a few villages down.'

'And Samsu?'

'His father only had one child left, so he kept him on a tight rein – encouraged him to be commanding, punish the guilty, reward the loyal. Samsu had a strict, military upbringing from then on. Hammurabi had ambitions to expand the empire, and his son needed to be able to hold it when he came of age. As a teenager, the prince notionally commanded the army, but was learning under experienced generals. He had a natural aptitude for it – he revels in blood and chaos. By his mid teens, he had the command in truth, and at age seventeen he took his first city for the King.'

'So how did he come to Nippur?' Eliana was eager to learn as much about this man as she could – any knowledge she could use to manipulate him into freeing her and Kisha was more valuable than the weight of the gold around her neck.

Ashan shrugged. 'As a gift on his twenty-first birthday, Hammurabi told him to choose a nearby city to conquer and reign from as crown prince. He chose Nippur.'

'And you? You never did tell me how you came to be here.'

'The prince and I grew up together, we are as close as brothers. When he chose his men for the conquest, he picked the Brute for his savagery, and me for my loyalty.'

They had reached the door to Kisha's rooms. Ashan pressed her fingers to his lips, turned, and melted away into the night. Eliana stared after him, her mind filled with all she had learned.

*

The two sisters reclined in the garden, Sarri rolling on the grass between them. Kisha's jaw dropped as Eliana finished telling Samsu's story.

'I had no idea!' she gasped.

'Did nobody tell you anything about him before you got married?'

'I never thought to ask. It was all quite irrelevant – we'd be married whether I liked his history or not. I try not to think of him beyond the times I have to see him. I'm just his brood mare. He barely speaks to me beyond orders and pleasantries anyway. He doesn't see me as a person, just a womb. But now that you've told me, I do pity him – perhaps he'd have been a better man if there had been a kind hand guiding him when he was young.'

'Well, I don't pity him!' Eliana responded hotly. 'In a moment of weakness, I pitied him as he told his story, but he swept it away as quickly as it came! He is not a pitiable man. Maybe his childhood *was* sad, but it's not what happens to us that defines us, it's how we react to it. If you hadn't been there to love me and keep me in line as I grew up, I would have been wilder for certain, but I would still be good at the heart. Bad things happening to you is no excuse to make misery for others.'

Kisha rubbed her belly, 'Maybe you're right. I don't see that it matters much – nothing that's happened in the past can change what's happening right now.'

Leaning her elbows on her knees and dropping her head into her hands, Eliana sighed, 'I'm just so angry with myself. If I had only submitted in the beginning, I might have been freed by now.'

'Elly, if you submitted, you would be a changeling.' Kisha smiled affectionately at her sister. 'No part of you is capable of true submission. It wouldn't matter how well you acted the role, you would be screaming against it on the inside, and Samsu would always hear that scream. He just *knows* when people are only pandering to him to get their own way.'

'That's why he wanted you then. You've always done as you're told.'

'If it means a quiet life and less conflict, then yes, I'll take a few instructions and let him use me for breeding. It's a small price to pay for security and comfort. I want children just as much as he does, only for a different reason.'

'But how does he treat you when he... you know?'

'Almost courteously, for him. He demands and orders, never asks or says *please* or *thank you*, but he does speak to me pleasantly, observes the niceties, does his duty and sends me back safety. He only uses me roughly when he's in a rage about something. Most commonly about you.'

Eliana opened her mouth to answer, but in that moment Mari appeared.

'Sorry to interrupt. The princess consort wants to see Eliana – you are summoned to Susa's rooms.'

'Both of us?' asked Kisha.

'No, my lady. Just Eliana.'

'I wonder what she wants.' Kisha picked up Sarri and stood.

'Who knows?' Eliana shrugged, getting reluctantly to her feet. 'I suppose I'll go and find out.'

'Try not to be rude to her – remember that she does hold some power over us.'

Eliana gave her sister what she hoped was a reassuring smile, and followed Mari to Susa's apartments.

She would not scuttle in like a cowed child – this woman would have to earn her respect if she wanted it, princess or not. Walking in with her head held high, she almost gasped.

The apartments were huge, nearly a match for Samsu's in scale and grandeur. They made Kisha's rooms look like a mud-brick hut by comparison. The walls were decorated with bright and cheerful paintings and hangings that must have taken weavers years to complete, depicting the stories of the gods and finished with gilding. The floor was a colourful medley of glazed tiles, blue silk floor cushions scattered at intervals around the place.

Vases of stone and pottery occupied each corner, all with pointed feet and set on cross-legged stands for stability.

For all the luxury, the only item in the room that Eliana looked at covetously was the magnificent lyre – highly polished and inset with semi-precious gems, it rested on a copper pedestal. It looked as though it had never been played.

Susa sat in a chair so large that it could be called a throne, with feet carved to look like the legs of an ox. Padded and draped in blue silk to match the floor cushions, it was truly fit for royalty. The woman who occupied it eyed Eliana with distaste.

She was suddenly uncomfortably aware of her appearance. Her gown was crumpled from lying outside with Kisha, and blades of grass still clung to her dishevelled hair.

Ever-conscious of her status, Susa was dressed immaculately – gown neatly pressed, greying hair oiled and swept back under an oversized feathered headdress, gold and gems dripping from every conceivable part of her. Spoiling the picture, her eyebrows knitted together in a frown, etching a deep line in her forehead. Her mouth was puckered, a thousand tiny lines surrounding it, drawn by years of displeasure.

She looked sour as an overripe lemon.

Ani sat on a stool at her feet, occupied with embroidery. She looked up at Eliana with her usual expression of smug spite.

Through narrowed eyes, Susa looked Eliana up and down. 'So, whore, are you impressed?'

She gazed back in sullen silence, refusing to answer to the epithet.

'I suppose you thought that all palace women live in the sort of storage cupboard you and your sister occupy?'

'It suits us well enough.'

'Yes, I suppose you are used to living in squalor. How fares the concubine in her pregnancy?'

'Just fine.'

She resisted the urge to add, *as long as you leave her alone.*

'No aches, pains, sickness? It is so soon after she bore the last little harlot-in-waiting.'

Through gritted teeth, Eliana replied, 'My niece is as much a princess as you.'

Susa's face purpled with fury, 'My bloodline is pure, whore. My mother was queen, the first wife of the King of Elam. To compare that whelp's blood with mine is to compare a mule to a thoroughbred.'

Eliana bit the inside of her cheek to prevent herself from retorting.

'And you? Perhaps you and your sister will deliver together. He could have a whore's child and a concubine's child at the same time. Has my husband had you yet?'

'I don't believe that is any of your business.'

'On the contrary girl, it is entirely my business. Duty will be something you understand little of; you are just a peasant's daughter, whatever petty provincial office your father holds. As the prince's *wife*, it is my duty to ensure that he has an heir to follow him, be it by my body or another's.'

'You have your own son – Kisha's is nothing to do with you.'

Susa laughed aloud at that. 'I do have my own son – a strong young man. But when the concubine's boy is born, he will be everything to do with me. He will grow up calling *me* mother – I may even exile your sister to a palace outside of this city to prevent her from interfering, not that she would dare.'

Eliana could not immediately think of a response. In all truth, Susa was probably right: Kisha was too placid. Any interfering would be done by Eliana herself, and they both knew it.

Their eyes locked and held – Susa knew that Eliana had understood her meaning.

'Very well then, whore. If my husband has not yet had you and you have nothing to report of your sister's health, you are dismissed. But I warn you, it is futile to withhold information from me. I have ears everywhere.' She waved her hand and turned her attention to Ani.

Grinding her teeth in a rage, Eliana turned on her heel and stalked out.

Chapter 11

The next time Eliana was summoned to Samsu's chambers, she knew her luck had run out.

He stood near the door, sober as a stone and waiting for her with a grim expression staining his face. The look in his eyes pierced her stomach and she felt her confidence draining away, replaced by a bubble of fear. She clenched her fists to stop her hands trembling and concentrated on breathing evenly to slow the gallop of her heart.

Ashan stood at his usual post. It lifted her spirits ever so slightly to know that she had a friend in the room; even silent support was welcome.

A light breeze blew in from the terrace behind him, stirring the blood-red gossamer curtains, making them swirl and dance.

Dressed in only a half-tunic, his scarred torso left bare, Samsu seized Eliana's upper arm in an iron grip, squeezing so hard that little darts of pain shot down through her fingertips. He pulled her to him and pressed his lips to hers in a possessive kiss; when he pulled away, he left a lingering taste of the onion and fish he had eaten at dinner.

However hard she tried to keep her expression blank, the revulsion was plain on her face. Samsu saw it – her free arm flew to block the blow he aimed at her head, taking some of the force from it, but still it felt like a thunderclap inside her skull. Her head snapped back as he gave her a violent little shake.

'You have delayed long enough, *karkittu*. This is the night I will have you, whether you like it or not. If you are good, I shall send you a little gift. If not, you will make the experience more unpleasant for yourself than it needs to be.'

She spat on the floor at his feet.

The spittle barely hit the ground before she did; he hurled her to the tiles and delivered a forceful kick to her stomach. All the air exploded out of her lungs with the impact and she struggled to draw breath, panicking, thinking that he might have broken her ribs, so sharp was the pain.

He stood over her, staring down as she fought to regain her breath. Winded, but not seriously injured, she recovered herself after several seconds. Samsu bent down and took her by the arm again, hauling her up and dragging her half-stumbling to the bed, where he sat and threw her back to the ground beside it.

'Do not make this harder for yourself,' he said coldly. Pulling up his tunic and exposing his member, he did not need to give any further instruction.

Eliana rolled her eyes insolently, but set herself to the task. If anything, it was less revolting than his kiss.

As his breathing became more laboured, she increased her pace and intensity, bobbing her head up and down. *Like a duck on the river* she thought, struggling not to laugh at the absurdity of it.

Samsu gave a gasp of pleasure. 'Stop!' he commanded.

She continued faster, hoping to make him spend himself now and prevent the invasion he planned.

'I said *stop!*' he growled, wrenching her head back by the hair. Pulling her up, he shoved her back onto the bed. The soft opulence of the silk sheets did nothing to give her comfort.

He dropped himself on top of her, pinning her down with his weight. He was not a large man, but he disdained excess, and every inch of him was solid muscle and sinew, crushing her to the mattress. Fumbling at her her dress, he pushed it up to her waist.

Eliana froze in horror – she had known this was coming, had known it for many moons, but the moment had finally arrived and panic flooded through her. She began to thrash beneath him, twisting like a cat to free herself.

He laughed. She might as well have been trying to fight her way out of a locked iron chest for all she was achieving. Catching both her wrists, he pinned them above her head easily with one hand.

She threw a desperate glance at Ashan, wondering if he was watching. Samsu spotted it in a heartbeat. Laughing again, he said, 'Ah yes, I've heard about your attachment to Ashan!'

Over at his post, Ashan forced a laugh to chime with Samsu's.

'Don't expect any help from there, *karkittu*. My stepson is more loyal to me than any blood relation ever was.'

Stepson.

Her jaw dropped.

Seeing her shock, Samsu threw his head back and gave a great long bellow of a laugh from the pit of his belly. 'You dog! Did you not tell her you are my wife's son?!'

Ashan laughed again. He hid his discomfort well, though inside he burned with shame. He had hoped to keep his secret from Eliana until the time was right to tell her.

'My naive little whore – you'll have to be clever if you want to survive here. You knew my wife had a son, yet you never thought to ask his identity. Well it's in Ashan's interest to see you miserable – if you and your sister fail to give me sons, he'll have my throne when I'm dead.'

'May Marduk grant you long life and many sons, sir,' Ashan responded immediately. His tone was flat, as though he had learned the words by rote and said them more times than he could count.

'Don't mouth platitudes at me, man,' growled Samsu. 'I can take it from anyone except you.' He still had Eliana pinned beneath him; gesturing to her with his free hand, he said 'Don't just stand there like a vase decorating the place – come and give the whore a few strikes. That should end her devotion!'

He slid off the bed and dragged Eliana up with him, holding her in front of him like a shield, gripping her wrists behind her back. She was numb with shock, staring at Ashan as though she'd never seen him before. He was no longer the one force of kindness in her life – the handsome and compassionate one who loved her; he was just another of Samsu's guards there to make her life a misery.

As the words left Samsu's mouth, Ashan would happily have taken out his dagger and plunged it into his prince.

But he knew that he couldn't. Even if not for the other guard in the chamber who depended on Samsu for his wages, he had never managed to defeat the man in combat in all the time he had known him. Samsu was unparalleled in the martial arts – being the best and seeming invincible made it far easier to inspire respect in your men.

Ashan respected Samsu as little as he respected himself in that moment. It even crossed his mind to use the dagger on himself, but he feared it would go worse for Eliana if he did. Taking his own life would be seen as proof of guilt, of coveting what was Samsu's. Eliana would certainly be killed, and his mother would be punished into the bargain.

With no sign of remorse or guilt to Eliana, he strode towards them as though he wanted nothing more than to follow orders.

No, Ashan! She thought, her gaze pleading as she stared at him. *Not you. Anyone but you. The Brute, Asag, Enlil himself – let it be anyone but you.*

There was not so much as a flicker of regret in his eyes as he drew back his hand and delivered a stinging slap at full force across her cheek, then swept it back across the other one.

Her eyes filled with easy tears such as she rarely shed when Samsu or the Brute hit her.

He followed it up with a punch to the belly so hard that her knees buckled beneath her – the pain was all the more nauseating for the blow landing precisely where Samsu had kicked her and a bruise had already blossomed. Samsu let go of her wrists and she fell to the floor sobbing, her mind racing.

How could he? He loves me. He loves me.

No, he doesn't love me. He's Susa's son. It was all part of some deception to get close to me. To gain access to Kisha's baby – if she has a son, he can put an end to it and protect his own position. Ashan! Why?

Samsu dismissed his stepson with a nod, and Ashan walked back to his place as though he didn't have a care in the world, so eaten up with self-reproach that he would willingly have thrown himself from the roof to escape the weighty demon of guilt that draped itself about his shoulders like a snake-dancer's python.

Picking Eliana up, Samsu dropped her back on the bed and forced his way inside her. She lay limp as a corpse, dimly aware of red-hot burning pain between her thighs and the stickiness of her virgin blood as he took her. Tears slid silently down her cheeks and into her hair. She was more conscious of her broken heart than her violated body.

Samsu laboured and panted above her, snorting with the exertion like an ox pulling the plough. Eliana saw the whole thing as if it was happening to someone else, her mind separating from her body. The ordeal passed in a haze; before she knew it, Samsu had gasped, shuddered, buried his face in her hair and spent himself inside her.

He lay still a moment before standing up and pulling down his tunic. 'There, *karkittu*. I told you it would go easier for you if you were good. Perhaps we are finally starting to wean you from that childish pride.'

Eliana did not move, did not even indicate that she had heard him.

'Get up, I am finished with you.'

It was like her body was being operated by someone else as she stood and pulled her dress back to her ankles. Her hair hung listlessly around her face, even the bounce of her curls flattened. Both cheeks burned with shame and the lingering sting of Ashan's slaps. There was a hand in her gut, kneading at her insides, making her feel nauseous. Whether it was from the blows to her stomach or the shame of losing her innocence, she couldn't tell. Most of all, she ached; between her thighs, in her secret places, and in her heart.

When Samsu sent her off with Ashan, the door had barely clicked shut behind them before she took off, sprinting away from him as if he were the demon Rabisu, who lurked in dark places to attack unsuspecting victims. She heard his sandals slapping the floor behind her as he gave chase, but she was swifter. He called out after her; she did not look back.

She burst into the apartments, fell into Kisha's arms, and sobbed as though her life was at an end.

Ashan at least had the decency not to follow.

*

The worst part of the heartbreak was that Eliana could not share it with her sister. She had not confided her passion for Ashan in anyone, but had carried it locked away inside herself as a personal comfort – something pure she could turn to when days were dark, unspoiled by anyone else's opinion or disapproval.

'There, there, Elly.' Kisha held her as she cried and stroked her hair as she used to when they were children. 'You knew this was coming – you were lucky to avoid it for this long. Surely it wasn't as bad as all that?'

She shook her head and wept all the harder for her sister's concern.

'The first time is always the hardest. It will get easier, and the less you fight, the less it will hurt.'

Eliana took deep breaths and tried to stem the flood.

Crying won't achieve anything, she told herself. *It won't lessen the hurt, it won't change things. Don't waste time with it.*

She sat up. Kisha pushed a stray curl off her sister's cheek and dried the tears with the hem of her dress. 'There now. I have some good news,' she couldn't suppress a smile. 'Samsu's father has sent emissaries to deal with some business – they're supposed to arrive tomorrow and there'll be a great banquet to welcome them. We're ordered to attend.'

'Us?' Eliana sniffed. 'Why?'

'Decoration, I suppose,' Kisha spread her hands. 'It doesn't really matter to me – you and I can finally attend a court occasion together. We'll dress up, eat well and share in the entertainments. This is what it's supposed to be, to be married to a prince.'

Eliana forced a smile. She didn't feel like celebrating, and she was sure she'd have to see Ashan at the feast. 'It will be good to have a distraction,' she said, trying to inject some enthusiasm into her voice. 'Are we expected to do or say anything?'

'No – Samsu's messenger just said we need to look our best, go where we're bid and keep quiet.'

'I think we can manage that.'

'Well, *I* can!' Kisha laughed. 'Are you sure you can do as you're told for one night?'

Eliana managed a weak chuckle, 'Well it all depends on what I'm told to do.'

'Come on,' Kisha wiped the last stray tear tracks from her sister's face. 'I'll feed Sarri and we'll get to bed. We can spend tomorrow making ourselves look pretty!'

*

The next morning, the two girls went down to the bathhouse to remind themselves of the benefits of palace life. After two hours of being soaked, soaped, scrubbed and massaged, they were more relaxed than they had been in weeks. Eliana finally felt that her sister was herself again as they giggled, traded silly jokes and reminisced about home.

Putting Ashan, Samsu and every other man in the world to the back of her mind, Eliana linked arms with her sister and went back to the apartments to prepare for that evening.

Mari had been practising her henna designs on the other maids in preparation for an event like tonight. The two girls stretched out on the grass in the sun in linen shifts as Mari patterned their hands, arms and feet in stunningly elaborate and intricate designs and left the paste to dry in the sun.

It was after midday before it was time to wipe away the excess henna and admire the motifs left behind – Mari blushed with pleasure as the girls praised her skill and exclaimed over the prettiness of the patterns.

A meal of cheese, bread and honey came and went; the girls only picked at it, anticipating a grander meal that evening. They went inside and Eliana began to arrange Kisha's hair, artfully twisting her oiled curls and secured them atop her head with gold-and-pearl pins.

As they switched places and Eliana sat to have her hair styled, they were interrupted by a knock at the door. Her heart plummeted through the floor.

Mari answered the door, and a familiar deep voice greeted her. 'Ashan for you, Eliana,' she announced.

Eliana's heart pounded unpleasantly in her chest as she stood and turned to face him, her eyes burning with a resentful fire.

He took half a step back as he was met with the full force of the hatred in her gaze. Clearing his throat, he said, 'The prince has sent me with a gift for you, my lady. As he promised last night.'

'Last night...' she repeated in a low voice, not trusting herself to finish a sentence.

Ashan held out a small red cushion and removed its covering, revealing a pair of exquisite earrings of beaten gold, fashioned to look like falling leaves and set with fragments of emerald.

'Samsu asks that you wear a green and gold gown this evening, to match the earrings and your collar. He appreciates your compliance, and hopes it is a sign of things to come.'

'My *compliance*,' she spat. 'I was in shock, you whoreson. If it hadn't been for you I'd have fought him all the way.'

She walked over to examine the earrings, her stomach twisting into knots as she neared him.

'Then we should be thankful that I was there. I won't tell him you said that,' Ashan said drily.

'Tell him whatever you like. I'm sure you tell him all sorts of things about me,' she snarled.

'Eliana...'

His use of her name snapped her fragile composure – she slapped him across the face with all her strength. His cheek reddened, showing the outline of all her fingers, but he did not so much as flinch.

Determined to get a reaction from him, she lashed out again, raking her fingernails down his face. She did not know whether to feel sick or triumphant as the skin split and blood dripped from his chin.

Ashan winced, but did not give her any more satisfying reaction than that. He put the cushion with its trinkets down calmly, turned and left without another word.

She turned back to Mari and Kisha, who stood aghast, mouths hanging open in twin pictures of astonishment.

'What was *that*?' said Kisha.

'Nothing,' mumbled Eliana. 'Just... do my hair, please. Mari – could you please fetch out the green silk gown, and maybe a bowl of wine from the kitchens? I need something stronger than honey and lemon, I think.'

She forced laughter and levity, trying to regain the carefree atmosphere of that morning. Kisha and Mari quickly realised that she would not discuss Ashan, and set about pretending to have forgotten the whole incident.

Eliana was grateful.

By the time the slave boy came to fetch them, they were ready. Both in gilded sandals, Kisha dressed in a gown of ivory silk trimmed with silver, and Eliana in her green and gold silk to complement the necklace and earrings. She resented the jewellery, but did not quite dare to not wear Samsu's gift. Her one gesture of defiance was to wear her mother's bracelet, the blue of the lapis clashing beautifully with everything else she wore.

Eliana's eyelids were dusted with gold powder, her lips tinted with vermilion, and her sophisticated hairstyle topped with a headdress of black leather and gold beading, fringed with a row of beaten golden suns hanging just above her eyebrows.

Kisha was similarly decorated, with pearl powder to match her ivory silk and a silver circlet set on her brow.

They smiled at each other in happy anticipation. Kisha kissed Sarri goodbye, leaving her in Mari's care, and the two girls followed the boy through the palace to the great hall.

*

It was as if the gods had brought the walls themselves to life.

The usually quiet palace was alive with music and voices. Eliana and Kisha gave a gasp of awe as they passed under the blue arch into the great hall. Lit by hundreds of flaming torches, their light lost as it stretched into the shadows of the cavernous ceiling, it had been decorated for the occasion with flowers and wreaths and every beautiful thing that Nippur could offer in order to impress Hammurabi's emissaries. Samsu was determined that they should return to his father carrying tales of the splendour of the prince's city and his skills as a ruler.

Tonight's company was a mix of every part of Nippur's elite – priests, scholars, officials, wealthy merchants, military officers – any man who could bring lively conversation to the table was invited.

Eyes followed the girls as they entered. Kisha held her head high, eyes half-closed in a serene sort of trance, hands clasped before her as she made her way through the throng. The crowds parted for her as a ship parts the waters, and Eliana followed in her wake, unsure where to put her hands, uncomfortable with the stares.

Several minutes passed before it dawned on her why they were receiving so much attention – they were the only women in the room. Tonight was a piece of diplomatic theatre to show off Samsu's wealth, possessions, leadership and citizens; Eliana and Kisha were possessions.

The boy showed them to their places at the long trestle directly beneath the high table at which Samsu would sit. Covered in white muslin cloth, set with great plates of beaten and engraved copper and strewn with rose petals and fragrant thyme, not a single detail had been overlooked.

They were seated with a handful of priests and scholars, none of whom paid them the least bit of attention. Samsu's attitudes to women, even his royal wife, were well-known; no man would waste his effort befriending the sisters when they did not have the prince's ear.

It suited them just fine – they could hold their own conversations and pass comment on the people around them without fear of being reprimanded as long as they drew no attention to themselves. They would be as a delicately woven tapestry – to be looked at and admired, but not engaged with.

A great gong was rung at the front of the hall, the music ceased and the guests moved to their seats, standing respectfully in their places waiting for Samsu to appear.

He emerged from the back of the hall, leading Susa by the arm. She was gorgeously attired in a tiered gown of purple silk studded with gems; her face was powdered, but even from this distance Eliana could see that it had settled unflatteringly into the deep lines around her eyes and mouth.

Behind Susa came Ashan in the ceremonial tunic of a Babylonian army general, leading Ani in a gown of rose pink. Bringing up the rear was the Brute. Eliana's stomach still knotted with fear whenever she looked at him, however safe the collar might make her.

They took their seats at the table on the raised platform, and Samsu gestured for the assembly to sit.

A young steward stepped into the centre of the room. 'His Royal Highness, Samsu, Prince of Babylon, *Lugal* of Nippur, has most graciously condescended to receive and feast the emissaries of his father, the mighty Hammurabi of Babylon. To show their gratitude to their most excellent prince, they wish to make a presentation of gifts.'

Samsu inclined his head, gesturing for the great doors at the side of the chamber to be opened.

Seven men filed in, ranging in age from beardless youths to salt-haired statesmen, all in the official white linen tunics of an emissary, crisply pressed and draped in immaculate folds over their shoulders. They stopped in front of the high table and bowed.

The first, the oldest, stepped forward. 'Your Royal Highness, I have known you since you were a boy, have watched you grow and mature into the man you are today; a conqueror in your own right and the greatest general in the empire after your father himself. In honour of your military might, I offer you this gift.'

He gestured, and a slave approached the prince, presenting him with a magnificent blade of polished iron mounted in a wooden handle, the hilt carved in the likeness of a roaring lion.

Samsu nodded and gave his thanks.

The ritual was repeated with each of the other six men; each stepping forward in order of his seniority and making some lengthy and gratuitously flattering speech in praise of his prince before presenting a gift. Twice, Eliana glanced at Samsu during the speeches. She caught the familiar gleam of irritation in his eyes, set in an expression of overwhelming boredom.

She struggled to repress a giggle as she turned her attention back to the emissaries.

The gifts were all exquisite, and not all for Samsu himself. He was presented with fifteen slaves for the running of his palace, fifty jars of Babylonian wine, an obsidian statue of Marduk, a set of perfectly balanced spears, and a war chariot; one of the men gave as his offering six bolts of silk for Susa, and one for Kisha as a token gift. Another gave a magnificent gold necklace and bangle set for Susa, with a matching bracelet for Ani.

Eliana received nothing, reinforcing her status as the whore, a slave.

She looked around the hall with mounting impatience as the speeches were made and the gifts given, taking in the faces of the guests, amusing herself with how many she could identify, and how many were new appointments since Samsu's regime had begun. Many of those present had attended her sister's wedding.

Her heart leapt as her gaze lighted on her father.

He looked just the same as he always had. A little greyer, a little more drawn, a little thinner, but still her father. His eyes were glazed and unfocused as he stared in the general direction of the ceremony.

She nudged her sister and nodded towards their father. Kisha did not react, but kept her attention riveted on the dull charade in front of her. She was determined to draw no attention to herself or give Samsu cause to reprimand her; she would be the perfect little wife, even if she must be the lesser wife.

Finally, the hall erupted into applause as the emissaries bowed and took their places of honour at the high table. The great gong sounded again, and a stream of servants and slaves flowed into the hall with steaming platters piled high with food.

The girls were half-starved after eating only lightly earlier in the day, but Kisha put her hand on Eliana's arm – a gentle warning to restrain herself. Ladies did not stuff themselves in public, she had taught her growing up. Not that Eliana had ever listened – she had always been an active child, and constantly hungry after a day of running around and getting into trouble.

Things were no different now, and it took the greatest willpower not to take as much as she wanted. She only held herself back for fear of drawing some negative attention to herself and not being allowed to attend an occasion like this again. Already it was unheard of for a whore to be out in public, let alone seated with a wife, even if they were sisters.

As it happened, she needn't have worried about being hungry. Course after course after course came into the hall in a never-ending procession – subtly flavoured barley and onion soups; fish spiced a dozen different ways; side dishes of chickpeas and lentils tossed with garlic; tender roasted gazelle seasoned with mustard; great loaves of flat bread still warm from the oven; baked and crispy wildfowl… every delicacy that Eliana could have imagined was placed before her.

She ate a small portion of each, but was soon so full that she wished she was wearing a gown that did not cling quite so insistently to every curve of her body.

Wine flowed freely with the food – servants stood to attention near each table, ready to refill empty drinking bowls with the sweet date wine favoured by the Nippurites and adopted by Samsu.

Kisha was quiet, so Eliana occupied herself with people-watching and examining the beauty around her, from the henna patterns on her hands, to the lions prowling the walls in their ceramic cages as the torches brought the mosaics to life. She was warm and full and utterly content as the wine worked its magic.

When the last of the food was cleared away, Samsu stood. The whole room stood with him. Some of the guests swayed a little on their feet. Eliana glanced at her father, he stood firm as a temple.

Toasts were raised to Samsu, to Nippur, to Hammurabi, to Babylon, to Susa, and finally to the child in Kisha's belly. She blushed and smiled, even though the good wishes were for the child she carried, not for herself.

When everyone had taken their seats once more, Samsu raised his hand again, and the entertainments began.

People laughed, drank, talked amongst themselves and watched the marvels unfold before them. The first act was a hypnotic snake-dancer. Barely clad, she twisted and writhed to high piped music with her drugged snake draped around her neck as though they were one being and she had absorbed its movements.

Eliana watched, fascinated, wondering what the girl's life must be – travelling freely and performing at royal courts and great occasions.

A troupe of singing eunuchs came next, their sweet voices filling every corner of the hall. Eliana glanced up at the high table during their song.

Samsu was deep in animated conversation with Ashan. She saw him gesture at his stepson's injured cheek; her heart sank.

Ashan waved his hands as if it were no matter, trying to deflect the question. She felt an unexpected surge of gratitude towards him, before swiftly pushing it back down, burying it under resentment.

Not to be diverted so easily, Samsu persisted, gesturing more vehemently at the cheek. Ashan dropped his hands and looked defeated as he replied.

Samsu's head snapped around suddenly and his eyes bored into hers, lit with rage. Her stomach lurched in fear. She dropped her gaze immediately to the table to hide it, cursing herself for losing her temper with Ashan, however much he deserved it.

There would be hell to pay for it now, she knew.

But Samsu would not interrupt his grand feast to condescend to speak to his whore, so she was safe for this evening at least. The sweet wine did its work and she was able to drown the fear, losing herself in the fire dancers that followed the singers as they whirled and tossed their flaming torches, lulling her into a trance.

The fire dancers were followed by tumblers and acrobats, more singers, a performing bear with shackles at his ankles who danced to his trainer's commands… Eliana fought to keep awake as the wine fogged her head.

People had begun to filter away and Kisha, distressed by the tormented bear, leaned over to Eliana and whispered, 'Do you want to go?'

She nodded sleepily, her head heavy with the effort.

As they made their way from the hall, she felt a pair of eyes on her and turned back to scan the room. Her gaze locked with her father's and her heart skipped a beat. In that moment, she would have given everything to again be able to run to him and have him enfold her in his arms and ruffle her curls before sending her off for a bath. Her heart ached to look at him and remember what their lives had been.

She gave him a little smile and touched two fingers to her heart.

With a grave expression, he returned the gesture.

Kisha tugged on her arm, anxious to be away from the bear, and she allowed herself to be led from the hall.

Chapter 12

His cheek still bearing the ragged red marks of Eliana's claws, Ashan appeared in the apartments the following day with another gift from Samsu.

She stepped forward to take it from him, shaking it out and holding it up to the light – it was a beautiful light gown of diaphanous gold gauze. She frowned, wrinkling her brow in confusion. After the look Samsu gave her at the feast yesterday, she certainly hadn't been expecting another gift.

'It's lovely, but I have nothing to wear under it, and no occasion to wear it for.'

'I don't believe you're required to wear anything under it. You're to put it on with the earrings he sent yesterday, and be prepared to come with me in a few hours.'

Her jaw dropped. 'I can't wear this!' she said indignantly. 'It's indecent.'

Ashan shrugged. 'You know I'm only the messenger.'

'Why does he want to see me again so soon? I suppose you told him about yesterday!'

'You left me with little choice. If you had vented your temper on my arms I could have bluffed some sort of believable story, but there was no convincing explanation for these rake marks on my face. I tried not to tell him, but he wouldn't be put off.'

She gave him a look of pure disgust. 'I thought you loved me,' she spat, turning away.

At that moment, Kisha walked in and began exclaiming over the lovely gown; Ashan had no opportunity to respond. Defeated, he left.

'What's this in aid of?' asked Kisha, allowing the fabric of the gown to run through her fingers like water, shimmering as it caught the light.

'I don't know,' Eliana said heavily. 'Samsu wants me to wear it to go to him this afternoon.'

'Elly,' Kisha put a hand on her sister's arm. 'What's happened between you and Ashan? Why is he so miserable? He was always our friend, but he's lost all his energy – he's just not himself anymore.'

'I haven't done anything,' she mumbled. 'I don't want to talk about it. Come with me to the bathhouse? I may be a whore, but I will not be called dirty.'

It hurt her to change the subject. She wanted nothing more than to confide in her sister and have her advice; but the less Kisha knew, the more credible she would be if anyone ever asked her about it.

She came back from the bathhouse clean, fragrant and full of dread. Slipping into the new gown, she stared down at her body and blushed deep crimson to see how little it hid. She sat in front of the polished obsidian reflecting stone with a heavy sigh, and began outlining her eyes in green malachite to match the emerald of the earrings.

When she was finished, her eyes glittered like the emeralds, the paint highlighting the unusual tilt at their corners. 'Laughing eyes,' her father had called them. She stood up, turning this way and that before the stone, smoothing the dress over her hips.

Mari gasped in shock, coming in behind her. 'That dress! You look...'

'... Like a whore.' Eliana finished bitterly.

When Ashan arrived to collect her, his face was drawn and taut, his expression pained. He said nothing, barely even looked at her as he escorted her to Samsu's rooms. His fists were clenched and he walked so quickly that Eliana had to hurry to keep up; she would not lower herself to ask him to slow down.

Samsu was waiting when she entered. His eyes lit at the sight of her – a goddess in translucent gold. He waited until she was in her bow before walking around her, taking in every detail of her appearance appreciatively.

'Sit up,' he ordered.

She obeyed, sitting back onto her heels, keeping her eyes on the ground, afraid to give away her anxiety if they met his.

'So, *karkittu*, it would seem that we haven't yet managed to tame you after all. You are as wild and feral as when you arrived. You used your claws against my stepson when he brought you my gift, like a stray cat run mad. Well, if you insist on behaving like an animal, you will have to be chained like one.'

Eliana looked up in alarm. Her gaze darted around the room… and came to rest on a pile of cushions against the wall beneath a torch bracket. From the bracket dangled a gilded chain.

Suddenly, she couldn't breathe – her heart raced in alarm. She panicked.

Leaping to her feet, she turned to run. A soldier was there in an instant, cutting off her escape through the door. He caught her full under the chin with his fist, sending her crashing to the ground. She scrambled up and tried another way, towards the door leading to Samsu's audience chamber. He laughed as Asag blocked her path – she struck out in blind hysteria. Asag caught her wrist and twisted her arm behind her, pushing her in front of him, forcing her towards the cushions.

Eliana twisted and kicked and bucked like a frightened horse, but he embedded his free hand in her hair, catching it and holding her head immobile as Samsu moved behind her. Her scalp burned as she heard the light jingle of the chain, and the crack of a padlock closing.

Asag released her abruptly, taking three rapid steps backward. She lunged for him immediately, stretching out a hand to rake his eyes with her nails, desperate to get past him.

She moved no further than two steps before the chain snapped taut and she was jerked back by her collar with such a bruising blow to the throat that she coughed and her eyes filled with tears. Asag laughed, standing just out of reach.

Trying again, she found that she couldn't move beyond the cushions. In the heat of her futile fury, she picked one up and hurled it at Ashan – he ducked.

Samsu roared with laughter. 'My wild *karkittu*! Be careful – if you throw away all your bedding, the nights will be uncomfortable for you!'

'Nights! How long are you going to keep me here?'

He spread his hands infuriatingly. 'For as long as it pleases me and you do not. Don't worry, you will be well-cared for. But if you are going to act like an animal, I shall keep you chained up as my little pet until you are house-trained. If you continue to be disobedient, you can be sure that I can make this far more uncomfortable for you.'

'How?' she spat, outraged.

Chuckling, he said, 'You have a warm and comfortable bed, for now. You will be well-fed, for now. You are clothed, for now. You have free use of all your limbs, for now. You have a long chain that allows you to lie down, sit, stand and move around, for now. Have some imagination, *karkittu*. I promise you that I have plenty.'

He turned away. 'Guard her, Asag. See that she doesn't try anything stupid. It's amazing what this one can come up with when trapped. Come along, Ashan. The emissaries are waiting.'

Ashan followed as he walked away, glancing back for one last look at Eliana. Their eyes met – hers blazed with indignant hatred, while his were full of pity.

As soon as they were gone, she flopped down onto the cushions, tipped her head back and gave a piercing scream of helpless rage.

*

She didn't sleep at all that night.

Curled up on the cushions, she tossed and turned, trying to find a comfortable position. The chain clinked every time she moved, reminding her of her confinement. However she settled herself, it seemed to get in the way. Terrified of getting it wrapped around her neck as she slept, she looped the excess length around her wrist, the gilded links cold and sharp against the delicate skin there. She kept forgetting about it until the next time she shifted position, when it would tug at her again.

She tried sleeping on her back, on her front, facing the wall and with her back to the wall – nothing was comfortable. In the end she sat up, her back pressed against the wall, and gazed out across the room through the terrace opening. A small sliver of crescent moon was visible, along with more stars than she could ever count – Suen's children. They winked at her from their warm blanket of sky, mocking her as she shivered. The temperature had dropped as soon as the sun went down, and she still wore nothing but the gauzy dress.

The only distraction was the changing of Samsu's guard at midnight – even when he slept, he had a sentry on watch, so terrified was he of assassination. His harsh snores were her only lullaby; she missed Kisha's warm body and gentle breathing beside her.

After what felt like an eternal night, the sky gradually began to lighten through purple, red and orange. Samsu was up before Utu was fully awake.

He greeted his guard when he got up, but didn't spare Eliana so much as a glance. She glared at him as he moved about the room, washing and dressing. She was surprised to see that he had no body slaves to tend him – he did everything for himself. Although she supposed that he was used to life on the battlefield; body slaves would just be extra mouths to feed.

Since conquering Nippur, he seemed to have lost his taste for war. Eliana wished that he would march out somewhere again; anywhere, just to get him as far away from her as possible. The sight of him made her flesh crawl.

Just before leaving the room, he turned back and gave her a smug look, amusement pulling at the corners of his mouth. She stared back at him with pure venom in her gaze, dark smudges under her tired eyes.

He chuckled and walked out, leaving the guard in there with her. It seemed she wasn't to be left alone for even a moment.

She studied her new gaoler. He wasn't as young as Samsu – he must already be past his thirtieth year. A jagged scar ran from under one eye to the centre of his jaw and part of one ear was missing. Eliana wondered if it was from the same thrust of the dagger.

Apart from the scar, he was almost indistinguishable from the dozens of other guards Samsu kept. He wore the standard military tunic, a dagger hanging from his belt, his body made up of scarred skin stretched over hard muscle. She would not want to cross him: his brows were drawn together in a fierce frown as he stood to attention and stared directly ahead – an image of discipline, he did not fidget once in all the time that Eliana watched him.

She cleared her throat. He did not even flick his eyes her way.

'Excuse me?' she called, when he didn't respond.

He might have been carved from wood for all the reaction he gave.

Eliana stood up. 'Hey! I'm talking to you!' she picked up a cushion and hurled it at him. It missed, skimming past his face and spinning away across the floor.

The man completely ignored her.

She sat down again in a sulk, leaning back against the wall and pulling her knees up to her chest and hugging them there.

So far, the worst part was the boredom. There was only so long that she could entertain herself with her own thoughts for – the largest part of the time was spent imagining gruesome and agonising ways to repay Samsu and his Brute for all the evil they'd done to her and her home. She tried to imagine Ashan with them, but some stubborn part of her mind couldn't bring her to picture him suffering.

As if she had conjured him with her thoughts, Ashan marched in with a plate of food when the sun was high in the sky and beating warmth into the ground.

'Relieved, soldier,' he barked at the man. 'Take a break, have your meal and be back here quickly. The prince needs me with him but he will not leave *her* unguarded,' he jerked his head at Eliana. Her feathers ruffled at his tone; she turned her head away in disgust.

The guard gave a curt inclination of the head, turned on his heel and stalked out.

Ashan's demeanour changed immediately. He moved slowly towards Eliana, as though afraid of startling her. Bending down, he placed a copper plate in front of her – on it was a bowl of honey and lemon drink, half a loaf of still-warm bread and a pot of chickpea dip.

She was ravenous, having not eaten since the banquet more than a day and a half ago, and the smell of the fresh bread made her mouth water.

'I don't want it,' she made herself say, pushing it away.

'Eliana,' he said, still using his commanding general's voice and pushing the plate back towards her, 'you have to eat. Don't be an idiot and refuse it. You'll only make yourself miserable and sick, and it won't endear you to Samsu or anyone else. A foolish little protest won't get you off this chain any quicker.'

'Don't talk to me like I'm one of your soldiers,' she flared up. 'I don't have to do what you say.'

'No, you don't,' he retorted, 'but you should. I only want what's best for you.'

'Like you wanted what's best for me when you hit me and then watched Samsu fuck me? Or when you told him I struck you? Or when you neglected to tell me who you were? That's where all this started – it's your fault I'm here!'

'That's not fair and you know it! If you could control your temper...'

'My temper! Tell me, Ashan – how do you think your *temper* would fare if you'd suffered half what I have?'

'Look, I know it hasn't been easy...'

'Ha! That's an understatement! And you've only made it worse.'

'I didn't have a choice!' he shouted, standing up, looming over her.

She quailed a little, pressing back into the wall and pulling her knees closer to her chest, as if they would shield her – she hadn't seen him angry before. 'That's what men always say when they've made the wrong one,' she said quietly, looking at the floor.

Ashan bunched his fists and took a deep breath. Bringing himself under control, he knelt beside her and looked into her eyes. 'How did you sleep?' he asked, gently.

'I didn't,' she snapped.

'Eliana, please don't make me an enemy. Let me help you.'

'If you want to help me, break this chain!'

'You know I can't. Samsu would know in a heartbeat who did it. Even if I freed you, there's nowhere for you to hide in the palace, and you'd never make it out alive.'

She dropped her head to her knees, hiding her face from him. There was a long minute of silence.

'Is there anything I can get you?' he tried again. 'Anything that would make you more comfortable? Think before you answer – be practical.'

She thought for a moment. 'A blanket,' she said in a small voice. Ashan had to strain to hear her.

'Pardon?' he asked.

Raising her head, she said, 'I'd like a blanket. It gets so cold at night, and I can use it to cover myself decently in this gown, and as a screen when I need to...' she tailed off, glancing at the painted clay chamberpot set beside her cushions. 'I haven't dared to use it yet – I don't have any privacy.'

'Anything else?'

She could have cried to see the pity in his face as she murmured, 'A jug of water, please.'

He put a hand on her arm and stroked it softly, arousing all her old feelings for him despite her determination to hate him. 'I'll see what I can do,' he whispered as her guard marched back into the room. Standing up, he gave the guard a brusque salute before striding from the room, leaving Eliana looking after him with longing in her heart.

After a few moments, the smell of the bread was too much. She grabbed it with both hands, dipped it into the chickpea paste and tore at it with her teeth. The whole thing was gone in minutes.

An hour or so later, a slave appeared to remove the plate. He carried with him a jug of cool, fresh water and a thick woollen blanket. Banging the jug down and dropping the blanket beside it, he collected the plate and left without a word, not even acknowledging Eliana's weak smile of thanks, though she was sure he'd seen it.

She took a long draught from the jug, then moved it over against the wall and out of the way where she would not knock it over. Curling up on the cushions and unfolding the blanket, she covered herself, pulled it up over her head, and wept.

*

Days dragged by in an excruciating pattern of boredom and loneliness.

The first few passed relatively quickly, as she expected to be released at any moment. But as the sun and the moon came and went, hope began to fade and desperation set in. Ashan, given the task of entertaining the Babylonian emissaries, had not visited since the first day. Samsu ignored her, and try as she might, she could not get any her guards to talk to her.

After four days of not even being looked at, let alone spoken to, even by the slave who brought her food and emptied her chamberpot, Eliana was in a frenzy for human interaction. Some acknowledgement of her existence, whatever form it took. She needed to know that she had not become an invisible *gidim* overnight.

She fought against her chain and collar, pulling and thrashing until her neck was black with bruises – the chain looked delicate, with its slender links, but beneath the gold finish it was made of iron. Even the Brute would have struggled to break it with his bare hands; Eliana stood no chance.

The guards watched her futile, frantic efforts and laughed themselves breathless. She attempted to draw them into conversation, tried everything she knew to strike up some sort of connection. She talked to them, questioned them, complimented them, insulted them… even, in her most despairing moment, tried to seduce them. It was all to no avail.

The one person she managed to make a connection with, eventually, was the slave man who looked after her. He was roughly of an age with her father, and she dared to hope that he might have a daughter too. On the seventh day of her confinement, as she saw him approach, she put on her best pathetic-little-girl voice, 'Um, excuse me, sir?'

The 'sir' caught his attention at once – it was a term of address that most slaves were unused to.

'Me, my lady?' he responded gruffly.

'I'm not a lady,' Eliana blushed as she gestured to her filmy gown and heavy collar, 'I'm a slave like you.'

'If you'll forgive me for saying so, your work is a deal less hard,' he grumbled.

'I know,' she said sweetly, thinking how stupid the man must be to think that fetching and carrying was more difficult than what she was subjected to, 'and I'm so very grateful for your care.'

He grunted.

'I hope you don't mind me asking, but could you possibly fill my water jug please? It has been empty for some time, and I'm terribly thirsty.' She allowed her voice to crack a little on the last two words, her eyes filling with tears. They were not feigned – the jug had been bone dry for three days. She had only drunk what had come with her food; to not be able to drink when thirsty was a deprivation she had never had to endure before now.

The man took in her pitiful state; a line of compassion cracked his brow. 'Seeing as you ask so nicely,' he said, picking up the vessel.

She rejoiced silently in her success as he walked away. The bond was as delicate as new-spun silk, but she could strengthen it – it was a starting point, if nothing else.

Within a few minutes, he returned with her jug brimming. She drank eagerly until she thought her stomach would burst. Putting it down, she gave him her prettiest smile. 'I can't thank you enough, …?'

'Resu,' he nodded. 'At your service, my lady.'

She took his hand and squeezed it in gratitude. Such a simple act, fetching her water, but how much it meant to her!

Thanking the mother goddess for small blessings, she settled back into her cushions and her thoughts.

No more than an hour later, a welcome silhouette appeared in the doorway.

'Ashan!' she cried in delight as she recognised him.

He gave her a scowl as black as the underworld. 'Quiet, whore!' he snarled.

Crushed, she folded in on herself and looked away to hide the shine of tears in her eyes. There was a surge of disappointment in her stomach as heavy as a stone. She heard him dismiss the guard; the man left, and Ashan's footsteps sounded on the tiles as he moved towards her.

He bent down and covered her hand with his. 'I'm sorry,' he said. 'I didn't mean it – but you must never seem pleased to see me. It will get back to Samsu and he will want to know why.'

She nodded silently, still looking away; she wiped her damp eyes with the backs of her fingers.

There was a smile in his voice when he spoke again. 'But hearing you call my name with such joy warmed my heart more than I can say.'

She turned back to him; his face was full of sincerity.

'Have you forgiven me?' he asked.

'It doesn't seem to matter very much at the moment,' she whispered, avoiding the question. Seeing him look at her with such intensity, Eliana was suddenly aware of how dirty and grimy she felt. Her hair was limp and tangled, the malachite she put on her eyes a week ago was still smeared about her face, and her dress was crumpled and spotted.

'Are they treating you well?'

'They're feeding me, if that's what you mean. I didn't have water for three days, but I do now, so I feel a little better.'

His face darkened. 'I will have words with someone about that – I expressly ordered them to keep you as comfortable as possible.'

Her heart leapt a little to hear it. 'Well, don't scold Resu – I think I made a breakthrough with him earlier, he was kind to me.'

'Is there anything else you need?'

'Just a bath,' she said, dejectedly. 'I don't think I've ever been so long without bathing before. I feel disgusting.'

Ashan thought hard. 'It can't happen without Samsu's permission,' he said. 'But I might be able to persuade him.'

'Oh, Ashan! Really?' She gave him a genuine smile of pure joy. To be off the chain, even for an hour! To bathe, to feel clean again!

'I'm on guard duty this evening until midnight, I'll bring it up then if I can. But keep quiet.' There was a warning note in his tone. 'I don't know what I'll have to say to bring it about – you might not like it, but if you speak out, you could jeopardise everything.'

'I'll be silent,' she promised. Then after a pause, 'How much longer do you think he'll keep me here?'

Ashan's face fell as he admitted, 'I just don't know. He hasn't given any indication at all, hasn't even mentioned you. He hasn't shown any interest in you since you've been here under his nose, but then he's been busy with the emissaries. They departed this morning. I wish I could tell you.'

'Don't worry about it,' she said, holding back tears.

The guard returned and Ashan had to leave to avoid arousing suspicion. He gave her hand one last reassuring squeeze and walked out without a backward glance.

*

Samsu gave Eliana a cold, appraising stare.

She held his gaze with her own for a few moments, her eyes full of sullen resentment, before dropping her head back to her knees and hiding her face.

'What do you think, Ashan?' he called to where his stepson sat on the floor cushions reading a tablet.

'Hmm? About what, sir?' he looked up.

'The whore. Has being chained improved her behaviour?'

Ashan hesitated; there was no answer he could give that would benefit Eliana. If he said that her behaviour was improved, Samsu would want to ensure she continued it. If he said that she had not improved, he would keep her there until she did. 'I haven't heard any negative reports from her guards. But whatever it has done for her behaviour, being chained has certainly not improved her appearance.'

'Explain.'

'Well, look at her, sir. If you don't mind me saying so, she could use a wash. Even a pet dog needs to be bathed once in a while. I wouldn't want her in *my* bed looking that dirty.'

Samsu scoffed, 'A visit to the bathhouse is a privilege to be earned. But if she has not been difficult this week, perhaps I could see my way to striking a bargain.'

Eliana raised her head a fraction to show that she was listening.

'Would you like that, *karkittu*? A visit to the baths. You are beginning to look and smell like a stray animal, after all.'

She nodded, not wanting to risk speaking and allow audible hatred to seep into her voice.

'Very well – you may go, under three conditions. Firstly, you will go with guards. They will stay with you at all times. You will not make any foolish and futile attempts at escape, because I assure you they will not go well for you. Next, you will not so much as look at or speak to another person while you are unchained. I will hear about it from your guards if you break this rule, and you will not be allowed out again. Lastly, you must come to me willingly afterwards.'

The last condition made her stomach turn; the thought of laying with Samsu again was sickening. Her spirit would never be willing, but for the sake of an hour's freedom, perhaps she could force her body to quiescence while he took his pleasure.

He would have her again whether she came willingly or not; she supposed she might as well be clean when he did.

She nodded again.

'Then we have an agreement. You will go under guard, bathe, and then pay the price for your privilege. Ashan, make the necessary arrangements.'

'Sir,' Ashan inclined his head and returned to his tablet, suppressing a triumphant smile.

*

True to his word, Samsu had two guards come for her the following day. The *chink* as the padlock opened and released her collar from the chain was the sweetest sound Eliana had ever heard. It took all her self-restraint not to run as soon as it dropped away – not because she thought she had any real hope of escape, but because she needed to spend her pent-up energy and feel swift and fleet again, moving her legs as fast as they would carry her. The guards would not see it that way.

As she was led to the bathhouse, she revelled in the simple pleasure of putting one foot in front of the other without being held back. It had been over a week since she had been able to venture more than three steps at a time; her knees shook a little, the guards following close at her heels. They didn't see a single living soul on their way there, and when they reached the squat white building, it was deserted.

Eliana stripped off the dirty gown shamelessly – it had hidden very little anyway – and plunged into the warm water.

It greeted her like an old friend, embracing every part of her body and soaking away the tension with the grime. She sighed and tilted her head back in the water, letting it saturate her hair and creep across her scalp with a pleasant prickle. Floating there for a few minutes, she absorbed the peace – the gentle sounds of water lapping against the stone sides of the bath pool; the play of sunlight on the ripples, reflecting Utu's rays onto the low ceiling and shattering them into a hundred dancing rainbows; the silken feel of the warm water against her skin.

Reluctantly, she picked up the soap and began to wash herself – she did not have long to spend here. If she took advantage, Samsu might not let her return. She was keen to stay on his good side; even if he would not give her freedom, she might be able to restore some of these small pleasures to her life if she learned to manage him the right way.

She massaged soap into her hair, wanting to get it as clean as she possibly could, painfully aware of not knowing how long it might be until her next wash.

After a final rinse, she sighed again, pushed her way through the water to the edge of the pool and hauled herself out. A clean sheet of linen and a dress had been left on a table for her. Wringing her hair out and twisting it into a wet knot at the nape of her neck, she dried off with the sheet and wrapped it around herself as she held the new gown up to the light to inspect it.

It was as flimsy as the gold dress she had just discarded. When she put her hand inside it and looked, the details of her nails were clearly visible, a sure indication that it would not hide any other detail either. She squirmed a little inside; she had worn the other gown for a week and had not once managed to forget that every secret part of her was permanently on display.

She blushed as let the sheet drop and dressed, the sky blue silk caressing her as it slid over her skin. Anointing her arms and legs with jasmine oil, she was ready to go.

Her legs felt leaden as she walked back to Samsu's apartments. She stood meekly as her chain was reattached; the gut-wrenching crack of the lock snapping back into place was almost unbearable.

She sat heavily back onto the cushions to await Samsu's pleasure. He had held up his end of their bargain – now he would surely call upon her to honour hers.

Night was drawing in when he returned to his chambers.

'All clean, *karkittu*?'

'Yes.'

'Yes, what?'

'Yes, *sir*,' she amended petulantly.

'And you remember your promise?'

'Yes, sir.'

'Then, when Ashan removes your chain, you will come over here, strip off your dress and spread your legs for me with no defiance?'

Her throat constricted. She swallowed hard and nodded.

'Very well,' he gestured to Ashan, who moved behind her and unfastened the chain.

No resistance, she told herself. *Go to the bed, strip off, spread your legs. It's not difficult. Just do it.*

Her legs refused her when she tried to move them at first, but through force of will alone she walked steadily towards him. Pulling the dress over her head, she shivered in the evening chill. She sat onto the bed, lay down on her back and parted her thighs, wanting to cry with the shame and embarrassment of it as he stared between them with his habitual amused smirk.

'You see, Ashan? I make her a bargain and *still* she cannot obey.' There was laughter in his voice.

She immediately sat up and closed her legs. 'I did exactly as you ordered!' she said indignantly, adding 'sir' as an afterthought.

'You did not. I made no mention of getting onto the bed, or lying down. Come here,' he beckoned.

Moving to the edge of the bed, she slid off and stood in front of him. He grabbed her by the hips and spun her around, facing her away from him, exposing her full front to Ashan. Her cheeks flamed red.

Samsu cupped a breast in one hand and her neck with the other – it was still bruised from where she had fought the chain; she winced. Burying his face in her hair, he inhaled deeply. He had been out riding that afternoon, and smelled of the summer

179

breeze mingled with horse sweat; to Eliana, it was the perfume of freedom.

Squeezing her breast, he bent her over at the waist.

Realising his intention with a jolt of horror, she bit her lip hard to stop herself crying out.

He leaned over her, pressing her into the bed. A hot whisper in her ear hissed, 'As I have you chained like a dog, I shall fuck you like one as well.'

Hitching up his tunic, he positioned himself at her entrance, holding her by the hips. She balled her fists in the silken sheets and whimpered as he drove himself inside her with a red-hot flash of pain. He did not wait for her to adjust, but thrust into her over and over, hard enough to give a sickening jolt to her stomach with each motion.

Biting down on her lip until the blood welled up from the soft flesh gave her a different pain to focus on. Her eyes were flooded with unshed tears, making the bed swim under her. She lifted her head; Ashan met her eyes, his face carefully blank.

Samsu moved faster and faster, wrapping the length of her hair around one hand. She yelped as he wrenched her head back and arched her spine; she felt rather than heard his amusement.

Giving an agonised groan of pleasure, he leaned over her and wrapped his free hand around her throat. He squeezed hard until she coughed and choked and began to fight to draw breath as her vision darkened at the edges.

With a shudder and gasp, he was spent. He stood there for a moment, panting, before pushing Eliana onto the floor and collapsing forward onto the bed.

He gave a breathy laugh as she lay curled up, shaken and disgusted on the cold tiles. 'If you are going to be this good, perhaps I'll allow you a bath every week, *karkittu*.'

She trembled violently, wishing there was a way to rid herself of his seed as it oozed uncomfortably between her thighs.

'Put your dress back on and return to your chain,' Samsu ordered. 'I'm finished with you, for now.'

Ashan clipped the padlock shut again with no hint of sympathy, though inside he was afire with rage. His loyalty to Samsu had always been unwavering, but this bold, brave girl made him see the prince for what he was, and he did not like it.

Arranging her cushions to create a nest, Eliana lay down with her back to Ashan, pulling the blanket up over her head, shutting the whole world out and creating a private shelter where she could be alone with her shame.

*

Days and nights blended into one, and Eliana lost track of the time.

Ashan helped her all he could, bringing little comforts when she asked for them, and even procuring a herb she desperately wanted; she stashed it under the bedding and mixed a little with her water every day. The taste was vile, but she would do anything to prevent Samsu's seed taking root inside her. She swore to herself that she would never bear his child, and gave thanks to the mother goddess every time her moon blood came.

She had bled twice since the chain was first put on – it was her only measure of how long she had been here. As the weeks drew on, she gave up asking Ashan when he thought she might be released, watching his face was all the answer she needed.

Samsu began to use her more frequently, sometimes two or three times a day. He did not always even bother to take her off the chain, just turning her over and taking her there on the cushions. There was no pattern to it – he just appeared as it suited his whim.

The insult never grew less, nor did the revulsion. Eliana began to live on edge, unable to relax, forever expecting the next assault, always watching the door for the dreaded sight of his silhouette. Her one comfort was her weekly trip to the bathhouse, where she could forget for just a little while as the water soothed her.

She told herself that it was just her body he violated, that nothing he could do would get inside her mind, but soon the night terrors returned.

It was a cool, crisp night when, as she slept, she pierced the air with a scream like a tortured soul of the underworld.

Ashan was on her immediately, clamping his hand over her mouth and nose. She woke thrashing and shrieking in a panic as she realised that she couldn't breathe.

'Hush!' he hissed, urgently. 'What's wrong? Are you hurt?'

'Quiet!' Samsu's voice cracked through the darkness like a whip. There was a rustle as he pushed his sheets aside and his bare feet slapped against the tiles as he came nearer. He sent Ashan flying with a strong shove and grabbed Eliana's upper arm, hauling her from her warm nest still sleepy and confused – she hadn't even realised that she'd screamed, her first awareness had been when she couldn't breathe under Ashan's hand.

He slapped her across the face and shook her hard, 'How *dare* you make that revolting sound in my presence? To wake me in the middle of the night?'

'Wh-what sound?' she stammered.

'Insolent whore!' he threw her back onto the cushions. 'You disturb me and then have the audacity to talk back! I'll teach you a lesson you won't forget.' He flipped her onto her hands and knees and pulled her legs apart before forcing himself in, taking her with even more violence than usual, his thrusts more calculated to hurt her than to bring himself pleasure.

Eliana buried her face in a cushion to muffle the cries of pain she could not stop.

As soon as Samsu was finished, he pushed her aside. 'Ashan – see that her food is withheld for three days.'

'That's not fair!' she cried without thinking, earning another stinging slap for her trouble.

'Five days.'

She clenched her fists and bit down hard on her tongue to stop herself from cursing him as he went back to his bed. Tears of helpless rage ran down her cheeks; she fought to keep herself silent as she wept.

As soon as Samsu's breathing became long and deep and steady and his snores began to ring out, Ashan moved back to Eliana. Sitting on her cushions, he drew her head onto his lap and began to stroke her hair.

The motion soothed her, his gentle hand a welcome balm running the length of hair, from the top of her head down to her waist. After a time, some of the tension began to seep from her muscles – she was almost able to imagine that the fingers running through her curls were Kisha's. She missed her sister terribly, wondering what she'd been told, and whether she was worried; she made a mental note to ask Ashan.

Every time she came to the edge of sleep, she forced herself back. She would not risk sleeping when Samsu did if she could help it – if the night terrors returned and disturbed him again she could find herself starved to death.

Ashan departed for his own bed at midnight when his relief arrived, but Eliana spent a long, wakeful night staring into the darkness, lying on the cold floor instead of her cushions, trying to keep sleep at bay. As soon as Samsu departed in the morning, she made herself comfortable, pulled up the blanket and fell into a dreamless sleep.

She was awoken by Ashan's gentle hand on her shoulder – he had come to check on her, dismissing her guard for a break, as always.

'Eliana? Are you alright?' he murmured.

She sat up and pushed the hair out of her eyes, 'In what way?'

'Your scream last night – it sounded like you were in agony.'

'Oh, that. I've had nightmares ever since Samsu's conquest of the city. I haven't had one for a while though.'

Ashan had the good grace to look embarrassed – he could not deny his own part in the conquest.

Eliana's stomach grumbled loudly. She blushed. 'I suppose I'll have to get used to that. Five days!'

Giving a wicked little grin that made her pulse leap, Ashan reached into the leather pouch at his belt and produced a chunk of bread and a handful of dates. 'It's not much, but I'll bring you what I can – just make sure nobody sees you eat it!'

'Oh, Ashan!' Eliana snatched the food and stuffed it underneath her cushions, concealing it with the herbs. 'Thank you!' she reached up and wrapped her arms around his neck.

Before either of them knew what was happening, their lips had joined in a heart-melting kiss. Eliana felt hot tears sting her eyes at the unexpected pleasure of feeling Ashan's lips against hers again. She opened her mouth a little, running the tip of her tongue along his lower lip. He gave a little shudder of arousal and she smiled into the kiss as his arms tightened around her waist and pulled her closer.

Somebody cleared his throat behind them.

Eliana's stomach plummeted as they sprang apart, whipping around to see who had caught them.

The guard that Ashan had dismissed for his break had returned. He leaned casually against the wall, watching them with an interested expression. 'The prince will cut your cock off for this, pretty boy,' the man drawled, an arrogant smirk on his face.

Ashan pulled himself slowly to his feet and walked towards the man with a measured pace, reminding Eliana of the dangerous dance of a scorpion before it strikes. 'And just how is he going to find out?' he asked calmly.

'I dare say word will get back to him somehow, unless you can make it worth my while to keep silent.'

Eliana shrank back against the wall, afraid of where this was going.

'What is it that you want?'

'Promotion,' the man answered without hesitation. 'And something for my troubles.'

'Like what?'

'That's a fine blade you've got at your belt – no captain of a household guard needs a blade that rich.'

'This one?' Ashan withdrew the dagger and held it out, still inching towards the man.

'That's it – you're too much of a woman to use it anyway. Talk amongst the soldiers is that you've never even killed a man. It's a sin to let a blade that beautiful live unblooded.'

'I dare say you're right,' said Ashan thoughtfully, examining the dagger. It was a fine one indeed, the bronze blade engraved with the arms of his mother's house, the polished bone handle marked with the symbols of warrior gods. 'This was my father's dagger.'

'And now it's mine,' the man grinned smugly, holding out his hand.

Ashan made his move.

He grabbed the man's hand and jerked him forward, knocking him off-balance. Twisting him around so quickly that Eliana didn't even see how he did it, Ashan opened the guard's throat from ear to ear, giving him a red smile to take to his grave along with their secret.

His life's blood cascaded down the front of his body like a waterfall, soaking into his brown military tunic and dying it a rich, deep crimson. Ashan dropped him; the man fell onto his knees before toppling forward with the dead weight of a hay bale, hitting the ground with a sickening thud. A dark pool spread along the tiles where he fell.

Eliana sat frozen with shock. 'Ashan,' she whispered. 'You killed him.'

Ashan wiped the blood from his dagger onto the man's tunic and put it back into his belt. 'I did, and I'd do it again. Nobody blackmails me.'

'But... I thought you...' she tailed off, her mind half-numb, trying to shut out what she had just witnessed.

'Thought what?'

She shrugged, 'I thought you were different.'

'I am, Eliana. I am not cruel. I do not rape and murder for fun. But I am a soldier; I am trained to kill. You think I just stood by and watched the conquest? That I never accompanied Samsu into battle before we came here? I have been trained since I was a boy to take vengeance on those who have wronged me, to defend myself against those who would hurt me, to destroy those who would harm my loved ones. I did it for you too, you know. Samsu would murder you without question; I flatter myself to think he might at least feel some regret over killing me.'

There was a horrified gasp from the doorway. Resu had come to bring Eliana's water; his eyes were wide as he took in the carnage.

'Ah, Resu,' Ashan said briskly. 'Go and fetch the prince for me, will you? Tell him it's urgent. There's a good man.'

Resu nodded, put down the water and fled.

'What will you tell him?'

'I'll think of something. I'll go to meet him now.'

He departed, leaving Eliana alone with the corpse. She could not bear to look; another man for whose death she was responsible, another *gidim* to haunt her dreams. Burying her face in the cushions to physically block out the grotesque sight, she prayed that Ashan would come back quickly.

Fortunately, he returned almost immediately; Samsu could not have been too far away. Eliana did not raise her head, hoping that Samsu would ignore her.

'... Caught him trying to use the girl, sir,' Ashan was saying. 'I ordered him away and he threatened her life. Said that you would never know he had borrowed her, so what did it matter. I tried to pull him off, and he was killed in the struggle.'

'Good man,' Samsu clapped his stepson on the back. 'I've no room for dishonest men in my service. You'll be rewarded for this.'

'No need, sir. Just pleased to have caught him in time.'

'Have the slaves clean this mess up. They can toss him on a dungheap for all I care.'

'And the girl? Shall I find another guard for her?'

'No. On balance, I think she is docile enough now to not need watching at all hours. What do you think?'

'She certainly hasn't been much trouble of late, barring last night's incident. Your training has obviously worked wonders.'

'Did you hear that, *karkittu*?' Samsu called across the room. 'I told you, didn't I? I have achieved with you what my father could not manage with my sister – I have taken a stubborn, prideful girl and taught her compliance.'

Eliana did not raise her head, lest Samsu should see the guilt in her eyes. She was grateful when he did not speak to her again.

'Well, good work, Ashan. Arrange for the mess to be cleared away and then come to find me; we have matters of state to discuss.'

'Sir.'

They both left the room, leaving Eliana alone with the cadaver again. Even when the slaves came to remove it, she did not look up. She would not lift her head until every last trace of evidence was gone and she could pretend it had never happened.

She tried to banish the picture of the man's body from her mind, to just absorb herself in what she had felt when Ashan kissed her. The memory made her warm with joy, from her heart right out to her fingertips.

Her stomach grumbled again. She thought of the food secreted beneath her cushions, but her appetite was gone.

Chapter 13

Eliana only slept during the daytimes now, when Samsu was out.

She felt more at ease without the eyes of a guard constantly watching her, and could finally stop trying to awkwardly balance herself at the same time as holding the blanket up as a screen when she used the chamberpot. The privacy was a luxury she had become unaccustomed to.

Although the atmosphere was more peaceful, she was still troubled by her dreams. The spirits of her past haunted her whenever she slept, their faces performing a grotesque dance as they drifted before her closed eyes, cackling with shrill voices; she recoiled and twitched as she slept. Mari's brothers, her mother, Isin, the foolish guard, countless men, women and children who had been put to the sword during the conquest – some of their faces were shadowy, others were as crisp as when she last saw them, but all were laughing at her.

Her mother's face was as blurred and indistinct as it had always been; whereas Isin's, with its expression of surprise, and the guard's, with its gaping red smile, were as bright and clear as a butterfly's wing.

As she slept that day, the fourth of having her food withheld and relying on Ashan for scraps, they whirled around her, spinning her, making her dizzy even in sleep. Their high-pitched chanting filled her ears – sounds halfway between a curse and an animal cry. Her mother stretched out dark arms, then danced away mockingly when Eliana reached for her. Isin's disembodied head stared at her accusingly, while the guard threatened to take her secret to Samsu.

They span her faster, closing in, reciting incantations in strange languages and anointing her with blood. The guard reached out a gory hand, straining to touch her. She stepped back, and back, edging as far from him as she could... until her foot stepped backwards into nothing, and she fell into the yawning nothingness of the underworld with a scream.

She was still screaming as she woke, damp with sweat and fallen off her cushions onto the cold floor. Shivering, she pushed herself back onto the bed and wrapped the blanket around herself. Her face was wet with tears. The room was empty, with no-one to see; she had never felt more alone. She longed for her sister's comforting arms, and could no longer remember what her little niece looked like.

The weekly visit to the bathhouse had not happened this week while she was under punishment. Her hair was greasy, her gown spotted, and the collar chafed at her throat. Eliana felt hungry, dirty, tired and, at that moment, utterly hopeless. She had been here for more than two moons now, and Samsu showed no signs of freeing her.

She was no longer living; simply existing. She could not bear it any longer.

Eliana slid the length of the golden chain through her hand, admiring and hating it all at once. In other circumstances it would have been a pretty thing. But now, what had bound her would free her.

Wrapping it around her throat above the collar once, twice, three times, she leaned away from the wall.

The links bit into her skin as the chain tightened. Nothing happened for a moment, but then she choked and gasped, her face beginning to tingle as her eyes bulged and the sound of the blood in her head increased to a thunderous hammering.

She looked out at the garden as her vision began to close in, a circular blackness blotting out nature's beauty like a cloud drifting in front of the sun.

The last thing she heard before drifting into unconsciousness was Ashan's voice, calling her name.

'Eliana?'

How fitting, she thought, that her mind should conjure him up now, so that he would be her last thought before Ereshkigal claimed her. The imagination was a powerful thing.

'*Eliana!*'

She had not imagined it – he had come to smuggle her what little food he could, and his heart skipped a beat as he saw her entangled in the chain, throwing all her body weight away from it, her face purpling as she slipped into the realm between life and death.

He had never moved as fast as he did in that moment, reaching her in seconds and fumbling desperately to unwrap the chain from her limp body.

Cradling her in his arms, he did the first thing he could think of – he grabbed the water pitcher and emptied its contents over her face.

The sudden cold shocked her back to consciousness.

Her eyes slowly regained their focus – was she dead? No, Ashan's face floated above her, a confusion of terror and anger. She turned her face into his arms; her throat still felt constricted, but now it was with disappointment. 'Just let me die,' she whispered.

'Never,' he growled. 'This is not you, Eliana. You are letting him win – I never would have believed it of you. Where is that strong, spirited girl I fell in love with?'

'Samsu killed her, just as he wanted. She died – let me go with her.'

'I will never let you die. As long as I am here, you're stuck in this world, and I'll continue to make it as bearable as I can for you. You have to trust me that one day, you'll be free of this chain and of this palace, but we must wait for the right time, or else we'll just make a bad thing worse. Do you trust me?'

She did not have the strength to nod or shake her head; even if she could, she was not sure what answer she would make.

Ashan laid her on the pillows and covered her with the blanket. As he did so, Samsu walked through the door.

He read the situation in a second.

Tutting, he shook his head. 'I admired your strength and courage, *karkittu*. I can't pretend that this is not a disappointment. Suicide is a coward's death, and you are no coward. With all your fortitude, I did not expect you to try to take the easy way out.'

She didn't react, just continued to lie there with her eyes shut, breathing deeply and trying to bring her heart rate back to normal.

'Well, you can put the idea from your mind,' Samsu continued. 'You will not be permitted to kill yourself as my Eshnunna did. She chose death over obedience, you will not. I shall have to set guards over you again. You will learn to live as a docile and compliant woman, and if anyone is to send you out of this world, it will be me.'

He collected the tablet he had come in for and looked at Ashan, 'Is she alright?'

'I think so, sir.'

'Good. Don't tell your mother, but I believe I'm growing rather fond of my little pet.'

Her stomach churned as his footsteps receded. *Fond* of her? She would rather he hated her as she hated him, then they would each know where they stood.

Ashan took out the food he had brought and stored it in her hiding place. With a gentle caress of her injured throat and a kiss on the forehead, he followed Samsu out.

Within minutes, before she could think about attempting the act again, a new guard was stationed in the room.

*

That night, there was a meeting in Samsu's chambers.

He, Ashan, the Brute, and two other generals that Eliana did not recognise sat on the floor cushions having a heated debate.

They spoke in the Babylonian dialect, but Eliana understood the sense of the conversation. Samsu was having trouble keeping his city safe. Slave raiders from the Sutean tribes were ravaging the cities of the Babylonian empire.

'It's an insult!' roared Samsu. 'I will not let it stand. These people belong to me, I will not have them stolen away and sold. Why can't any of you dung-brained beasts find a way to stop them? You are supposed to be the best that Babylon has to offer.'

'We have tried all we can, sir,' said one of the unnamed generals. 'We simply don't have the men to increase patrols empire-wide.'

'It's unacceptable! You will find a workable solution or I...'

With her heart in her mouth, her throat still sore from this morning's trauma, Eliana croaked from her place against the wall, 'I have a suggestion.'

The Brute leapt to his feet, infuriated that she should dare to interrupt. He strode towards her with his arm raised, ready to strike. 'You dare to speak when men are talking, little girl?' he hissed, his voice full of menace.

He was within range when Samsu called, 'Stop!'

Freezing in place, the Brute twisted his head on its thick neck to look at his prince. 'Sir?'

Samsu's mouth was contorted in an amused smile. 'Let us hear what she has to say. It may have some comedic value, if nothing else.'

Eliana ignored the last remark. 'Pass a law prohibiting citizens from buying slaves that originate from any of the Sumerian city states. If the raiders can't sell the slaves, they might move on and bother someone else. If you cover the honey, the wasp flies elsewhere.'

'Idiot girl!' the Brute drew his hand back to strike her.

'Hold!' barked Samsu. 'If there is an idiot here, it is you. All of you. A chained-up whore can think of a better solution than any of you! You ought to be ashamed. You are all dismissed; useless, pig-headed morons to a man.'

The soldiers filed out in silence, the Brute shooting Eliana a poisonous look as he passed. She was not concerned – he would not hurt her while Samsu forbade it. She knew little enough of the man, but she could be sure of that.

After the last man had left, Samsu came to stand over her. She looked up at him and could not decipher the expression on his face. 'Perhaps you have a brain after all, *karkittu*. I was beginning to think that you were quite stupid.'

'I'm an *Ensi*'s daughter, sir. I have a little understanding of things.'

'Well, I may come to you from time to time to see if your way of thinking is an improvement over the same old ideas that my men come out with day after day. *But*,' his voice dropped to a growl, 'if you *ever* presume to offer unsolicited advice or to contradict me, I will deal with you accordingly. Do you understand?'

'Yes, sir,' she nodded, feeling more hopeful than she had for many weeks. Perhaps if Samsu found a use for more than just her body, she could begin to make a difference to people's lives as she had always wanted.

'Good, now turn over.'

*

Over the next couple of moons, Samsu began to use Eliana for her mind almost as frequently as her body – she was finally starting to feel that she might have been brought to the palace for a higher purpose, and gave thanks to Enlil every day.

Sometimes her suggestions were met with scorn and a slap, but more often with a nod and a hint of admiration.

It was necessary to tread a very careful line when offering her advice to Samsu; she made a game of it – making him feel like her ideas were his own. She must never appear too intelligent to him – he was paranoid at the best of times, and she was sure that seeming clever would only fire his overactive imagination.

Gradually, he was coming to rely on her advice. Growing up in Nippur, she had always taken an active interest in the city's problems and the solving of them – her father had taught her that the meaning of life was a life of meaning, and she had always intended to give her life meaning by improving things for others as he did. Now, at last, she had that opportunity. She often thought about her father as she set her mind to the conundrums she was given – wondering what he would do in each situation, and whether he recognised her influence in Samsu's new policies.

Though he wanted her ideas, Samsu was ever-keen to make sure she remembered her place in his life. He began to take her to his daily audiences to give her a broader view of the issues the city faced, allowing her to hear from the citizens first-hand; but he had her there his own way. She sat on a cold stone step at his feet, commanded to silence, the golden chain still attached to her collar as a sure indicator of her status as his pet. He held the other end in one hand, making a show of his ownership as he sat on his great throne of exquisitely polished Lebanese cedar, listening to pleas and dispensing judgement.

For Eliana, the worst part of it was that he would not allow her more decent clothes. She was still a whore, he said, and she would be attired as one. She blushed when her father attended audiences and studiously avoided looking at her in her creased and semi-transparent gowns, a deep line of pain appearing between his heavy, greying brows.

But it was worth the humiliation, for what she learned was invaluable. Hearing the problems of the Nippurites from their own mouths was what she had always enjoyed about working with her father. Important details about which street was being plagued by pickpockets, or which field the crops were failing in, or precisely where the canal needed repair, were often overlooked by Samsu in his impatience to have the audience finished with.

As her political influence grew and Samsu came to trust her a little, the terms of her confinement were considerably eased. They had an unspoken agreement: she would keep her privileges and extra freedoms so long as she did not try to escape or conspire against him. It was an uneasy truce, but one she was happy to maintain for the moment.

She still could not quite believe her fortune – at Ashan's suggestion, Samsu had agreed to allow her off her chain for a walk in his own gardens every day. Granted, it was only for half an hour, and her every step was followed by a guard, but it was a tentative move towards freedom.

The first time that she was allowed out was a moment that she would never forget. As the sun warmed her face, a cool breeze lifted the curls from her neck and the grass tickled the soles of her bare feet, her heart swelled with pure joy. The simplicity of nature and the sheer pleasure it could bring was something she never ceased to be thankful for. She had always felt most at peace in the garden, and to be able to move about freely outside and turn her face up to the wide open sky was a luxury she was certain she would never again take for granted in her lifetime.

When Ashan accompanied her on her walks, she was able to set off at a run, burning off the energies and frustrations that she had been forced to store up for so many weeks. The other guards would not tolerate it, but Ashan always trusted her to return.

Her walks with him were special – even under the cover of the trees she did not dare to take his hand or speak of anything dangerous, but to be together with some degree of privacy, to laugh and joke and flirt and pretend to be carefree lovers strolling the city gardens like a real couple… it was paradise.

Samsu's garden was aflame with red flowers of every hue – each petal seeming to have been kissed by Utu, dipped in the rays of the rising sun and set alight. There was no other way to achieve such a richness of colour, Eliana was sure. They walked amongst the blossoms together, inhaling the intoxicating perfume, and it was like nothing else in the world existed.

Ashan laughed at Eliana as they crossed the terrace and she ran to the grass, dropping to roll in it like a gleeful horse, heedless of the stains she was adding to her dress.

It became harder and harder to return to her chain after tasting freedom, but she knew better than to complain. Ashan had convinced her to accept that escape now would avail her nothing: even if she escaped the palace, even if she escaped the city, where would she go? For leagues around, there was nothing but the Babylonian empire – she could not evade him for long. She could not hope to survive the desert trek between cities alone. The roads were hazardous, populated by bandits and slave raiders – she would simply be trading her golden chain for an iron one.

Even on her chain, she now had a small pleasure in which to indulge – in passing, she had mentioned her love of the lyre, and Samsu had immediately commanded her to play something for him. Resu had been sent for Kisha's instrument – her sister preferred weaving to music anyway – and Eliana had played him a haunting lullaby from her childhood, the very one that Kisha sang her to sleep with when she suffered from her nightmares.

Her eyes filled with tears and her voice trembled as she sang, bringing a depth of feeling to the sweet notes that she could never have feigned.

Samsu had shown no emotion, but nodded brusquely and told her to keep the lyre – he would hear her play sometimes at the end of the day.

'I'm so much happier,' she told Ashan as they walked in the gardens. 'Perhaps Enlil had a purpose in sending me here after all. I am even beginning to hope that I might be free from the chain soon.'

'Perhaps,' Ashan gave nothing away, but offered an affectionate smile. 'It is good to see you laugh again.'

'My sole regret now is that I can't be there for Kisha during her pregnancy – she must be almost full term now?'

'Around eight moons, I believe. She misses you terribly.'

'And I miss her,' Eliana's eyes were pricked by unexpected tears in the midst of her happiness. 'Do you think... would it be possible that she might be allowed to visit me?'

Ashan frowned. 'I could bring it up with Samsu. He might allow it as a reward for your good behaviour recently.'

'Oh, say whatever you have to!' she pleaded. 'To see Kisha again before she gives birth would be...'

She tailed off, she could not think of the words to express how much she longed for her sister's embrace.

'I'll see what I can do,' Ashan smiled, plucking a flower and tucking it into her hair.

She blushed as red as the petals and walked on.

*

Ashan was on duty in Samsu's chambers again that evening.

Eliana plucked at the lyre, weaving a sweet tune of her own composition as Samsu reclined on the cushions, reading a tablet bearing his father's seal, his forehead creased in concentration.

He shook his head, put the tablet down and leaned back, closing his eyes to better absorb the music. The final notes of the melody quivered in the air, before melting away into nothingness.

Silence stretched out, settling over the room.

Ashan cleared his throat.

'What is it?' asked Samsu, not opening his eyes.

'Sir, if I might mention a small domestic matter...'

'Go on.'

'The concubine is nearing her final month of pregnancy.'

'Come to the point.'

'She has been anxious for several weeks now, concerned about the whore, though I told her that she was well-cared for and there was nothing to worry herself about.'

'And?'

'The physician has advised that an unhappy mother breeds an unhappy child. If she continues to pine and fret, your son may come forth sickly and weak.'

Samsu opened his eyes and sat up, 'Why has nobody mentioned this to me before?'

'We had hoped that she would come to accept the situation, sir. But she is worse than ever, and the physician advises that this is a vital time for the child.'

Ashan spoke with a perfectly straight and serious face; Eliana wondered how much of what he said was true. Was Kisha really worried?

'Well I will not release the whore, so she can give up that idea immediately. She can join her if she likes – I'm sure there's room for two chains over there.'

Eliana's heart sank – no, no, no! That was not the way it was supposed to happen. She bit her tongue to prevent herself from speaking and ruining everything.

'I would not have dreamed of suggesting it, sir.' Ashan said, respectfully. 'I merely meant to suggest that the concubine be permitted to visit the whore if it might stop her worrying.'

Samsu frowned as he thought – Eliana could see that he was torn. He did not like being coerced into giving her an extra privilege that he would consider a gift to be earned, but if his son was weak and sickly, the future of the empire could be at stake.

'Do you believe you have earned a visit from your sister, *karkittu*?'

'I've tried to, sir,' she answered tactfully.

'And would you be willing to give up another privilege in order to see her?'

'If it is your wish.'

The words grated in her throat, but she must be deferential, must be respectful; it was the only way to manipulate him into giving her what she wanted.

'It is. You will give up your garden walks for the next two days in exchange.'

'Thank you, sir.'

She returned her attention to the lyre and struck up another tune, a little irritated that she would be stuck here for two days, but rejoicing in Ashan's clever playing of Samsu. She was beginning to learn that by massaging his vanity and presenting ideas carefully, it was possible to get almost anything out of him.

Anything but her freedom.

'Very well. Ashan, arrange it.' Samsu picked up the tablet again and resumed reading.

*

She fidgeted impatiently on her cushions, waiting for Ashan to return. He had been gone for almost half an hour.

Her heart leapt as the door finally creaked open on its hinge; belly huge with child, her face drawn and pinched, her sister walked in.

'Kisha!' she cried, leaping up impulsively to run to meet her. She ran two steps before being yanked back viciously by the chain; she stumbled, and regained her balance.

Kisha walked quickly towards her with her arms outstretched, 'Oh, Elly! I've missed you so much!'

Enfolding her in an embrace, tears began to run down Kisha's cheeks. Eliana breathed deeply, pressing her face against her sister's shoulder as she savoured the soft, loving arms around her, the steady heartbeat, the sweet rose perfume. As they held each other, the baby in Kisha's belly gave a hearty kick.

'Oh!' cried Eliana, laughing. 'I felt that, you naughty thing!'

'My boy is impatient,' Kisha grinned, pulling away. 'He is strong, and gives me no rest. Oh – your poor neck! Are you alright?'

A bruise was blossoming already where Eliana had forgotten the chain and run. 'Oh, it's fine,' she gave a rueful smile. 'You'd think I'd be used to this thing by now!'

'I would never expect you to get used to something like that. How much longer do you think he'll keep you like this?'

'Oh, not too much longer,' said Eliana brightly, trying to sound optimistic. In truth, she had no idea, but she didn't want to burden her sister any more than necessary.

'Good – I'm so hoping you can be with me for the birth. You were such a help last time.'

'Susa hasn't sent Ani again, has she?'

'No, no. It's just me and Mari. Though the physician has been out to examine me a few times.'

'Why?'

'A few twinges, nothing much. He says that my son is impatient to be out in the world, and my womb is preparing to help him on his way.'

'Well I hope you are resting enough.'

Kisha grimaced. 'It seems I do nothing *but* rest. Mari takes very good care of me.'

'I'm sure she does,' said Eliana carefully. She had never been entirely able to shake her suspicions about Mari and her motives. 'How is she?'

'She's well,' smiled Kisha. 'There's been a little romance with one of the gardeners – she seems very happy at last.'

'I'm pleased to hear it. How about Sarri? I miss her almost as much as I missed you!'

'She's beautiful,' Kisha positively glowed with pride. 'Walking and babbling and as mischievous as you were when you were tiny!'

'I wish you could have brought her,' said Eliana wistfully.

'Me too. But hopefully you'll see her soon enough – oh!'

Eliana took her sister's arm in concern as the older girl doubled over in pain, 'Are you alright?'

'Fine, fine,' Kisha was pale as moonlight. 'Just another twinge.'

'Come and sit,' Eliana guided her to the cushions and settled her comfortably.

'Don't worry about me, Elly,' she gave a weak smile. 'Tell me about your life here.'

Eliana launched into the story of how she had solved the slave raider crisis for Samsu, and how he liked her to help with the basic running of Nippur and play the lyre for him, skipping over the more unsavoury details of her present state, trying to distract Kisha from her pains.

'You've always been so good on the lyre,' said Kisha. 'I'm glad he likes to listen to you play – I miss hearing you while I weave.'

'I can play, but I've never had the sweetness of your voice,' smiled Eliana. 'How about I play something now? You can sing for me.'

Kisha grinned and nodded. It was just like when they were children – Eliana's fingers flew over the strings, plucking out the intricate melody of their lullaby, while Kisha sang the words in her beautifully rich voice.

All too soon, Ashan reappeared in the doorway looking apologetic. 'Sorry, ladies. It is time for Kisha to return to her rooms.'

The sisters hugged as if they would never let each other go – each one feeling how much the other needed her. At length, they broke apart, all unwillingly.

'Take care of yourself,' whispered Eliana, feeling foolish. The words seemed so inadequate.

'You too,' replied Kisha, as Ashan took her arm and led her away, leaving her sister alone with her thoughts again.

*

The next day was a long and boring one for Eliana. She slept in the morning after Samsu departed, as she always did, but her afternoon was quiet and dull with no walk to break it up. Ashan was being kept busy by his duties and did not find time to visit, so she sat with nothing to turn to but her own mind.

She spent most of the day reliving Kisha's visit. Despite her drawn face and the paleness of her complexion, her sister had looked beautiful. Pregnancy suited her.

Eliana did not forget to pray that day; she prayed to Enlil to intercede with the other gods for Kisha – to send her an easy birth, for her child to be the little prince so desired by both his parents, and to be freed in time to be with her sister at the birth.

When Samsu returned to his rooms after dinner, the evening passed in much the usual way. He lounged on his bed reading, picking at a dish of honeyed dates as Eliana played a soothing tune. If it hadn't been for the Brute at his guard post and the chain about her neck, she was sure that it might have passed for a scene of domestic bliss.

A knock at the door shattered their harmony. 'Enter!' barked Samsu, displeased by the disturbance.

The door edged open and a short man stepped inside, wringing his hands nervously. His frame was spare and wiry, with eyes that seemed over-large for his face, a beak-like nose and thin wisps of copper hair plastered to his head; he distinctly resembled an owl. Eliana struggled to repress a giggle as she looked at him.

The laughter died in her throat when he spoke. 'Sir, your concubine is in labour.'

No, no it was too early. The baby had weeks to go yet.

'How long?' asked Samsu sharply.

'She began in the early hours of the morning, before the sun was risen.'

'And? Out with it man – physicians do not usually attend me to tell me when my women are in labour. I only need to know about the outcome, not the process.'

'The baby is stuck, sir.'

Chapter 14

Stuck.

The word echoed in Eliana's ears, repeating itself until it was nothing but a deafening thrum filling her mind. Another word began to creep in, growing louder and louder, beating in her head as steady as a drum.

No. No. No, no, NO!

'What is the danger?' Samsu was saying.

'You may have to choose, sir. The life of the mother or the child.'

'The child then,' he answered without hesitation. 'Children take months to grow, but new concubines are easily found. Cut it out of her if you have to; I need an heir.'

'No!' screamed Eliana, leaping to her feet. 'You can't! Not Kisha – no!' She thrashed against the chain, trying to snap it, pull it from the wall, break her collar – anything to get to her sister's bedside.

Samsu gave her a mild look and turned back to the physician, 'But before you do, bring this one a sedative. I cannot abide hysteria.'

'Sir,' the physician bowed and retreated.

'Let me go!' shrieked Eliana in a frenzy. 'I have to go to her. You can't keep me here!'

He chuckled, 'I think you'll find that I can.'

'No!' She fought harder against her restraints. 'She needs me!'

'She *needs* to deliver my son safe and intact.'

'You heartless bastard! If you ever loved your sister, you'd let me go to mine!'

Samsu raised an eyebrow and gave a nod to the Brute at his post. He walked towards Eliana, flexing his fingers. She was too full of fire and desperation to care, pulling against her chain, leaning out to meet him in her anger.

He aimed a vicious blow at her face – she ducked at the last second and he struck only air.

She barely had time to register the surge of triumph before the Brute brought his fist down on the back of her head – with a blinding flash of pain, her knees buckled and she fell onto the cushions. Within seconds the Brute had her on her back, pinning both her arms with one powerful hand, using the other to steady his balance against the wall and kneeling across her legs with a weight so crushing she thought her bones would turn to powder.

Still, she fought; heedless of the pain, she writhed and twisted like a snake, thrashing her head and torso. The Brute bared his teeth and laughed at her.

The physician's owl-face appeared above her, a drinking bowl in his hand, his brow wrinkled in concern. 'Sir, I cannot administer the draught while she moves so much.'

'Sedating a whore should not be a three-man job.' Samsu sighed and slid from his bed. He twisted his hand into the hair at her scalp and held her head immobile, pulling it up a little so that the physician could tip the tincture down her throat.

Keeping her mouth firmly closed, Eliana stared at Samsu, her black eyes burning with a hatred deeper than she would have ever known she could feel. She knew that she was fighting the inevitable, that he would have her sedated one way or another, but every moment the physician was here was another moment of life for Kisha – perhaps giving the baby precious time to right itself and come unassisted into the world.

Samsu rolled his eyes and pinched her nose, preventing her from breathing. She held out for torturous seconds, perhaps half a minute or more, her lungs aflame and screaming for air, before her body betrayed her and her mouth burst open to suck in a quick gasp of air.

The physician moved like lightning, tipping the bitter mixture down her throat the moment her mouth opened so that she inhaled as much of it as she swallowed. It burned and stung – she coughed and spluttered as she tried to clear it from her lungs, fighting to free her hands so that she might sit up and force herself to vomit before the potion could begin its awful work.

Samsu saw her intent. 'Hold her until it takes effect,' he commanded the Brute, letting go of her hair and nose and moving to resume his relaxed posture on the bed.

The physician disappeared to tend to Kisha.

Eliana screamed and fought as long as she was able; within minutes, the draught affected her. Her screams became whispers, and her limbs grew as stiff and heavy as tree boughs. The world began to dim and she could fight no longer as the blackness crept over her eyes and slowed her heart rate.

*

Her head throbbed. It was dark outside. Torches flamed in their brackets; the dancing light hurt her eyes. She felt like her brain was made of unspun wool, and her arms and legs might have been iron.

A pulse of nausea tugged at her stomach, and a black shadow seemed to be pressing down on her. Something terrible had happened, but she could not remember what it was.

She lifted her head weakly, looking around. The room was as neat and in order as it always was. Ashan sat on the floor cushions a short distance away, discussing a tablet with… Samsu.

At the sight of him, all her memories came flooding back.

'Kisha!' she tried to shout, tried to stand, but her knees would not support her weight, and the shout was barely a sigh.

Nonetheless, Samsu heard it.

'Ah, *karkittu*. You're awake, I see. Have you quite recovered from your hysteria?'

'What have you done with Kisha?' she tried to sound strong, but her voice rasped out of her throat as though it had been dragged over sand all the way.

'I have not done anything with your sister. I've been here the whole time, watching you sleep, and very peaceful you looked, too...'

'Tell me!' she was almost in tears.

He sighed in exasperation. 'The physician cut the baby out of her, as I ordered. The concubine is dead...'

Eliana screamed – a high-pitched wail of grief that tore from the very heart of her.

'... And all for nothing. She bore another useless daughter – a sickly thing unlikely to live out the night.'

She collapsed, sobbing wildly.

'So, it would appear that I have a marital vacancy. Perhaps I'll take you to fill it.'

'No,' she gasped between sobs. 'Please no – let me see her. I don't believe you! You're just saying it to be cruel. Let me see my sister. Please...' she tailed off, struggling for breath.

'Sir, perhaps it might be best to let her go,' Ashan murmured.

Samsu growled, 'I suppose so. I cannot put up with this all night.'

Ashan moved to her and bent to unlock her chain. As soon as she heard the click, Eliana tried to leap to her feet and run – she dropped forward onto her hands and knees; her legs still would not hold her.

Catching her around the waist, Ashan lifted her to her feet as though she were weightless as a *gidim*. He offered his arm as support and began to walk her towards the door – each step was an exhausting effort for Eliana as the drug lingered in her body.

As they reached the door, Samsu called after them, 'See that you return immediately, Ashan. We still have business to tend to.'

'Yes, sir,' Ashan called back over his shoulder, stepping through the door and closing it behind them. As soon as it was safely shut, he picked her up in his arms and strode through the darkness to Kisha's rooms, putting Eliana down just over the threshold.

She stumbled her way to Kisha's bedroom, struggling to maintain her balance and avoid the obstacles in the dark.

A light flickered through the door to the bedchamber.

Clinging to the doorframe, she took in the scene.

The only light in the room came from the lamp burning beside Kisha's bed, the orange flame vividly illuminating sheets so saturated with blood that they were almost black. Mari sat on a stool beside the bed, keeping vigil, clutching a tiny bundle in her arms.

Though the sheets were bloodied, Kisha was clean. She had been carefully sponged off, and her face looked at peace. Eliana approached the bed and tentatively touched her sister's arm. It was already cold, the skin waxen and unreal in the quivering lamplight.

She gave another heartbroken wail and fell to her knees at the bedside, sobbing as she clutched her sister's lifeless hand.

Mari and Ashan exchanged uncomfortable looks.

Eliana sensed them watching and turned to face them, her eyes blazing with sudden fury. 'Get out!' she cried. 'Both of you – go! Leave us alone.'

'Are you sure?' Ashan asked, his voice soft.

'I was chained up,' she hissed bitterly. 'What's your excuse? Both of you were free, and neither of you saved her.'

Mari opened her mouth to protest – there was nothing they could have done, Eliana knew it as well as they did. Ashan caught her eye shook his head in silence – the agony was fresh, and she must blame someone, anyone, everyone for it.

They left quietly, closing the door behind them.

Eliana sobbed herself into exhaustion. When she had no more tears to shed, she climbed up onto the bloodied bed and curled up against Kisha's cold body, as if she might infuse her sister with some of her own warmth and life.

When she woke in the morning, her gown and skin were stained with Kisha's blood. Numb and half-dead herself, Eliana was too full of grief to think. The first thing her eyes took in when she opened them was Kisha's face – for a moment, she could have been sleeping, but she was too pale, and the metallic-smelling stickiness beneath her brought the reality back with crushing misery.

A small bundle had been placed between them – a tiny, tiny baby. Eliana sat upright, picked the child up and cradled it in the crook of her arm. It struggled to breathe – each inhalation sounding harsh and laboured.

'She still needs a name.' Mari sat on a stool in the corner of the room, watching over Eliana and the baby.

Looking down at her newest niece, Eliana was stunned that she had survived the night. She was perfect in every detail from her littlest toe to the delicate whorl of her ears, but so small, so delicate… almost translucent.

Eliana shook her head. 'Later. I'll name her later. Where's Sarri?'

'She's playing quietly in my room – she's been calling for her mother.'

'And what have you told her?'

'I've given her excuses – mother is busy, sleeping, bathing… anything but the truth. I don't know how much she understands.'

Eyes filling with tears again, Eliana thought of these two tiny, defenceless girls alone in the palace, with no mother to protect them and an aunt no better than a slave. They had been robbed of their mother as she had been robbed of hers… only far more cruelly – they lost theirs by their father's word.

'It is for me to make her understand,' Eliana said heavily. 'I owe her that much. Help me change my gown – I don't want to go to her stained with her mother's blood,' she glanced down at the babe in her arms. 'It's time she met this little one. I only hope that she looks after her baby sister as well as Kisha did.'

*

Eliana dressed Kisha for eternity – a sapphire-blue tiered gown, gilded sandals at her feet, a circlet of gold set on her brow as a marker of her status. Her blue-black curls were washed and brushed out until they shone, forming a soft bed beneath her body. As a final touch, Eliana clipped their mother's lapis bracelet around Kisha's wrist in the hopes that it might give her a smile when she reached the underworld.

Perhaps it would also help their mother to recognise Kisha's shade – she had been so very small when they last saw each other.

Kisha was taken away to be entombed, the bed was cleaned, every trace of blood was washed from the floor, but the rooms would never feel like home again. The sun that warmed them had been extinguished.

Trying to make Sarri understand had been so difficult. She welcomed her new baby sister with a delighted squeal, and her aunt with a wary gaze. It had not occurred to Eliana that her niece would no longer know her – she had been away for more than five moons, almost half the girl's life – she had only celebrated her first birthday six weeks before. Too young to understand the finality of death, but old enough to understand that Eliana was not her mother, Sarri had wailed for hours when Kisha did not come.

Eliana cried with her.

Eventually, Sarri quieted and snuggled into her aunt, snuffling and hiccupping occasionally as she caught her breath. She was a pretty little thing, with a cloud of dark curls and big black eyes like her mother's, framed by long lashes. She would be a beauty when she was older.

Eliana was almost grateful that the girl was so small that she would not remember her mother as she grew. It would be less painful for her that way.

By turns numb with grief and fired with anger, Eliana tried to keep herself occupied – with a lively little one and a newborn in the rooms, there was plenty to do, and always a child to watch. Sarri had grown so much in her absence; she was pulling herself up on the furniture and toddling about, trying out her favourite word, telling anyone who would listen, 'No!'

Everything was interesting to her – Eliana and Mari had to be careful to keep everything not meant for her little hands well out of reach.

Just four days after Kisha's body was taken away, Ashan knocked at the door.

Mari answered it while Eliana sat watching the newborn have her feed from a wetnurse. Her heart sank as she looked at Ashan's face – his expression was grim; this wasn't a social call.

'What does he want now?' she cut straight to the heart of the matter, not bothering with a greeting.

'He wants to see you – you're to come with me now.'

'I'm busy. He can wait.'

'He doesn't wait.'

'Well he'll have to. I refuse to go.'

Ashan sighed. He had hoped that she wouldn't be stubborn – now that her chain was off, she was asserting control over her own movements again.

'You can't refuse – you know that he'll get you there one way or another.'

She shrugged, uncaring. Her hatred for Samsu was eating her alive – he was entirely to blame for her sister's death, and she could not be sure what she would do when she next came face-to-face with him.

'Eliana!' Ashan barked, using his military voice. 'If you do not come with me, the prince may send his Brute after you, and then the girls will be in danger. Is that what you want?'

She shot him a withering look, 'Of course it isn't. Don't be ridiculous.'

'Then you'll come?'

'Fine!' she stood abruptly, handing the baby to Mari. 'Take them out somewhere,' she instructed. 'Anywhere. The gardens, the bathhouses, I don't care. Just take them somewhere that isn't these rooms, where they can't be immediately found and used as leverage over me.'

Mari gave her a suspicious look, 'What are you planning?'

'I'm not *planning* anything, and therein lies the danger. I don't know what I'm going to do or say, so get these girls out for a walk.'

'Don't do anything stupid,' pleaded Mari, going to collect Sarri from her playroom.

Without waiting for Ashan, Eliana turned and strode from the room, towards Samsu's apartments. He chased after her, 'Don't be an idiot, Eliana. He's well-disposed towards you, for now. Don't jeopardise it!'

She didn't answer.

When she reached the door to Samsu's rooms, she barged straight in without knocking. 'You wanted to see me, *sir*?' There was just a hint of a sneer in her voice.

If he heard it, he ignored it. 'Yes, *karkittu*. I've decided that I will take you as my new concubine. The ceremony will take place next week.'

'When Utu falls from the sky, it will,' Eliana fired back, quivering with rage.

His eyes narrowed dangerously. 'I beg your pardon?'

'I will never give my consent to this marriage.'

'Fortunately, I do not require your consent.'

'You'll have to drag me there – I'll kick and scream all the way!'

'If that's what it takes,' Samsu raised his voice, beginning to get irritated. 'Ungrateful whore! You should be honoured.'

A smug feeling of triumph at his annoyance smothered any fear she might have felt. 'Well I am not *honoured*. I am disgusted. You murder my sister and seek to put me into her place? I will not.'

'You will, if I command it,' he growled.

'You can force me to the altar, bind me to you with your strange ceremonies and foreign ways, but I will never love you, never respect you, never willingly obey unless I choose to. I don't even think I fear you anymore. You will find no easy, pliant wife in me as you had with Kisha.'

'I do not want an easy, pliant wife,' he said, coming to stand so close that she could feel the heat radiating from his body. 'I want *you*, may Marduk have pity on me. You may never love me; that, I do not demand. But you will respect me, and you *will* fear me.'

Slowly, deliberately, she spat at his feet.

Every muscle in him tensed.

'Have you forgotten how to bow, *karkittu*?' he hissed. 'Perhaps you've been too long in my company, grown too accustomed to taking liberties. Bow!'

She did not move, did not step back, but continued to stare him full in the face, her eyes full of insolence.

'I said, *BOW*!' stepping swiftly to one side, Samsu drove his foot into the backs of Eliana's knees, knocking her to the floor.

She immediately got to her feet. He clenched his fist and delivered an iron blow to her stomach.

The pain was so intense that sparks danced before her eyes as she doubled over, stifling a groan. Forcing the air back into her lungs, she straightened up to face him again.

He raised an eyebrow, 'A smart whore would stay down.'

'Then I suppose I am a stupid whore,' she retorted. 'Why would you want to marry a stupid whore?'

'Because I say I do!' he slapped her face; her head snapped back with the force.

Whipping her head straight again, she did something she would never have dared had she thought about it first – she slapped him back.

Striking him across the cheek with all her strength, a satisfying *crack* resounded about the room. His cheek reddened within seconds.

He exhaled slowly, his eyes blazing now. An unexpected hand of panic gripped her gut – she had pushed too far.

His hand snaked out and caught her forearm, gripping painfully tightly; he yanked her up onto her tiptoes, so that her eyes were level with his. Catching a glimpse of the sudden fear, he bared his teeth in satisfaction. 'I told you that you would fear me.' He threw her to the ground so hard that her head bounced – she felt the skin split where her forehead struck the tiles; blood began to seep down the side of her face.

Samsu drove a brutal kick into her face. Her lip split to match her forehead, stickiness oozing over her chin. He followed it with a boot to the midriff – she felt a crack in her chest with the impact.

Pulling herself into a ball, she tried to protect her head and stomach as the blows landed on every side with sickening force, pain exploding all over her body.

'Sir!'

She heard Ashan's voice as if from a great distance – muffled and vague-sounding. 'She is no use to you dead!'

Samsu grunted and stamped on her leg with all his weight. 'Take her away,' he growled. 'Ungrateful bitch. See that she's kept out of my sight until the wedding.'

She whimpered in pain when Ashan picked her up as gently as he could. It was a blessed relief when her consciousness began to slip away – she did not fight it, but let the darkness claim her.

*

Eliana's next fortnight was spent in bed.

The obsequious, owl-like physician had come to examine her, diagnosing two cracked ribs, a split lip, severe bruising and a broken skull. For her pain, he left some more of the potion that had drugged her the day of Kisha's death. She had Mari pour it into the chamberpot – she would never drink anything he gave her. He ordered two weeks' bed rest for her.

Eliana felt a little guilty; confined to her bed, she could do nothing to help Mari, who now had her hands full as the sole carer for two small girls and an invalid. No visitors were permitted to the apartments, with the exception of the physician, and Eliana would have preferred never to see him again.

But she did not regret standing up to Samsu, whatever the outcome. She had said what she longed to say, and she had struck him. Hatred was slowly overcoming fear.

The two weeks of quiet were good for Eliana. They gave her time to come to terms with her loss – she wept, she mourned, she raged, she remembered. She waited for Kisha to come and tend her, as she always had during times of sickness. Only her shade visited – Eliana dreamed of her sister the night of Samsu's attack; they had clung to each other, bidding their final farewells. As Kisha began to melt into the shadows, she whispered one word – *Kisuri*.

The newborn had a name at last.

At the end of the fortnight, Ashan came to visit.

Eliana was dressed and sat up on the bed playing with Sarri when he arrived. He gave a tentative smile, as if not sure of his welcome. She beckoned him over and called for Mari to take Sarri away.

'What brings you here now?' she asked.

'The prince sent me to see if you're well enough and looking pretty enough to be married in two weeks.'

'And what will you tell him?'

'What would you like me to tell him?'

'I would *like* you to tell him that I will never be well enough to marry him… but if you cannot tell him that, tell him three weeks instead of two.'

He smiled briefly, but his expression turned serious again. 'You won't try anything like that again, will you? With Samsu, I mean. He might kill you next time. When the red mist descends, he's like a wild animal – he barely knows what he's doing. If I hadn't been there…'

'I might,' she sighed. 'I don't care if he kills me – I won't be trampled over any longer. I hate him with every part of my being.'

'Hush!' he urged. 'Do you hate him because of what happened to Kisha?'

'Of course! And for a dozen other reasons besides.'

'Well, ask yourself: if Kisha had been given the choice – what would she have chosen?'

'Life!'

'But life for whom? It was her life, or the baby's. Whose would she have chosen?'

Eliana looked away, tears clouding her vision. 'The baby's,' she whispered.

Ashan took her hand, 'Kisha's daughters need you. The people of Nippur need you. *I* need you. Don't defy Samsu and die pointlessly – you can do so much more good in the world if you live.'

'But I can't live without her,' the tears spilled down Eliana's cheeks.

He wiped the tears away. 'She would want you to, Elly.'

His use of her sister's pet name for her was a shock – she forgot to breathe momentarily, trying to decide whether the diminutive sounded right or wrong on his tongue. He leaned in and tucked a stray curl behind her ear, his breath sweet and warm on her cheek.

Before she knew what was happening, they were kissing. It was urgent, intense – not the soft and gentle kisses she had had from him before. She liked it – there was an edge of desperation, of need.

She twined her fingers into his hair and kept his mouth on hers until she felt faint; losing her balance, she toppled backwards onto the sheets, pulling him down with her, barely aware of the pain in her half-healed body. He looked at her in surprise.

Not giving him time to think, she kissed him again, arching her back to press her body down the length of his.

Ashan groaned in response, sweeping a hand from her neck, over her breasts, into the curve of her waist and down the side of her thigh. It was as if his hand was alight, for every part of her that he touched was set afire with longing for him.

He kissed her again, deeply, her lips opening under his and encouraging him. Touching her, caressing her, Ashan seemed on the very edge of self-restraint.

Giving a frustrated sigh he pulled away. 'We shouldn't be doing this. Is this what you really want?'

'Yes,' she whispered. 'Is it what you want?'

He began to fumble with her gown in reply, pushing it up to her hips and freeing himself from his tunic. He brushed lightly against her, teasing as he positioned himself. Even then, he stopped to ask, 'Are you sure?'

Eliana grabbed his shoulders and arched her hips into his in response. He slid in easily – she gasped, shivering with an arousal she had never felt before in her young life. Holding his weight carefully on his elbows so as not to further damage her ribs, he made love to her as she had never known it could be done. Tender and considerate, he listened to her responses, seemed keen to give her the pleasure that she had never known was possible. For just a moment, she felt truly, uniquely happy.

When Ashan was spent and she was exhausted, they lay together in silence for several minutes, their hearts beating as one. For the first time, Eliana did not feel dirty. She had given herself to Ashan, not expecting to enjoy it, because she wanted to make him happy – she hadn't been expecting to feel like he had given something of himself to her, too.

There was a little pang of sadness in her stomach as he slid from the bed. 'This can't happen again, can it?'

He shook his head, and murmured, 'But I'm glad it happened once. I love you, Elly.'

Placing a little kiss on her forehead, he drew the sheet up over her as she drifted into sleep.

Chapter 15

The day of the wedding came around far too quickly for Eliana's liking, even with the extra week's grace that Ashan had won her.

She knew very little of what to expect from the ceremony, beyond what she had seen of Kisha's wedding almost three years ago. From what Ashan had told her, this would be a far grander affair than her sister's marriage. He could not explain why – perhaps it was an indication of Samsu's respect for her, he suggested. When she pulled a disbelieving face, he shrugged, adding that it might be an attempt to gain some popularity with the people by putting on a grand spectacle for them.

That sounded more likely.

A wedding would traditionally take place in the house of the bride's father, as responsibility for her wellbeing and ownership of her person passed from father to new husband. For Eliana, it would have been farcical to be married in her father's house – Samsu owned her; he had made that clear on the day he fastened the collar around her neck.

She had grown used to it now, the warm metal almost a comforting shield at her neck. She could barely remember what it felt like to be without it – it had been part of her for over a year.

The ceremony, Ashan said, was to take place at the base of Enlil's temple, now given over to the worship of Marduk. To ensure a son this time, Samsu wanted the marriage blessed by his god, and so it would take place in sight of his house.

A dressmaker was sent to measure Eliana for a gown worthy of the occasion, and what he produced was truly magnificent. The golden shimmer of the fabric was like liquid sunlight, the tailoring exquisitely crafted to Eliana's shape, and the five tiers of the gown were so encrusted with beading that the creation could almost stand unassisted.

On the day of the wedding, Mari helped her into it, straightening and arranging each segment so that it lay perfectly under the next. Eliana's hair was washed and combed through with jasmine oil before being pinned into an elaborate and ornamented style so that some curls were plaited atop her head and secured with gold and emerald pins, while others were left to flow freely down her back or fashioned into soft spirals to frame her pale face.

Eliana lined her eyes with malachite, darkened her lashes with kohl and applied subtle vermillion to her lips and cheeks. Her entire body had been decorated with breathtaking henna designs yesterday – originally, Mari had only intended to decorate her arms and legs, but they had had so much fun over the patterning and symbolism that they soon got carried away, and Eliana's skin became a living canvas for Mari's art.

She wore the gold leaf-shaped earrings that Samsu had given her when she had first pleased him so many months ago. With her collar being so eyecatching, there was no need for more jewellery, though she felt a little twinge of regret at having buried her mother's bracelet with Kisha. She would have liked to have a little piece of her family with her on this day. Although she had resigned herself to the fact that it must happen, she still felt a knot of nerves in her stomach at the thought of being at the centre of such a ceremony.

She was nothing more than an ornament, she told herself. She must stand and look pretty, and follow where she was directed. Everything would be fine.

It was almost midday when Ashan's knock sounded on the door. He had come to collect her for the procession through the city to the temple. She slipped her feet into gold-and-beaded sandals, and was ready to go.

His eyes widened when he saw her, his thoughts written on his face. She looked like Inanna come to earth – the goddess renowned for her transcendent beauty. Wordlessly, he offered his arm. She took it and followed him with her head held high, projecting a confidence she did not feel.

He led her through a part of the palace she had never seen before, bringing them out into the front courtyard where Samsu waited for her upon his towering chestnut stallion, surrounded by a mounted guard. In contrast to his wedding to Kisha, he had dressed for the occasion. The tunic he wore was a match for her gown, created from the same fabric that could have been spun from the rays of the sun.

Samsu nodded in satisfaction when he saw her. 'Good, let's go.'

Ashan lifted her onto a roan mare and the procession set off through the imposing north gate – when she entered, it had been through the servants' small eastern gate. It felt like a lifetime ago.

A band of slaves and heralds went ahead to clear the streets, closely followed by Samsu, surrounded by his mounted guards. A short distance after, Eliana followed, enclosed by four armed guards of her own – they walked alongside her, keeping perfect step with the horse.

She was a beautiful little mare, the ghostly paleness of her coat contrasting starkly with her blaze of red mane and tail. Snorting, she tossed her head impatiently and curvetted, eager to trot, to canter, to gallop. She chafed at the stately pace of the procession. Calming her with a gentle hand on the neck, Eliana knew just how she felt. She had not been outside the palace walls for almost two years – the old familiar sights of the city warmed her heart beyond words. It was all she could do not to leap from the horse and run off to explore – she wanted to see if the baker still conducted his business from the lopsided shop down that side street she had just passed, whether the merchant's wharf still bustled alongside the canal, and the farmers still employed the small boys of the street to chase the crows from the fields of new-planted seeds.

The citizens of Nippur lined the dusty streets to watch Samsu pass – they did not cheer, nor did they create trouble. The tension simmered like water over the fire. Eliana was grateful that the Nippurites were sensible enough to keep the peace, even if they did not give Samsu precisely what he wanted.

They smiled at Eliana though, many making encouraging gestures of blessing and good wishes. She smiled back at them, giving little waves where she could, though her guards shot her unpleasant looks when she tried to engage with the crowds.

In truth, she was startled by what she saw. The city's buildings were in a considerably worse state of decay than when she had last seen them, and evidence of increased poverty was all around her: half-starved children with wide eyes; unmended damage to property; the patched and torn clothing of a formerly fashionable and proud people.

She did not let her shock show, but continued to smile and wave while plotting how she might sway Samsu to policies that might improve the everyday lives of the average Nippurite.

The procession wound its way down the main thoroughfare. They rounded a corner, and the entrance to the great house of Enlil came into view. The *ziggurat* was a lofty pyramid constructed entirely of red brick, seven tiers high and faced with yellow glazing, it was a truly breathtaking sight. *Ekur*, the house of the mountain, was aptly named. Atop the *ziggurat* sat a modest temple – the house when Enlil dwelt, and no mortal man dared to venture. It was said that even the High Priest of Enlil was forbidden access.

As the dwelling place of the gods, the temple complex was not traditionally a place for communal worship or public ceremonies, but since it had been given over to Marduk, the Babylonian customs were beginning to take root.

Still, only priests were permitted to set foot on the *ziggurat* or in the rooms at its base. The marriage of Samsu and Eliana would take place in the forecourt – within sight of Marduk's house, and so close that he could easily make his displeasure known if he did not wish to bless the union.

Part of Eliana still hoped that the Babylonian god would intervene where her own had failed. Perhaps he would not approve of her. Perhaps he would send some sign of anger and the ceremony would be halted.

She knew that she was hoping against hope. The gods had not taken much interest in what she wanted so far.

They reached the temple and dismounted outside. Samsu took Eliana's hand and led her through the great arched entrance. An altar had been set up in the centre of the courtyard – before the purification pond. The open space was flanked by aisles along either side; rooms for the priests led off the aisles, along with innumerable small temples to the pantheon of gods and goddesses that formed Enlil's court.

A podium and a mudbrick table for animal and vegetable sacrifices were set at one end of the forecourt. Eliana was relieved to see the table laden with produce – it would not be necessary to spill blood, even animal blood, on her wedding day. Behind the podium lay the granaries and storehouses.

Fish leapt in the pond, and Eliana was taken back to that moment on the day of Kisha's wedding where they had held hands and gazed into their father's pond together. A bittersweet memory.

Back then, she could never have dreamed what would happen in the few short years to come. Now she stood in her sister's place, and Kisha lay cold under the earth.

The guests had been allotted their places before Samsu's arrival, and the priest stood ready at the altar. The prince wasted no time, marching her straight up to the altar, leaving his Babylonians to fall in behind him and arrange themselves in the remaining space on the benches. Eliana's heart gave a little leap to see her father amongst the Nippurites assembled there. He was given a prominent position, his face greyer and more drawn than ever. She pitied him – this was a painful finality for her father, a confirmation of the fact that he would never have either of his daughters back. One was buried in the ground, the other entombed behind palace walls.

The nerves built as she approached the altar, but she forced herself to keep putting one foot before the other as Samsu propelled her along. This was it; she was to be sealed inside the gilded cage. Samsu had claimed ownership over her by right of conquest, but now he would have her in law.

She forced her mind to quiet – she would think about it later, when the deed was done. She would think about it tomorrow, when it was too late to change. If she thought about it too hard now, she would bolt like a frightened horse.

Releasing her in front of the altar, Samsu looked at her pointedly. With a jolt of realisation, she remembered Kisha's bow at the start of the proceedings and sank to her knees, touching her forehead to the floor.

Samsu raised her up and nodded to the priest.

The rites were just as they had been for Kisha's wedding. Beginning with the invocation of Marduk and a plea for his blessing, followed by the sprinkling of the grain and a prayer for Eliana's fertility, the priest went on to bind Eliana's hand to Samsu's with a coarse hair rope. The sensation of her bare skin pressed against his still made her stomach churn with revulsion. In Marduk's name, the priest commanded her to faithfulness, honesty, loyalty and obedience before anointing the pair and their binding with holy oil, untying the rope and repeating the prayer he had opened with.

It was all so familiar to Eliana, and she lived through it as though she were a spectator again, imagining that it was Kisha stood at the altar, alive and well, with endless life stretching out before her.

She was snapped out of her trance when Samsu did not immediately drag her back up the aisle to return her to captivity in the palace. Instead, he raised he hand and made a curt beckoning gesture. Ashan stepped up behind him, a slave at his heels.

Ashan held out a small, golden key. Eliana's heart leapt – she did not quite dare to believe in what she hoped was about to happen.

Samsu reached behind her, fitting the key into the lock of her collar. To Eliana, the smooth click as the mechanism released was the sweetest note ever sounded. He lifted the heavy gold from her narrow shoulders and handed it to Ashan. She felt curiously light without it, as though she might float away into the ether without its weight to keep her grounded. Enlil was god of the wind, perhaps he hadn't entirely abandoned his house; his breeze on her bare skin was the sweetest kiss she had ever felt.

'A slave no longer,' Samsu intoned. 'Now, my wife.'

What's the difference? Eliana wondered, but she had the sense not to speak.

The slave stepped up from behind Ashan, extending a cushion. Samsu picked up the slender golden circlet that sat atop it. It was not unlike the one she had buried Kisha in, but this one was set with emerald and fashioned to look like a crown of leaves and flowers – a perfect match for the earrings.

He placed it on her head, settling it amongst her curls so that the leaves banded her forehead. She tilted her head back and looked him in the eyes. As their gazes locked, she could have sworn she glimpsed some warmth.

It was gone as quickly as it had come.

Samsu took her hand and marched back up the aisle – the ceremony complete, he had no desire to linger. As she turned from the altar, her heart stopped momentarily. A pair of familiar figures hovered in the shadows. She knew their silhouettes very well – Kisha smiled gently at her sister, hands clasped over her belly; half a step behind her, his arm protectively around her waist, Isin's accusing stare was gone, replaced by an expression of soft compassion.

She caught sight of them only in a fleeting glance as she turned, when she twisted her head to look back over her shoulder, they were gone.

As Eliana was led back to the palace only half a horse behind her husband, the crowds cheered her again. Samsu was pleased, allowing himself to believe that their acclaim was for him. She smiled graciously at them – she was still only a concubine, but she could be the mother of their future ruler. In her, the citizens of Nippur saw a better future for their children.

As they rode back to the palace, Eliana was beginning to feel quite self-conscious. Though she had been a focus of attention for hundreds of people over the course of the day, she only felt uneasy now, under Ashan's gaze. Almost every time she glanced at him, he was staring at her. As soon as she caught him, he would look away. She tried to read his face in the split second before he wiped it clean of emotion – there was a strange sort of hunger in his eyes that made her squirm.

He tried to stop himself from looking at her, tried to occupy his mind elsewhere, but his gaze kept sliding back to her, riding her fine pale horse as well as any man, shimmering in the sun like a gilded statue. Utu's rays reflected from the gold of her gown, her circlet and her hair ornaments, creating a bright halo; it was as if the divine light of a goddess emanated from within her.

He watched her, remembering the unearthly joy of being in her bed, her warm thighs wrapped around his back, pulling him deeper. His mouth pressed to hers, stifling her breathy gasps of pleasure and delight, urging her to quiet. The softness of her breasts under his palms. The way she writhed with arousal when he had kissed the tender skin of her neck. He had an almost unbearable desire to be with her again; it was all he could do to keep his hands from her, let alone his eyes.

He was becoming a danger to himself, he knew. He could not let his desire for one woman be the death of him; for it surely would be, if Samsu noticed.

It had been agony, standing there impassively, watching her at the altar being bound to a man she hated, the man he had grown up with as a brother. Though she had belonged to Samsu in word before, she was truly his property now, in deed and in the sight of Marduk. The great god had witnessed the bond and blessed the marriage. To be with her now would be to risk his wrath... and Samsu's.

There were few things Samsu took so seriously as betrayal. Once, when they were children, Ashan had repeated a secret of Samsu's to his mother; always the better fighter, the older boy had beaten him bloody for it in their next combat training session.

As the wedding party re-entered the palace through the magnificent north gate, Ashan couldn't help but notice the slight droop in Eliana's shoulders.

It was like an iron cloak being draped around her as they came through the arched gate, a great weight of sadness pulling her down. She had felt alive again, out in the city; now, she couldn't help but wonder how long it might be until she would be permitted to leave again.

The Brute lifted her from her horse, setting her on her feet a little harder than necessary. Samsu beckoned – she went to him. He took her arm to lead her to the great hall for the marriage feast.

Eliana felt Kisha's absence keenly as she sat on a lower chair to the left of Samsu's great throne, a full head below him. An empty chair, smaller, but still a polished and carved throne, was placed to his right. Susa had snubbed the ceremony and the celebratory feast. She would have no part of it, she said. It shamed her husband's noble line for him to marry a whore.

With Asag on her other side, Eliana had nobody to talk to. Nerves and loneliness twisted her stomach – she could not relax, sat between these two men who had brought her nothing but misery. The banquet was less grand than the one for the emissaries, but there was still good food in vast quantities, an assortment of high-ranking guests draped in bright silks and glittering jewels, and a wild array of eclectic entertainments. She picked politely at the dishes that were set in front of her, but for once she had no real appetite; instead, she focused on the performers or watched the people as they drank and laughed, argued and flattered, danced and brawled.

Nobody paid her the slightest bit of attention, despite the fact that the feast was ostensibly in honour of her marriage. Still, she was on the dais – a vast step-up from where she had sat at the last celebration. Kisha had never been accorded these honours. She supposed that Kisha had never earned Samsu's respect in quite the same way. Her ribs still ached when she breathed too deeply, or sneezed, or coughed, or laughed. The respect was hard-won.

The party seemed interminable. The wine flowed as freely as if the canal was suddenly flooded with it, and the empty jugs began to stack up against the far wall. Innumerable dishes of delicacies were paraded out – more food than a congregation twice this size could ever hope to consume. Her blood boiled a little as she thought of the starving children she had seen on her procession route earlier that day.

She had lost track of the hours by the time the last entertainment finished and the dishes began to be cleared away. Samsu, roaring drunk and telling some boisterous war anecdote in the midst of a crowd of his soldiers, did not notice as a pair of female body slaves came to take Eliana away.

They were to prepare her for the marriage bed, they told her. Eliana snorted, 'That's ridiculous! It's hardly going to be the first time he has had me, nor even the hundredth.'

'We merely obey the great prince, my lady,' the girls said, softly, apologetically, as they guided her with insistent hands to the bathhouse.

She was washed, scrubbed, purified and perfumed all over again. They slipped a sheer gown over her head – she shuddered as it touched her skin, reminding her of her humiliating slave dresses. She should be used to them by now, she supposed, but she would never get used to the fact that her body was not her own property.

The girls decorated her, painting her eyelids with gold and using ochre to give her cheeks a maidenly blush, despite her scoffing at the idea. Leading her to Samsu's chambers, they helped her up onto his bed and arranged her prettily for him to find – straightening her skirt and smoothing her hair over one shoulder. They reclined her and placed a cushion underneath her, forcing her to arch her back, creating an attractive line that emphasised the dip of her slender waist and the swell of her breasts.

When they were satisfied that they could do no more to please Samsu, the girls bowed and took their leave, and Eliana's wait began.

After half an hour, a head peered around the doorframe.

'My lady?' Resu's gruff voice was a sound to soothe the ears.

'Resu! Forgive me if I do not stand to speak to you – those girls spent so long arranging me that I should hate to move and spoil all their hard work. I feel like a lump of clay that they have spent all evening moulding into shape.'

He smiled, 'And very well they have done their work too, my lady. I just wanted to offer my congratulations on your marriage. The prince had me clear away your cushions and your chain – I do not think he intends to keep you here again.'

'No,' she agreed. 'He has me bound by a different chain now.'

'I found some personal belongings under your bedding – I returned them to your chambers during the festivities this afternoon.'

'Oh, thank you! I had completely forgotten. I don't even remember what I had.'

He shrugged, 'Just some odd bits and pieces. Herbs, and the like.'

Her smile froze in place, 'Well thank you again, I'm so grateful.'

'My lady,' he disappeared as quietly as he had come.

Her herbs! She hadn't taken them since the day before Kisha died, almost six weeks ago. Quickly, she began to count the weeks.

She counted twice. She should have bled more than a week ago.

A little spark of joy warmed her from the inside; any child she might be carrying could only be Ashan's – she had bled since Samsu last had her.

The spark quickly died, chased away by panic. Samsu knew she had bled – she must endure his attentions stoically for a couple of months before she could plausibly make him believe that the child was his.

But still, the realisation was enough to make her want to hug herself. She said a quiet prayer to the mother goddess that her courses were not merely late, as they sometimes were.

The door creaked open – Samsu's silhouette swayed in the frame, giving Eliana a chill of dread. He walked heavily over to the bed, leering down at her, licking his lips wetly.

'So,' he slurred, 'I have freed you, married you, and honoured you far above what any concubine could ever dream of. Do you have any affection me yet – your new-wedded husband?'

'No,' she said quietly. 'I am not free – I am married. That is the same as being a slave. You forced me into this bondage as you forced me into the chain. I did not choose it, you have simply found a new way to bind me.'

He grunted, 'Ungrateful whore.'

Climbing unsteadily onto the bed, he reached out to touch her face. 'Beautiful whore,' he murmured, his voice thick with wine, eyes lit with anticipation.

Pushing her back, he tugged her gown up to her waist and clumsily pushed his way inside her. She squeezed her eyes tight shut against the pain.

'Open your eyes,' he growled. 'I will have you look at me – you are mine by right, as your husband, whether you will it or not.'

She did as commanded, her clear gaze locking with his. It seemed to arouse him more than ever – he gasped and began to thrust hard.

Eliana fought to keep her eyes as opaque as coal, to hide her disdain and disgust.

Still… she might be imagining it… it might be the drink… or it might just be that she was getting used to his ways, but the ordeal did not feel quite so rough as usual.

The wine sped him on his way, and he spent more quickly than she would have dared to dream. As he rolled off her and sprawled on the bed beside her, already asleep, her heart lifted with a painful twist of hope. She could be carrying Ashan's child – it was too early to be sure, but it was possible. Almost drowned out by the deafening snores, Eliana repeated her whispered prayer to the mother goddess.

Chapter 16

It was time.

'The Lady Eliana,' the herald announced, '*Sekrutu* to His Royal Highness Samsu, Prince of Babylon, *Lugal* of Nippur.'

Sekrutu. Her new name – meaning *harem woman*, it was no less a barb than *karkittu*. Samsu still called her by his insulting pet name in private, but *Sekrutu* would be her public title.

After two and a half months of marriage, of enduring his attentions almost every night, she was finally ready to tell him. She would announce it in front of the court, to save the news spreading by the servants and palace gossips. She smoothed the violet silk of her gown over her hips, wincing as she brushed over a tender new bruise – another token of Samsu's affections.

Walking slowly, with as much dignity as she could muster, she held her head up and ignored the venomous stares from Susa, in her seat next to Samsu, and Ani and the Brute as they stood off to one side of the dais. Ashan stood with them, trying to keep his face expressionless as he watched her.

She approached the throne and knelt before it, waiting for permission to speak.

'You may rise,' Samsu sounded bored. He chafed against the inactivity of government – he preferred to be out on the battlefield, leading an army. His was a mind for strategy, not mundane matters of politics.

Eliana lifted her forehead from the ground and stood slowly, bringing her head up last. It would not do to have a dizzy spell before him if she stood up too quickly.

'I am with child,' she said, loudly and clearly for the whole room to hear. The audience burst into spontaneous applause as her words took effect – on the dais, Samsu's eyes lit up, while Susa's face contorted as though she sucked a lemon. Ani merely scowled, her expression a perfect reflection of the Brute's.

Ashan's face remained bland, but he felt as though he had just taken a blade to the gut. He had lost her forever. She was truly Samsu's now – she carried a piece of him within her, and when she gave birth, she would forget she had ever loved Ashan; all her love would be for the child.

Samsu nodded. 'You shall be moved to bigger rooms, nearer my own, along with your maidservant and my daughters.'

'Thank you, sir.' Eliana inclined her head, and Samsu waved his hand to dismiss her. She moved to the edge of the room, standing with the other petitioners whose business was concluded.

She took a keen interest in the Nippurites as they came and went with their problems – this one disputed a piece of land with his neighbour, while that one complained that the price of bread had risen too high to feed his family, and another begged a position within the palace for his son. The queue seemed endless.

Her mind worked rapidly through the problems as she heard them, throwing out solutions and compromises, though she kept her tongue still. If Samsu wanted her advice, he would ask for it in private, well away from any who might construe it as weakness. Sometimes he would resolve a matter in exactly the way that she would have, and sometimes he would make it worse with a harsh retribution. Occasionally, his decreed 'justice' made her physically bite her tongue – she *must* not interfere, however unfair he seemed. She wished with all her heart that she might be able to sit up there on the throne in his place, protecting the people from him as Enlil never did. The great god had truly abandoned his holy city.

When an unfortunate, half-emaciated man with wild hair and wilder eyes was dragged in behind a farmer, her heart went out to him. He had attempted to steal a goat, been tried and found guilty, and had nothing with which to pay the fine.

Samsu condemned him to death, according to his father's code of law. Eliana knew that in doing so, he also condemned the man's family to death, for they would surely starve with no-one to provide for them.

She fought back tears as the judgement was pronounced and the man's heart-rending wail shattered the air. Samsu nodded to the Brute, who stepped forward and seized the man by his skeletal upper arm, dragging him through a side door. He screamed again, the sound cut short, followed by a wet thud as the body dropped to the floor.

The Brute walked back out, shaking the blood from his dagger, and returned to his place.

As the afternoon drew on, the stream of petitioners slowed to a trickle. 'Any other business?' called a steward.

'Sir!' Ashan stepped forward. His mother gave him a questioning look. Whatever he had to say, he had not discussed it with her.

'What is it, Ashan?' Samsu was less than pleased, having hoped that the audience was at an end.

'Sir, we are all aware of the recent troubles in Lagash – if we do nothing to curb their vexing behaviour, they may rise up and pose a threat to other Babylonian cities in the region.'

'And what do you propose?'

'I would like to volunteer my services as emissary. Demand a tribute from them in exchange for not razing their city to the ground. Your reputation goes before you, sir. They will capitulate, and fill your coffers without the need to tax the people of Nippur.'

Eliana struggled not to gasp – that was *her* idea. She had suggested that a levy be extracted from another city, to save the money of struggling Nippurites, but she had never imagined that Ashan would volunteer himself.

'Very well. An excellent plan, Ashan. You do yourself credit.'

'Thank you, sir.' Ashan nodded. He and Eliana had discussed that he would put the plan forward as his own, but they had not intended to venture it so soon. He had to get away – could not trust himself around her. She would be great with child when he returned in a few months – she would have other things to think about. He could take himself a wife, and their paths need no longer cross except on court business.

He felt sick to his very stomach to think about it – not to have daily sight of her lively eyes and mischievous spirit. But it must be done – to protect them both, it would be done.

'Leave immediately – I want it settled as soon as possible.'

Ashan gave a curt bow and left.

'Is there any other business?' Samsu called again, his tone daring anyone else to respond.

He was answered with silence.

'Dismissed.'

He stood to leave and took Susa's hand to lead her out as the whole court bowed as one. She shook her head, indicating that she wanted to speak to someone in the hall.

No, no, no! He can't leave! Eliana's heart pounded as she forced herself to walk calmly after Ashan. *I have to tell him – he has to know.*

Her exit was blocked by Susa's shrivelled form. The older woman scowled up at Eliana as she tried to pass. It took every ounce of Eliana's self-control not to shove her aside and run after her love.

'So, whore. You have finally allowed my husband's seed to take root in your belly.'

Eliana's jaw dropped – did Susa know about the contraceptive?

Reading her face, Susa laughed. 'Those herbs were procured from my own physician – did you think it would not reach my ears?'

Eliana closed her mouth immediately, remembering to keep her face blank, whatever Susa said.

'Well, I hope that you are better at producing heirs than your worthless sister was. Perhaps you will bear another daughter to add to the little harem of harlots,' Susa goaded her.

She clenched her fists and took the bait. 'I shall certainly be better at producing heirs than you are. My body is a fertile field, ripe for planting. Yours… well, your womb may as well be made of clay, for all the use it is to Samsu.'

'I have borne a strong and healthy son,' Susa spat. 'As you well know. Now only one question remains about your brat – not the question of gender, but whether it will look like my son or my husband.'

Eliana's heart nearly beat out of her chest and her hands shook with the effort to control herself. Her stomach plummeted – Susa knew. 'It will look like the husband we share, of course,' she forced herself to say.

'Well, that remains to be seen. At least my son has had the sense to take himself away from this court, away from your vicious seductions and lustful ways – all to be expected from a shameless whore.'

Seeing that there was no way through Susa to chase Ashan, Eliana turned on her heel and stalked down the length of the hall to exit through the petitioners' door. She felt sick with the injustice of the last comment. As if she had asked for any of this! If she did not leave now, she would surely do Susa some serious harm. That would do her no favours with Samsu or with Ashan.

The moment she exited the audience chamber, she began to run. She had to tell him, she just had to. But she had no idea where to find him. She ran blindly, chasing Ashan as a child chases a butterfly.

After an endless time of searching up passages and down corridors, through gardens and across courtyards, she was forced to concede defeat. Ashan may already have left by now, and there was no sign of him anywhere. She went back to her apartments.

Crossing the terrace, she made for her favourite spot by the stream. The delicate singing of the water as it bubbled along always calmed her and helped her to think.

Her heart stopped as she crossed the little bridge and saw a shape waiting for her in the grass.

'Ashan!' She ran to him, throwing her arms around him as he sat up. She was so pleased to see him that she did not even register the hurt in his eyes.

'What took you so long? I have been waiting here almost an hour.'

'I was looking for you!' she cried. 'What's wrong? You look angry.'

He turned his face away from her. 'Why do you think that might be?'

'I have no idea! Ashan, I have wonderful news.'

'What?' he asked, bitterly. 'Have you decided to name the baby after Samsu?'

She clamped a hand over his mouth. 'It's *yours*, you great idiot!' she hissed.

Beneath the flesh of her palm, she felt a slow smile spread across his face. She removed her hand to see it better.

'Are you sure?' he whispered.

'Positive. There's no way it could be otherwise. I bled just before Kisha's death, and I had already missed my next moon blood before Samsu married me.' She grinned, 'It's a little you! A little piece of you and me.'

The smile faded from Ashan's face. He put his finger to her lips. 'Eliana, this is very serious. If this child is a boy, he will inherit the throne of Babylon.'

She tried to speak, to tell him that it would be his son who inherited the throne. He silenced her.

'You must not speak a word of this ever again. The baby is Samsu's, to all intents and purposes. If he ever finds out that the child is of my blood, all three of us will die. Make no mistake about it. He will not spare our child in its innocence, and not one of us will receive a quick or painless death.'

'But...'

'No buts!' he quieted her again. 'Samsu will claim this child, raise it as his own, pass his inheritance to it if it is a boy. If we are lucky, it will have more of your features than mine. Fortunately, Samsu and I do not look so very different. If you were having a child by Asag...'

She gave an exclamation of disgust.

'... It would be very difficult to hide the resemblance.' he finished.

There was silence between them for a moment.

'You're going away,' said Eliana, sadly.

'Yes, I can't be near you – you're like a poison to me. A sweet poison, but no less deadly for it.'

She crumpled a little, crushed by his words, but what came next lifted her heart again.

'I love you, Elly. I will always do my utmost to protect you and our child. My going away is for the best – I hope you'll believe me. The most help I can give you right now is to not endanger you – even the wrong sort of look passing between us could get us both killed.'

'I know,' she said, miserably. 'But I wanted to share this experience with you.'

He took her hand. 'It's not my experience to share. It's Samsu's.

We can never be an ordinary couple, not while he lives.'

'And how long will he live?'

Ashan shrugged. 'Who knows what the gods have in store? He cannot die by my hand – I swore an oath to his service. I bound myself in blood to him in an ancient rite of Marduk when we were just teenagers. The god does not hold oath-breakers in high esteem, and neither does Samsu.'

Eliana hung her head. 'I've created a bit of a mess for you then,' she said in a small voice.

'You have,' he smiled. 'But I would not change it now. The gods have their plans for us all.' He kissed her forehead and stood to leave. 'You make me *feel*, Elly. Happy to be near you; angry that I cannot protect you without breaking my vow; conflicted between loyalty to one who is like a brother, and one who is like the other half of me; joy when I see you smile... it will kill me not to see you while I am away, but know that I only have your best interests in mind.'

'Just – before you go – can I ask you a question?'

'I think you just did.'

'Be serious – why are you so good to me? You would inherit if Samsu had no heirs.'

'I don't want power.' He spread his hands in a helpless gesture. 'I never have, though I am as much a prince as Samsu – grandson of King Simash of Elam. Growing up firstly in Elam and seeing my family obliterated, then in Babylon and seeing Samsu's tear itself apart for control... it's all too ruthless for me. I am only ruthless when I have to be – it brings me no pleasure. I'm not meant to sit a throne.'

'What does bring you pleasure, then?'

'Diplomacy. Solving a problem with words, not swords. That is why I must go to Lagash and persuade them to send *something* to Samsu – anything to keep him from destroying another city, another populace. You are not the only one who still has nightmares about the conquest.'

'Stay safe,' she urged.

'Don't worry – I'll be back before you know I've left.' He gave a reassuring smile, and left her to her thoughts.

Chapter 17

A fortnight after her announcement, Eliana was moved, along with her nieces and Mari, to a vast suite of rooms that almost rivalled Susa's for luxury. Her jaw dropped as she was ushered through the doorway – sun streamed through the expansive windows at the far end of the room, where the doors to the terrace stood wide open to allow a cool breeze to ripple through, carrying the scent of blossoms from the gardens.

The walls had been painted with vibrant scenes illustrating Samsu's great victories – Eliana supposed that he wanted his children reminded of their father's greatness every time they glanced around. The living space was equipped with every luxury – the stools and tables all had legs carved to resemble those of an ox, just as Susa's throne did. A great copper plate was set on a broad table near the middle of the room; it in, flower petals drifted in fragrant oil.

Not one detail had been overlooked. This was clearly a reward for her pregnancy – she wondered if he would take it all away again if she was delivered of a girl.

Mari followed in behind, carrying Kisuri and holding Sarri's hand. She gasped, stunned, and immediately went off to explore the other rooms.

They were as lavish as the first – there was a well-equipped nursery for the two girls, with a room leading off it for Mari, as well as a grand bedchamber and dressing room for Eliana.

She looked at the bed with just a hint of melancholy – it was enormous, hung with rose-pink curtains and draped with matching silken sheets; it looked inviting and comfortable... but she missed the bed she had shared with Kisha. The bed she had shared with Ashan.

Somehow, it felt that by leaving that bed behind, she left behind her last traces of physical connection to Ashan and Kisha. There had been a strange strength in sleeping in the bed that Kisha had died in, a feeling that somehow, they still slept together. She wandered from room to room, gazing around sadly; her surroundings were beautiful, but Kisha had never set foot here. It would never be home.

All her possessions had been moved on ahead – there was no need to unpack or fuss over where things should go, it had all been arranged for her. She sank onto a plush cushion and studied the walls, searching for Ashan in the paintings. Eliana missed him desperately in those first long weeks. She felt his absence more as her belly began to grow.

Perhaps it was best that he was gone. The added space and grandeur of her new apartments came with the distinct downside that she was much nearer to Samsu – it would be far harder and riskier to snatch a private moment with Ashan now.

Less than half a day after their arrival, they had visitors.

The Brute and Ani arrived together, bearing gifts.

They made no pretence at civility. Ani stepped forward first, a cold smirk on her lips. 'My mistress thought you might appreciate this, in your current state.' She thrust something small and black towards Eliana; she recognised it immediately, with a heave of revulsion in her stomach.

Slowly, deliberately, she reached out for the statuette of Lasmashtu. The last time she had seen it, it had been tied to the neck of the dead and decaying dog that had shocked Kisha into labour. She was not so easily frightened as her sister.

Ani held out her hand to drop it into Eliana's – at the last moment, Eliana drew her hand away. The statuette tumbled to the floor with a satisfying crack as it broke into three pieces on the tiles.

'Oh,' Eliana gave a falsely apologetic smile. 'Such a pity – do tell your mistress I am sorry. I truly appreciate her gift, and accept it in the spirit in which it was given.'

Glaring through narrowed eyes, Ani made no reply. Eliana turned to the Brute. Her palms sweated a little and her hands trembled – every time she looked at this man she could feel nothing but the terror he had inflicted on her as he had systematically stripped away her pride, her dignity and her innocence. She was fully under Samsu's protection now, but it brought her little comfort when the Brute could so easily kill her with a well-landed blow.

'The prince sends this, with a summons to attend him in his rooms tonight. Bring it with you.' He thrust a large object towards her, wrapped in red silk.

She took it and drew off the cover, revealing an elegant lyre of gilded wood, carved with the snake-dragon of Marduk and inlaid with panels of lapis lazuli and shell. It was breathtaking.

Running her fingers tentatively over the strings, she smiled. It was perfectly in tune.

'You may thank the prince from me,' she said briskly, turning away from the pair, walking towards the terrace with her gift.

Ani glanced down at the floor and gave a spiteful kick – one of the pieces of the childbirth demon came skittering across the floor towards Eliana's feet.

She ignored it.

Taking a final look around, no doubt to inform Susa of her rival's new situation, Ani and the Brute left without another word.

Mari popped her head out from the nursery, taking in the beautiful lyre and the shattered statuette. 'That's lovely,' she nodded at the instrument. 'Samsu?'

'Yes,' smiled Eliana. 'The first gift he's ever given me that I might actually want.'

'He's winning you over, then?'

Eliana looked up sharply, 'Never.'

'And what's that on the floor?'

Looking down at the pieces of jet at her feet, Eliana shrugged. 'Just Susa. Nothing I can't handle.'

*

When she went to Samsu that evening, she was determined to be pleasant, if he was. She would never forgive him, never let go of her hatred for him, but perhaps she could learn to live under some sort of peace banner until some better option presented itself.

'Ah, *karkittu*,' he beckoned her in when she appeared in the doorway, not bothering to stand from his cushions. She walked over, set down her lyre and bowed.

His eyes lit to see her in his favourite posture – prone, submissive, compliant. He stood then, and walked around her – she grimaced as he bent, gripped her buttocks in both hands and squeezed hard. He delivered a stinging slap across her backside for the sheer pleasure of hearing her yelp in pain and surprise.

'Sit up.'

She sat, her cheeks burning with the degradation, knowing what was coming. Her pregnancy afforded her some little protection, but she must still satisfy her husband in other ways. He hitched up his tunic and stood before her.

When he was satiated, he rearranged himself and went back to the cushions, patting one nearby in an invitation to join him. Eliana stood and moved over to him gingerly, feeling slightly nauseous. It didn't matter how many times she had performed the act, it still left her feeling soiled and sick to her stomach.

'Are you pleased with the lyre?' he asked.

'Yes, very pleased, thank you,' she gave a weak smile. 'It will give me many hours of pleasure.'

He nodded, 'A reward for the many hours of pleasure you have given me.'

She repressed a shudder – those hours had not been given, but taken from her.

'There are a few matters I wish for your opinion on,' he continued. 'Certain issues that arose at yesterday's audience.'

It was all the usual problems – shortage of food, decreasing population as people moved away from Nippur, fewer people to tend the land, fewer skilled labourers.

'... Of course, the lack of farmers will be less of an issue when Susa's temple is erected on the common land...' he was saying.

A warning bell clamoured in Eliana's head. 'What temple is this?' she asked evenly, betraying no hint of concern.

'Nothing much. My wife wants the common land to build a temple to some mother-goddess from her homeland. She just wants the revenues from visitors to the temple, of course, but it looks good to the people.'

'It does not!' Eliana burst out, regretting it immediately.

Samsu glared at her.

'It does not, *sir*,' she amended, trying to regain her calm. 'It's not the farmers who use the land. The poorest people of Nippur need it to survive – if they cannot grow food there, they'll starve. I beg you, don't let her have the land.'

He shrugged. 'I have already said yes, in principle. It just has to be finalised at audience.'

'Please, don't let her take it from the people who need it most – block her.'

'Why should I?'

She thought quickly, remembering how he had craved acclaim on their journey through the city on the day of their wedding.

'Because the people will love you for it,' she tried. 'You will be the wise and benevolent ruler who saved their land and protected them from starvation.'

He was silent for a moment. Then, 'I'll think about it. I suggest that if you do want to challenge Susa for use of the land, you do so at the next audience.'

His tone told her that he would brook no more discussion of the matter tonight. She took a few deep breaths, pushing it to the back of her mind, where she could draw it out later to think on when she was alone. She cast about for a subject to lighten the conversation.

'Sarri is walking now,' she ventured.

'Who?' He was barely paying attention as he scowled at another tablet.

'Your eldest daughter. She's very bright, interested in everything and learning new words every day. And Kisuri is thriving too, considering that she was not expected to survive her first night in this world.'

Samsu looked up, taken aback, as though he'd forgotten he had one daughter, let alone two. 'Oh. Yes, good.'

He paused. Eliana could almost hear the machinations of his mind. 'Bring them to audience next week and present them to the court. Wear something tight, show the swell of your belly. It will be good to remind people that I am a part of something more permanent than their petty troubles – a great line of kings stretching back for generations, one that will endure as long as time itself. My daughters' presence, with your pregnant belly, will showcase my fertility, prove I am blessed by the gods.'

'Sarri has nothing suitable to wear, sir.'

'Then take a bolt of silk from the store cupboards and have something made, just bring her next week. Now, amuse me. Play something for me.'

*

One week later, Eliana stood before the door to the audience chamber, clad in an indigo gown fringed with silver. A slim circlet of gold and pearl sat on her brow, and matching bracelets jingled at her wrists. Balancing beside her on still-unsteady legs, Sarri was a perfect miniature copy of her aunt, right down to the gold circlet nestling amongst her tangle of black curls.

The little girl tugged impatiently at Eliana's hand – she wanted to explore. Now that Sarri was walking and running, it was becoming ever-more difficult to keep her out of trouble. She was inquisitive, wanting to smell, touch, and taste everything she could get her tiny hands on. Yesterday, Eliana had gone into her dressing room and immediately noticed that her paints and powders were in disarray. A cloud of pale face powder still hung in the air.

A giggle came from underneath the table – Eliana peered underneath to discover a little ghost laughing at her with mischievous eyes. Sarri had got the powder everywhere – in her hair, on her gown, on her face and in her mouth. They had both needed a bath by the time Eliana finished cleaning up.

The herald banged his staff on the tiles. 'The Lady Eliana, *Sekrutu* to His Royal Highness Samsu, Prince of Babylon, *Lugal* of Nippur; and their Royal Highnesses, the Princesses Sarri and Kisuri, daughters of Babylon.'

The doors were flung open – Eliana took a step forward, Mari at her heels in a good wool gown, cradling Kisuri in a gown to match her sister's and aunt's, wildly inappropriate for a four month old baby. The silk was already watermarked where she had dribbled onto it.

They took a few steps into the hall. Sarri dug her heels in, freezing in fear.

Giving a reassuring smile, Eliana prodded her niece gently,

'Come along,' she whispered.

Sarri stared around with wide eyes. Eliana could not imagine how boundless this room must look to such a tiny girl – a vast, glittering cave filled with unknown beasts and silent, watchful faces.

'No!' Sarri wailed, turning to bury her face in Eliana's skirts and holding up her arms. The assembly laughed; Eliana looked to the dais, Samsu and Susa were not smiling.

Scooping her niece from the floor, she cuddled her and stroked her back, walking smoothly towards the thrones.

She knelt carefully, bowing her head. Behind her, Mari did the same. Neither of them could bow fully whilst holding the girls, and they prayed that Samsu would not make anything of it.

Eliana exhaled a soft sigh of relief as he motioned for them to rise. She stood and set Sarri on her feet on the floor, where the little girl clung to her leg. She took Kisuri from Mari, and rested her free hand on Sarri's head.

'Your Royal Highness, may I present your daughters, Sarri,' she gestured, 'and Kisuri.'

He nodded and grunted acknowledgement. 'Are they strong and healthy?' he asked.

'They are, sir. And within a half-year they will have a vigorous brother to join them in the nursery.' She took her free hand off Sarri's head and placed it protectively over her belly, glaring defiantly at Susa.

Truthfully, Kisuri was not healthy. Still small for her four and a half months, and struggling with her breathing, she was pale and delicate as a rare orchid. For all that, she looked just like her mother, and Eliana's heart melted a little every time she looked at her. The two sisters were as different from each other as Suen from Utu – while Kisuri was pale and still like the moon, Sarri blazed with energy, like the sun, her quick mind and playful spirit already apparent.

Samsu waved them away. Mari stepped forward to take Kisuri again, Eliana picked up Sarri and they moved off to the side.

The petitioners began in earnest, with Samsu dispensing judgements and justice at a rapid pace, eager to get off the throne and into a saddle. For once, Eliana paid scant attention; she was too busy trying to amuse her niece, keeping the bored girl quiet as her father worked. She slid off a bracelet and played with it, dangling it in front of the baby.

Only when she became aware of a change of atmosphere in the room did she look up.

Two men stood before Samsu. One in his middle age, the other in the prime of his youth. Their faces shared the same almond-shaped eyes and slightly hooked nose.

'You *struck* your father?' said Samsu, his voice soft with danger. Eliana knew that tone well, and her stomach knotted with dread.

'Well, yes, but he...'

'Do not make excuses!' Samsu snapped at the young man. 'It is an unpardonable crime, to strike one's own father. He would be within his rights to disinherit you.'

The man opened his mouth again, 'I-'

'*Silence!*' roared Samsu. 'Babylonian law is very clear – "if a son strikes his father, they shall cut off his fingers".'

'No!' cried the man, 'I beg you, please!' He fell to his knees.

'My prince, I would not have him punished so severely.' The older man intervened.

'What you would have is of no consequence,' sneered Samsu. 'The law is the law.' He snapped his fingers.

Two guards stepped forward, crossing their spears between the father and his son, preventing any interference. The Brute stepped forward with his dagger.

The young man's piercing wails were the only sound in the hall.

Sarri wriggled in Eliana's arms, distressed by the noise, trying to twist around to see what caused it. Eliana focused wholly on her niece, trying to block out what was going on before her. The man's cries of fear changed to screams of pain, and there was a sickening crunch as the Brute's dagger took his first finger.

One.

She stared straight into Sarri's eyes, pulling a face to make the baby giggle.

Two.

She danced from side to side.

Three.

Bouncing up and down on the spot, she hummed a little tune.

Four.

It worked – Sarri ceased to listen to the mounting screams of the tortured man and the anguished shouts of his father, she gave all her attention to Eliana.

Five.

It was done. Father and son were reunited and sent on their way, the younger man leaving a stream of blood in his wake as he staggered from the hall. Eliana felt a wave of nausea and a tightness in her throat, threatening tears. Such a waste – a man mutilated for life, all because of a heated response to a probably minor quarrel. His injuries could kill him, if they festered. She wished she had heard the whole of the story, but she swallowed down her pity – this was no time for softness. The last petitions were finished and her moment was approaching. She set Sarri back on the ground.

The herald banged his staff. 'In her benevolence, Her Royal Highness, Susa of Elam, Princess Consort of Babylon has requested a small piece of land in order to build a temple to Pinikir, mother-goddess of Elam, that her blessings might extend to Nippur and its people.'

'Any objections?' called Samsu.

Eliana took a deep breath, and stepped forward from the crowd. Susa's eyes narrowed with rage as they lit on her.

'Please, sir, I have an objection,' she said.

Samsu turned to her. 'What is it, Lady Eliana?'

'Sir, if I may… which piece of land specifically does the Princess request?'

'It is the common land on the south bank of the canal.'

'Forgive me, but there is already a shortage of food in Nippur. The poorest citizens scratch what little food they can from that land – if it is taken from them, you condemn hundreds of innocent souls to a wretched death by starvation.'

Susa laughed, 'What matter if there are fewer rats on the streets? I say I shall be doing a favour to the populace at large. They ought to thank me.'

Eliana looked as Susa with contempt, seeing the feeling mirrored on the woman's own face. Everything about her proclaimed greed, from the richly feathered gold-and-green headdress over her neat hair, to the jewelled bands clasped around her ankles. She only wanted the temple erected so that she could collect its revenues to lavish on more expensive luxuries while the destitute went wanting.

Turning back towards the crowd, Eliana beckoned Mari forward with the children; she spoke from the heart. 'Sir, Mari is a loyal servant, a talented healer and an excellent nursemaid to your daughters. Without this common land, she would have starved to death following your glorious conquest.' Those words almost choked her, but she would say what she had to, if it meant winning.

She took Kisuri into her arms. 'Dozens of babies as sweet and innocent as your daughter will go to the underworld without ever really having tasted life, and who knows who they might otherwise grow up to be? What use they might be to you and your empire? If you allow this temple to go ahead, children like Sarri and Kisuri will perish. For the love of your people, sir, I beg you not to build.'

Handing Kisuri back to Mari, Eliana reached up and removed the circlet of gold from her head, before sliding the bracelets from her wrists. She got to her knees. 'If it please you, I will sell my own jewellery and the few possessions I have of my own to purchase the land for the people.'

Susa swelled up like a toad, purple with rage as Samsu nodded. 'You are right, *sekrutu*. The people are better served by this land in its current state. I forbid the use of the common land for a temple. Further, I forbid you sell your jewellery for it. I gave you those as gifts, I will not have you sell them on like a coarse mercenary. The land shall be given to you, to use it as you feel best.'

A beaming smile lit Eliana's face; she dipped into a full bow. 'I cannot thank you enough, sir. Your people will sing your praises from now until the end of time.' She knew that he had only acquiesced because he wanted the acclaim of the people; honestly, she did not care what his reasons were, so long as he gave her what she wanted.

She remained in her bow. There was a pause.

'Is there something else, *sekrutu*?'

'Only a small matter, sir. I am a simple woman, inexperienced in the complexities of managing land. Might I ask that the land be turned over to the *Ensi*, my father, to govern wisely in my stead and manage it more effectively than I could ever hope to.'

'Granted.' Samsu gestured for her to get up, clearly delighted by her show of being rendered inferior by her sex.

She had known that would please him. Though she was as capable of managing the land as her father, she particularly wanted it turned over to him. He was out in the city every day, seeing those on the lowest rung of society. He would know how the land was best to be used.

Flushed with her victory, she stood and moved back into the crowd; her legs and hands shook a little as excitement coursed through her, the thrill of defeating Susa.

The woman glared daggers at her as she passed. With only a vague sense of unease, smothered by the intoxicating joy of success, Eliana sensed that her actions may have consequences. She had the distinct feeling that a full-blown war was about to erupt.

She placed a hand over her belly as Samsu drew the audience to a close.

Chapter 18

Eliana determined to stay away from audiences for a few weeks, to allow time for Susa's rage to calm. There was no shortage of ways to occupy herself – now nearly five moons through her pregnancy and with two children to keep out of trouble, there was always something that needed doing. She kept herself so busy that two weeks flew past almost without her notice.

'You need to take more care of yourself, my lady,' Mari warned. 'If you do not rest enough, you'll do the baby harm.'

'The baby is fine, Mari,' smiled Eliana. 'I don't have time for rest – Sarri has the energy of a young gazelle, and Kisuri needs constant attention. When they are not placing demands on me, Samsu is – he always wants some new song, or my take on a problem in the city, or… some other form of relief.'

'I know you feel fine, but I'd feel better if you would take some tonic.'

The worry on Mari's face was enough to get Eliana to agree. The girl chewed at her lip, and her brows knitted together in concern. 'If you really think it will help, I will.'

Mari twisted her fingers together nervously. 'I'll bring you some with your dinner.'

Eliana was anxious to soothe her. 'I really don't know what I'd do without you looking after all three of us – you've been such a rock to me, through everything. If I ever have any real power, I promise I'll free you as soon as I can.' She gave a little laugh, 'perhaps you can even go off and marry your gardener! Kisha mentioned that you were seeing somebody.'

To her great surprise, Mari's eyes filled with tears. 'Excuse me, please, my lady,' she mumbled, darting off to her room.

Whatever is the matter with her? Eliana wondered. *Perhaps things have gone wrong with her gardener – I won't mention him again. Not for a while, anyway.*

When the girls were in bed and she brought Eliana's dinner that evening, Mari looked more unwell than ever. Her skin was pale, her eyes wide and feverish. 'Are you alright?' Eliana asked, concerned.

'Fine, thank you my lady,' came the short answer as Mari poured liquid from a painted clay jug into a red glazed drinking bowl.

'You don't look at all healthy.'

'I'm fine. Really.' Mari passed the bowl to Eliana with shaking hands.

Taking the bowl, she raised it to her nose. For a split second, she was almost sure she saw Mari flinch. Perhaps she had imagined it.

She took a deep breath; inhaling the fresh sweet smell of the tonic. 'It smells delicious, what's in it?'

'Just some herbs and fruits, my lady,' she mumbled.

Eliana lifted the bowl to drink. Just before the liquid touched her lips, Mari let out a strangled cry and leapt forward, slapping the bowl from her hands and making her jump. It tumbled to the floor, shattering on the tiles, splashing tonic up Eliana's gown and staining the silk.

Thoroughly taken aback, she was stunned into silence for a moment as Mari fell to her knees and curled into a ball, sobbing.

'Mari – what on earth…?'

The slave girl shook her head and sobbed harder. Eliana knelt on the floor before her and took her hands. 'You can tell me,' she said, kindly. 'Was it poisoned?' She forced the words out calmly, but her heart hammered. She prayed Mari would not have done such a thing.

Her heart plummeted as Mari nodded miserably.

'But… I trusted you. Why would you do it?' she asked, bemused.

'S – Susa,' she gasped out, trying to calm herself.

'Hush – breathe deeply, then tell me.'

Taking long, shuddering breaths, Mari took a few minutes to bring herself under control. Eliana felt sick as she waited – there were only two people in the world that she had felt she could trust – one of them was leagues away in Lagash, and now the other had betrayed her. She thought hard, wondering how she might have offended Mari, why the girl might have tried to harm her.

As if she read her mind, Mari said, 'Susa promised me my freedom if I gave it to you. I'm – I'm so sorry.'

Through her personal hurt, Eliana's heart went out to the girl. Susa had placed her in an impossible situation – she couldn't be sure what she would do herself if someone offered her freedom at such a terrible price. Of all the changes that had been forced upon her, she could get used to everything but the loss of freedom. To ride out, to visit the market, to wander the city and talk to the people… express her opinions openly, speak to whom she chose, not care what she looked like… all freedoms she had taken for granted, and would give anything to have back.

Anything? She wasn't sure. Would she really murder for them? She supposed it would depend on who she was told to kill.

'It was not a deadly potion,' Mari was saying. 'Not for you, though it would have made you sick.'

'For the baby?'

She nodded.

She clenched her fists, shaking with rage and fear. It made sense. Susa wanted her to miscarry. Their husband would suspect foul play if she suddenly dropped dead, but women lost babies every day. Thank Enlil that Mari had had a last-moment crisis of conscience... but this was merely Susa's first attempt.

'I'm so sorry, my lady,' tears began to fall down Mari's face again. 'I can't believe I even considered it – you have always been so good to me.'

'I don't know how I can ever trust you again,' said Eliana, sadly. It was true – she would view every morsel put in front of her with suspicion from now on.

'Please, please let me do something to make it up to you,' the girl begged.

'What can you do? I may never eat or drink without fear again.'

'Then... let me be your taster. I'll try everything before it touches your lips.'

Eliana considered for a moment. Mari put herself at risk by offering – they both knew that Susa would not stop at the first failed attempt to rid her rival of a potential son. She would be as stubbornly bent on her course as a rushing river.

'You would do that?'

Mari gave a vigorous nod, her hair sticking to her damp cheeks.

'And there's nothing else I need to know? Do not hide anything from me now if you ever hope for my trust again.' Her mind returned to poor Isin, and the plan that she had hatched with Mari. The private conversations she had had, her feelings for Ashan... all the things that Samsu and Susa had come to know about inexplicably.

'My gardener...' she hesitated, tailing off.

'Yes?' Eliana prompted.

'He's not a gardener... it's... it's Asag.'

Eliana gasped, 'That beast! Oh, Mari! How could you? He's so vile, inside and out. He's the ugliest man I've ever seen, and glories in cruelty almost as much as the Brute.'

'He's not so bad, really,' Mari shrugged. 'Once you get used to his looks. He is kind to me, he talks to me like a real person, not as a slave. And he pays me – most of the soldiers would never consider such a thing. I thought I might be able to save up to purchase my own freedom… then Susa offered it.'

'And… you told Asag things about me?'

'I did not mean to, my lady, I swear it! Susa and Samsu paid him for any information he could get from me, and he gave me a share – it was just fragments, like when I saw you and Ashan so comfortable with each other, I didn't think it would do any harm. Once I found out, I made sure to keep my mouth shut.' The tears fell faster.

'But, what about Isin? You sacrificed him for pocket money?' Eliana could have wept for him all over again, dying so senselessly, sold out by a greedy girl.

'No! Never! I truly wanted Sarri safe and away. But I do know how Isin came to his end.'

'How?' She was not sure she could bear to listen.

'Asag told me – Isin went to his favourite tavern the night before he died, with his fellow scribes. For farewell drinks on his last night in Nippur. Samsu suspected him, was having him followed. He sent men to the tavern – they bought Isin's drinks all night, until he was roaring drunk and dropping hints all over the place, so pleased with himself, so looking forward to his new life as a father.'

Eliana dropped her head into her hands. So Isin had all but killed himself! Stupid boy – letting his tongue run away with him.

She sighed heavily. 'I can't hear any more, Mari. Can we just… pretend that none of this happened? Start afresh? If you agree to be my taster, I shall agree to trust you, as far as I can.'

Mari gripped Eliana's hands. 'Truly, my lady? You would do that? I swear you'll have no more loyal friend in the world.'

Eliana nodded. 'Prove it so, and I promise I'll find a way to free you. If you ever give me cause to mistrust you again… well, I don't know what I shall do. But I hope I never need to think of anything.' She got to her feet and went to her bed with a sorrowful heart and an empty belly, leaving her food untouched on the table, and Mari still weeping on the floor.

*

For all that she had said, Eliana couldn't bring herself to fully trust Mari. She tried to give her the benefit of the doubt, but uncertainty lingered.

The girl had been true to her promise to taste everything that came to Eliana's table, and the incident had not been mentioned again, but still she could not eat or drink without a little flutter of worry in her belly. She kept quiet about it, not wanting to make Mari feel worse; she did seem genuinely repentant.

Eliana could only hope that her own good nature would not be her downfall. She had even considered telling Samsu, but the blame would certainly fall to Mari as Susa tried to deflect suspicion. Eliana shuddered to think of the girl's fate – Samsu would be obliged to believe his wife over his concubine's slave.

So far, Susa had not attempted any retribution against Mari, but Eliana could not help but be nervous for her. The flutters continued for more than three weeks – she put them down to almost everything else before she realised what they were.

It was as she lay on the bed one afternoon, resting in the midday heat as the two girls took their naps, that she felt it. An unmistakeable thump against her ribs.

She cried out and sat up in alarm, placing her hand where she had felt the kick.

Everything was still for a moment. Mari came running, 'I heard you shout, my lady. Are you alright?'

'I think so,' she said, cautiously. Then, 'Oh!' Another thump in the same spot.

A slow smile spread over her face and she felt a warm glow diffuse through her body. 'It's the baby,' she said. 'Come, feel!'

Mari almost ran to the bed. Eliana took her hand and placed it over the spot. The baby obliged with another hearty kick.

'Oh!' Mari laughed. 'He is strong!'

A fist of fear gripped Eliana's stomach. 'You said "he". What if… if it's *not* a boy?'

'It will be,' said Mari, with absolute conviction.

'You can't know that. If it's a girl… I'll go back to being Samsu's whore. There'll be no hiding from him. He slapped Kisha when she bore him a daughter, and he's more intense with me than he ever was with her. I can't bear it – the not knowing. Building my hopes for months. At least if I could know, I could accept it. Prepare for what might be coming.'

Mari dropped her voice to a whisper, 'There could be a way.'

'How? What way? Nobody can know.'

'There is a priestess in the city – I knew her back when I was free. She serves Ninlil – a goddess who should have great sympathy for you.'

'Enlil's wife? Why should she?'

'Think about it, my lady. You share the same plight. Ninlil was forcibly taken by her husband, ravaged and impregnated. She conceived a boy-child from her ordeal, perhaps in her sympathy, she will send one to you, too. The priestess could tell you – Ninlil speaks to her.'

'As Marduk spoke to Samsu and promised him a boy with Kisha?'

'Marduk is a false usurper – Enlil truly rules the pantheon. His wife is queen and mother of his sons. She will take pity on you.'

'I hope so. If you think you can get your priestess here, I will happily see her,' Eliana conceded. 'Anything to set my mind at rest.'

*

It took only a few days to make the arrangements. Mari sent Resu out to find the priestess, with instructions to disguise her as a midwife. She would enter the palace under the pretence of examining Eliana.

She was admitted with minimal fuss. Satisfied that she was not carrying a weapon, the guards at the gate sent for Mari to verify the woman's identity and escort her inside.

The woman arrived in their chambers shrouded in a black hooded cape and veil. She bowed.

'Please, no need,' said Eliana immediately. 'Stand, make yourself comfortable. What is your name?'

The woman removed her hood and veil. Eliana gasped – when she heard the word 'priestess' she had expected a wizened old crone. This woman could not be past twenty-five years. Her hair fell straight and fine past her shoulders in a startling shade of red that could not be natural, and she stood a head taller than Eliana.

'Matima, my lady.'

'Please – we are all women here. Let us speak as equals.'

The woman nodded. 'Do you have the items I require?'

Mari produced a linen cloth, a copper bowl and a jug of water. 'Good. Please, lie down, Eliana.'

She did as she was told – Mari came to sit on the bed beside her, holding her hand for comfort.

Matima took a small pot from the folds of her cloak, liberally sprinkling a purple powder from it into the water. She stirred it into the water, turning it a vibrant shade of violet.

She took the cloth and dipped it into the water, then gestured to Eliana to pull her dress up to expose her belly.

Chanting mysterious words in a language that Eliana did not recognise, Matima rubbed the linen over the baby bump before withdrawing a yellow crystal on a fine gold chain from another hidden pocket in her robe. She began to swing it above Eliana's belly in a hypnotic, pendulum-like motion.

The women watched the crystal swing; the silence extended for several minutes before Eliana could bear it no longer. 'Please, what is it? Can you tell?'

'The signals are mixed,' grumbled Matima. 'Ninlil is unclear. I sense first a boy, then a girl, then a boy again.'

'What could that mean?' asked Mari, anxiously.

'Any number of things,' replied the priestess. 'I get the strongest feeling that there is more than one baby present in this room – that is what is most likely to confuse the signs.'

Eliana looked at Mari in shock. 'Mari, are you…?'

The girl looked away, ashamed. 'I had not decided whether or not to keep it. I have some of the potion that Susa sent, still.'

Eliana gripped her hand, 'You *must* keep it. Is it Asag's?'

She nodded.

'Then your baby will be the child of a Babylonian – born free and guaranteed a lifetime of Babylonian privilege. And you will be protected – a slave who has borne a master's child cannot be sold.'

'I know all that… but, when I have a baby, I would like it to have an assured future. Asag may choose not to acknowledge the child.'

'I'll see that he does,' said Eliana, darkly.

Beside the bed, Matima cleared her throat. 'Perhaps, Mari, I could ask you to leave the room. Ninlil may be clearer without the spirits of two babies vying for her notice.'

Eliana gave Mari's hand a final squeeze, 'We'll talk later,' she promised.

Once she had left, Matima began to concentrate again, swinging her crystal back and forth, muttering in her foreign tongue. Eliana was captivated as the light danced through the facets, throwing rainbows onto every surface.

The words had an almost musical timbre – she longed to know what they meant.

'The signals are still confused,' Matima frowned. 'I sense both male and female.' She sat back and sighed. 'Ninlil refuses to be clearer on this – her voice blows with the wind, first one way, then the other. I am afraid, my lady, that you will simply have to wait and see. All I can tell you is that the child is healthy. Its heart beats strong enough for two. This will be a child that thrives – its thread of destiny is woven. Ninlil tells me that it shall have its mother's courage and spirit, and its father's strength and bravery. It will be protected by Ninlil herself.'

Eliana felt threatening tears of disappointment. She swallowed them back. 'Thank you for trying,' she said, trying to keep her voice from breaking. Usually she would not be so prone to tears – the pregnancy played havoc with her emotions. 'Please, Mari will pay you and see you back to the gate.'

'May Ninlil bless you and keep you, Eliana,' said Matima gravely. She took out a charm and placed it beside the bed. 'This will shield you in childbed.'

Picking it up and examining it, Eliana could not help but be intrigued. Made of shell inset with fragments of the same yellow crystal the priestess had used over her belly, the creature had the head of a dragon, the wings of a bird, and the body of a lion.

She did not recognise the beast, but something about the amulet gave her comfort. She clutched it to her breast. 'Thank you,' she whispered.

'One further thing,' Matima said. 'Ninlil warns of a man with the strength of a bear and the cruelty of a snake. His shadow looms large – he poses great risk to the child.'

'Thank you,' she said again.

Matima bowed and took her leave.

Eliana turned the amulet over in her hand, thinking of all she had been told. The baby had a great destiny, strength of spirit, would be protected by the mother goddess, was at risk of harm at the Brute's hands... and still could be either male or female. The priestess's words tumbled through her mind, wrapping around each other until they were so hopelessly entangled that she could hardly remember which order they were supposed to go in.

She missed Ashan keenly in that moment. Missed his calming words, his reassuring presence... his blade that would not hesitate to flash against those who tried to hurt her.

*

The pregnancy progressed normally, and Eliana scarcely noticed the months passing. She continued to be summoned to Samsu, to attend audiences, and to learn how to be a mother as Sarri and Kisuri demanded ever-more of her attention.

Her body thickened, growing heavy and cumbersome. It irritated her that she was no longer lithe and agile enough to flit through the gardens like a hummingbird or run and climb amongst the trees. She was sure that Kisha never grew this fat when she was pregnant.

She missed her sister more than she could admit – to herself or to anyone else. If she thought too deeply on it, she would open the floodgates and the tears might never stop. She needed Kisha's calming presence at her side, to hold her hand and tell her everything would be fine. To be with her through the birth, to give advice, to reassure her... to see how fast her little girls were growing up.

Sarri was almost two years old now, and stubborn as an ox. She spent a lot of time in the gardens, and was constantly running back to show Eliana and Mari what she had found. A curious child, she was making extensive use of her new favourite word: 'Why?'

Eliana always tried to answer patiently, remembering how frustrating she had found it as a child to ask a question and be answered with 'Just, *because*'. But as her pregnancy grew increasingly exhausting and she became more irritable, it was difficult to keep a good humour. This was something that Kisha would have excelled at, she knew.

Kisuri was still small for her age. She tired easily, and still shuffled around on her stomach rather than crawling. She coughed frequently, and Eliana could not help but be worried for her health.

She worried about both girls, and whether Susa would target them in her campaign against Eliana. They were probably safe; as nothing but daughters of a dead concubine, they were no threat to Ashan's position. Still, they were a weapon that Susa could use against her at any time, and she could not rest easily when she thought of them.

She knew that Susa suspected the identity of her child's father; but in that, at least, she was safe. Ashan was Susa's ticket to power, and she would never put him in danger, even if it meant destroying Eliana. She would keep the knowledge as quiet as Eliana did herself. She hugged the secret to herself, telling no-one, not even Mari. Especially not Mari. It was her secret. Hers and Ashan's. The knowledge may make Susa feel powerful, but she could do nothing with it.

The pregnancy neared full-term, though the palace believed that she had another month to go, and she began to miss Ashan so much that it hurt – a deep ache within her that she was reminded of with every kick from his baby. The ordeal of childbirth drew nearer, and she needed him at her side. Though, with every day that passed, she began to feel a little safer from Susa – she had surely left it too late to act against Eliana now. She would not be able to kill the baby without killing the mother too, and Mari still tasted everything, despite her own pregnancy.

Just three months behind Eliana, Mari was also beginning to get too big to chase around after the energetic Sarri. She was more cheerful about her pregnancy now – Asag had agreed to acknowledge the child. Eliana thought that he was secretly grateful to have found a woman to bear his child; few women would be able to look past his ugliness. His skin had the colour and pitted texture of a sun-baked brick, his lips were too large and thick for his face, and a battle-wound had taken off his right ear and part of his nose. Mari was not a beauty, but she was attractive enough, with a pleasant face, rosy cheeks and kind eyes; Eliana hoped for the child's sake that it would have its mother's looks.

She considered asking Samsu for another maid. With Sarri's increasing energy and Kisuri's need for constant attention, and more babies coming to the nursery within the next few months, she was not sure how they would manage.

As she eased herself into the bed with just a week or so of her pregnancy remaining, her baby gave her a strong kick in the ribs. She winced – she would be black and blue inside. It was definitely time to beg another maid from her husband. For Mari's sake as much as hers. They would both need looking after.

Exhausted, she settled into the bed and turned onto her side, propping a pillow under the great mound of her belly. She soon drifted into uneasy sleep.

It felt like she had barely been asleep for five minutes before she awoke in a panic, sitting bolt upright in the bed, her heart racing. She pushed her unruly curls back from her face and listened – had she heard a noise? What had woken her?

'Mari?' she called.

She waited. There was no response. She listened for a few moments more, before putting it down to a movement from the baby and paranoia brought on by the pregnancy. Taking a few deep breaths, she tried to bring her heart rate back to normal.

She was about to lie down again when her eyes snapped to a movement in the shadows. A huge form stepped out, silvered by moonlight, the dagger in his hand flashing as it reflected Suen's rays.

His silhouette was unmistakeable. The Brute.

Every muscle in her body tensed. She froze, her limbs turned to stone, too terrified to scream.

He laughed aloud, dragging Mari out into the light beside him. She was gagged, her hands bound behind her, eyes huge and frantic with fear. The Brute pushed her down onto a stool, advancing slowly on Eliana.

'The Princess will not risk you having a boy child, whore. She has paid me well to ensure that it never happens.'

Eliana willed herself to move, but she was paralysed by panic. 'You – you would never dare to – to hurt me. Samsu would kill you if … if you harmed his child.' The words staggered out like a drunkard, she was furious with herself for letting him know she was afraid.

'Samsu will never know,' sneered the Brute. 'I will make it look as though *she* did it,' he jerked his head towards Mari, 'and then killed herself. Breeding puts all sorts of strange madnesses into women's heads. It is known that they are often beset by demons when a child grows within them.'

He approached the bed, his dagger glinting.

The baby gave another strong kick, spurring Eliana into action. Her limbs sprang free, and she threw off the blankets and tried to scramble away.

He really means it. He's going to kill me. He's not just here to scare me. Oh, gods, help me! Strike him down! Send me a weapon! Anything.

As she tried to roll away, her huge belly got in the way; he caught her by the ankle and dragged her back, his eyes glittering sharp as black diamonds in the moonlight, a smile on his lips. 'I love nothing more in this life than seeing the spark of fear in a woman's eyes. Apart from watching the life ebb out of them. I will be almost sorry to kill you, I've had so much pleasure out of you.'

Her stomach lurched sickeningly – it made her nauseous, how he revelled in cruelty and misery.

He pressed his dagger against her belly, hard enough to split the skin a little. Blood seeped out and stained her nightgown. She knew that he only wanted a more fearful reaction from her. She would not give him the satisfaction.

Drawing on reserves of courage she didn't know she had, she drew back her hand and struck him. He hardly seemed to notice.

She did not dare to try to wriggle free – she had learned her lesson about that in the past, and she would not risk accidentally plunging the dagger into herself.

He chuckled, 'Do you have anything more to do or say before I cut this child from you and send you to the underworld with it?'

Desperately, she spat, 'You'll never get away with this! Samsu will find out. You'll regret it.'

The Brute merely laughed again, 'Dead women tell no tales.'

He tensed as a blade appeared at his own throat, 'And dead men tell no lies,' growled a familiar voice.

Eliana's heart leapt. Ashan! The gods had heard her prayer, and sent her a weapon.

He did not acknowledge her; every ounce of his attention was focused on his opponent, ready for a counter-attack.

'Don't be stupid, boy,' snarled the Brute. 'What matter to you if the whore lives or dies? Her child threatens your place.'

'It matters to me because it matters to Samsu. And it matters to Asag whether his child and its mother live or die.'

Asag stepped forward from the shadows, his bow and arrow at half-draw, trained on the Brute.

Ashan's voice was low, taut with danger as he said, 'Unless you are going to disarm and kill all four of us, perhaps arrange us in a pretty tableau for Samsu, you should leave now. Perhaps there'll be no need to involve the prince if you comply. You might escape this mess with all parts of your body intact.'

Giving Eliana a look as hard and cold as iron, the Brute turned on his heel and marched from the room without another word; Asag followed him to the door, bow and arrow still at the ready, to ensure that he did not try to harm the girls as some sort of consolation prize.

Ashan went to cut Mari's bindings, and Eliana exhaled deeply, her breath shaking. She unclenched her fists, realising that her hands were trembling. 'How did you know?' she whispered.

'I have spies in mother's household,' replied Ashan, shortly. 'I have only been back from Lagash for a couple of hours. My servant gave me the report as soon as he could – I ran for Asag and we came straight here. Just in time, by the looks of it.'

Asag came back in, his weapon lowered and at rest. He went straight to Mari; Eliana was surprised to see him take her tenderly into his arms, as though he really cared for her. In the past, she had only ever seen him acting on Samsu's orders, trying to be a soldier as hard as the rest of them. The more she looked at him, the more she saw a gawky boy with an unfortunate face, who had probably fallen in love with the first woman ever to be kind to him.

As her panic began to subside, she became aware of a warm fluid soaking the sheets between her legs, now cooling. She blushed a brilliant crimson, thankful that nothing could be seen in the black and silver of night.

Shameful, to wet herself in fear. She had not even felt it happen.

Suddenly, an agonising pain gripped her belly, like an eagle's talons embedding themselves into her womb – she cried out in shock.

'What's happening?' asked Ashan, urgently. 'Did he hurt you? I swear to Marduk, I'll kill the bastard with my bare hands.'

She could not reply, gritting her teeth against the spasms.

Mari's voice came out of the darkness, quiet and wavering still, 'She's in labour.' The girl was pale and shaking, but she took charge as though nothing had happened. 'You had better leave before anyone finds out you've been here. Bring a bowl of clean water, some sheets and some wine, then go. This is women's work.'

Eliana caught Ashan's hand, whispering, 'I'm afraid.'

Ashan knelt beside the bed and gripped Eliana's hands in his. 'You'll get through this, my brave one. I'll be back with you soon.'

And our child, the words remained unspoken, but Eliana heard them. She nodded. He wished he could say more, she knew, but they could not be too cautious, even in front of Mari and Asag.

Giving her hands a final squeeze and beckoning to Asag, Ashan left, pausing in the doorway for one last look back at her as Mari set to work.

Chapter 19

Eliana screamed as the baby fought to be free of her. She was being ripped in two from the inside out – it felt like the child was dragging her innards out with it.

The labour had progressed quickly, and before Utu was fully risen in the sky she was ready to push. The birthing chair had been brought in a hurry by two sleep-addled slaves. Mari helped her into it, and she gripped the arms of the chair, placing her hands just where Kisha had when she had sat here.

With Mari busy at her lower end, preparing to bring the baby into the world, the space beside Eliana felt horribly empty; she wanted her sister, Ashan, even her father – anyone to hold her hand and give her courage. Through the long, dark hours of pain since her waters had broken, there were only two thoughts in her mind: to get the baby out of her, and to survive. Lasmashtu, the childbed demon, hovered at her shoulder. She had already taken Eliana's mother and sister – the fear that she would take her too was overwhelming, suffocating. She was not ready for the underworld.

'Breathe, my lady!' called Mari from her position near the bottom of the chair. Her voice sounded muffled in Eliana's ears.

But one whispering voice was clear in her mind: 'Push, Elly. It'll be alright, I promise.' The faintest breath of warm breeze caressed her cheek, and she felt Kisha there beside her, shielding her from Lasmashtu.

Gritting her teeth and gripping the arms of the chair so hard that her knuckles threatened to split the skin, Eliana bore down as hard as she could, straining to free the baby from her body, suddenly filled with a desperate longing to meet it – Ashan's child – to hold a little part of him in her arms, to discover whether she had delivered her own saviour, a boy child, or whether she must face Samsu's wrath.

With a final strain, a wrench and a cry, it was out. Eliana collapsed against the back of the chair as Mari moved rapidly, cleaning and swaddling the baby and cutting the cord.

She lurched forward again as her body gave another great heave, expelling the afterbirth with another spasm of gripping pain.

When it seemed to be over at last, Eliana slumped back against the chair. 'What is it, Mari?' she asked weakly.

'A daughter, my lady,' Mari said in a near-whisper.

'Oh.' Eliana was so filled with disappointment that she could find no other words – the bottom seemed to have dropped out of her stomach; her eyes filled with tears as she reached for the child.

As she was about to take the bundle of linen and yowling infant from Mari, her stomach suddenly contorted again – she doubled over with a cry of pain as another gush of bloody fluid flooded from her, spattering the stained tiles beneath the birthing chair.

'What's – what's happening?' she gasped, panic-stricken, hazy with pain and fear.

Mari rushed to set the screaming baby in her arms gently on the bed; she hurried back to inspect her mistress. 'I think... I think there's another one coming!' she cried, eyes wide with shock.

'Twins?' whispered Eliana. 'I'll never survive it!'

Mari was at her side in a moment, gripping her hand hard. 'You will, I swear it. I won't let you go to Ereshkigal. You shall live to see your lover again and watch his babies grow up.'

Eliana's jaw dropped. 'You know?' she whispered.

Laughing shortly, Mari said, 'I am not a fool. I promised you could trust me, my lady. The secret goes to my grave with me.'

'And Asag?'

'Has no idea.'

Nodding, Eliana opened her mouth to speak again, but a guttural scream was all that came out as her stomach contracted.

Mari disappeared back to the other end of the chair. 'I see it! Push!'

With the last ounce of her strength, Eliana strained against the chair, struggling to free her body of its burden. Finally, first one shoulder, then another appeared, and the baby slid silently into Mari's arms.

Her daughter still screamed alone on the bed, tugging at Eliana's heart. She did not have the strength to move, though she longed to hold the baby, to comfort her.

The girl's cries were the only sound in the room.

'Mari?' she called, voice cracking with the worry, trying to sit up. 'What's happening?'

'The cord is wrapped around his neck.' Mari answered shortly, her back to Eliana.

'His…?' Eliana's heart leapt.

'A boy, but he's not breathing.'

The world seemed to disintegrate around her, and every aching muscle tensed. 'Not… breathing? Is he…?' She didn't dare to speak the words, to make them real. Surely Ninlil would not be so cruel as to send her a boy and then snatch him away in the same instant. Her body contracted again, pushing out the second afterbirth with a final shudder – she barely felt the pain. All her thoughts were for the child in Mari's arm's.

She waited, not breathing as Mari worked frantically over the child, blowing on his face and massaging the chest.

Another cry tore the air, and Eliana went limp with relief as her son's wails joined her daughter's.

Triumphantly, Mari turned to face her mistress. She brought the boy over and placed him at Eliana's breast, before going to fetch his sister and placing her beside him. Against their mother, the twins quieted into gentle snuffling breaths.

With an overwhelming rush of love, Eliana kissed first one, then the other, marvelling at every little detail, feeling the warm weight of them against her, inhaling the newborn scent.

She held them like that, in blissful stillness, for long minutes as Mari put the room to rights, mopping up the fluid from the floor and wrapping the afterbirths in sheets for burial.

Everything was back in order when Samsu strode in, Ashan at his heels. He looked down at Eliana, still in the birthing chair. 'Well, *karkittu*?'

'Twins, sir,' she smiled. 'One of each.'

Over his shoulder, she saw Ashan's face soften.

'Which is the boy?' asked Samsu.

Eliana lifted one shoulder, indicating which side she held him on. Samsu reached down and plucked him from her breast, cradling the child as gently as though he were a vase of the most delicate alabaster.

Unexpectedly, his face split into a wide grin. 'I have a son! Well done, you shall be rewarded for this. Ashan, come here and meet my boy.'

He turned, and Ashan reached out a tentative finger, stroking the downy hair atop his son's head. 'He takes after you, sir, don't you think?'

Samsu gave a short bark of laughter, startling the boy, who began to wail again. 'Perhaps. He certainly has my lungs. Here, take him back, *karkittu*, I cannot bear that noise.'

He placed the baby back on her chest.

'Do you have names for them, sir?' she asked.

'Eshu, for my son.'

'And for your daughter?'

Samsu shrugged. 'Name her what you like. As soon as you and he are strong enough, you and Eshu shall be taken on procession through the city – we will show the people their future ruler, and remind them that his blood is half Nippurite.'

'If you will it,' she smiled, delighted at the prospect of another trip out into the city. 'If it doesn't displease you, I will name the girl Nisala, for my mother.'

'Fine,' Samsu agreed. 'Ashan, prepare the procession for one week's time. That should be sufficient. And have a message sent to my father.' He looked back at Eliana, noticing her tangled, sweat-matted hair, and the blood smeared up her legs and on her gown. 'Well done, *karkittu*. Now get yourself cleaned up, you look a mess.'

He left without a backward glance, expecting his stepson to follow. Quickly bending over the chair, Ashan kissed both of his children, and then Eliana. He pressed his forehead lovingly to hers, before turning and going after Samsu.

*

Her head was spinning, but she gripped the side of the chariot determinedly and waved to the people lining the streets of Nippur.

She had lost a great deal of blood during the birth, and was still paler than usual. She tired easily and had dizzy spells. Mari assured her it would ease after a time. Taking part in the procession through the city was not optional though, so she pasted a smile to her face and gritted her teeth at every jolt and rut in the street.

They rode in Samsu's great war chariot, drawn by a matched team of four roan horses, their red coats flaming in the sun. He held the reins in one hand, and cradled Eshu in the other, thin lips curled into a smile, black eyes flashing with pleasure at the cheers of the populace.

Eshu, born in silence, was by far the quieter of the twins. Nisala had been left behind with Mari, Sarri and Kisuri. Her twins were easily as small as Kisuri had been at birth, and Eliana couldn't help but worry that they would be as frail. Thus far, neither of them seemed to have Kisuri's breathing problems – they appeared to be as strong and healthy as Sarri. Still, every sneeze set sparks of anxiety smouldering.

Mari had just smiled indulgently when she expressed her fears. 'Every new mother feels this way about her baby,' she said.

Eliana's tiered gown was a perfect match for Samsu's tunic – bright crimson edged with gold. Her curls tumbled freely down her back, a wreath of red roses and yellow sunflowers woven into her hair as a sign of her fertility – a woman so blessed by Ninlil that she had brought forth two babies at once. Eshu, sleeping quietly in the crook of Samsu's arm, was swaddled in a blanket of red shot with gold to match his parents.

Heralds marched before them, clearing their path; armed guards surrounded them, and they were followed by a vast retinue of officials, priests and scholars – a calculated display of Samsu's wealth and influence.

He had been worried about the possibility of trouble in the city; despite his marriage to Eliana, a favoured daughter of Nippur, the people still loathed him as an oppressive conqueror, and he knew it. In a moment of inspiration, Eliana had suggested dispensing free wine and bread prior to the procession. With their bellies full and their cups overflowing, the crowds were too merry to protest.

They processed to *Ekur*, the house of the mountain where Eliana and Samsu had been married. As King of the Pantheon, Enlil had had the right to confer the overall kingship of Sumeria on whomsoever he chose – for generations, kings had come to Nippur to carve their names into the bricks of Enlil's temple, and Samsu had been no exception.

He had carved his name on the *ziggurat* on the very day that he claimed Nippur. Today, he would carve Eshu's name beneath his own, recognising the boy and sealing his place in the line of succession. With Enlil now displaced from the head of the pantheon by Marduk, it would be in the Babylonian god's name that today's ceremony took place.

Ashan swore that he was happy to be displaced, and even happier that it should be his own son to do it, but Eliana could not help but feel a little tug of guilt that it moved him a step further from the throne. She did not say it aloud, but she had no doubt that Ashan would be a far better ruler than Samsu – he had a greater understanding of people, and a greater capacity for empathy and friendship. He would not have won the city as effectively as Samsu had, but he would certainly govern it better.

He was somewhere nearby, mingled in amongst the other armed guards, keeping a sharp eye out for trouble in the crowds. It had been a fine line to tread: giving the people enough wine to make them merry, but not so much that they grew disorderly.

They drew up outside the temple gates, where Samsu handed the reins to a slave and stepped from the chariot; Eliana climbed down gingerly after him, taking care not to move too quickly, not wanting to risk a dizzy spell. Not now, with so many eyes upon her. She followed Samsu through the arch and into the forecourt. To her great horror, the mudbrick table was laden with grain and vegetables as at her wedding, but alongside it were chained dozens of animals, and six gaunt and desperate-looking men.

She felt sick, and swayed a little on her feet. Sacrifices.

A warm hand appeared under her elbow, steadying her. Trying to focus her vision again, she looked up at its owner: Asag. Still wary of this man she had always thought of as an enemy, she gave him a grateful nod and went to stand beside Samsu at the altar, where a squat, balding priest was readying himself as the guests arranged themselves about the courtyard.

She glanced around as they waited, searching for her father's face in the assembly. He must be among the retinue that had followed them, but she could not see him. It would do her so much good to speak to him again, to embrace him, to tell him what she had named her daughter. She knew it would please him.

The priest cleared his throat.

The Babylonian naming ritual was strange to her. In Nippur, they made a simple offering to Enlil and begged his blessing for the child. Whether it was because they were foreigners, or because the child was a prince, Eliana was not sure, but the ceremony was long and complex, and her aches and pains increased steadily under the hot sun as the minutes dragged into hours.

Beginning with a lengthy invocation, the priest was in his element. Prayers followed, with the Babylonians reciting the responses on cue as the Nippurites shifted uncomfortably, not knowing the words.

From there, the priest set light to a copper bowl of sacred oil atop the altar; a sweet fragrance, like frankincense, but stronger, filled the courtyard. Taking a pinch of powder from a leather pouch at his waist, the priest tossed it into the flames. A great cloud of acrid purple smoke billowed from the bowl as strange words were chanted over it.

Smothering the flame, the priest dipped his fingers into the oil – Eliana gasped, but the man seemed to feel no pain. He moved to where Samsu was holding Eshu, squinting into the baby's face before anointing his forehead with the oil.

'Great Marduk, we call upon you to protect Eshu, your son; to guide him, to raise him up to be a great and powerful ruler whose accomplishments will surpass even his earthly father's. Help him, great Marduk, to be strong as the wind, wise as the stars, long-lived as the sun, strong as an ox, fierce as a lion and constant as a mountain. Let him expand his empire to the ends of the earth. We etch his name upon your house, and offer you rich sacrifices in poor exchange for your generous goodwill.'

The forecourt was overwhelmed with noise as the sacrifices began; screams of pain and terror saturated the air, and the heavy stench of blood mingled with the perfume of the sacred oils and the flowers in Eliana's hair. She squeezed her eyes shut, unable to watch as animal and human gore ran together. Swaying again, she focused her mind on remaining steady.

The screams dwindled to silence. Eliana opened her eyes.

Corpses were heaped beside the sacrificial table. His companions all dead, only one man remained on his feet, mouth open in a silent scream, eyes wide with terror as he stared Ereshkigal, goddess of the underworld, directly in the face.

With Eshu still in his arms, Samsu approached the man, his blade drawn.

Every muscle in her body went rigid – it sickened her that her son must be exposed to murder and death at just one week old. It was Babylonian custom, she was told. A prince must kill his first man in infancy, to earn the great god's respect.

She said a silent prayer to Enlil that he might forgive her son for his part in the ceremony, all unknowing and helpless, and closed her eyes again as Samsu touched the flat of the blade to Eshu's head before plunging the point into the stomach of the chained prisoner, who doubled forward with a strangled cry and swiftly expired upon the flagstones at his prince's feet.

Eliana wondered what the man had done to warrant such a fate, and prayed that, in her realm, Ereshkigal would treat him with kindness he had been denied in this.

Samsu held the bloodied blade above Eshu's head, allowing a single dark drop to fall onto the baby's face, before moving to the wall upon which were carved the names of kings of centuries past. Using the gory dagger, he carved the boy's name in blood and stone.

The gods would recognise Eshu as rightful ruler of Sumeria, when his time came.

By the time the rituals were concluded, every part of Eliana's body ached. She longed for the comfort of her bed – an oasis of cool calm when the curtains were drawn and Utu shut out.

Beckoning to Eliana, Samsu made his way back out of the forecourt and into the city. The people had assembled outside, and he raised his free hand to acknowledge the cheers for the child in his arm. The cheers grew louder when Eliana appeared behind him, a vision of beauty, despite her delicacy.

He climbed back into the chariot and took the reins, and she stepped carefully up behind him, trying to find a handhold.

As she adjusted her grip, he flicked the reins – the chariot lurched forward. Eliana was jerked off-balance and tumbled backwards, landing in the dust with a bruising thump. The crowd gasped, and two men rushed forward to help her to her feet.

She stood, trembling with the shock, but laughing outwardly, telling the men not to worry and thanking them for their consideration as she dusted herself off.

Samsu would notice, eventually, but she wouldn't injure her dignity more by chasing after him. Her head was reeling, so she took slow, cautious steps as she followed the chariot, talking to the people along the way, blessing the children, greeting old friends. There were smiles on every face, and good wishes on everyone's lips – people reached out their hands to touch her as she passed, calling out for her attention. One woman showered her with rose petals as she passed.

Through the heat and press of bodies, through the jollity and the festivities, Eliana noticed a lone child crouched in the shade of a wall.

It was a little boy, gaunt, almost skeletal, clothed in a half-tunic that barely covered his decency. He was curled up, wrapped in his own misery, oblivious to the merriment surrounding him.

Eliana murmured to the man next to her; he handed her a chunk of his bread, and cleared a path through the crowd for her. She made her way through and crouched beside the child.

'Hello,' she smiled, kindly. 'What's your name?'

The boy looked up nervously with wide eyes, not sure if she was speaking to him. When he saw her gentle expression, his trepidation vanished. 'Kenu, miss.'

'How old are you, Kenu?'

'Seven summers.'

'So big!' she grinned. 'Are you hungry?'

He nodded eagerly. She handed him the bread – he tore at it, barely even chewing. She watched him with pity in her heart.

'Do you know who I am, Kenu?'

He shook his head, then thought hard. 'A princess?'

'I am a wife of the prince,' she allowed. 'But my father is *Ensi* of this city – if you go to the civic hall on a normal day, you should find him there. You ask for the *Ensi*, and tell them Eliana sent you. He'll make sure you have food.'

The boy stared at her as though she might be some demon sent to tease him.

She gave a reassuring smile, 'What name will you give them?'

'Eliana,' he whispered.

She placed a hand on his hand and ruffled his hair. 'Good boy.'

A voice behind her barked, 'Eliana!'

Standing slowly, she turned around to see Samsu waiting for her, his hands fisted on his hips. He strode forward and seized her by the arm, 'How dare you sneak off like that? I've had half the palace guard off looking for you. Talking to filthy beggars – you'll catch some disease.'

She glanced back over her shoulder to see Kenu staring after her, a stricken look on his face. 'Please, sir – I didn't "sneak off", I fell when the chariot moved. By the time I got back to my feet, you were too far ahead.'

Lifting her back into the chariot, he growled, 'Well hold on this time!'

Word of her good deed spread like wildfire as they made their way back up the packed street, travelling faster than the chariot. The people shouted out to her: '*Rubutu* Eliana! *Ibti* Eliana!' – divine queen, beloved, they called her. She was their hope – if she raised her son to be as compassionate as she was, then perhaps their own sons and daughters would have a better life. She had always been a great favourite with those who knew her and her father, but she was beginning to win the love of the whole populace.

Mari would have adored this, she thought, a little sadly. The noise and bustle of the streets, where she was most at home.

Suddenly, she remembered that she had a favour to ask of Samsu. Now seemed the best time – he was in as good a mood as she had ever seen him.

'Sir, might I ask something of you?'

'That depends what it is,' he said, suspiciously.

'Nothing much, just another maid to help out in the nursery. With four little ones all under the age of three, and my own maid about to have another, we have our hands full.'

'Of course, of course. Take two – one for each of our children.'

'Thank you, sir,' she smiled graciously as they came back through the north gate of the palace, shutting out the city behind them.

As they climbed down from the chariot, a steward hurried towards Samsu. 'A messenger arrived in your absence, my prince. He claims to have an urgent communication from Babylon.'

Samsu sighed and handed Eshu to Eliana. 'Return to your apartments,' he ordered, striding off after the steward, towards the audience chamber.

Never had a newborn felt so heavy as Eliana trudged back to her rooms. Eshu's face was still smeared with the blood of the sacrifice – she couldn't wait to wash him off and change her finery for something simple. She hoped that Mari could cope alone if she went to lie down for an hour or two.

Her heart sank as she stepped through the door. There, sat in the biggest chair in the room, was Susa. Ani stood at her back, constant as a shadow. With a sickening lurch, Eliana focused on the bundle in Susa's arms – Nisala.

'So, the whore has returned to her nest.' Susa sneered. 'Did you enjoy making a spectacle of yourself and my husband today?'

'Give me back my daughter,' said Eliana, shortly.

'Oh, this one? Please, I have no interest in her. I will gladly exchange her for the one in your arms though.'

Eliana's arms tightened around her son, 'You will not have either of my children. Nor Sarri, or Kisuri either.'

Susa laughed; a thin, brittle sound. 'What would I want with them? You will hand your son into my custody – I told you many moons ago that if your sister had a boy child, I would have the raising of him. Why would yours be any different?'

'You have no right to him. You are the first wife, but you are not queen yet.' Eliana tried to be reasonable.

'Not yet,' agreed Susa. 'But it is only a matter of time. I am a princess born; you are a common catfish that my husband caught in a palace pond.'

'Better a catfish than a trout!' Eliana snapped back. 'You are a bitter old woman, intent on stealing my child because you cannot give Samsu one of your own! Well you shall not have him! Give Nisala over to Mari.'

From the doorway to the nursery where Sarri and Kisuri were napping, Mari edged tentatively forward, certain that it would not be so easy.

'And better a trout than a whore!' hissed Susa. 'My pride and my dignity are unsullied – I never gave my body to a man who was not my husband.'

'I did not *give* it, it was *taken*.' Eliana shook with rage at the implication, trying to keep her temper under control for the sake of her daughter, though her blood boiled.

'Enough!' Susa shrilled. 'I will not tolerate this insolence. Your sister knew her place, know yours, whore. Give over the boy, or you will find that some *accident* befalls this pretty girl of yours. Perhaps you don't realise how easy it would be? A slip of the finger, stroking her face, and she is blinded... a twitch of the arms, and she is dashed on the floor.'

She made to open her arms, giving Nisala a jolt and waking her. The little girl began to wail. Susa laughed again to see how Eliana had flinched when she thought the child would fall. 'You will comply, or there will be dire retribution. I will remove the boy by force and kill the girl, if that's what it takes.'

Eliana clenched her fist and gritted her teeth, wondering what her chances would be if she simply charged the woman and snatched her daughter from those bony arms. She kept her feet rooted to the floor – it was too much to risk injuring Nisala.

'You'd never get away with it,' she snarled. 'Samsu would have your head. He may not care for her as a daughter, but he cares for her as his property. You should know as well as I that he cannot abide other people damaging his belongings.'

Susa's eyes lit up with cold malice. 'Yes... Samsu. Perhaps he will have an opinion on who should raise his son.'

Her heart stopped momentarily as she realised Susa's intent; Eliana was stunned into silence. Samsu surely would have ideas about who should care for his son. Given that he still called her *karkittu* in private, and accorded her little more respect in public, she thought it unlikely that his decision would go in her favour.

Reading Eliana's face, Susa knew that she had struck a nerve. She stood and placed Nisala on the seat behind her; Mari hurried to pick her up and soothe her pitiful cries.

Susa made for the door, followed closely by Ani. 'I think I'll go and ask him now,' she laughed over her shoulder. 'Don't go far, whore. I'll be sending Ani back for the boy within the quarter-hour.'

'No!' shouted Eliana in desperation. 'You can't! Anyway, Samsu is in urgent audience, he'll never see you now!'

If Susa heard her, she did not acknowledge it, but sped off in search of Samsu.

Turning wildly to Mari, Eliana cried, 'What do I do now?'

Mari took Eshu from Eliana's arms. 'You fight,' she said. 'Go after her. You are high in Samsu's favour at the moment, he might take your argument into account. You know how to handle him – be humble and prostrate yourself, perhaps he'll listen!'

Eliana nodded, turned and fled after Susa. She flew across courtyards and down passageways, not paying attention to where she was going – her feet knew the way. She caught up with Susa just as the audience chamber doors were opening; the woman threw her a spiteful look before stepping over the threshold to her announcement.

Without waiting to be invited, Eliana dashed after her, every inch of her trembling.

Susa stalked up to the dais and stood before Samsu, tall and proud. 'Husband, I have come to demand that the prince Eshu be given into my custody for his raising and education. It is not appropriate that the future King of Babylon be brought up by a whore.'

Elaina ran to the throne with a mind full of Mari's advice – no matter how it demeaned her, she would do what it took to keep her son from the claws of this wretched woman. She threw herself into a bow at Samsu's feet. 'Please, please, sir – I beg you, don't take him from me!' she looked up, her eyes full of tears. 'He belongs with me.'

Ashan stood behind the throne, his face drawn taut at the

open conflict between his mother and his love; for once, Eliana barely even saw him.

Samsu regarded the two women gravely. The atmosphere in the room was sombre. 'This is a matter that I have already given a great deal of thought to,' he said. 'I had thought to make the announcement at a more pertinent time, but seeing as my wife has forced the issue, and in light of recent events...'

'Please,' Eliana implored him. 'I am his mother – I promise to raise him exactly as you wish, just allow him to remain in my care.'

'Silence,' commanded Samsu. 'The decision is already made. Stand up.'

She pulled herself to her feet, clasping her hands before her to stop them from shaking, staring at the floor as she willed herself not to collapse from sheer fatigue and anxiety.

Susa looked across triumphantly.

'It is only fitting that the new Queen of Babylon should raise the prince,' said Samsu, looking at Eliana. Her stomach heaved and her head reeled – Ashan's son would be taken away from her, would know her only as a distant stranger, would no longer be her child.

'Queen of Babylon?' said Susa. 'King Hammurabi...?'

'Dead,' said Samsu, abruptly. 'Last week, on the very day of my son's birth. I am now King of Babylon, and my son will be raised by the queen I have chosen.' He was still looking at Eliana.

A ray of hope began to break through her fug of grief as realisation dawned. 'You mean...?' she whispered, not wanting to speak the words, to sound foolish if she had misunderstood. She did not quite dare to believe it... it could be a sick joke.

Susa laughed harshly, 'You jest! Very funny!'

Turning a hard stare on her, Samsu said, 'Madam, we have been married for more than twenty years. When have you ever known me to jest?'

The woman's face contorted with fury, 'No! You cannot be serious. You would raise this *whore* up to be queen? I am daughter of a king, born to the position! *She* is a wanton slut who weaselled her way into your bed and your affections.'

Eliana was overwhelmed – her, queen? She must have misheard, misunderstood. Any moment, Samsu would laugh at her, tell her she was stupid, his foolish *karkittu*, believing she could be queen. He would sent his Brute to hit her, would punish her for her idiocy.

She struggled to stand on shaking knees as the argument raged over her head.

'You are nothing but a bitter and twisted old woman!' Samsu bellowed. '*You* have only ever been interested in affairs of state for the sake of your own power. *She,*' he jabbed a finger towards Eliana without looking, 'cares about politics only for the sake of the people, only wants to improve their lives. And they *love* her. She brings *me* their love. What do you bring me?'

'She is a *whore*!' screamed Susa. 'The great whore of Babylon! Putting a crown on her head won't change that. You may as well crown a stray cat!'

'Well that cat would still make a better queen than you!' roared Samsu. 'You think that just because I have been chained to you since I was a child, you have some sort of claim over me? Some sort of power over me? Well, madam, the power is mine to bestow upon whomsoever I choose, and it is time you learned that!'

Almost purple with rage, Susa turned and spat at Eliana. It fell short, dropping near the hem of her gown. 'She will never be a queen. She will never be more than a jumped-up harlot who has played you for a fool.'

'She is Queen of Babylon, and you would do well to show her the proper respect. And if any attempt is made to harm her, be sure that yours shall be the first head to roll.'

Susa stormed out, Ani scuttling at her heels like a tame dog.

The long day, the festivities, the rituals, the stresses and strains, the terror and excitement… it was all too much for Eliana. As the reality of Samsu's choice began to sink in, her vision darkened and her knees buckled. She staggered.

'Ashan!' barked Samsu.

Her lover sprang off the dais and caught her under the arm, holding her upright.

'Take her away. Keep your thrice-damned mother away from the queen. Have her rooms guarded. I will speak to her when she is well – the day has been a trying one for all of us.'

He dropped heavily onto his throne as Ashan guided Eliana from the hall.

Chapter 20

The news of Samsu's accession threw the Red Palace into uproar. The comfortable routines of the last weeks and months were blown away in a heartbeat, and suddenly every servant from the most senior steward to the lowliest kitchen maid had a role to play in packing up the place for the move to Babylon.

Samsu was determined that they would arrive in Babylon in time for *Akitu* – the fortnight-long harvest festival that celebrated Marduk's victory over the water demon Tiamat. On the fifth day of the festival, the Babylonians had some traditional ritual in which the king must submit publicly to Marduk, and so it was vital that he be enthroned before then.

Life for Eliana had never been so hectic – there were still the four children to look after, and now she had to supervise the careful packing and transportation of all their clothes and belongings, as well as her own. Mari was less and less mobile, and Eliana was beginning to think that Samsu had forgotten his promise to send her two more maids, though she supposed there would be a whole army of staff when they reached Babylon.

On top of all that, Samsu insisted that she have a wardrobe befitting a queen when they made their entry into Babylon – she was plagued by dressmakers and goldsmiths, bowing and scraping to her as they measured and fitted and plied their wares.

More than anything, she could not get used to her new honorific. Whenever somebody called her 'Your Highness', she failed to answer – it just did not seem natural that they might be speaking to her.

The one thing that stuck in the back of her mind in the midst of all the preparations was her father. He would be left in charge of Nippur, as he had been before the conquest, but now subject to Samsu. Adab would be expected to send regular reports to Babylon, but unless they contained stories of rebellion and trouble, they would no doubt end up buried in the vast mountain of reports that must pour in every day from all over the empire. It was with a bitter pang of sadness that Eliana realised that she was going to Babylon as queen; it would become her new home, and she might never see Nippur – or her father – ever again.

Though she had not had more than a handful of glimpses of him in the three years since her arrival in the Red Palace, it was painful to think that she might never speak to him again. She would so like to say goodbye – to speak to him, and show him that she had matured into a daughter to be proud of.

She confided this to Ashan when he visited to congratulate her on her new status, and ask if there was anything he could do for her. They both knew the real reason for his visit – he held both his children, kissed them fondly, gave them his blessing, and looked longingly at them when it was time to leave. Still, he had said nothing when she expressed a wish to see her father – she supposed it was impossible, and he did not want to upset her by saying so.

The days passed in a frenzy of activity, and before she knew it, she was waking up in a near-empty room on the day of their departure.

The royal party was to meet at the north gate an hour after sunrise. When Eliana stepped through the huge thick wooden doors at the front of the palace, from cool dim passageways into dazzling sunlight, the forecourt was alive with noise and frantic activity. Her appearance did not go unnoticed.

A steward banged his staff as she stepped out, 'Her Highness, Queen Eliana of Babylon,' he called.

All activity stopped, and every servant of high or low estate paused to bow to her as she passed. She tried to greet old friends, people who, just a few months ago, had recognised her as an equal, a slave as much as they were. Now they all averted their eyes, murmured deferential nothings with insincere voices. It infuriated her.

Spying Resu amongst the crowd, she stopped before him. The old man kept his head bowed, showing her his thinning hair instead of his weatherbeaten face.

'Resu,' she smiled. 'I hope you are accompanying us to Babylon?'

'No, Your Highness,' he muttered, uncomfortable with the attention.

'Oh,' her face fell. 'Well I wish you all the best here in our absence.'

'Thank you, Your Highness.' He did not raise his eyes; he did not dare, lest he be seen behaving disrespectfully towards the queen.

Eliana did not want respect, she wanted her friends. Thankfully, Mari had not treated her any differently. Eliana had watched the Brute slay Mari's brothers during the conquest, still saw them in her nightmares, and that bound them. They had known each other when they walked the streets of Nippur together in search of problems to solve – it felt like a lifetime ago, but Mari would never forget that they came from the same place, and Eliana was glad of it.

She gave up trying to speak to Resu. She genuinely wished the old man well – he had been kind to her in her hour of need, and that was not something to be taken lightly inside the Red Palace. She walked on. Servants cleared a path for her as she approached until she reached Samsu, already mounted on a great black war charger.

He nodded in greeting, his face clearly approving of her choice of attire for the grand departure. She wore a flowing silk gown of peacock blue, a heavy sapphire collar at her throat, and her arms moved with a pleasant tinkling music as her dozens of thin gold bangles bounced off each other. Atop her curls, fresh-washed and bouncing blue-black in the sunlight, was set a blue-feathered gold headdress. Her eyes were lined with kohl and her cheeks dusted with gold powder. She looked like a queen, even if she did not yet feel like one.

Asag appeared beside her and gave a deep bow, as though he had not once seen her sprawled half-naked on the bed, at the mercy of the Brute and in the early stages of labour.

He lifted her up onto the mare she usually rode, and after what seemed like an eternity of waiting, the assembly was ready to depart.

Eliana rode at the head of the cavalcade, just half a horse behind Samsu as she had after their wedding. Mari followed behind with the children as the party wound its way through the city to the docks, where the royal ship waited to take them up the canal, northwards to Babylon. Citizens cheered them as they passed through, although Eliana was sure they were simply cheering Samsu's departure. Things could never be as they had been before the invasion; indeed, some people no longer remembered the time before the conquest, but for those who did, a semblance of normality would return.

Whether the good days of peace and prosperity would return with it remained to be seen.

A pleasant breeze blew off the canal as they approached and dismounted. Her horse was led away, and Eliana was left gazing up at the vessel that would take her to her new home. The ship that was like nothing she had ever seen – a huge wooden craft that almost filled the width of the canal, its railings and bow decorated with boughs of leaves and flowers. She had never been on a boat before, let alone a ship – the sight of this floating palace, the anticipation of riding in it, took her breath away.

A quiet cough behind her caught her attention; she turned to find Ashan smiling down at her. He said nothing, only bowed and stepped aside.

Behind him stood her father.

Her eyes filled with tears as she threw herself into his arms, heedless of who was watching. He embraced her tightly, stroking the curls that spilled down her back.

'I've missed you,' she choked.

'And I, you,' he murmured. 'Don't cry, darling. You are queen now – you must not cry in public.'

'Of course.' She shook her head, blinking back the tears. It would not do to smudge her paints.

'I'm proud of you, Eliana. Your natural kindness and goodness has won you the acclaim of the people and the respect of the most ruthless man I have ever known. You have outgrown your childish stubbornness and impetuosity to become a strong and clever woman. I'm certain you will thrive as queen, and leave a legacy that all the people of Nippur can be proud of.'

She bit her lip to keep from welling up again. 'Thank you,' she whispered.

Her father kissed her hand, bowed and walked away.

She turned to face Ashan, her eyes still shining. There was no need for words.

Samsu called her over; taking her hand, he led her up the gangplank and onto the ship's deck. It swayed a little beneath her feet. It was all she could do not to giggle at the sensation – she kept having to remind herself that a queen did not do this, or that, or the other, but must be proper and circumspect at all times.

It was certainly a challenge.

Stood on deck, she breathed in the distinctive smell of the city – dust and spices, people and animals, incense and herbs – and took a last look at Nippur as the rest of the party boarded and the ship's crew prepared to cast off. The canal was sufficiently wide here for the oars to start them on their journey; where it became narrower, ropes would be thrown to the banks, and oxen and slaves would pull them on their way.

A great cheer went up from the crowd on the wharf as the oars emerged from the sides of the ship and dipped into the water; the deck lurched beneath Eliana's feet as they began to move. Tears threatened again as she said a silent goodbye to her home, her childhood, her family, and looked forward to an opaque future as queen.

Scanning the crowds with her eyes, she sought one last glimpse of her father. She found him – stood slightly apart, a sad smile on his face, hand raised in farewell. Half-obscured behind him stood a skinny child, a little boy of no more than seven years, stuffing a date into his mouth. With his clean clothes and impish grin, he was almost unrecognisable – Kenu, the little boy from the parade on Eshu's name day.

Adab laid his free hand on the boy's head and ruffled his hair, just as he used to do to Eliana. Her spirit soared – he would not be alone; he had a child to take care of again. More importantly, he had a child to take care of him as he grew older. A huge burden lifted from her shoulders, and she said a silent prayer, thanking the mother goddess for bringing the two together.

Now it was with a lighter heart and a more optimistic mind that she waved goodbye to all she had ever known, before following a steward to the rooms that would be hers during the journey.

She was shown to a suite of three small rooms – pretty enough, with windows looking out over the banks of the canal. The shutters were thrown open and the low-ceilinged reception chamber was flooded with light and suffused with a cool breeze. The rooms were near to Samsu's, the steward told her, as though that would please her. She smiled brightly and thanked the man.

As he withdrew, she couldn't help but think: this steward was the same man who had ignored her as less than a dog during those dark months when she had sat at Samsu's feet in chains, and now he bowed and scraped as if he could never do enough to please her. The ways of the gods were strange indeed.

So, her rooms were near her husband's. She fervently hoped that was mere coincidence, and he did not want to keep her close for any more amorous reason. Her body was still sore and tender from the trauma of the birth just a fortnight ago. With any luck, Samsu would give her a few weeks' respite yet. He would be busy, after all.

A tentative voice behind her said, 'Your Highness?'

She swung around – two girls stood in the entrance to her rooms, probably in their mid-teenage years. They were stark opposites in their bearing. The first girl was plain and homely, a little on the plump side, but she had a pleasant demeanour and an open, friendly smile. The second girl was a pretty thing, short and slight, with long, elegant fingers and a slender neck; her full lips were pursed in a sulky pout, and her face bore an unmistakeable scowl. Something about the girl bothered Eliana.

'Yes, can I help you?'

The plainer girl spoke. 'We have been sent by the prince...'

'The king,' Eliana corrected, gently.

'The – the king,' the girl stammered, blushing. 'We are your new maids. Happy to serve, Your Highness.'

So, he had not forgotten. 'Very well, and what are your names?'

'I am Tabi, my queen,' smiled the first girl.

'And I am Adra, Highness,' said the sullen one.

As she spoke, Eliana realised what it was that bothered her about this girl, where she had seen her before: Susa's rooms. Her heart sank as she recognised Adra for what she was – a spy sent by Susa. She sighed inwardly, would the woman never give up? No doubt she was cooped up somewhere on the ship, in smaller rooms than she felt entitled to – Ashan had promised to try to keep them apart as far as possible, for the sake of the peace.

'Welcome!' Eliana forced a smile. 'I am very glad to have you – Mari and I have had our hands quite full, with four children and Mari's own on the way. Tabi, find your way to the nursery and help Mari – tell her that I've given you into her charge.'

'Yes, Highness,' Tabi gave an obedient little curtsey and disappeared.

'Adra, you can tend to me.'

'What should I do?' the girl asked, insolently.

It was all Eliana could do not to roll her eyes. A rude teenager was not what she had hoped for when she'd asked Samsu for a new maid – Susa's hand in this was plain to see.

'Fetch me some food and a jug of water,' she said, firmly.

Adra gave a barely noticeable incline of the head and left.

Eliana sank into a window seat and dropped her head into her heads, enjoying the peace. Given the choice, she would have rathered keep Tabi as her maid and send the surly Adra out of sight to the nursery, but she did not dare to have Susa's spy around her children. She half-expected her own food to come back poisoned, though she was determined not to fall into paranoia. Samsu had been quite clear that if any harm came to Eliana, Susa would be the first person upon whom the blame would fall; she must take that as some sort of security. She would keep Adra nearby, where she could keep an eye on her.

It was strange, Eliana thought, that the plain girl, Tabi, should be so much less pretty than the sour Adra, and yet be so much more attractive.

'Ah, *karkittu*,' Samsu said briskly, striding in with the Brute at his heels, 'I see you've found your rooms. You will come to me tonight – bring your lyre.'

Her heart sank. She hoped he would only want her to play for him. 'Yes, sir, I'll have the new maid dig it out.'

'I sent two. Are they suitable?'

'Yes, thank you. I've sent one to the nursery to help care for the children, and I'll keep the other for my own needs.'

'Good. You should also know that I'm posting Ashan and Asag at your door. There are bandits up and down the canal who might try to target this ship. I'll keep him for my own guard,' he jerked a thumb towards the Brute, 'and I've posted two more at the nursery. The royal family of Babylon is the most valuable cargo aboard – if there is trouble, they'll be looking for someone to kidnap and ransom.'

'Thank you,' she bowed graciously, wishing he would go.

He nodded and left. Shortly afterwards, Adra brought her food. It was simple fare – bread, dates and a wedge of cheese, but Eliana preferred it to the rich palace foods.

She took the platter and dismissed the girl, with instructions to search out her lyre, before returning to her window seat.

As she ate, she gazed out, watching the oars dip in and out of the water, enjoying the seductive sway of the boat as it pushed north, and the fresh breath of air that lifted the tendrils of hair at her neck and soothed her with a gentle caress. Fields and fields of crops drifted past her window – barley and wheat, standing tall and ripe, ready for harvest, shining golden in the sun. Strong, sun-browned farmers and their field hands stopped to stare at the magnificent wooden beast as it glided up the canal.

The hours slipped away from her, and the sun had begun to lower towards the horizon before she realised the time and hurried to find the nursery. By the time she arrived, the children were all fed, bathed and ready for bed, and Mari and Tabi sat chatting companionably, as though they had known each other for eternity. Eliana felt a curious pang of jealousy – it felt odd to not be a part of that camaraderie any more. She consoled herself with the thought that at least the nursery in the palace of Babylon would adjoin her own rooms, and she could see the children as often as she liked. Ashan had assured her of that – he remembered the place well from his own childhood and adolescence.

She went to each of the children in turn. Even Sarri was worn out with her day's adventure – she was usually so difficult to get to bed, but her head lolled against Eliana's arms as she embraced her niece and kissed her goodnight.

Once she was satisfied that the children were down for the night, she returned to her rooms, where Adra brushed out her hair, perfumed her and handed her the lyre.

She made her way along the dark deck to Samsu's rooms with a heavy heart, an aching body and a stomach full of butterflies.

It was a struggle not to breathe an audible sigh of relief when he beckoned her over to the bed with the words, 'Come, *karkittu*. Play to me – I am too exhausted for sport, but you can always soothe me with your lullabies.'

He was asleep before she reached the end of her second song, and she was glad to creep away to her own bed.

The days of the voyage passed quickly as the boat made its way steadily up the canal, further from Nippur and nearer to the future.

They were still several miles from Babylon when she began to notice people lining the banks, cheering and acclaiming Samsu at the tops of their voices. The crowds thickened the nearer they drew to the city, and the approbation grew louder with every passing hour. Samsu, stood out on deck, positively glowed under the praise – this was his glorious homecoming. He had begun life as a third son, left the city as crown prince, and now returned as king.

Even Eliana, unaccustomed to the cheering, could tell the difference between this and what they had heard on the streets of Nippur. These people truly loved him – their applause was wholehearted and genuine.

As the ship passed under a grand arched water gate set into the city's thick stone walls, the noise grew positively deafening. The city must be five times the population of Nippur, and it seemed that every single citizen had turned out to welcome the royal family home. The sound was like the roaring of strong wind in the ears – a loud, steady thrum, punctuated by whoops and whistles.

Eliana's own dresses looked horribly awkward and old-fashioned beside the Babylonian women. The fashion here was for gowns that draped over one shoulder and fell in elegant folds to the feet – her tiered and fringed dresses would be wildly out of place. The jewellery, too, was heavy and ornate. Eliana had always preferred lighter, more subtle styles.

She stood out beside Samsu on the deck as the ship made its way towards the palace. The canal flowed directly up to the royal residence, which had its own private wharf so that the family would not have to mingle with common people when they took ship.

The city even smelled different – it had the same tang of dust and spice as Nippur, an aroma that cloyed and clung to the back of the throat, but somehow it wasn't the same; the spices were strange. It smelled… foreign. She could not place it.

Finally, they came around a bend and Eliana caught her first glimpse of the palace. 'The Palace of Gold', the people called it, and it was easy to see why. Constructed entirely of sandstone, the stepped sides rose up from behind high walls, gilded by the sun's rays. Creeping vines made their way across every wall, and flat terraced roofs had been turned into delightful gardens of potted trees and flowers – 'the garden palace' would have been a better name, she thought.

Suddenly, she was filled with apprehension – she wanted nothing more than to turn tail and run all the way back to Nippur. Who knew how things would go for her inside the palace?

What the future held? What freedom she might be permitted, or whether she might ever be allowed to leave? Would she go behind those walls and remain there until death?

Questions swamped her all at once. She forced herself to stand still, beside Samsu, smiling and waving to the populace, but all she wanted was Ashan. In the cramped, close-quartered environment of the ship, she had barely had the opportunity to catch his eye, let alone snatch an embrace.

She took a deep breath and steadied herself against the railings as the oars were withdrawn and the ship pulled up to the wharf to dock. There was no turning back now. May the gods give her strength to face whatever they had planned for her future.

*

If Eliana had been impressed by the size and grandeur of Susa's rooms in the Red Palace, they were nothing compared to the queen's apartments in the Palace of Gold.

The floors were tiled in elaborate mosaics of every imaginable colour symbolising health, happiness, fertility and fidelity; the walls were gorgeously painted with deity stories enough to keep her amused for weeks. Shell lions prowled across bright lapis lazuli plains, and statues of the Babylonian gods occupied niches all around the rooms, watching with judgemental eyes of semi-precious stone.

In all, the apartments were bigger than the entirety of her father's house back in Nippur. They did not have the lush private gardens of the Red Palace, but there was a roof terrace with trees and plants and flowers of every colour and description.

Her belongings had not yet been brought up, and she wandered from room to room, feeling the emptiness keenly. Every footstep echoed off the walls and disappeared into the cavernous ceiling. Once the babies were here, things would be better, she told herself. The rooms would not feel so vast when they were filled with the cries and laughter of children.

There was a knock on the door, and Ashan entered to discover her looking like a lost little girl, separated from her mother on market day. His heart went out to her, and he wanted nothing more than to go and put his arms around her, make her feel found again. He had fond memories of these rooms from his days as a child at the palace – he was eager that she should feel as at home here as he had.

A dressmaker entered immediately behind him. They bowed and straightened as one.

'Your Highness,' began Ashan. 'I have come to brief you on the arrangements for the king's coronation next week. You must have some new gowns made in the native fashion. His will is that you should look and behave as much like a Babylonian as possible.'

'Highness,' the man inclined his head. 'Might I take your measurements?'

'Of course,' Eliana gave a weak smile. 'Do what you need to do.'

She was still tired from the journey, and overwhelmed by the newness, the unfamiliarity of everything. She had not even had time to adjust to becoming a mother before she had become a queen, uprooted and dropped alone here in an expanse of luxurious nothingness. She was so dazed that she would have agreed to anything at that moment. The whole world seemed to have turned upside down.

The dressmaker scurried about her as she stood still for him to do his work. He had a closed-in, ferret-like face, beady eyes scrutinising her as he pulled a thin strip of fabric about her in all different places, marking in paint where the ends overlapped. His face twitched as he worked, clicking his tongue and occasionally baring sharp little teeth.

Ashan ignored the man completely as he began to give Eliana details of the coronation.

'The most important thing that you really need to know, is that your presence is not required,' he said.

'Oh,' Eliana did not know whether to be relieved or disappointed – she had been looking forward to getting out into the city, but would be grateful for the time to rest. 'Why is that?'

'Queens are not crowned, merely proclaimed. You would have no part in the ceremony, which is purely a religious rite. It is not the Babylonian way to make a great public spectacle of private communion between gods and man – Marduk has chosen to ordain Samsu as king, and the ways of the coronation are known to a precious few. It preserves the mystery of kingship. I will be present, along with a few of Samsu's most trusted men, but no women will be present at all, to my knowledge.'

'So, do I have to do anything at all?'

'Well, Eshu will be taken to the ceremony and invested as crown prince at the same time. Afterwards, as mother to the heir, you will be required to appear on the balcony before an assembled crowd, to receive their homage. You'll need to look your very best. Samsu wants the citizens to see the royal family all together on coronation day – past, present and future.'

'Who will be taking care of Eshu in all that time?'

'I will,' Ashan could not resist a grin. They could say no more, with the dressmaker present, but Eliana felt his joy radiating out – it would be the longest time he had spent with his son since the birth.

She nodded, enjoying the moment.

The Brute stalked in unannounced, and the atmosphere immediately felt thick, laden with tension. He bowed slightly, though it looked like the very movement pained him.

Ashan's hand went immediately to his dagger, and he took a step between Eliana and their unwanted visitor.

Rolling his eyes, the Brute said, 'I've come to see her.' He pointed to Adra.

For all the girl's sullen rudeness, Eliana immediately pitied her. Had the Brute found a new target? She looked over at her maid.

She was shocked to see the girl's eyes lit up with joy at the sight of this monster. Adra scrambled to her feet, bowed to the queen and hurried away after him without even waiting for permission.

Eliana's mouth hung open. She turned to Ashan, 'She looked as though... as though she were *happy* to see him.'

'I thought that,' Ashan frowned. 'I suppose you know she is one of my mother's?'

'Of course, I recognised her almost immediately.'

'I don't think she's a danger, but I'm glad you haven't sent her to the nursery.'

'Not a hope of that,' Eliana shook her head vehemently. 'I would rather she endangered me than the children. I don't think she will try anything, she seems to be just a pair of eyes and ears. It seems more trouble than it's worth to go to Samsu and try to have her removed.'

Ashan agreed, 'Seeing as he sent you that specific girl as a gift, it would be best to keep her for the time being. He probably agreed to send her to mollify my mother.'

There was a pause. Eliana sighed, 'Do you think she will ever accept it?'

The corners of his mouth turned down. 'Never. She has always cared more for power than anything else on this earth. I was her ticket to that – then you came along and bore a son to push me away from the throne.'

But that son is her grandchild! Eliana wanted to protest. She could not say it in the dressmaker's presence, and she already knew Ashan's answer. Eshu was Susa's grandchild, but more importantly, he was Eliana's son. Susa would have no influence with him while he remained in the care of his mother. That was the way things must remain.

The dressmaker rolled up his fabric and gathered his paints. 'My work is concluded, Your Highness. Do I have your leave to depart?'

'You do, thank you.'

The man bowed himself out of the room, closing the door softly behind him.

Eliana and Ashan were left alone together. She could not say who moved first, but they were drawn to each other as if by an ever-shortening rope.

His arms slid around her body, feeling like paradise as the heat from his hands warmed her body through the thin silk of her gown. He bent his head and kissed her neck – the merest brush of lips against flesh, but it set her afire and sent a prickling sensation along the hairs at the nape of her neck. Her stomach tightened with longing as he raked his hands through her hair, giving a gentle tug.

She trailed her fingertips over the hard muscle of his arm, enjoying watching the trail of gooseflesh she raised as her hand travelled. Lifting her head to his, she met his eyes; they blazed with intensity, black as polished jet. Tousled hair fell across his face; she reached up to push it away as he bent to kiss her again.

The kiss was gentle, slow at first, as though he was afraid of frightening her away. Something inside her screamed impatiently – she pressed harder against him, opening her lips under his and searching for his tongue with her own.

His hands travelled, caressing her as though he would touch her everywhere at once. Ignoring the protests of her aching body, she slipped a hand up under his tunic and began to stroke him where he was already hard and aroused; he groaned deep in his throat, loosening the shoulders of her gown and allowing his fingertips to drift inside, lightly grazing the soft swell of her breasts.

Breathing hard, Eliana guided Ashan's hands to her shoulders, silently urging him to remove her dress.

As he was about to throw it off altogether, a knock at the door froze them in place.

Heart pounding like a war drum in her chest, Eliana sprang back from Ashan, eyes wild with horror. She gestured frantically at him as she smoothed her hair and pulled her gown back to its place.

Ashan knew this place inside and out – he remembered a favourite hiding place of his as a child, and slipped into the alcove behind a great statue of the mother goddess of Babylon.

'Come in,' called Eliana, trying to steady her voice.

Adra entered, her hair dishevelled, her face flushed, and a blue-black bruise blooming on her upper arm.

The girls eyes and expression had softened, as though she had just seen a glimpse of happiness, but the bruise belied it.

They paused for a moment, staring, taking each other in. Looking at Adra, Eliana saw a girl in love. She would have to be blind to not recognise the symptoms.

She wondered what the maid saw, looking at her queen; wondered what she was thinking.

Adra made to move further into the room. Eliana thought quickly – she needed to get rid of her, to get Ashan away. Her hands shook as she said, 'Ah, Adra. Go to the kitchens, will you? I am thirsty after the journey – fetch a jug of honey and lemon.'

The girl's eyes narrowed suspiciously. 'As you command, Highness.'

She left, closing the door behind her again.

Ashan emerged from behind the statue, his expression dark with anger, brows knotted together. 'That was too close.'

Eliana could hardly force the words out. 'We can't do this again, Ashan. You and I must never be alone together again – we can't control ourselves. I just… I want you too much. It frightens me.'

'You're right,' he nodded. 'We're endangering the children now, not just ourselves.'

'We have to say goodbye. Forever. The twins will be a reminder of the love we once shared, but it's time to bury it. We can never be together while Samsu lives, as you once told me.' Her stomach lurched and her eyes filled with tears. She clenched her fists to hide the shaking.

'Not while he lives,' said Ashan, softly. 'But nobody lives forever. No matter how long it takes, if I outlive Samsu, I will be waiting for you when you are free.'

The tears threatened to spill over. It was too much – she could not dare to hope. While hope remained, love and longing lingered. She must quash it once and for all. To cover her bitter disappointment at a moment of happiness snatched away, she snapped, 'You assume that *I* will outlive Samsu? He may kill me yet. I might never be free; do not fill my head with false hope. I am your queen now; you must treat me as such, as if I were any other queen, in public *and* in private. Do not overstep the bounds. Let us take the children as testimony to our one-time love, and leave it at that. I will not see you privately again.'

She saw it: the moment that he put on his soldier's face to mask his pain.

'As you say, *Your Highness.*' He bowed brusquely, turned on his heel and marched from the apartments.

Absolute silence reigned in his wake. Tears spilled down her cheeks.

Adra would be back at any moment, Eliana knew. She must not be seen crying – it would get back to Susa within the hour. The aching knot of misery in her throat threatened to choke her as she moved out amongst the trees in her garden terrace, taking deep breaths as she fought to bring her emotions into check.

When she emerged several minutes later, she was pale-faced and dry-eyed, ready to face the world with one fewer friend at her side.

Chapter 21

The first few days were the hardest. She could barely look at her own children – every glance reminded her of *him*. She couldn't even think his name without recalling his expression as her haughty words broke his heart. His absence was agonising, and all the worse for knowing it was permanent, and of her own making.

With everyone now in their rooms and beginning to settle into their new home, Eliana could be grateful that she at least had Mari back near her. Any friendly, familiar face was welcome now. She even welcomed Asag when he visited, and he came often to see Mari and her bump. It was clear that he was utterly besotted with her – he made no secret of his affection for a slave, though the other guards mocked him for it.

Since the night he had helped to save them both from the Brute, he had redeemed himself in Eliana's eyes. She dismissed his past crimes as the follies of a boy trying to impress hardened men, and a soldier obeying his orders.

Mari positively glowed; she was the most content Eliana had ever known her. All she lacked to complete her happiness was her freedom. Eliana had approached Samsu to ask permission to free Mari, but was rudely rebuffed and given no explanation. She didn't push the issue. Her husband was more on edge and unpredictable than ever now that the pressures of kingship had been placed upon his shoulders. She was frightened to cross him, lest he return to treating her as he had when she had first been taken captive. Memories of the weight of her collar and the dull *chink* of the chain were as strong as if it had been only last week, though it had been almost a year since she'd been freed.

Which meant… almost a year since Kisha's death. When she thought of it, there was a painful stab of grief in her belly, and she felt almost crushed by the weight of her sadness. A year… how much had changed. And how much had not.

Whatever else changed in her life, with Kisha gone she would always feel as though her shadow was missing.

She did not have much time to dwell on her sadness. No sooner was the coronation over than the harvest festival began. The twelve days of *Akitu* were the highlight of the Babylonian calendar, Asag told her. It was a time for celebration and feast as the barley was cut and the Babylonians marked Marduk's victory over Tiamat.

The high priest of Marduk came down from *Esagila*, his huge temple complex in the north of the city, and three miserable days of dirge-like prayers and penitence followed. Interminable hours of recitation and response – the people expressing a sad fear of the unknown, the priest begging Marduk's forgiveness, pleading with him to protect the people and his holy city.

If this was what passed for a festival in Babylon, Eliana would have hated to see an occasion for sobriety. She had always thought of the Babylonians as barbarians, and first-hand experience of their biggest celebration was doing nothing to change her opinion. Where was the cheer, the warmth? The thanks to the gods, the gratitude for all that they had? Festivals in Nippur were full of life and colour; they celebrated the present and were thankful for the past, not filled with pessimistic laments about the opacity of the future.

These rituals, known as the *Secret of Esagila* continued throughout the fourth day. When darkness fell, Eliana dressed in a gown as deep in colour as the night sky and walked with Samsu at the head of a torchlit procession of hundreds of Babylonians making their way to the temple to hear the Epic of Creation, *Enuma Elish*. The full tale was said to be more than one thousand lines long, over seven impossibly huge clay tablets. Eliana was keen to learn more of Babylonian culture, but she was already numb with boredom in anticipation of the lengthy reading.

They entered the great round tower of *Esagila*. Flaming torches burned in their brackets and the vaulted ceiling was lost in darkness; reed mats rustled underfoot – every step crushed the aromatic herbs strewn across the mats, releasing their sweet perfume until the air was thick with torch smoke and heavy scent. Samsu led her to two thrones of elaborately carved cedar wood set on a dais scattered with petals and sat her upon the lower one.

She settled herself against the cushion as the priest took up his position; there were some advantages to being queen. She and Samsu were the only two present who were permitted seats.

'When the sky above was not named, and the earth beneath did not yet bear a name,' the priest droned, 'and the primeval Apsu, who begat them, and chaos, Tiamat, the mother of them both, their waters were mingled together, and no field was formed, no marsh was to be seen; when of the gods none had been called into being...'

Already Eliana could feel her eyelids drooping. The hour was late, and it was warm and dark inside the temple. The smothering perfume and close press of bodies inside were doing nothing to help.

She forced her eyes open, sat bolt upright and leaned away from the back of the chair. It was unthinkable that she should doze off – she dreaded to imagine what Samsu would do.

Throughout the reading, she felt him shoot sharp looks at her, making sure she was still paying attention. She forced her spine rigid, made her eyes look bright and interested.

On and on the priest drawled in a flat voice that seemed to have just one tone. He was a tall, thin man, all angles and elbows, with a nose as sharp and pointed as a reed stylus. His watery eyes were too close together, giving him something of a cross-eyed look. If she had not been so afraid of the consequences, Eliana would have giggled to look at him. But she forced her face into a serious expression as the priest recited the story.

Tiamat, goddess of chaos and the ocean tried to prevent her husband, Apsu, god of fresh water from destroying the younger gods whose noise and babble disturbed him. To prevent it, Tiamat recruited Ea, the most powerful of the gods, to put Apsu into a coma and kill him. Ea became king of the gods, and had a son – Marduk.

As a child, Marduk was given the wind to play with. The dust storms and tornadoes he created disrupted Tiamat's great oceanic body, leaving all the gods residing inside it unable to sleep. Frustrated, they persuaded Tiamat to take revenge for the death of her husband, not knowing that hers had been the hand behind it. As her power grew and traitorous gods flocked to her banner, she prepared to fight Marduk. She created eleven monsters in the hopes they would help her win the battle, married again and elevated her new husband to supreme dominion...

Eliana gave up paying attention and let her mind wander as the priest went into a lengthy description of how some of the other gods felt threatened by Kingu, the new husband, and his position of power.

Only when she felt Samsu's critical gaze on her did she remember to pay attention again.

Marduk offered to save those gods from Kingu if they would agree to appoint him as their leader and allow him to remain so after the threat had passed. The gods agreed to Marduk's conditions, selecting him as their champion against Tiamat.

The great Marduk challenged Tiamat to combat, and utterly

defeated her. He ripped her corpse into two halves, fashioning the earth from one half, and the skies from the other. He then set about creating the calendar, organising the planet and stars and regulating the moon, the sun and the weather.

Those gods who had pledged their allegiance to Tiamat were forced into labour in the service of those who sided with Marduk, until he destroyed Kingu and created humankind from the vanquished god's blood...

To keep herself amused, Eliana tried to picture it all in her head, to imagine the faces of the gods – their anger, their jealousy, their betrayals... but it all blurred in her mind as the hours drew on and the moon rose high in the sky outside the temple.

By the time the ritual was concluded and they processed back to the palace, Eliana was almost asleep on her feet. But it was done. This was the explanation of Marduk's might and the source of his power; it was the beginning of the preparations for Samsu's submission before the god. It would take place tomorrow, on the fifth day, and Eliana was eager to see her proud and arrogant husband brought to humility before his god.

*

It seemed to Eliana as though the whole of the city was crammed into the temple. The voices of hundreds mingled as one in prayer, rising to the vaulted ceiling like the swirling incense smoke. Amongst these people, she felt very much like the foreigner she was. She did not understand their words, their customs, their prayers, or their gods. Watching them from her high, lonely throne, she felt as detached as a guest watching entertainments at a banquet.

Samsu waited outside the temple doors, adorned with every trapping of a king, impatient to get the ritual over and done with. He had seen his father do it every year of his childhood, and it had always made him cringe with embarrassment to see the mighty Hammurabi reduced to the level of an ordinary man.

The silver-haired high priest waited on the dais, wearing an ivory mask of Marduk and clutching the chief god's signature lightning bolt. For the purposes of the ceremony, he *was* Marduk – when Samsu spoke, the god would answer.

A gong was sounded, the deafening metallic crash echoing around and around the temple; huge double doors at the far end of the nave swung open to reveal Samsu, flanked by half a dozen lesser priests of Marduk, wearing the traditional red robe of their order.

Samsu was the very image of kingly might. Standing a head taller and half a man broader than any of the priests, he was a giant amongst dwarves. He positively glittered in the torchlight – his yellow half-tunic was edged with gold, a matching headdress rose two feet above him, making him look even taller, and not one part of his person was left unjewelled. He looked like a raven dressed in peacock feathers – the lavish costume was ill-suited to the man she knew he was. In his right hand he held the golden sceptre of his reign, topped with a black diamond that drank the light; in his left he carried the orb.

He marched up the aisle with his glare fixed upon the high priest. Eliana was amused to see the man quail a little under his king's stare. She knew exactly how he felt – the difference was that this man was in no danger. He represented Marduk on earth; he was inviolable. Any crimes committed as a legitimate part of his duties were considered null.

Samsu stopped before the dais and squared up to the priest. The nervous man stepped down and approached his king, where he began to strip the sovereign of every symbol of rule, every marker of status.

First to go were the rings – each one was removed and dropped into the waiting hands of a lesser priest. Next his gold cuffs came off, followed by the chain of office that he wore about his neck. It took two priests to remove the weighty headdress, and another two moved forward to take the orb and sceptre, whilst one slipped the sandals from his feet.

Eliana almost laughed. Suddenly, with his clipped black hair all askew from having the crown removed, and his arms, head and feet bare, all his grand feathers had been stripped away and he resembled nothing so much as a plucked chicken.

She stifled it. Not one motion or sound she made would go unnoticed tonight, and nothing that was noticed would go unreported. Samsu was keeping a close eye on her to see how she was taking to queenship, to ensure her behaviour was what he expected of a consort.

Finally, the moment that she had been waiting for arrived. The high priest stood directly before Samsu, his face completely concealed behind the carved ivory, only his pale eyes visible through the slits.

He slapped the king with all his might, drawing back his hand and releasing it with such strength that the *crack* of skin on skin echoed in every corner of the sacred space. Eliana smothered a smile of satisfaction as Samsu's head rocked back on its thick neck with the force of the impact.

The king got to his knees before Marduk and spread his arms wide, baring his chest. When he spoke, he hardly raised his voice, but it was powerful and clear enough for even the worshippers at the very back of the temple to hear every word. In his general's voice, he recited, 'Oh great and strong Marduk, chief of all the gods, I pray you, hear me and answer my plea. I submit myself to you wholly and beg your forgiveness. I have not sinned at all, O lord of the universe, and I have never neglected your heavenly might.'

Once again, Eliana fought to contain herself. If Samsu's actions since his conquest of Babylon did not constitute sin according to the laws of this martial and ruthless god, she dreaded to imagine what did.

Marduk spoke through his priest: 'Do not be afraid of what I have to say, my son, for I am pleased with all you do. I hear your prayers, extend your power and increase the greatness of your reign. Your empire will extend to the ends of the earth, and your son shall equal you in might and power.'

Samsu rose back to his feet and stood impatiently as the priests fussed around him, returning his raiment and jewellery, restoring him to the status of a king before Marduk, replacing everything but his headdress.

There was a sharp *whip-crack* as the priest slapped Samsu again to conclude the ritual. If the slap before had been hard, this was ferocious, but Samsu did not flinch: one cheek reddened with the force of the blow, while the other remained deathly pale.

Asag had explained this part of the ritual to Eliana – the priest hoped that his king would shed a tear, to express more complete submission to Marduk and deeper respect for the great god's power.

If the high priest thought that a mere slap would cause Samsu to shed a tear, he was greatly mistaken in the man's character, thought Eliana. She did not think that her husband was capable of forming tears.

As a final symbol of Marduk renewing and refreshing Samsu's power, two priests stepped forward to replace his headdress.

Eliana could not mistake the anger in his eyes as he stalked to his throne beside her and sat heavily. Samsu was not a man used to humiliation by man or god. His fists were clenched on the arms of the chair throughout the rest of the ceremony.

She kept her face carefully blank and impassive, not even wincing when he gripped her by the hand hard enough to make the bones crunch as he led her to the waiting horses at the end of it all.

A great feast followed, to celebrate Marduk's continuing favour upon Babylon, its people and its king. Samsu drank hard and fast. Eliana eyed him worriedly as he drained bowl after bowl of wine and signalled for more. There was no cheer about him – he sat in brooding silence for the most part, only giving monosyllabic answers when spoken to and venturing no conversation himself. He seemed to grow more detached as the evening went on; his eyes shifted suspiciously, his paranoid gaze falling on everyone in turn.

She breathed a sigh of relief when he stood abruptly and turned to march from the room, retiring for the night.

The relief died in her chest when a page boy brought the summons she was dreading.

Following the boy from the room, she tried to swallow her dread. Perhaps Samsu just wanted a soothing song on the lyre, or to talk over something that had been troubling him.

She knew she was wrong as soon as she entered his chamber. He stood in the centre of the room, as tall and unyielding as a monolith, glaring at her as she walked in.

Eliana gauged his mood immediately and went to her knees in a bow. In a good humour, he did not require it of her anymore… but he was not in a good humour. She breathed deeply, trying to slow the anxious gallop of her heart.

'Get up,' snarled Samsu. 'Don't show me your false reverence. You'd have laughed at me just like everyone else today, if I hadn't been watching you.'

She sat back on her heels with lowered eyes, not daring to speak in case she said the wrong thing.

'Well? Say something!' he slurred.

'I have nothing to say, Sir.'

'Well, that is a first. Perhaps you have finally learnt humility.'

'I am a mother and a queen – I have learnt dignity.'

'You only have what I give you. I choose to give you dignity.'

'And I thank you for it,' she replied, through gritted teeth.

He stared at her for a moment. 'Get up on the bed.'

Doing as she was told, she settled back against the cushions, still not sure what he wanted of her tonight.

'You are the only one in this whole gods-forsaken world who speaks the truth, except for Ashan, perhaps. There are so few I can trust to tell things as they are.'

'I hope I shall always be able to tell you the truth,' she said, carefully, a small pang of guilt tugging at her stomach as she thought of Ashan and their children.

'Then tell it to me now. I have given you everything – wealth, jewellery, status, children, even a crown. Do you love me?' he demanded.

Eliana laughed, taken aback. 'No, why would you think that?'

She could have bitten her tongue out as she saw the red mist of fury descend on Samsu. He stepped up to the bed and seized her by the throat with bruising force.

His face inches from hers, he hissed, 'How *dare* you laugh at me? Insolent, ungrateful piece of dung! You are only what I allow you to be – I have given you everything, and you repay me with nothing!'

Her eyes widened – she tried to choke out a reply, but his hand crushed her windpipe with such brutality that she could not draw breath. Pinpricks of light began to dance before her eyes.

'What do you have to say for yourself?' he barked, easing the pressure on her neck.

Drawing an unsteady breath, she whispered, 'I repay you with truth. If you desire false love and sycophancy, I can oblige.'

His fist landed on her cheekbone like a mallet against stone with shattering force, stunning her as pain exploded inside her head. The rings that he still wore tore at the soft flesh of her face and she was vaguely aware of a warm trail of blood snaking its way down her cheek.

'The truth,' growled Samsu. 'You like the truth?' He grabbed her hard between the legs, '*This* is your truth. *This* is why you're here. The people love you, you have some good ideas, I'll concede that much, but without *this*,' he squeezed again, 'you're nothing. Without the two children that came from here, you'd still be chained to my wall – my plaything and my pet.' His breath reeked of wine, and he stumbled over his words. He breathed heavily as he glared down at her. 'You have been getting above yourself, *karkittu*. I made you queen, I can unmake you just as easily. Now get on your hands and knees and please me!'

Trembling, her head still reeling from the blow, she turned herself onto all fours, burying her face in the bed as Samsu ripped her gown open and forced his way inside her. It had been almost a year since he had had her, and the first thrust was a stab of agonising white-hot pain she had almost forgotten. She balled her fists in the sheets as he drove himself in and out with a madman's frenzy. He wound her hair around his hand and pulled, arching her back and burying himself so deep that her muscles clenched and spasmed in protest at the violence of it.

When the ordeal was over, he pushed her off the bed and onto the floor where she lay curled up, angry and disgusted, not daring to move for fear of more violence. 'Let that be a lesson,' he panted. 'Be grateful for what I give you, for I can reduce your status again in a heartbeat. You will learn to love me, or you will live as a slave again until you do.'

A familiar tightness pricked the back of her throat. She would not let the tears flow; she bit the inside of her uninjured cheek to hold them back. Things had been so much better since the birth of the twins – perhaps she had been foolish for thinking they could stay that way. Samsu had been kinder lately, in his own way, and now she understood it – he was trying to win her love. The old pride that she had fought so hard to bury was clawing its way back to the surface.

Slowly, she struggled to her feet. 'I'll never love you,' she said, her voice unemotional. 'You stole me, imprisoned me, took away my innocence, violated me, chained me, killed my sister and separated me from my father. All that – it's unforgiveable. You can take away all you have given me – my jewellery, my status, my dignity... even my children. But for all that you can take by force, you can never have my love – *that* is a gift that must be freely given.'

Samsu rose from the bed and stood over her, staring her down. 'Said your piece now, have you?'

'Yes.'

'Good,' another swing of his fist connected with her other cheek and sent her sprawling, hitting the cold tiles with a crack. 'Another little speech like that, and the children shall be taken out of your care and given to Susa.'

She whimpered, feeling her face begin to swell where he had struck it, and sick to think of Susa so much as looking at the children.

He was drunk, she knew. This was not a man who took kindly to public humiliation, and so he repaid the favour in private, to make himself feel better. Her female parts burned and throbbed.

The depth of loathing she felt for him was no longer a surprise to her. The fact that he could still increase that loathing *was* a surprise. Each time she thought she couldn't possibly hate him any more than she already did, he proved her wrong.

'Get out,' he sneered, leaving her to pick herself up from the floor and limp back to her apartments, feeling revulsion in every ache of her ill-used body, longing for Ashan's arms around her, his soothing voice murmuring into her hair; she wished with all her heart that she had not closed and barred that door.

*

Akitu went on around her as if nothing had happened. As though all she thought she had achieved in the past year hadn't just been torn down around her ears.

The following day, Samsu made no reference to anything he had said or done. Statues of gods arrived by boat from all over the empire to accompany that of Marduk's son, Nabu, in his mission to free his father.

Eliana did not fully understand it, but the tradition went that Marduk had been imprisoned by the evil gods, led by Tiamat, after renewing his favour upon Babylon, and awaited rescue by his son and an alliance of other brave gods.

She was forced to walk with Samsu back to *Esagila* at the head of a huge procession of citizens, carrying the statues of the gods, led by Nabu, and chanting, 'Here's he who comes from afar to restore the glory of our imprisoned father!'

People stared at her as she passed, the bruises on her face shining like beacons, livid and swollen. She cringed with the shame of it – to have to appear in public in this state. The people would be in no doubt as to what had happened; they would certainly be wondering what she had done to provoke him to it. The markets would be full of slanderous gossip before sunset.

And this was just the sixth day – Akitu was only half complete.

On the seventh day, a mock-battle took place at the gates of *Esagila*, which the king and queen were required to attend. Inside the temple complex, the evil gods swirled and chanted as they protected their precious quarry – the high priest, once again in the guise of Marduk, fought them tirelessly. He was surprisingly nimble for an old man, Eliana thought. Outside the barred gates, the hero gods worked to batter their way inside.

The gates burst open, the heroes streamed inside. A tremendous choreographed battle ensued – statues of the gods swaying, embellished costumes of their handlers fluttering in the breeze and sparkling in the hot sun.

Eliana wiped her brow as sweat trickled down her face from underneath her heavy headdress. Her neck ached ceaselessly – whether from the weight of the crown or the force of yesterday's blows to the face, she could not say. She only knew that her head hurt, and she wanted nothing more than to sleep in a cool, dark room with her babies.

She had barely seen the children since her arrival in Babylon, and the hectic schedule of the festival fortnight left little time for visiting. It felt as though someone had cut off one of her arms – like she was missing a part of herself. Mari sent regular reports of her babies, but it was not the same as holding them every day.

A great cheer went up from the crowd as the evil gods were overcome and, one by one, fell to the ground. Nabu emerged victorious, freeing the mighty Marduk from his imprisonment; finally, she was free to return to the palace.

The festivities seemed never-ending. On the eighth day, the entire court was required to gather in *Ubshu-Ukkina*, the Hall of Destinies, where the 'gods' deliberated between themselves and decided to join all their forces together and bestow them upon Marduk. Samsu implored each of them in turn to support and honour Marduk, supreme commander of the gods and wielder of all their powers. The great god was unique in his position – receiving submission from all the others as recognition of his strength.

The victory of Marduk over Tiamat was celebrated the following day, in yet another procession, this time to the House of Akitu, outside the city walls. The squat stone temple was immaculately kept, with trees carefully cultivated and beautifully laid out to show respect to the god who granted life to nature.

There was a feast at the House of Akitu on the tenth day; to add insult to injury, Eliana was not only required to attend, but was demoted from her place at Samsu's side. She sat in silence throughout, seething and eating nothing, arrayed as a queen, but looking for all the world like she was severely out of Samsu's favour, with her bruises and her lowly position at the table.

It was all part of the ritual, Asag had explained. The tables were arranged around the statues of the gods as at a wedding feast, and Marduk, in the person of Samsu, was to marry the goddess Ishtar, in the person of the highest priestess of *Esagila*, a noble girl from a Babylonian family.

Eliana had been forced to watch their 'marriage' ceremony earlier that day – she loathed her husband, but there was no joy in watching him stand beside a lithe and nubile girl who looked up at him with such puppy-like devotion that he almost smiled at her.

The pair recited love poems before an assembled congregation, and sealed the union with a chaste kiss. It was this noble girl who sat on a throne beside Samsu tonight. The love between Marduk and Ishtar symbolised a union of heaven and earth, and would bring forth life when the new crop of barley was planted.

Samsu directed smug glances at Eliana throughout the evening, watching carefully to see if she exhibited any signs of jealousy. She did not attempt to curb her sulkiness – if he perceived it as jealousy, perhaps he would begin to believe that she loved him after all. It had not taken her long, as she sobbed herself to sleep the night of his attack, to decide that if his believing that she loved him would ensure the safety of her children, it was a small price to pay. He could believe whatever he liked – it would not make it true.

The priestess sat to Samsu's right. To his left was Ashan.

Her stomach somersaulted every time she looked at him. She could break off their love with words, but never in her heart. His tousled hair fell about his sun-bronzed face, his teeth gleaming white in his easy smile. He ate and drank as though he had not a care in the world.

She masked her own pain, pretending not to notice him, unsure if he had even seen her. Perhaps he hadn't recognised her, displaced from her position and with her face swollen and disfigured. Or perhaps he hated her now. It was a heartbreaking thought.

The final ritual took place the following day, as the gods met again in the Hall of Destiny to decide the fates of the people of Babylon. The happiness of the gods could never be complete if their servants, the humans, were not happy. After much stilted and scripted speech-making, it was decided that a human's destiny was to be happy, on condition that they served the gods. With this decision, Marduk's covenant with Babylon was renewed, and he was able to return to his house in the heavens.

For the first time, Eliana wondered if she was serving the wrong gods. Maybe Marduk *was* superior to Enlil. If her destiny was to be happy as long as she served the gods, she was failing in her duties to them somewhere, that much was evident. It was time to add a Babylonian goddess to her prayers. If Ninlil could no longer protect her in this foreign land, perhaps Ishtar would take pity on her.

She breathed a deep sigh of relief as, on the twelfth and final day, the statues of the gods were taken down to the boats to be returned to their own temples, and normal life could resume at last.

It was bliss to spend a few days in her apartments, visiting the nursery and watching the children grow. Sarri was an imperious and demanding toddler, but fiercely protective of her fragile baby sister and utterly fascinated by the twin babies. Eliana spent hours each day, playing with her and holding and talking to the others. Between her, Mari and Tabi, there were plenty of hands to see to the children's needs now.

Her bruises had almost healed and her tranquillity almost returned within a week of the end of Akitu. She had not seen

Samsu, nor been summoned by him, nor been required to leave her apartments.

The respite was temporary, she knew, but she was grateful for it. She had begun to include Ishtar in her daily prayer ritual – perhaps the goddess of love had something to do with it.

When he eventually visited, he took her entirely by surprise, bursting in while she crouched on the floor with Sarri, playing with a little cloth doll.

'*Karkittu!*' he barked.

She leapt to her feet as though pricked by a dagger. 'Yes, sir?'

'You will attend audience with me tomorrow. Emissaries are arriving from Nippur – I would have you hear what they have to say.'

'Yes, sir.'

'And do you have anything else to say?'

'No, sir. Should I?'

'Well, you were so talkative at our last meeting, I wondered if you had decided to reconsider any of your words.'

'Oh, yes,' she thought quickly, trying to pull the right falsities into her mind, searching for the words that would satisfy him. 'I spoke rashly, of course. I was strained and tired. My... my great *affection* for you cannot be overstated. You are right, you have given me everything, and I have no wish but to please you in every way I can – though I can never sufficiently repay you for all you have done.'

At least the very last part was true, she thought.

Samsu nodded, grunted his satisfaction and left without another word.

Relief washed over her like a cooling breeze. The man may profess a desire to hear the truth, to hear things as they were and drink his medicine with no sweetening, but he was as shallow and foolish as any other man – only interested in hearing of his own importance.

It was a lesson she would not soon forget. She had told him what was in her heart when asked for it, and the punishment had been severe. Flattery and beguiling words were all he wanted.

She got back to the floor and resumed her game with Sarri, wondering what her father's emissaries would have to report tomorrow.

Chapter 22

'Sarr-eeeee!' Nisala wailed, chasing her sister across the room.

'Can't catch me!' sang Sarri over her shoulder, running for the nursery door. 'You can't – oof!'

She ran straight into Eliana and ricocheted back off her, catching her heel in her gown and nearly tumbling over backwards.

'Woah!' Eliana caught her niece under the arm.

Sarri steadied herself, laughing breathlessly as Nisala caught up. Eliana kept hold of the older girl's arm, asking, 'What's going on here?'

'She's – got – my doll – AGAIN!' panted Nisala, bottom lip sticking out in a sulky pout.

Eliana gave her niece a stern look. Sarri rolled her eyes, 'Oh *alright*,' she sighed. 'I was only playing!' She held out the doll; Nisala snatched it back and stormed off.

'Sarri,' said Eliana, softly. 'What am I going to do with you? Nisala adores you, you know. She idolises you. Must you always fight with her?'

The girl shrugged, looking at the floor. 'I was bored. I only wanted a laugh. She's so easy to agitate – didn't you ever fight with my mother?'

'All the time,' smiled Eliana, 'but we were not royal princesses. You *must* learn to behave yourself. It's a lesson we've all had to learn.'

And some of us learn it in harder ways than others, she thought, sending Sarri on her way.

Eight years had now passed since her arrival in Babylon. Sarri had grown into a precocious and mischievous beauty of eleven, with curls that cascaded to her waist and dark expressive eyes that tilted up at the corners – her mother's eyes. It still gave Eliana equal pangs of joy and grief when she looked at Sarri and saw Kisha's image reflected back at her. The girl had her mother's looks, and her father's sharp intelligence. She also had his sharp tongue, when it suited her; Eliana was trying to curb that at every opportunity. Sarri may be a princess, but she must grow up humble and sensible – Eliana felt a duty to her sister to make sure of it.

Kisuri, on the other hand, was as fragile and delicate as the day of her birth. She could not walk any great distance without tiring; while the other children ran about the gardens, she would sit under the shade of a tree with Eliana and watch with a gentle smile playing about her lips. She was almost ten years old, but she had the wise eyes of a much older woman. Where Sarri was flirtatious and coquettish, Kisuri was quiet and shy. The girl had a talent for the lyre and composing poetry, and she was always ready with a willing ear and soothing words if any of her siblings had a secret to share. She was already a princess to be proud of – Eliana prayed only that Kisuri would be married to a husband whose nature matched her own. She would never survive a man as robust as her father.

Though she loved her two nieces as dearly as her own children, the twins were Eliana's pride and joy. Now eight years old, they were strong and lively, with adventurous spirits and kind natures. It annoyed them that they were forced to spend more and more time apart as they grew, with Eshu's education being taken over by the tutors who would mould him into the sort of prince that Samsu expected.

Well, the tutors could mould him into Samsu's idea of a prince, but Eliana was determined that she would mould him into her own idea of a man. He was already showing signs of being a better man than Samsu could ever hope to be – the boy was stern with his sisters when they were being silly, but knew when to have fun, when to be serious, and, most importantly, when to be compassionate.

He and Ahat were thick as thieves, as close as Samsu and Ashan. Mari's son had been born on a stormy night not two moons after Akitu. The gods had seen the boy safely into the world, and his mother had recovered quickly. He was not an especially attractive child, but his looks were not as unfortunate as his father's.

Asag doted on the boy. Now risen to be a commander in Samsu's army, he was more mocked than ever for his continuing liaison with a slave woman. But, to his credit, he did not abandon Mari; in fact, his love for her seemed to grow stronger than ever. More than once, Eliana had heard him lament the fact that he could not marry her while she was still enslaved. Samsu would not countenance freeing her – she was too good a guardian to the children, and too good a nurse to lose from the palace staff.

For all that had changed, Samsu had not. After her harsh lesson that first Akitu in Babylon, Eliana had learned to be constantly alert around her husband, giving him the words he expected to hear, making her ideas seem like his own, and giving every appearance of being the dignified and acquiescent queen he wanted. It had been difficult, at first, suppressing her own nature to gratify his, but it soon became a force of habit. If it kept the children safe, it was worth it. She had no regrets there.

In fact, the only regret that she could call to mind… was Ashan.

She had kept to her word – they had never been alone together since that awful day she had arrived in the Palace of Gold. For all the long years that had passed, she had never managed to get over her love for him – only to bury it, smother it beneath other concerns. And for what it was worth, she could not be sure that he no longer loved her – he had never taken a wife, despite much pressure from Samsu, and a good number of eligible beauties hanging around him at every opportunity.

If she could change just one thing about her time in Babylon, it would be to allow Ashan to spend more time with his children. But it had never felt safe, and their wellbeing had to be her top priority.

Still, Ashan was now responsible for his son's military education – it warmed Eliana's heart to watch them cross wooden blades in the practice arena or to see their identical black-haired heads bent over a map of the empire, discussing strategy.

Military strategy was becoming an ever-more important feature of Eshu's education. There were rumours of rebellion in the empire. A man named Rimsin had risen up, proclaiming himself the heir of the troublesome city of Larsa, and the revolution was spreading fast.

Asag burst into the room, intruding on Eliana's thoughts.

'My apologies, Your Highness, but the king would see you in his audience chamber immediately.'

'Is it so urgent?' She could not help feeling a little alarmed.

He nodded gravely, and she followed him quickly through the sprawling halls and passageways of the palace to the audience chamber.

Samsu stood at a great table set in the centre of the room, deep in intense conversation with Ashan, the Brute and three of his most trusted commanders.

He looked up as she entered. 'Ah, there you are. It took you long enough.'

'Apologies, sir,' she bowed. 'I came as soon as I received your summons.'

Waving his hand impatiently, he said, 'I am leaving – it's war.'

She froze, momentarily speechless. After long seconds, she managed, 'War, sir?'

'War,' he nodded. 'Rimsin has rallied twenty-six cities across the empire – from Rapiqum in the north, right the way down to Ur in the south.'

She gasped – truly the whole empire had risen against Samsu's rule. Though she did not care for Babylonian rule, Samsu's kingdom was her son's inheritance.

'I have to leave immediately – within the week. There is no time to make detailed arrangements. Asag will be left behind with a small guard – my generals and I will march south to quell the rebellion in the most troublesome cities. I will do whatever it takes to preserve the empire my father built.'

'Of course,' she said, weakly.

'You and Eshu shall be left as joint regents in my absence,' he continued.

This time, her jaw dropped in shock. 'Regents?'

'Yes. Your judgement is second to none in this palace, and no-one's interest is more closely tied to the boy's than your own. You will teach him the ways of ruling, keep up the weekly audiences for as long as you deem them safe, and make the minor decisions regarding the wellbeing of the people. I shall have a document drawn up before I leave to outline the extent and limits of your powers.'

'Yes... sir.'

'Very well, you are dismissed. I won't have time to see you before I depart. I shall send a messenger to let you know precisely when we intend to leave, and you will dress in your finest and bring the children to see us off. The city will turn out to see the procession, and I want a full display of the might of the royal family – a glimpse of their next ruler with the sisters who will make grand dynastic marriages to strengthen their house.'

She bowed, still mute with the unexpectedness of it all, and allowed Asag to escort her back to her apartments to break the news to Eshu.

The boy was thrilled at the chance to play at being a king. Eliana did not think he fully grasped the truth of war, the fact that Samsu could die, and the play might easily become reality. The king took little interest in daughters, but he had always been tender towards Eshu, and the boy revered him as almost a god.

She did not wish to put a dampener on his excitement; she would cross that bridge if they reached it. If Samsu survived the war, and there was no reason to suppose he would not, broaching the subject now would only cause Eshu distress. He was a clever child, but not yet ready to rule – it was difficult to imagine any eight year old boy who would be.

The week seemed to fly past – hours and days all melding together, until the moment of the army's departure was upon them and Eliana and the children stood on the royal balcony overlooking the palace gates, dressed in their finest silks and jewels.

The crowd gathered below them roared and cheered as Samsu stood in his saddle and stabbed his dagger into the air in salute to his family, the sun glittering on his blade. Eliana, Eshu and the three girls raised their hands in response.

Samsu wheeled his horse around and set off through the gates at a smart trot, surrounded by his personal guard, the Brute to his left, Ashan to his right.

Even after so many years of marriage, Eliana cared nothing for Samsu's safety for the man's own sake, but she said a silent prayer to Ishtar to bring her husband and her love both home safely. Samsu's death could spell disaster for Eshu at a time when the empire was threatened and disintegrating; it needed a strong hand on the reins. And Ashan's death simply did not bear thinking about. A little part of her would die with him. She still harboured a secret hope that she would one day be able to reveal the truth of the twins' paternity to them, however unlikely that was.

As a cloud of golden dust kicked up by their horses' heels obscured the army, Eliana turned to go back into the palace. She had not felt so free since before Samsu's invasion of Nippur, and her heart positively soared at the thought of weeks, maybe months, without her husband's oppressive shadow hovering at her shoulder.

*

The freedom from Samsu was utter bliss; Eliana finally felt able to relax without fear that she might be summoned at any moment or called to audience at a minute's notice. She could even stop taking her herbs at last, after forcing down the bitter drink every day without fail since Samsu's assault on her during their first Akitu in Babylon.

Though she adored children, the idea of carrying any child of Samsu's was utterly abhorrent. The thought that she might not be able to love it as well as she loved her children by Ashan terrified her – she could not bear to imagine that the child might suffer any sort of neglect just because of its paternity. It was far better to prevent any such child from ever existing.

At first, Samsu had been mystified by her failure to conceive, then he had been angry, and finally, after several years, he had accepted it. He still took her to his bed once or twice a week for sport, but she believed he had resigned hope of Eshu ever having brothers.

It was quiet in the King's absence. The palace felt deserted – it was possible to walk through a whole wing without hearing anything but the eerie whistle of the wind through the passageways.

The weather was beginning to turn – the temperature was dropping and the wind was rising as the season changed. When Eliana took her daily walks in her rooftop garden, she was forced to wear a cloak to keep out the biting chill. Still, she made sure that she took a walk every day. Knowing that Samsu could not call on her meant that it was of little importance if she was windswept or rosy-cheeked – there was no-one around to care.

It was as she took one of these walks, just a few days after the army had marched out, that Adra came running and screaming for her; eyes wild, and hair damp with sweat.

'Your Highness!' she shouted, racing out to the garden.

'Adra? What is it?' Eliana called back, every nerve suddenly alive with fear.

'It's Eshu,' the girl panted. 'He's had a fall.'

Eliana's heart seemed to stop beating, and the world around her slowed down. 'What do you mean, "a fall"?' she pressed, urgently. 'Is he alright?'

Adra shook her head, 'Down some stairs... he's, he's hurt...'

Grabbing the maid hard by the shoulders, suddenly blind with panic, Eliana cried, 'Where?'

'He's in the account-keeper's office – it was the nearest room...'

Eliana was off at a sprint, tearing along without a moment's hesitation towards the small office on the ground floor of the palace.

Why was he near the account-keeper's office? He knows not to go to this side of the palace – it's almost deserted most of the time. What could have taken him there? Dozens of questions chased through her mind, almost drowned out by one overriding thought: *please be alright. I beg you Ishtar, please let my little boy be alright.*

She burst through the door of the little office, not knowing what to expect, her heart hammering so hard that it burned her chest.

Eshu was not there.

Where she had expected to find her little boy, her darling prince, twisted and crippled, there were only two men. Young men, by their stature and posture, probably servant boys, by their clothes, but it was impossible to tell for sure; they had lengths of cloth tied around their faces.

The door slammed closed behind her. She wheeled around – a lined and careworn face stared back at her: neat grey hair smoothed back beneath an oversized headdress, malicious eyes glinting above pursed lips.

Susa.

'What are you doing?' Eliana tried to keep her voice calm, steady. 'Where is my son? What have you done with Eshu?'

'Your son has come to no harm,' said Ani, from the corner. 'You, however…'

With a vicious grin, baring teeth like fangs, Susa said, 'You have stood in my way for too long, whore. They can call you queen, dress you in gold and silks, but you'll never be more than the jumped-up daughter of a petty official. It's time you made way for the true queen.'

Despite the rising tide of fear for herself, Eliana was overwhelmed with relief to hear that Eshu was not injured. The truth of the situation began to dawn on her though: she had rushed headlong into a trap.

'I *am* the true queen, and have been so for these past eight years,' she said. 'You have been silent on the matter until now. Why would you suddenly choose to start creating trouble?'

'Because *suddenly*, my husband is leagues away from here, and occupied with more pressing concerns than the safety of his little whore. I have been a good, accepting wife for so long now that he will never suspect my involvement.'

'Who else would he suspect?' Eliana tried. 'You'd be a fool to think you'll get away with it.'

'But we will,' smiled Susa, her voice full of malevolence. 'You are like a cornered rat. These men will take you and do their work – the physician will tell my husband what I pay him to say about the cause of your death, and you will be interred and well out of the way before Samsu ever hears a whisper of your demise.'

Panic began to flutter again in Eliana's chest. She forced it down, telling herself to remain calm.

She opened her mouth to reply, to try to talk some sense into Susa, but a hand seized her arm through the cloak, and a second pair of hands clutched at her waist.

Immediately, she began to writhe, twisting and bucking like a frightened horse. By sheer accident, she caught one of her assailants in the shin with the heel of her foot; he let go of her, crying out in a voice barely broken into manhood.

With one more determined twist, she slipped from her cloak and ran for the door. Susa tried to grab her, but she easily sent the older woman flying against the wall with a powerful shove, wrenched the door open and fled.

She ran blindly, not caring where her feet took her, hearing the slap of sandals against the tiles behind her, hot on her heels.

Darting around a corner, first left, then right, sprinting down a corridor and up a curving flight of stairs, along one passageway, around another corner, up another passageway, down a flight of stairs, across a courtyard, vaulting over a low wall and charging across a second courtyard… she was thoroughly lost.

In desperation, she stared around, looking for a room she could hide in until she was certain that the servant boys would not find her. She spotted a small door at the base of a tower – she ran to it, forced back the long-rusted bolt, and slammed it behind her.

Inside the tower was pitch-black. She leaned against the door, her heart thudding so loudly in her chest that she was terrified it would give her away – it must be audible to half the palace!

She took a few deep breaths, closing her eyes, allowing them a moment to adjust to the gloom. The air around her was cold, musty and damp. She shivered as the sweat began to cool on her skin.

When she opened her eyes again, Eliana could see that this tower used to be sumptuous, before it fell into decay. Daylight streamed through a narrow window high above her, illuminating a flight of stairs that twisted up and vanished into the darkness. The steps certainly used to be grand – the bright tiles were dulled by a thick coating of dust, but the vibrant patterns beneath were still just about visible.

She looked about her; there was nothing but the tower steps. Still eager to put as much distance between herself and her assailants as possible, she began to climb.

As she went up and up, her footsteps were muffled by the dust, and there was no sound but the rustle of the bats in the alcoves, the pounding of the blood in her ears, and her own laboured breathing as her already-exhausted body made the ascent. The dizzying climb seemed endless – as though the steps rose up to the very gate of Marduk's house. There were landings and rooms on the way up, but the doors to all of them were locked.

It took an eternity, but Eliana finally reached the top... only to be confronted by a bricked-up doorway.

She sagged against the wall in disappointment – all this way, for nothing.

The bricks moved beneath her weight as she leaned against them – she gasped and jerked forward again, afraid of toppling backwards with it if the wall fell.

The bricks were plain mud, hastily fired. They crumbled beneath the touch. This wall was plainly not put here for decoration – it was built in a hurry.

She brushed at the mortar; it flaked away under her hands.

Suddenly overwhelmed by curiosity, she began rubbing hard at the mortar, loosening the bricks until she could pull them away and toss them aside, one by one. She worked feverishly: anything to distract herself from her run-in with Susa; she couldn't think about that yet.

Her hands were sore and bleeding by the time she finished. A beautifully preserved door was in front of her. Lightly running her fingertips down the polished wood, she allowed them to linger on the handle before she tried it, holding her breath.

The door opened.

The room beyond was beautifully decorated – round, following the curve of the tower, and elaborately painted with bright images of young lovers and scenes from the life of Ishtar. The furnishings were moth-eaten now, but Eliana could see that they had been luxurious – almost as luxurious as her own. Silken cushions, sheets, curtains and bed hangings dominated the chamber in a very feminine way. The bed was immaculately made.

It was dim inside, and the air was dry and cloying. There were a pair of shutters tightly closed across a window on the far side of the room – she crossed the floor, leaving footprints in the dust, and threw back the shutters, allowing light to flood the room.

She could immediately see whereabouts in the palace she was – this was the tallest tower in the place, with a perfect view of the temple *Esagila*. On the bench below the window was a little token of carved stone – rough-hewn lovers holding hands. She picked it up and turned it over in her palm.

She spun back into the room and screamed, the little stone token clattering to the floor as her hands flew to cover her mouth.

There, half-sprawled across a shrine to Ishtar, was a girl with her back to Eliana.

'I – I'm so sorry,' Eliana started, shakily. 'I didn't know that anyone was –'

She paused, taking a closer look. The girl was utterly still, her black curls fallen across her face, kneeling at the foot of the shrine, her head resting on her arms atop it. She wasn't breathing.

Eliana took a tentative step forward – the skin was a dull grey, and pulled tight on the bones. The girl was dead, and had been for some years.

Poor thing! Eliana thought, horrified. *Bricked up and left to die! Just like...*

Eshnunna.

She remembered the story she had been told almost a decade ago. Here was Samsu's sister, still lying in her prison-tomb after all these years.

Afraid to touch her, Eliana knelt at the shrine beside the girl. This poor child had been sentenced to death for her love and spirit, and had died praying to the goddess of love. With tears streaming down her face, Eliana completed the girl's last prayers to Ishtar, and said a silent one of her own to Enlil and Innana.

She stayed there for a long while, until the sun began to go down and she remembered that she would be needed in the nursery. With great reluctance, she got to her feet and made her way to the door.

As she descended the stairs, she was overwhelmed with sympathy and respect for the girl who had been brave enough to die rather than live a life dominated by cruel men. Eliana had not had that luxury – with a father and sister's wellbeing dependent on her good behaviour, and then her baby nieces and eventually her own children to think about, death was not an option. There were too many who relied upon her. In an odd way, she rather envied Eshnunna; not her death, but rather her freedom to choose it.

It did not take Eliana long to find her way back to her own apartments, now that she had been able to get her bearings from the tower window. She crept back in the shadows, half-terrified of meeting another of Susa's assassins. She would need to double her guard, she realised, and not leave the apartments unaccompanied for any reason. Nor must any of the children be left alone for any length of time.

Samsu's absence now felt as much of a curse as a blessing.

Slipping back into her apartments with a glare at Adra, whom she was certain had been party to the whole trap, she decided to arrange Eshnunna's interment as soon as possible. That poor child had lain unburied for too long.

*

Asag listened gravely as Eliana related the story in a low voice out on the roof terrace. She had sent Adra off on some menial errand to be assured of privacy.

'Will you arrange Eshnunna's burial?' she asked.

'I shall certainly see if there is space for her in the royal catacombs,' he said. 'But I have a few other things to arrange first.'

'That's fine,' she nodded. 'As long as the girl receives a decent burial. I'm sure she can wait a couple more days, after thirty years.'

'Indeed, Your Highness,' Asag stood up. 'Is there anything else I can do for you?'

'No, thank you Asag.'

He bowed and retreated.

The next day, she was utterly dismayed to learn what his 'few other things' were. He had been charged with keeping law and order in the king's absence. While Samsu trusted Eliana's judgement as far as matters of general policy were concerned, he had always been of the opinion that she was too soft, too womanly to ever be a true politician. The document that he had drawn up on departing had left matters of governance to Eshu and Eliana, and matters of justice and punishment to Asag.

Taking his responsibilities seriously, Asag had hunted out the two slave boys who had acted as Susa's henchmen and hanged them above the palace gates, and Adra had received a whipping.

When Adra limped in with a bitter stare and a torn and bloodied dress, Eliana had coaxed the story from her before sending for Mari to treat the wounds.

She summoned Asag to her chambers.

'I did not ask you to do that!' she cried. 'Those poor boys were probably offered money, or even their freedom, by Susa to do what they did.'

'They did not have to accept it,' Asag was unapologetic. 'They have broken the law, and been punished accordingly.'

'Are you aware that, many years ago, she bribed Mari similarly?' demanded Eliana. 'If I had taken your approach, your beloved would be dead, and you would never have had your son.'

Asag shrugged. 'Then I am fortunate that you are a gentle queen. But the king left me in charge of law and order. I take my responsibilities seriously. I cannot apologise for upholding the law, Your Highness.'

She gave a frustrated sigh, knowing that his responsibilities were only part of the reason he had been so harsh. If she died, Mari would never be freed, and he could never marry her. As long as Eliana lived, there was hope.

Reprimanding Asag would not bring the boys back, or heal Adra's wounds, but it made her feel a little better. 'I didn't even have any *proof* of Adra's involvement,' she said, 'only a suspicion. It was not fair to punish her without it.'

'The attempted assassination of a queen cannot be pushed aside as a matter of no consequence. The state of relations with Elam is delicate – they teeter on the brink of joining the rebellion. I cannot touch their princess for fear of making the situation worse, but chastising her spy sends a clear message, and I have set a spy of my own to watch her in case that message goes unheeded.'

Eliana turned away. 'I would not have chosen this retaliation,' she murmured.

'I know, Your Highness. That is why the king left matters like this to me,' said Asag, softly.

'Very well,' she sighed. 'You are dismissed.'

There was no point arguing, she knew. The deed was done. Adra moved around the apartments gingerly, clearly in pain, darting resentful glances at her mistress.

Eliana ignored them; but, remembering the agony of her own flogging soon after she was taken by Samsu, she placed fewer demands on the girl for a couple of weeks.

The time flew by at an alarming rate whilst Samsu was away. Eshu began to come into his own at the weekly audiences – after just a couple of months, the solutions he began to propose were making Eliana proud. He made them tentatively at first, as if afraid of being laughed at or scolded for being wrong, but his mother was quick to praise him for trying, even when she needed to correct him when his ideas were misguided or needed more thinking through.

Reports from the army came once a fortnight, carrying news of the rebellion and Samsu's movements. He travelled south through the empire, crushing the resistance city by city, making his way down to Larsa, where Rimsin was rumoured to be massing his own army.

It was after the first attack on Larsa that news of Samsu's injury came through. There were no details of the circumstance, the messenger merely said that the king had suffered a serious wound to his leg, and that it had festered. He knew nothing more, he swore.

She kept the news from Eshu. There was nothing the boy could do – it was useless to make him fret when the outcome was so uncertain.

Waiting anxiously for an update, her feelings were mixed as she considered the possibility of Samsu's death. In a way, it would set her free – she would no longer be subject to his whims and tempers. But on the other hand, it would certainly plunge her into a power struggle that she had only the faintest hope of winning. Susa would act swiftly, that much was certain. Eliana had the title of queen, as well as custody of the crown prince; but Susa had wealth, royal blood, an adult son, and, perhaps the strongest weapon of all, the Brute. He commanded his own men, and his ruthlessness was second to none, not even Samsu.

A decade ago, she would have been certain that Ashan would not accept the throne if it was offered to him, but now… it had been so long since their time together – who knew how the years and his experiences in this war might have changed him?

She wanted to plan for the event of Eshu's succession, take advice on the best course of action, but the only one she could ask would be Asag, and she could not be certain where his loyalties lay: to her, to Samsu, to Babylon… or to himself. If Samsu did not die and discovered that she had been making plans for the eventuality, his anger would be unlike anything she'd ever seen; of that much, she was sure.

The reports dried up for several weeks, and the possibility of Eshu becoming king loomed large as she began to fear the worst for Samsu.

Finally, a messenger arrived, dusty and travel-strained – he fell to his knees at Eliana's feet.

'Your Highness, the king has won a great victory at Larsa. The pretender Rimsin is defeated and captured, the city of Larsa sacked and torn down. Nothing remains there but rubble and corpses. Your husband is on his way home to you as I speak.'

'Marduk be praised!' Eliana smiled, meaning it. Relief flooded through her as she realised that she would not have to fight for her son's throne just yet. 'When should we expect the king?'

'He is little more than a week behind me,' replied the messenger. 'His train is lighter of men, but substantially weighed down with the spoils of war.'

Eliana nodded her thanks and waved the man away.

Eight days later, she and the children waited in the forecourt of the palace as the dusty and worn procession straggled through the great gates – a stark contrast to the paragon of shining strength that had ridden out almost a year ago.

Samsu had to be helped down from his horse. It shocked Eliana to the core – she had never seen her husband accept assistance from anyone, for anything. He limped towards her, leaning heavily on a wooden staff. His leg was heavily bandaged, and the flesh above and below looked angry and inflamed. He grimaced with every step.

'Welcome home, sir,' Eliana bowed, the children following suit. 'We are so glad to have you back with us, and victorious.'

'Did you ever doubt it?' he snapped. 'I'll bet you were quietly hoping that I would not return.'

'Not for a moment, sir,' she lied, smoothly. 'We always knew that you would…'

'Quiet!' he barked; she flinched. 'Your chirping irritates me. Where is my son?'

'Here, father,' Eshu stepped forward.

'You have grown in my absence,' he nodded. 'Have you grown in wisdom, too?'

'Yes, father. I have learned a great deal about government from Mother and my advisors.'

Samsu grunted, 'Good. I shall talk with you when I am rested.'

'Father,' Eshu bowed and stepped back as Samsu stalked past towards the palace door, not even acknowledging his daughters. They should have been used to it, but looked crushed nonetheless.

Hot on Samsu's heels was the Brute, looking immensely satisfied, leading a man in chains.

This could only be Rimsin, Eliana knew. Brought all the way back to the palace for the sole purpose of executing him before half of Babylon. The man was in appalling condition – he was missing several teeth, his nose was flat and bloodied, and one arm hung crooked and useless by his side. He limped as badly as Samsu, and his tunic was torn and bloodstained.

There was a sharp crack, the clatter of breaking pottery, and an adolescent cry of pain near the door of the palace – Eliana wheeled around to see a slave boy stagger sideways, clutching at his head, a drinking bowl lying shattered on the ground in a pool of wine, red as blood.

'Idiot!' shouted Samsu, lowering his stick and resuming his slow progress to the door.

Eliana glanced back towards the horses, where Ashan was just dismounting. Their eyes met for a moment and they exchanged looks of concern.

Despite the seriousness of the moment, her heart beat a little faster as she looked at him. His face was more careworn, with lines of strain etched around his eyes and mouth, but his skin had been burnished dark copper by long months out in the sun, living in an army camp. His body was leaner, more defined, any trace of the softness of palace life long-vanished. Hair tangled to his shoulders, a little longer than it had been. It suited him.

She smiled a little as memories blazed within her, tinged with sadness that their love had been ensnared in a complex web of responsibilities, loyalties and circumstance.

Asag went to greet his old friend with a brotherly clasp of the hand. Bending his head, Ashan muttered a few words to him before clapping him on the shoulder and stalking after Samsu.

Coming back to his queen, Asag whispered, 'Ashan needs to speak to us both this evening. Avoid the king; do not seek him out.'

She nodded, her stomach fluttering a little at the thought of being so near Ashan again.

*

After dark, the three of them met out on Eliana's roof terrace, lit by a mere sliver of moon that reminded her of the night she had first been captured, stupidly falling into a palace pond.

Adra had been delighted to be dismissed for the night, and had quickly disappeared to spend the night with the Brute, Eliana supposed. Mari was keeping Tabi busy, so they could be assured of some degree of privacy.

Close enough to feel the heat of Ashan's body, smell the scent of his hair, Eliana felt part of herself come alive again. She wished it would not; he was brittle and formal with her, oblivious to her discomfort. She was ashamed that she had ever held onto even the smallest shard of her love for him – his for her was clearly long-dead.

He came straight to the point, 'The king is half-mad. His leg is putrid – the pain is debilitating, and makes him irrational and irritable, but it is more than that. Paranoia consumes him.'

'How did it happen?' asked Eliana.

'During the first assault on Larsa, one of the archers miscalculated – he shot an arrow straight into Samsu's leg. The king was sat atop his horse – it panicked and bolted. He fell hard, hitting his head and falling unconscious. The shaft of the arrow was snapped off in the fall and became wedged inside the leg. He did not regain his sensibility for two hours, and his leg had to be cut open to remove the arrow.'

Eliana recoiled as she imagined the pain.

'The physician stitched him up, but the wound never healed properly. Samsu grew fevered and delirious. At the height of his madness, he accused us all of plotting his death, trying to assassinate him. He forgave the archer in the beginning, but as fever took him, he ordered the man executed: shot with all the arrows in his quiver.'

'And now…?' she feared to hear the answer.

'His paranoia grows. He has never questioned the loyalty of his men before now, but he began to dole out harsh punishments for the most minor transgressions, making life difficult for the men. His battle plans became nonsensical and illogical – hundreds of men died because of them, and dozens more defected. Had he not won that final battle, the war would have been lost. So many men were killed… we could not have afforded another victory such as that one.'

'Has he said anything about me? About the children?' she asked, anxiously.

'He suspects everybody of deception and treason. He trusts no-one but me, and is more violent, irrational and unpredictable than ever. You must do nothing to upset him. Nothing to make him suspect you.'

She glanced at Asag; his lips were pressed together in a tense line.

An awkward silence descended over the trio, and for just the briefest moment, she longed to reach over and take Ashan's hand, as though she could wipe the last decade clean from their minds and return things to the way they used to be.

*

Eliana managed to take Ashan's advice, and was able to avoid Samsu for several days. It was not until the following week that she had to face him, when she, along with the entire court, was summoned to audience. Sitting beside him on her smaller throne, it felt odd to be a mere spectator at the audiences again, rather than leading them. Eshu sat on Samsu's other side.

The steward banged his staff against the floor, and an expectant hush fell over the assembly. 'Rimsin, the vile pretender,' he announced.

The huge doors at the end of the hall were flung open, and the broken man was marched up and thrown to his knees before the dais. The man's decency was barely covered by his torn and decaying tunic, and every inch of bare skin was smeared with dust, mud, and dried blood. He raised his head and stared directly at Eliana – a silent plea for mercy. The haunted look in his eyes pierced her heart, and she quickly looked away. Even she could not be such a soft fool as to try to interfere with the king's justice.

'Do you have anything to say for yourself?' asked Samsu in a dangerous voice.

'I am a lowly and wretched creature,' croaked the man, forcing out his rehearsed speech. 'I have greatly transgressed against the rightful king, and I beg your royal forgiveness and mercy.' His voice broke on the last word.

'Denied,' snarled Samsu. 'You take me away from the business of government for a full year, raise my country in rebellion against me, and cause the deaths of hundreds of men, then have the audacity to beg mercy?'

'But, you promised…' begged the man. 'If I gave myself up… gave your word…'

'As a promise from a traitor is worthless, a promise to a traitor is no promise at all.' Samsu gestured to Rimsin's guards. They stepped forward with a thick wooden post, taller than a man, made stable by the cross it was mounted on. Chains hung from the top.

They set it down and swept him up from the floor, attaching the manacles to his wrists – he cried out in pain as they forced the useless arm above his head to secure it.

Samsu gestured again. The Brute emerged from the crowd, a look of great anticipation on his face as he flexed his fingers and advanced on the helpless man.

Staring into Rimsin's eyes, the Brute wrapped his fingers around his throat and began to squeeze, slowly increasing the pressure, eking it out, watching the life begin to drain away.

The man's face reddened, then purpled. His eyes bulged and he began to flail weakly, uselessly, choking out his final, indistinguishable words. Eliana forced herself to watch – Samsu would criticise if she looked away, would accuse her of having sympathy for the traitor. Every second made her feel physically sick, but she must pay attention. She wished that she could protect Eshu from having to see this; giving him a quick glance, she saw that he was pale, but he kept his eyes fixed on the execution, his face expressionless.

As a final insult, the Brute spat in Rimsin's face just before the man lost consciousness. When he slumped from his chains, the Brute took the head between his hands and gave a sharp twist.

There was a nauseating crack as Rimsin's neck snapped in two.

His work done, wearing an expression of immense satisfaction, the Brute moved back to his place as the guards removed the body and the post.

When everything was cleared away, Samsu raised his hands. 'Marduk has been good to me, this last year, guiding me to victory at every stage of the campaign. His generosity must not go unrewarded. As thanks, it is my intention to give him my eldest daughter, Sarri, when she turns thirteen next year.'

Eliana was stunned – she had not heard so much as a whisper of this. She looked around to see shock on every face.

Poor Sarri, Eliana thought. *The girl was never meant to be a priestess. She will find the life insufferably dull. She needs excitement and challenge. Kisuri would make a far better priestess of Marduk – it would suit her down to the ground. Perhaps I can persuade him...*

Of all the faces in the assembly, Ashan's stood out, horror plain in every line of his body. Eliana was surprised at the strength of the reaction all round – she knew Sarri, knew that the life would not suit her, but nobody else was close enough to realise that. Being a priestess was not such a terrible fate, it was just not the one she would have chosen for her headstrong niece.

It was with a slow-dawning anxiety that she began to wonder if she had interpreted Samsu's words correctly.

Chapter 23

Ashan confirmed her fears that evening.

'The king intends to sacrifice Sarri to Marduk when she comes of age,' he said. 'He has it set in his mind that the god will not be good to him again unless he offers proper thanks.'

Eliana heard his words as though her head was under water. The world seemed to slow down around her, and she felt like she was trying to breathe through damp silk.

Her knees buckled beneath her – Ashan stepped in and caught her around the waist. For once, his touch barely registered in her mind. There was nothing else but Sarri.

'How – how can we stop him?' she whispered.

'I'm not sure we can,' he said seriously. 'There's no reasoning with him any more – he is worse than he's ever been…'

His voice caught in his throat, as if he was going to say more, but thought better of it.

Eliana looked up at him, saw the hesitation before he could wipe it from his face. 'What?' she pressed, her voice urgent. 'What else is there? You're keeping something from me.'

'He… he is talking about marriages. Mine. And Nisala's.'

If it was possible, her heart sank even lower. She had always known that she was foolish to cherish any hope of being with Ashan – he could not remain unmarried forever. That was painful in itself, but worse was the thought of losing her daughter to some unknown man – Nisala was only nine years old.

'To whom?' she asked weakly.

'To... to – each other,' he choked out.

Her jaw dropped – she stared at him with undisguised revulsion. 'No!' she whispered. 'But you're – you're...' she remembered the servants in the room at the last moment, finishing pathetically with '... so much older than she is.'

She wanted to scream, *You're her father! How can you even speak of it?*

He nodded. He knew exactly what she wished to say.

'We must stop him,' she said. 'First Sarri, now this... how many more wild ideas will he have?'

'I know,' he muttered. 'Things are becoming dangerous. And not just for us – he will tear this fragile empire apart with the new policies he talks about.'

'I can't be interested in policy just now. How can we protect the girls? It will be impossible to change Samsu's mind, and dangerous to try. The only thing that could stop him is...' she hesitated, afraid to finish her sentence.

Ashan gave her a quizzical look.

'Death,' she breathed.

'Pardon?'

'Don't you see? He has to die – we will never be safe while he lives. Our *children* will never be safe.' She was barely audible, so afraid was she of being overheard, though no servant stood anywhere near them.

Ashan stared at her with blank horror, forgetting all courtesies. '*Kill* the king? Eliana, if we failed...'

She looked him in the eyes. 'We must not fail. You said to me many, many years ago, that one day I would be free of my chain... when the time was right. *Now* is the time. If we do not act soon, it will be too late. I could do nothing to save my sister – I *can* save her child.'

Before Ashan could form a response, Tabi burst into the room and ran to them. 'Your Highness!' she called, her voice frantic. 'Is Eshu with you?'

Eliana leapt to her feet, 'No! Have you lost him?'

'We haven't seen him for hours – I asked Adra, she said the Brute took him for exercise after the audience, and he hasn't been seen since.'

Ashan's military side immediately took over; he began issuing orders. 'Tabi – go with Mari down to the exercise yard and start asking questions. Ask every person you find if they have seen the prince. Eliana, you come with me – we're going in search of the Brute.'

Tabi ran off to fetch Mari, and Ashan turned and marched from the room; Eliana had to run to keep up. Her heart pounded, she could barely think straight. 'Where will he be?' she panted, chasing him down stairs and along passageways.

'We'll start at my mother's apartments,' he growled. 'If anyone put the Brute up to this, it will have been her. Try not to panic; this is likely just a ploy to put the wind up you. To keep you afraid. Asag told me about her attempt on your life, and how your love for Eshu was used as part of the trap.'

They charged into Susa's rooms unannounced. Sure enough, the Brute sat laughing with Ani on a bench; water dripped from his hair, and his tunic was damp.

Ashan strode up to him. The Brute stood as he approached, looking down on him. The atmosphere was suddenly thick and tense.

'What have you done with the prince?' demanded Ashan.

'I took him for exercise, as the king commanded,' replied the Brute, smoothly.

'And where is he now?'

'Still swimming, I presume.' He folded his arms smugly.

'Swimming!' cried Eliana, from the doorway. 'Eshu can't swim!'

The Brute shrugged, 'If he couldn't before, he should be able to by now. The little whelp cheeked me – I left him down there to learn by himself.'

'Where were you swimming?' roared Ashan, his patience snapping.

'The canal,' smiled the Brute.

Eliana was immediately off again at a run, heading for the palace wharf.

'I wouldn't bother hurrying yourself,' Ani called after her, spitefully. 'He's probably drowned by now!'

Ashan was close behind her as they sprinted through the dark passages that led down to the canal. The air became noticeably cooler as they drew near, and the smell of the water grew stronger.

They burst onto the wharf, looking around wildly for any sign of their son in the water.

'Eshu!' screamed Eliana. 'Eshu! Answer me – *Eshu!*'

The merchants on the wharf stopped to look at her in astonishment. Ashan rushed to the edge of the canal and peered down.

'There!' he shouted, springing to his feet and running alongside the water. Eliana gave chase.

She threw herself to her belly beside Ashan and leaned over the edge. There, in the water, half-frozen and terrified, Eshu clung tightly to a mooring ring set into the bricks of the canal wall.

'Eshu!' she cried, overwhelmed with relief to see him alive. 'Are you hurt?'

'N-no mother,' he shivered, teeth chattering.

'Hold on!' she called.

Ashan had run back to the wharf and snatched a length of rope from a merchant without so much as a word of explanation. He twisted it into a noose as he rushed back to where Eliana lay on the bank.

'Here, son,' he said, trying to keep his voice calm for the boy's sake as he lowered the rope. 'Slip this over your head and under your arms – I'll have you up in a moment.'

Eliana watched on as their son did as he was told and Ashan began to haul on the rope, hand after strong hand, gently bringing their boy back up. The seconds seemed like hours.

Finally, Ashan brought him over the edge, and Eliana gathered him into her arms and hugged him as if she could never let him go again. Water from the canal seeped into the silk of her gown – she hardly noticed. Cold, pale and almost sick with the amount of water he had swallowed, her little prince was safe.

Scooping Eshu into his arms, Ashan strode off back towards the palace, Eliana at his heels. He turned to her, 'Run to the exercise yard and let Tabi and Mari know that we've got him,' he said.

She hesitated, not wanting to leave Eshu's side.

Ashan saw her indecision in a heartbeat. 'He'll be fine with me – safer than with anyone else. I won't let any harm come to him.'

With one last, yearning glance at Eshu, she did as she was told.

When she found Mari and Tabi, they sagged against each other with relief to hear that he was safe, and only a little worse for wear for his misadventure. The three of them made their way back up to the apartments. As they neared the doorway, Eliana stopped. Ashan stood there, Eshu still in his arms, talking to Samsu.

Waving Mari and Tabi away to the nursery, she approached cautiously.

Samsu looked around sharply at the sound of her footsteps. 'There you are,' he growled. 'Is it true, what Ashan tells me? Did my man do this?'

Eyes on the ground, she responded quietly, 'Yes, sir.'

'Ashan also tells me that this is not the first time he has threatened the lives of my children – that he tried to kill them in your belly just hours before you birthed them?'

'That's true, sir.'

'Right.' Samsu's eyes glittered dangerously. 'Get inside your rooms, now. Ashan, put my son down, and fetch that traitorous dog here. We'll settle this.'

She followed them inside, and fussed over Eshu while they awaited the Brute's arrival. Anything to stop herself from thinking – she must keep busy. Wrapping the boy in a blanket and drying his hair, she stripped off his wet clothes and sent Tabi to fetch him a hot drink from the kitchens.

By the time the Brute arrived, some colour was beginning to return to the prince's cheeks – he sat up straight beside his father, staring defiantly at the man who had left him to drown.

'You have served me well over many years,' said Samsu, coldly. There was no preamble, everyone knew why he was here. 'By rights, the crimes you have committed demand execution.'

The Brute folded his arms. 'The boy cheeked me, sir. I left him there to teach him discipline.'

'DO NOT lie to me,' bellowed Samsu. 'Of all the insults you have offered, do not crown them with lies and forfeit my mercy.'

The man stared at him in cold silence.

Ashan appeared in the doorway, six soldiers at his back.

'Because of your years of loyal service, I could commute your sentence to exile in exchange for your word that you would never raise a weapon against me. My father advocated equal justice for all, but I would feel some regret over your death, after all we have been through. Your crimes against the queen put me in a very difficult position – I am forced to make a choice.'

The Brute looked straight at Eliana with a smirk on his face. 'Perhaps you should offer the choice to the queen,' he said, mockery in his eyes. He thought her soft, she realised. Knew that she abhorred suffering and pain, particularly any of her own making. She stared at him and remembered every moment of agony he had ever caused her – the way he had forced himself on her when she was young and innocent, the way his eyes had flashed like his dagger in the moonlight when he tried to kill her that night, the suffering he had inflicted on her at every opportunity… what he had done to Eshu.

'Kill him,' she said.

The laughter in his eyes died. His jaw tightened, his fists clenched. He took a menacing step towards her.

Samsu gave the signal, and Ashan's six soldiers leapt forward to bind the Brute and take him away. He swung round violently, catching one of them around the head with his outstretched fist, sending the man sprawling. Ducking another blow, Ashan drew his blade and, in less than the time it took to snuff out a candle, had it at the Brute's throat.

'Go on,' the man snarled. 'Kill me – deny that whore the pleasure, not that you have ever denied her *the pleasure* before, I'm sure. You smarmy little princeling – you're just like the boy. Perhaps he's yours.'

Her heart galloped in her chest, but Eliana kept her expression carefully blank, kept the alarm from her eyes.

Ashan pressed the blade harder against the Brute's neck as the five remaining guards snared him with ropes and bound his arms.

'Even a lion is no match for six dogs,' snarled Samsu. 'Take him away.'

Eliana felt awash with triumph as one of her greatest enemies was dragged away, bound and helpless. She had expected to feel some twinge of guilt as she sentenced a man to death – examining her conscience, she found nothing.

*

She was not required to attend the Brute's execution, but she chose to go nonetheless. He was a demon who had haunted her nightmares and her waking hours equally for well over a decade. If she didn't see him die with her own eyes, she could not believe him truly gone.

Her world was changing – the time for softness was past. The Brute had gambled on her gentleness, had mistaken it for weakness. He had lost his gamble, and she would see him pay the price.

With not so much as a flicker of emotion in his face, he stared at her as he was led out to his death. Her insides went cold. In that stare, she felt every moment of terror he had ever caused her – from the first time she laid eyes on him as he murdered Mari's brothers, to his vicious assaults when she first came to the palace; from beating and restraining her so that they could kill her sister, to attempting to murder her in her bed. There was joy in knowing that every smug look and savage blow he had ever given, he would pay for in this moment.

But when the moment arrived, she could not watch.

Samsu had ordered him torn apart by horses, and the court had gathered in the exercise yard to witness it. The Brute had few allies, and fewer still who would be sorry to see him die. Of all the court, only Susa, Ani and Adra seemed to be in mourning – Susa had reportedly collapsed when she had heard the news, and Adra had not spoken a word since the condemnation.

Guards, former comrades, forced him to the dirt, chaining each limb to half-wild stallions who champed impatiently at the bit, prancing in place, anxious to run. His torso secured to the ground, he was ready.

He raised his head from the ground and shot a look of pure, unadulterated hatred at Eliana. It was a look that would have made her tremble in other circumstances, now she met his eyes with a steady gaze as clear as her conscience.

Her body betrayed her. As Samsu gave the signal, the four riders raised their whips and brought them down on the horses' flanks with stinging cracks and the beasts lurched into a gallop... her eyes squeezed shut of their own accord.

Her ears, she could not close so easily. The man from whom she had never heard anything but taunts and insults gave one chilling, piercing scream, straight from the depths of the underworld – it tore the air and cut to the quick, echoing in her mind long after the sound had faded. It would stay with her until her dying day.

When she opened her eyes, he was the Brute no more. The man who had had the power to maim, to terrify, to kill… he was just a mass of meat, his torso still twitching and convulsing as the horses trotted back, each dragging a limb behind.

He was as mortal as anyone else. She was almost surprised.

Samsu stood. 'Thus die all those who threaten Babylon, her king, or his family,' he said, turning and making his way painfully down the steps of the dais.

Left alone up there, Eliana suddenly could not bear the sight of the corpse or the smell of blood – her stomach turned and she felt ill, but she could not – must not – show any sign of weakness on a stage before all the court.

She rose gracefully and descended the steps after Samsu, then walked away in the opposite direction, heading for a favourite path that followed the entire perimeter of the palace walls.

By the time she had walked a complete circuit, she felt calm and at peace, confident that she had made the right decision and seen justice done not just for herself, but for Mari, the people of Nippur, and everyone else he had wronged.

There was an ominous silence as she entered her apartments. They were usually a hive of activity, with servants and messengers coming and going at all hours. Now, they were deserted.

A bolt of pure panic shot through her and she ran to the nursery door. It stood ajar.

Mari and Tabi were nowhere to be seen, but there, in the middle of the room, Samsu stood examining her daughter.

He had Nisala stood on a bench before him, to raise her up

to his eyeline. Scrutinising her from every angle, he pinched at her face and arms, poked at her waist, tugged at her hair. The girl had her eyes squeezed tight shut, clutching her doll, tears running down her face. Against the far wall, Sarri and Kisuri huddled together.

Eliana had to restrain herself from running over there and snatching her daughter from the bench, away from his probing hands.

She forced herself to speak calmly, 'Is everything alright, sir?'

Samsu turned blazing eyes on her, 'She *is* mine, I suppose?'

Keeping her face mild and impassive, she said 'Of course. I belong to you, and you alone, as does Nisala.'

'I wonder,' he sneered. 'You started your career as a whore – the Great Whore of Babylon, the people called you – who in their right mind would expect fidelity from a whore?'

She felt her anger rising dangerously, but maintained an even tone, 'Your *unwilling* whore, sir. I was never loose or light with my morals.'

Grabbing Nisala's chin, he twisted her head, forcing her face towards the window. 'She doesn't look like me,' he snarled suspiciously.

'Children do not always take after their fathers,' she shrugged, trying to seem nonchalant.

'The traitor said she and Eshu could be Ashan's. In certain lights, I see it.'

'I do not,' she replied, the lie coming easily, forcing down the rising terror. 'There is no reason that they should look like Ashan. You heed the words of a known traitor over your most trusted commander?'

'*He* was one of my most trusted commanders, until he was proven a traitor,' shouted Samsu. 'Who's to say if any of these are mine?! Marduk alone knows.' He gave Nisala a violent shove, sending her stumbling backwards off the bench. She hit her head on the floor as she fell, lay stunned for a moment, then began to cry loudly in pain and fear.

Eliana went running to her daughter, dropped to her knees and gathered her up in a hug. She pressed her fingers lightly over the sore spot – there was a lump forming, but no blood. There seemed to be no lasting harm. She rocked Nisala gently, arms wrapped protectively around her, shushing her as they knelt at Samsu's feet.

'You are a *whore!*' he bellowed. 'Once a whore, always a whore! I was a fool to make you my queen, to acknowledge children you cannot prove are mine!'

'You cannot prove they are *not* yours!' she retorted, regretting it instantly as he swept his walking stick across a nearby table, bringing its contents crashing down around her.

'May Marduk strike you down if they are not!'

He picked up a little porcelain vase and hurled it across the room – it hit the wall above Sarri and Kisuri and shattered, raining shards down on their heads. The girls pulled tighter together, Sarri trying to block her fragile little sister from the worst of it.

Eliana seized the opportunity; she scrambled up and ran to them, dragging Nisala with her. She pushed her daughter in with her nieces, and stood with her body as a shield between them and Samsu as he ranted incoherently, spraying spittle everywhere, his face turning purple with fury as he smashed the room to pieces.

Behind her, the girls wept and trembled – they had always been afraid of their father's coldness and sharp tongue, but they had never seen him in a blind rage before. Eliana held her arm behind her, and three small pairs of hands seized it, seeking comfort.

She did not think he would kill them – in her experience, his killing was a result of cold calculation; when he was in a frenzy, his instinct was to hurt people. She prayed that he would not assault her – not here, not in front of the girls. She did not want them to have to see it. He would do it, she was sure, if it was not for the pain in his leg that often prevented him from becoming aroused now, which only added to his anger and frustration.

'Whore!' he shouted again. 'You may masquerade as a queen, but you're a whore! The people should see you for what you really are – I'll punish you, I'll make them see. They must see, before you meet your downfall.'

The words struck fear into her belly, 'My downfall, sir?'

'Aha! Now I have your attention! Marduk has shown me a vision of you – a beast with seven heads and ten horns, that's your downfall!'

He was raving like a madman. She could not think what she might say that would calm him – his every word, every action was unpredictable.

Asag appeared, returning his own son and Eshu to the nursery after their daily combat training. He stopped in the doorway; his jaw dropped in frank astonishment to see his king throwing a child-like tantrum, ranting like a lunatic.

At first, Eshu did not seem to know what to make of the situation, but one look at his terrified mother and weeping sisters told him what was going on. He went to the king, put a hand on his arm. 'Father, we have been studying great victories today, and our tutor said we might benefit from hearing about your glorious conquest of Nippur. If you have time, would you mind telling us the story?'

Samsu stared down at the young prince as though a cushion had suddenly started talking to him – he had not even seen him come in. Then, slowly, reality began to work its way back into his clouded mind, and recognition dawned on his face. 'My son – yes, of course. Go, wait for me in my office with Ahat – I will show you the maps. Tell you all about it.'

With a last anxious look at his mother, he left with Asag's son.

Taking a couple of limping steps towards Eliana and his daughters, Samsu hissed, 'Don't think I've forgotten – I will show the people what a whore you are. Put you and the little harlots on public display.'

The hatred in his eyes took her by surprise – he had looked at her in many ways before, but never with hatred.

Asag left with his king, hurrying him away without seeming to do so. As they departed, Eliana thanked Enlil, Marduk, and every other god she could call to mind for her son's quick-thinking – appealing to Samsu's ego to lure him away. The boy may only be nine years old, but he was already a skilled reader of people.

*

When Samsu decided on her 'punishment', she accepted it with stoicism and dignity. The three girls were to be included – it was a good lesson to teach them, she supposed, that what could not be changed must be endured with as much grace as possible.

It was made easier by the idea that had taken root in her mind just before Eshu's disappearance. The king had run mad – he was dangerous, was incapable of ruling effectively. The notion that he had to die grew ever-stronger in her mind – it was the light that sustained her through her darkest moments. All she awaited was an opportunity.

With Ashan back and the Brute no longer a threat, she could feel confident that Eshu's succession was assured. All she needed now was to know whether Ashan was with her, for the sake of their children, or whether his love for her was truly dead and buried, and he would side with his mother. Even if Ashan did the unthinkable and took the throne for himself, Eshu was still his first-born son, his heir.

What would happen to Eliana and the girls remained to be seen.

But for now, Samsu sought to humiliate them. He had Eliana dressed in purple and scarlet, decked with gold, pearls and precious stones from her hair to her ankles. The three girls were dressed in miniature copies of her outfit.

They were sat upon donkeys, and had tablets hung about their necks. Eliana's read *The Great Whore of Babylon, mother of harlots.* Sarri's, Kisuri's and Nisala's all simply read *Harlot.*

A golden cup was forced into Eliana's hands before they set off, full of blood, offal and things so vile that she did not want to think about what they might be. The stench was appalling, and she tried to breathe through her mouth to avoid retching at the smell.

They set off on procession through the streets of Babylon, preceded by a herald with a bronze gong – he gave her an apologetic look as he beat it, calling the citizens out of their houses to see her pass: 'Here comes the great whore!' he cried, looking embarrassed. 'The woman who has committed fornication with kings, and seduced the people with the wine of her misdeeds. She is drunken on the blood of martyrs, and has brought forth abominations and harlots. The beast with seven heads and ten horns shall be her downfall.'

The people exchanged uneasy looks and muttered as she passed; wondering what had possessed their king to order such a spectacle, to present them with such nonsensical ramblings.

Sarri was almost weeping with the degradation when they returned to the palace. She was of an age where her appearance and reputation were beginning to matter a great deal to her, and her father had swept it all away in a heartbeat. If she knew that he planned to snuff out her life in sacrifice to his god, she would weep a great deal more.

Kisuri and Nisala, being a couple of years younger, took it all very much in their stride. They were mortified by the abasement, but knew that tears would change nothing.

As Eliana shepherded the girls back to the nursery after the trial, she made up her mind that she must speak to Ashan alone, breaking the vow that she had made so many years ago. It could not be avoided – they had much to discuss.

*

With Mari's help, she arranged a meeting.

Samsu was already suspicious and paranoid – she dared not risk meeting Ashan out in the open, or even when any of the servants might notice. Instead, the meeting was arranged for the dead of night, out on her roof terrace.

As she rose from her bed and slipped on a hooded woollen cloak, Eliana's heart pounded so loudly that she was sure it would give her away. Surely half the palace must be able to hear it.

She went to the agreed meeting place and waited, pulling the cloak tightly around herself against the chill. Tilting her head back, she gazed up at Suen and his children, illuminating the clear night sky. She wondered what it would be like to be a star – so high up, so far removed from everything, able to see the whole world at once…

A quiet cough behind her interrupted her thoughts. Her heart began hammering again as she turned slowly.

There he stood, just out of reach, his features silvered by the moonlight.

She left the hood up, keeping her face in shadow, the better to hide her expression. She was sure that her eyes would betray her longing for him.

'I thought you swore you would never see me alone again,' murmured Ashan.

'I did,' she said, smiling into the darkness, 'but desperate times call for desperate measures.'

'Are you so desperate?'

'You know I am – he endangers the girls, he suspects that Eshu and Nisala are not his children, he plans to sacrifice Sarri... he is too dangerous. If we do not do something, he will destroy us all.'

Ashan nodded, 'You're right. I swore many, many years ago a blood oath to protect and serve a man – that man is long gone, and a lunatic has taken his place.'

'He was always mad,' grimaced Eliana.

'No, not mad. Cold, yes, calculating and cruel, certainly; but never mad. There was always some logic to his actions in the past, however ruthless he was.'

'Well, that's not the case anymore,' she said, thinking of the demeaning ride through the city.

'No,' he agreed. 'It's just a matter of time before he turns on us all, one by one. He seems to slip deeper into insanity every day. He has to die, before he kills us.'

Eliana hesitated. The idea of taking a life grated against everything she had ever been taught. The Brute's execution had been different – that was a punishment according to the law, decreed by the king. This... it was cold-blooded murder.

'Does – does he have to *die*?' she asked, tentatively. 'Could we perhaps just lock him away somewhere?'

'After all he has done to you, you would spare him?'

'It's just... I will have to live with his blood on my hands for the rest of my life. I don't know if I can.'

'Your life will be a lot shorter if you don't,' he said harshly. 'Eliana, see sense. This is not the time to be squeamish. Eshu's succession will have no legal standing if Samsu still lives, and former kings always become figureheads for rebellion, sooner or later. People become dissatisfied under the new regime and start to imagine that things were better under the old – it's an invitation for chaos.'

'Perhaps he would abdicate?' she suggested, hope in her voice. 'His grandfather abdicated, didn't he?'

Ashan laughed aloud, 'His grandfather was a weak old man who turned the throne over to a son who would have taken it by force had he not abdicated. Samsu would never abdicate of his own free will – he'd rather die. You know that as well as I do.'

She was forced to admit defeat. There was a brief silence before she asked, 'Do you think Eshu is ready to rule?'

'With a strong regency council, I think so. He's a clever boy – bright, good with people, quick-witted, wise beyond his years...' Ashan's voice warmed as he praised his son. 'With the right guidance, he'll grow into an excellent king.'

'You don't think there'll be any opposition?'

'Not with me at his side. If there was going to be opposition, it would be trying to put me on the throne, as the only other available heir. I will lead the regency council, advise him, help him learn to rule, but I will not take the throne.'

She exhaled slowly, a long sigh of relief; she had not realised she was holding her breath.

'But there is one thing... Eliana...' his tone grew serious.

'Ashan?' she breathed.

He came half a step closer, almost within touching distance.

'If Eshu is to be king, we will see a lot more of each other – with me leading the council, and you having a prominent place as queen mother.'

'Yes...' her body became painfully aware of his nearness. She had thought that these feelings were dealt with years ago, but now they resurrected themselves without her permission. This Ashan was stronger, more powerful, more confident than the man she had fallen in love with as a vulnerable girl. He was no longer afraid of Samsu, and she had faith that he would do what was necessary to protect her children and Kisha's.

'You have broken your vow – you swore never to see me alone again. I just want you to know – I can't work alongside you without telling you – I have never broken mine.'

'Yours?' she was baffled for a moment.

'My vow. The one I made the day you broke my heart. I respected your wishes, kept my distance for the sake of you and the children, for your safety; but I promised you that, no matter how long it took, I would wait for you, and I have kept my promise. No matter how aloof you were, how haughty, I kept a spark of love for you burning in my heart. There has never been anyone else for me, but you.'

'Oh, Ashan.' She took a step towards him, closing the gap that separated them.

'If you don't feel the same, that's fine,' he rattled on, quickly. 'Just say so, and I swear I'll never bring it up again; but all these years I have held out in hope of you, and now I need to know whether to let it go for good, or...'

'Hush!' she smiled, lowering her hood. 'I love you, too. I told myself that the love was gone, but it never truly was. Please, tell me you understand why I did it.'

'Of course I understand,' he wound his arms around her waist, resting his chin atop her head. 'But it didn't make it any easier to bear.'

She slipped her arms underneath his, clasping her hands behind his back and standing with her head resting against his chest. It was harder, more muscled than she remembered, but his scent was the same, and it set a wildfire of memories blazing through her blood.

Pulling back, she stretched up on tiptoe as he bent his head to meet hers; their lips came together in a kiss full of a heat and passion that she had forgotten she could feel, that she had only ever felt in his arms.

He slipped his hands under her cloak, sharing her warmth and pulling her closer to him. She reached up and entangled her fingers in the hair that fell across the back of his neck, grazing her fingertips against the fragile hollow beneath his ear and allowing them to trail across his shoulder and down his bicep. He groaned and tried to pull away, 'How do you always have this effect on me?' he growled. 'Almost ten years, and you can still make me desperate for you with the lightest touch.'

'It's only fair,' she laughed, holding onto him. 'You do the same to me.'

'Let go now,' he said. 'You are not free yet.'

She shook her head, 'No. We have to be together again, just once. In case we fail.'

'We can't go inside – we might be heard.'

She took his hand and led him around behind some potted trees to a favourite bench of hers. 'Will this do?' she smiled, wickedly.

In answer, he pushed her down on the bench and covered her body with his own. One hand cupped her face as their lips met, his tongue searching hers as his other hand brushed lightly over her breasts beneath the cloak.

She was suddenly overwhelmed with need – she had to know that he loved her, that he truly wanted her. Reaching down between his legs, she pulled up his tunic – he was hard, ready for her. She began to caress him.

In answer, his hand snaked down between her legs, fumbling with her gown as he pulled it up to her waist. He began to stroke her with such gentleness that she felt she might explode with frustration.

'Take me, Ashan,' she whispered, urgently.

He did not need telling twice – in moments, they were making love. It was only the second time in all the years since he had first confessed his feelings for her, yet it felt as though their bodies had known each other forever. As he moved inside her, the memories flooded back – she remembered that there was pleasure to be had in this act, that a man could make her feel good, could take her to the very gates of heaven.

When he could hold out no longer, he brought his head to her shoulder and kissed her neck as he shuddered to his climax, struggling valiantly to keep himself silent. He lay panting against her chest; she stroked his hair as the sweat cooled on her skin.

'Thank you,' she said.

He raised his head, surprised, 'For what?'

'For keeping faith,' she smiled.

He answered with a kiss.

When they had recovered, they began to make their plans. It would have to be poison, they decided – they would bring Mari in on their secret. With her great knowledge of medicine, she must have acquired some skill with the darker herbs along the way. They would require something fast-acting, something that left no visible sign of their crime.

Eliana would invite her husband for dinner – a quiet, family affair, under the pretext of Eshu wanting to spend more time in his father's company, to learn from him. In his increasing paranoia, Samsu trusted no-one but Ashan to serve his food and wine. The responsibility of slipping the poison into Samsu's drink would lie with Ashan, and if they failed, he alone would take the blame.

She had protested this last part at first, until he made her see that the children needed her – he could bear whatever agony Samsu chose to inflict to end his life, as long as he knew that they were safe, that he had a son to continue his legacy.

They would give it out that the king had died choking on his food – an ignominious death for a once- revered warrior.

When their plans were thought out to the last detail, they returned to their beds.

Eliana lay awake until Suen retired and Utu lifted his golden head above the horizon. She had no sleep that night – her mind raced over all the possible outcomes of the situation.

There was no turning back now, and no possibility of failure.

She must not allow her courage to forsake her. They had one chance at this, and one only – any blunder would mean certain death.

As soon as the sun was fully risen, she sent for Mari.

They sat together on the bed, closing the door and shutting out the rest of the world. As Eliana whispered the details of the plan, Mari was at first horrified, then thrilled; she lapsed into thoughtful silence for a moment.

'It must be quick, potent,' she murmured. 'It would not do for him to have time to recover. A few years ago, I would not have believed it possible that we could kill him, but now… his health is much weakened as a result of his leg. We must give him enough to be a fatal dose, but not so much that he can taste it… this will be a risky operation, Your Highness.'

'I know,' said Eliana. 'But if we succeed – and we *must* succeed – it will mean freedom for all of us.' She gave Mari a meaningful look. A slow smile spread across her friend's face as she took the implication. 'So, I can trust you?' asked Eliana.

'To the death, my queen,' said Mari. 'Leave it with me – I'll get what we need.'

Chapter 24

A messenger was dispatched to Samsu, begging him to attend a dinner with his queen and his son. The prince was eager to hear more of his military exploits, he was told. Eshu was showing much promise as a soldier and strategist, and would benefit from hearing more of his father's tales of war.

It was half the truth. Eshu was indeed growing into a brilliant young man, and showed a great deal of interest in military successes and defeats, studying what had happened to bring about the final results. He thought the world of his father, though the incident with his mother and sisters had shaken his confidence in the king somewhat.

But he was delighted at the prospect of this quiet dinner with both his parents, reconciling them to harmony and accord, he thought.

If all went according to plan, it was Eshu that Eliana would feel pity for. The child would witness the death of the man he believed to be his father, and then have the weighty responsibilities of kingship thrust upon him. The murder of Samsu would bring about the end of the boy's childhood. Though she consoled herself with the thought that his carefree days would have come to an end on his tenth birthday anyway, when he would be removed from the nursery and his training as king-in-waiting and a soldier would begin in earnest.

A date was set, and the days leading up to it began to crawl by. Eliana found it more and more difficult to go about her daily routine as the event loomed, casting its dark shadow of anxiety over her more intensely with every passing hour.

On the day itself, when it finally arrived, she was a fidgeting, nervous wreck.

Mari recognised it immediately, feeling the same way herself. Though she would have no actual part in the assassination attempt, the powdered aconite sitting innocuously in its small clay jar amongst the rest of her medicines seemed to scream out to her.

She approached Eliana cautiously, 'My queen, it is a beautiful day. Perhaps I could persuade you to join me and the girls in a picnic out in the gardens? If you have no more pressing duties, of course. They are so disappointed about not being invited to dinner with their father tonight that I thought this might cheer them up.'

Eliana smiled gratefully. She was sure that she would not be able to eat a thing, her stomach was in such turmoil, but the chance to escape her rooms, get out under the sky and spend some time with her girls was too good to pass up. 'Yes, thank you, Mari. I believe I will. I have no engagements today that cannot be cancelled.'

Dismissing the servants, she changed into simpler clothes and plain braided leather sandals, tying her hair back with a ribbon and leaving all her jewels and face paints to gather dust on her dresser. She felt lighter, freer – the years dropped away, with their weight of memory, responsibility and trauma, and it was as if she was once more that simple young girl, just a couple of years older than Sarri, who would run and climb and speak without a second thought.

That girl would not recognise the woman I have become, she thought, sadly. *But then, that girl might have killed herself if she had known what would turn her into this woman.*

As she set out, holding Kisuri's hand on one side and Nisala's on the other, she left the shadows behind and stepped out into the sun for a few hours' blissful peace.

Watching Sarri toss her curls and gesture excitedly as she talked, Eliana was reminded of why she must do this thing. Her niece was blossoming into a woman so fast. Her mannerisms were just like Eliana's at her age, but her looks were all her mother's.

As the girl chattered away, absorbed in the story she was telling, Eliana could not switch off her mind; she imagined Sarri being dragged screaming to the sacrificial altar, her gown being cut away, the flash of the blade in the sun as it descended to her heart...

All her resolve returned, and suddenly she was looking forward to the dinner that evening. What kind of man would do such a brutal thing to a young girl, and his own daughter at that? Babylon might be full of sophisticated and beautiful things, but its people and customs were still barbaric beneath their glamour.

It was only as they were walking back to the palace for Eliana to dress for dinner that she realised: if this endeavour went wrong, this would be the last time she ever spent with the girls. She smiled to herself – if that was what the gods had in store, then they had truly blessed her with some perfect final moments as a family.

When they reached her apartments, the first thing she did was retreat to her bedroom to say a prayer to the mother goddess of her childhood that everything would go well, and if it did not, that the girls would be safe and protected.

Her hands shook with the anticipation as she readied herself. She could hear the clattering of the table being laid in her dining room – her stomach turned somersaults.

The hour approached.

Eshu arrived in her rooms. Tabi had dressed him in his best tunic and combed his hair out neatly, though an untidy tuft still stuck up stubbornly at the back. He ran to his mother, alight with excitement. 'Am I dressed properly, mother? Will father be pleased?'

She smiled and stroked his cheek affectionately, 'You look the perfect prince. I don't see why your father would not be pleased.'

Samsu arrived shortly after.

He had made no special effort with his appearance, but then, she had not expected him to. He limped in, leaning heavily on his walking stick, wearing his usual military tunic. Eliana stood with her hand on Eshu's shoulder – they both bowed as he entered.

Grunting in acknowledgement, he stumped past them and went to the dining chamber without a word, Ashan coming close behind. He did not so much as look at Eliana; he did not dare.

His presence was like a drug to her, and she felt herself beginning to relax a little, knowing that he would do all he could to keep them safe – even if her own life must be forfeit, he would protect their son to the death.

She squeezed Eshu's shoulder – his disappointment at his father's greeting was plain to see.

They followed the king through and took their seats at the table. Samsu eyed his wife suspiciously, 'You were keen to get me alone. You usually avoid me,' there was a hint of accusation in his tone.

Eliana smiled brightly, 'No, sir. I enjoy your company, and Eshu so wanted to spend time with you.'

'Hmm. How are you, boy?'

'I am well, father,' grinned Eshu. 'I have learned so much recently. In today's combat lesson...'

He babbled on, reciting his lessons as Adra and Ashan began to serve them. Eliana's heart was in her mouth. She barely noticed Adra placing drinking bowls before her and Eshu and filling them with watered wine; her eyes were all for Samsu's drinking bowl as Ashan filled it with a strong wine from a separate jug.

Samsu saw her looking. 'You want some stronger wine?' he growled.

'No, thank you, sir,' she smiled, quickly thinking of a lie. 'I thought I saw a chip in the side of the bowl – I must have been mistaken.'

His eyes narrowed as he looked at her; his fists clenched on the table. 'Perhaps,' he said slowly, 'I do not care for strong wine myself, this evening.'

Her stomach plummeted – no! No, no, no!

'Does the strong wine not help with your pain?' she asked, trying to appear sympathetic.

'Sometimes. Tonight, I choose to drink watered wine. Swap drinking bowls with me,' he ordered, his tone brooking no argument.

Her mind screamed against it as she handed the bowl over, taking his in return, attempting nonchalance. She had signed her own death warrant – if she did not drink, she confirmed her complicity in Ashan's guilt; if she drank, the poison would claim her.

She clenched her fists in her lap to stop them shaking, looking down at the food on her plate. The smell made her nauseous as fear and disappointment crashed through her.

Forcing a false smile, she turned her attention to Eshu as he continued to chatter – she could not have been more grateful that he gave his father something else to focus on. He had not even started on his dinner, he had so much to say.

Eliana barely touched her food either – she feared her volatile stomach could not hold it. Samsu looked at her with a laugh in his eyes as he ate and drank with gusto. Within minutes, he had finished half his meal and almost drained his – Eliana's – drinking bowl.

There was triumph on his face as he watched her, 'What is the matter?' he asked, almost gleefully. 'Do you not want your –'

He froze.

She looked at him, alarmed. 'Sir, is everything alright?'

Bringing a hand to his face, he said in a thick voice, 'My throat is numb, my mouth too.'

Eshu fell silent, suddenly afraid.

After a few moments, Samsu's face contorted – he began frantically clawing at his neck and chest. 'It burns!' he rasped. 'Make it stop! Do something!'

He fell from his chair, writhing in agony on the floor. Eliana leapt to her feet, staring in horror at the table. 'Eshu! Don't touch anything – there is poison here!'

She was beyond shock – she could not understand what was happening. Had Ashan poisoned her bowl by mistake, or worse, on purpose? Had she been mistaken in him? Surely it was impossible – he had not come near her when the meal was being served.

'Father!' Eshu cried, his face pale as bone.

Samsu thrashed on the bright tiles, 'I am being flayed alive!' he screamed, choking on the words. He turned to Ashan, his gaze desperately pleading for help as he drew a guttural breath.

Ashan stood behind Eliana's chair and looked steadily back.

Realisation dawned on Samsu's face – he stared at Eliana and Ashan with accusation written in his eyes. He opened his mouth, tried to speak, to condemn them, but the words would not form.

His limbs twitched, then trembled before he began to convulse, shuddering grotesquely in his agony, his eyes rolling back into his head.

Ashan and Eliana watched in dumbstruck silence.

As Samsu's convulsions subsided and his gaze became fixed, he exhaled one last, rattling breath and was still.

Eshu gave a piercing scream and collapsed into sobs.

Eliana and Ashan stared at each other – his face showed just as much bewilderment as hers, answering her unspoken question. He could not explain what had just happened.

Adra had shrunk back into a corner, white-faced with panic, staring at the dead man on the floor.

'What just happened?' whispered Eliana, unable to make herself believe that her husband was really dead – that she was free, and he would not suddenly stand up and begin to make her life a living hell once again.

Ashan could not answer. He was stunned into silence.

Gradually, Eshu's sobs began to seep into her consciousness. She walked over to him, put her arms around his shoulders, kissed him atop the head.

'Come along, son,' said Ashan. 'Come with me – we'll go to find the guards.'

Eshu looked up through swollen eyes and nodded vigorously; he could not bear to be in the same room as the corpse. He got up and staggered around the other side of the table.

'I'll find Asag,' Ashan muttered to Eliana as he passed, one hand on Eshu's back.

She was left alone with Adra, both in a state of utter shock. She was finally free, but she could not take it in; could not fathom how. How had he been poisoned?

She was so absorbed in thought that she did not notice when Susa entered.

Head held high, wearing her usual expression of smugness and self-satisfaction, she stalked in unannounced. Catching sight of Eliana stood there, healthy and full of life, the meal abandoned on the table, her jaw dropped. As her eyes followed Eliana's gaze to where their husband lay dead on the floor, she forgot all composure and gave a pitched wail of despair that echoed from every surface.

Eliana's head snapped up. 'You!' she cried. 'What are you doing here?'

Susa stammered, 'I – I came – came to...'

She couldn't think of a lie quickly enough.

Before she could say any more, Adra ran from her place in the corner and threw herself at Susa's feet, 'My lady! I'm sorry! I did just as you said – followed your instructions exactly, but the king… he swapped bowls with the whore, suspected her of trying to kill him. There was nothing I could do!'

Realisation came slowly to Eliana; '*You* were trying to poison *me*?' she was disbelieving at first, then began to laugh long and loud, bordering on hysteria. 'You stupid woman! *You* killed him.'

'No!' Susa cried, shaking her head. 'No! It was an accident! You poisoned him first – with your wiles and your seductions. You've sat in my place for too long – it was past time to get rid of you for good, and your wretched little princeling.'

'That *princeling* is your grandson,' spat Eliana. 'As you well know!'

'Of course I know – I'm not an idiot. He looks exactly as Ashan did at that age – Samsu knew it too, in his heart; he would have come to accept it eventually, would have put you both to the blade.'

Eliana looked pointedly at Samsu's body, cooling on the tiles a short distance away. 'Fortunately, you have spared me that fate. Now my son will be king. Ashan's son will be king.'

Susa screamed, 'No! *Ashan* will be king!'

'No, I will not, mother.' Ashan walked in. He crossed the room and went to Eliana's side, wrapping an arm around her waist, making it clear on whose side he would stand.

'The poison was meant for me,' Eliana explained, 'and Eshu too. She would have killed us both.'

Ashan looked at her, aghast. 'You would kill your own *grandson*?'

'I would do whatever it takes to put you on the throne,' Susa said, pleadingly. She stepped forward and reached up to touch his cheek. 'My beloved son…'

Letting go of Eliana, he slapped his mother's hand away and stepped back. 'And what of *my* beloved son?'

'A whore's whelp – we will find you a proper bride, you will have many strong sons to follow you...'

Ashan shook his head in disbelief. 'Eliana is no whore – I have loved her since she first arrived in the palace. She is strong, spirited, courageous... you lurk in the shadows, spreading malice.'

Four guards appeared in the doorway, led by Asag. They froze, all of them staring horror-struck at their dead king.

'Asag!' called Ashan. 'Arrest my mother – she poisoned the king in a foolish and misguided attempt to kill the queen and the prince.'

The men looked at each other, baffled. Asag barked at them, 'You heard him, arrest her!'

When Susa made no move to resist arrest or deny the accusations, the guards stepped into the room and surrounded her.

'Take her to –' Ashan paused for a moment. Her rooms were not secure, but he was reluctant to send his own mother to the dungeons, whatever her crimes.

'Eshnunna's tower!' Eliana burst out. 'She can live out her days in comfortable isolation.'

'Eshnunna's tower,' nodded Ashan. 'Take her there, and see that she sends no messages and receives no visitors. We will discuss the terms of her confinement later. Take the maidservant too.'

Utterly defeated, Susa allowed herself to be led from the room, with the sobbing Adra being dragged along behind.

Ashan looked at Eliana. 'You didn't tell her that there was poison in Samsu's wine, then?'

She shook her head, 'Of course not. Nobody ever needs to know – our hands are clean of blood in this, however close we came. Your mother is the murderess. Our secret will remain between you, me and Mari.'

'Can you be assured of Mari's silence?'

'I think so,' she smiled. 'It is finally within my power to give her something she has long desired.'

He did not answer, but pulled her close, bringing his lips to hers in a kiss full of promise and hope. For the first time, she could fully relax in his arms, without fear of being discovered and punished.

She sighed deeply. It had been many years since she had truly believed it could ever come to pass, but she finally allowed herself to feel it, to revel in it: freedom.

Epilogue

'*Nahasu!*'

The little party of guests raised their bowls in the air, and drank a toast to the health of the bride and groom. Mari and Asag positively glowed with happiness – she finally had her long-promised freedom, and he his bride.

Eshu had willingly granted his permission to set Mari free from the bonds of slavery. She had been a second mother to him, and he prized her happiness almost as highly as Eliana's.

She was proud of him. The boy had taken on the mantle of kingship without so much as a grumble. He was heavily guided at the moment, by Ashan, Asag and other members of the king's council, but he was balanced and fair, listening to what everyone had to say before coming to a decision. She was confident that he would be a king that history would remember for all the right reasons, unlike Samsu.

Once Eshu had discovered that the man he believed to be his father planned to sacrifice his beloved eldest sister to Marduk, his grief had quickly turned to anger. With Samsu dead, people were no longer afraid to speak. The more Eshu heard, the more his disbelief grew, the more he was ashamed of ever having looked up to the man. He had sworn publically in the audience chamber before the entire court that he would never be a man such as his father was, that he would rule guided by wisdom and justice, like his grandfather Hammurabi.

A storm of applause and cheers had broken out in the chamber, continuing for some minutes as Eshu sat and beamed.

He would not be crowned for several years to come – likely not until after his fourteenth birthday, when the council would be set aside and he would be judged fit to rule alone. In the meantime, Ashan was official regent, and consulted Eliana at every opportunity.

It had been more than six moons since Samsu's death. With his passing, the passageways and corridors no longer felt full of lurking dangers and shadows, and Eliana was growing quite bold again, able to walk around without fear of spies and punishment.

She would never be as bold and fearless as she had once been – too much had happened to change her. Looking at Mari, she thought back to when they had first met – Mari a half-starved orphan, and Eliana a lost child, searching for purpose after losing her sister to Samsu. Would those two girls recognise the women who stood here now?

Eliana was grateful, in a way, for all that had happened. For all the dark times, she felt stronger, wiser and more useful than ever before – each moment of fear, every tear shed, had helped to mould her into the woman she was. The proud and spirited girl was gone, but like a caterpillar transformed, she had emerged from her confinement free and confident, ready to soar.

She stood apart from the others, looking around at the little party. They were gathered in the gardens of the new apartments she had given to Mari and Asag; a small, informal group – all friends and allies gathered together.

Looking at them each in turn, she smiled, feeling grateful to be alive. She knew that without these people, she might not have survived. The only people missing were Kisha and her father.

She had received a message from her father when the news of Eshu's succession reached Nippur. Though it was carefully worded, as was his way, she could still read between the lines. He congratulated her on her new-found freedom, and her elevation to the role of queen mother. Nippur was thriving, he reported, without Samsu's oppressive thumb holding them back, the citizens had begun to regenerate the city. Migrants were flowing in from all corners of the empire, swelling the population and tending the farmland with all the care and devotion it required; with enough men to till the fields, the famine had come to an end.

Kenu looked after him well, the old man said, and he thanked whichever god had brought them together. The message finished on a loving note – Kenu was a fine son, he said, but would never replace the daughters he loved so dearly. There would always be a place for her in Nippur, should she ever choose to return.

Holding back the tears, she had smiled at that. She would never return to Nippur, she knew. Not to stay. Her place was here now, in Babylon, with her children and her love. Eshu was king here, and he needed her. She would not desert him.

Despite that, she had not given up hope of seeing her father again. She hoped he would come to visit, perhaps to attend her own wedding. He would be proud of his grandchildren, she knew, and she would dearly love him to meet Kisha's girls, to see how she lived on through them.

Sarri sat aside, on a bench with Ahat. Dressed in her finest purple silk with golden ornaments in her hair, she flicked her head as she talked, and pouted as she listened. Eliana was sure that the girl was not unaware of the effect her flirting was having on Asag's son, as the boy sat and listened all agog, hanging on her every word.

The little minx.

Kisuri sat with Nisala under a tree, plaiting her younger sister's hair. They chattered softly, as close as Eliana and Kisha had ever been.

She watched Kisuri for a moment – she was so like her mother, both in looks and in temperament. Kisha was not truly gone, she knew. She was like a phoenix – burst into flame and died to be reborn as her own young.

For just a fraction of a second, she thought she saw Kisha sat there on the grass behind her daughter, one hand on Kisuri's shoulder, a smile on her face.

Her heart melted at the sight. Then she blinked, and her sister was gone.

Ashan, Eshu, Mari and Asag stood together in a little group, talking and laughing. Asag had his arm draped around his bride. She was big with their next child, due in just two moons.

Eliana shared their excitement, bringing her hand to her own belly and resting it there, where a swell would soon appear. She was already three months gone.

Seeing her looking, Ashan detached himself from the little group and came to stand beside her.

'It will be our turn next,' he whispered.

She smiled up at him, warming at the thought. 'Eshu and Nisala need to know first,' she said, suddenly serious. 'They need to know who they really are.'

Ashan nodded, went to get the twins.

Taking them aside, sitting together on the grass, Eliana moved a little closer to Ashan. He covered her hand with his.

'We have something to tell you,' she said.